I0778859

CALL OF THE CHATHAMS

Call of the Chathams

Val Croon

Croon Publishing

Copyright © 2024 by Val Croon

All rights reserved. No part of this book may be reproduced in any manner whatsoever without written permission except in the case of brief quotations embodied in critical articles and reviews.

Val Croon asserts the moral right to be recognised as the author of this book.

This is a work of fiction. Any references to historical events, real people, or places are used fictitiously. Names, characters and events are products of the author's imagination, and any resemblance to actual persons living or dead is entirely coincidental.

A catalogue record of this book is available from the National Library of New Zealand.

Soft Cover ISBN 978-0-473-70829-0

Cover by Evelyn Doyle

Printed in Australia
by Croon Publishing
21 Port Hutt Rd
Chatham Islands 8016
New Zealand

First Printing, 2024

Contents

To the people of the Chathams.

PART ONE

PART ONE

1

THE LIVERBIRD

The crew of the Merchant ship, Liverbird, were on high alert as they head punched into a northeast gale heading up into the North Sea from Liverpool. The heavy swell lifted her bow as she crashed into the huge wave with the sound of violent thunder that hurled her back, stopping her momentum. She gave a shudder as though mortally wounded, then came a pounding from the engine-room as her stern lifted, causing her propellers, with less water resistance, to spin in the air. She lurched forward as though in violent insanity, then faced head on to challenge the next wave that once again, crashed into her bow.

The German U-Boats and Raiders ran a blockade north of the Mersey targeting the defenceless British Merchant ships. These merchantmen were transporting fuel, machinery, weapons etc from their USA to the UK via Liverpool then returning with coal mined in Yorkshire and Wales. This was 1940 and the USA had not yet entered the war against Germany but had answered the call from Winstone Churchill.

'Give us the tools and we will do the job.'

The less dangerous route out of Liverpool was to embark at night into the strong to gale force wind from the North Sea. These Merchantmen would keep to the north into the eye of the storm and stay with the low pressure system that tracked to the north and west where they would link up with the Royal Navy protected the convey of merchantmen. Calmer seas increased the risk of encountering the German U-Boats and Raiders looking for a soft target.

As the storm abated the engine-room crew took the opportunity for some relief from the intense heat, heavy diesel fumes and the deafening noise of their claustrophobic workplace in the heart of the ship. The engineers, in turn, would emerge from the bowels of the ship onto the deck to deep breathe in the icy air and the expanse of grey gun-metal sky and troubled seas.

Dan leaned on the cold steel rail with one foot resting on the gunnel rolling a cigarette with grease-stained fingers. He cupped his hands and using a wax match lit his smoke. He deeply inhaled cigarette smoke and the icy air as his thoughts meandered far beyond the horizon to home and family in their sparsely furnished and unheated Liverpool flat.

At this very moment they would be sitting down to their rationed meal. If they were fortunate it could be a tin of bully-beef, maybe a few potatoes or a cabbage. Liverpool was experiencing continued nightly blackouts so his family would prepare for another long and lonely night without their father and husband. Nights were filled with the horror of the German bombers with their night raids across England and especially Liverpool. Liverpool was targeted for being the main port for the imported goods to keep the war machine wheels turning. These dark nights were nights of horror for Rose: to settle herself and children she told the stories and fairy tales of ancient Ireland as told to her by her Mother, Myfanwy. They would drop off to sleep one by one only to be wakened in fright by the terrible sound of the air-raid sirens that would proceed the noise and flashing lights of exploding German bombs. Sometimes it was too late to run to the air-raid shelter and they would have to huddle in fear in their cold-water flat until the blitz was over.

As Dan leaned over the ships rail he was joined by the Second Engineer, they didn't speak as they both gazed with unseeing eyes at, and beyond the horizon, each lost in their own thoughts. Memories of a life without danger or fear, trying to imagine life after the war, that's if there were fortunate enough not to be blown out of the water by a torpedo. They didn't actually converse, random memories would arise and be put into words that had been stumbling through the brain. Back to the days of a carefree youth, love and lust, past deeds, some to be proud of and others to be ashamed of, agreeing that those good and not so good times were part of the experience of being human. They shared the constant fear of the safety of their loved ones and the possible wartime destruction of their homes. These ramblings came from within with unabashed honesty, when an unseen enemy could, without warning, shatter their lives, be it at sea or on land.

To lighten up the mood Dan told the story of the Navy sending a probe with a camera deep into the Atlantic to explore the Titanic which was laying on the seabed approximately where their convoy was at that time. The probe discovered that the Titanic's swimming pool was still full.

They both agreed that they would not want to be interred in a cold and merciless sea but preferably a place in a secluded sunny churchyard, under a yew tree smothered in the daffodils and bluebells of an early spring. They were adamant that drowning or cremation was not an option.

The Engineer told the story of the wife and the death of her philandering husband who requested his ashes to be scattered in the sea. She flushed his ashes down the toilet.

The were both at ease in their own company and idle thoughts. One said that Hitler had only one ball, the other responded that Goering had none at all. Eva Bruin was once, and still is a hooker. Chamberlin had no guts and Churchill was a war monger. Eisenhower was a greedy German who would not enter the war because the Americans were selling steel to both the British and the Germans. As for the evacuation of Dunkirk, what a monumental fuckup.

The day was cooling as it eased into a late afternoon gloom when Dan sensed before he actually saw a smudge of grey about 2,000 yards off the starboard beam. As he opened his mouth to shout a warning he saw the wake of the torpedo. He froze, almost instantly there was a huge explosion amidships, then a second.

The Liverbird shuddered, then lurched as if she was trying to free herself from a giant predator, she rolled to one side taking in water through two large jagged holes on the waterline amidships. Sirens screamed as if in agony, then a recorded announcement over the loudspeaker system...

'Abandon ship, abandon ship...'

A third explosion, this one was from the heart of the Liverbird as the engine died. A brief silence, and then came the screams of the men trapped down below, these desperate screams quietened, seemingly one by one. The stern rose as the bow plunged as if the ship was hurrying to escape the pain of being permanently wounded, she quickly disappeared into the oil blackened sea to rest in her watery grave.

The German Raider, 'Aquarius' turned her back on the devastation and disappeared into the darkening horizon.

2

MYFANWY

was the fifth child of 11, brought up on a subsistence farm a few miles outside the village of Delancey. Her parents came from a line of once sustainable land-owning farmers able to produce their own food with surplus to sell in the market square of the nearby large town of Killarney. Myfanwy's ancestors were able to enjoy a relativity comfortable lifestyle as their forefathers had done for many generations. Potato was the staple crop of most Irish landowners along with other crops such as wheat and oats. Protein came from poultry, mutton and pork that were farmed and traded providing a reasonable cashflow some of which went into the coffers of the Catholic church.

That was until the English colonists invaded Northern Ireland resulting in thousands of farmers being evicted from their land. These people faced certain poverty and starvation unless they agreed to pay rent as tenant farmers to the English who claimed ownership of the land through conquest. The rent these tenant farmers had to pay was crippling and any breach of tenancy was met with fines or eviction. Thousands of farming families were thrown off their land and onto the streets of the towns and cities, many homes were destroyed as the English consolidated these family farms into larger blocks then rented them to compliant Irish or English settlers.

The invaders were quick to realize that, along with collecting rent they controlled the sales and export of the higher valued produce like animals and wheat which was more profitable than potato. The colonists ordered the Irish Catholic tenants to eat only potatoes and all other farm produce was owned and controlled in the marketplace by the colonists from which they paid their tenants a pittance.

To lessen the risk of any insurgence many of the young men were removed from the land to work in the factories and mills of the cities. Catholics were not allowed to own land, own a horse, or to eat the highly valued meat; education was severely restricted and they were certainly not allowed to vote.

In the late 1800s, a devastating disaster struck the people of Ireland. The English landlords had ignored the farming practices of the tenants and forbidded the rotation of crops and grazing land for higher-valued produce, this concentrated farming practice caused the spud crop to contract the disease of potato blight resulting in total crop failures. This resulted in about 1.5 million Northern Irish people dying of starvation and a huge exodus of the population emigrating to America, Canada and Australasia. The English government refused to help in any way during this famine fearing the Irish would use the money to buy arms and revolt. Those who survived were filled with hatred of their English invaders giving birthbirth to the IRA and its political arm, Sinn Fein.

This was the backdrop which Myfanwy and her family had survive on their subsistance farm.

Her mother, Maureen, was a large, heavy-boned, broad-shouldered good-natured woman of Welsh descent, hence the name Myfanwy of her eldest daughter. Maureen had an easy smile, often followed by a hearty laugh. Her happy disposition flowed through to her children who were eager to take part in the running of her sometimes-unruly household. There was never enough food, especially for the teenage boys; although whenever she was able there was something in her cast iron pot bubbling on her peat-fired stove for friend or stranger in those hard times.

Myfanwy's dah, Pat Fitzgerald whose surname translated to 'Son of a Norseman', through his lack of formal education his ancestry was unknown to him. He was renowned throughout the County for his skill in the distillation of the fermentation of potatoes to make the illegal Irish whiskey called Pointin. The name was derived from a small pot and the Irish word for a hangover, 'poit'. His copper still was hidden in a hilly forest about two hours walk from the farm; he also had a spud crop in a clearing surrounded by a thicket of thorns to feed his still. The English authorities, were ruthless in the prevention of the production of Pointin, simply because they were unable to collect the alcohol excise tax.

Pat had a weakness for the product that he produced and over the years he did little else other than work his still. He would sell or try to sell his illegal whisky in nighttime visits to Delancy. The problem was that most of his customers didn't have any money, so he would drink with them free of charge anyway. More often than not he would be too drunk or hungover to return to his family at night.

This left the family to run the farm, with the older boys doing the heavy work of growing spuds, wheat, oats and digging peat for fuel. The younger ones were responsible for egg production and tend the vegetable garden. Most of the farm production would have to be sold through the English owned and operated 'Irish Company' in Killarney.

Unlike her siblings who were of heavy build, inherited from their parents and developed by hard work, Myfanwy was of slim adolescence approaching womanhood. She had long dark hair, deep green eyes that hinted her Scandinavian heritage. Her intelligence often annoyed her parents and siblings because of her continued questioning. Why, how, when, she was always looking for other ways of doing things. Her family teased her with the nursery rhyme, 'Mary Mary, quite contrary...'

Although not beautiful in the sense of the word her attractiveness came from within as she matured. She was oblivious to all this; her only mirror was the duck pond at the back of the house. Although her family were desperately poor, where clothing was always hand-me-down, Myfanwy had the ability to make something out of nothing. A bow, an apple blossom for her hair, a splash of colour, she always insisted on wearing shoes, to do so she was adept at sowing fine shoe leather. She would unpick and remake clothing from material she mysteriously scavenged from who knows where. She had an artistic touch which was evident throughout the house, a bunch of flowers here, a touch of nature there, an odd bit of junk creatively recycled into something artistically useful. She took control of the house garden that became her passion. Her garden was always with colour, even in the dark days of winter. Her dah and brothers would complain that they couldn't eat primroses, daisies, winter roses or the vibrant spring flowers that she grew.

Education was, for Catholics, restricted, therefore schooling for most, and especially for the poor was practically non-existent so the church took a limited role in education with the emphasis of the secular. The visiting priest recognized Myfanwy's intelligence and groomed her to be able to give to her siblings some basic education. From a young age she walked the five miles to the 'Church of Ignatius', where she was taught the three Rs of reading, writing and arithmetic, this basic education she was able to pass onto her siblings. Unbeknown to her, the Priest and Nuns were grooming her for a life within the church by teaching her Latin along with Catholicism. After instructions Myfanwy had a series of daily chores to complete in the Vestry under the suspiciously watchful eye of the Priest. No free lunches in those days, especially if it involved the church where guilt reigned.

In the evenings after dinner Myfanwy would coax her family to a rudimental education, including her mother who could not read or write. The older boys were not interested and when they became of age they emigrated to Boston where jobs for the illiterate were hard to come by, like many Irish, these immigrants entered into a life of crime.

Eventually Myfanwy's insistence won over, her younger siblings learnt to read, write and count, yes count. It is hard to understand in this day and age when, back then, most farmers were unable to count their sheep and would engage a person who could count. He became known as an accountant. Actually, nothing much has changed, we still employ an accountant to count so we can pay taxes.

And then the unexpected happened which was to change Myfanwy's life forever.

On her daily journey home after church lessons and chores she had to ford a bubbling stream using steppingstones. One afternoon while crossing the stream she stopped to look upstream into a glade, she vaguely saw the form of a male sitting with his back supported by a large sun-drenched lichen covered stone, he must have sensed he presence and lifted his eyes from his book, she quickly turned ansd hurried home. About a week or so later she saw him sitting in the same position, she hesitated in the middle of the stream and could see that his head was down, reading a book. She became intrigued and every day she looked to see if he was there. As spring turned to summer, she found him in that same place several times, sometimes reading, sometimes just gazing sightlessly, maybe just soaking up the sun; when she did see him, she quickly hurried out of sight.

One very warm day he was sitting on the bank of a deep part of the stream with his feet and lower legs dangling in the water. He was side on to her, so she felt it was safe to stop to have a closer look at him, he turned toward her and in fright she hurried back to the crossing and headed for home.

She had not seen him for three or four weeks as it dawned on her that she began to doubt that he may have been a figment of imagination. The day was still and hot, he wasn't sitting in his usual place, nor was he on the bank of the stream. Without thinking any further, her body, with a mind of its own, took her closer to the glade, to her shock and horror he was sitting in the shade of the rock, reading. He sensed her and looked up; his movement caught her unsuspecting eye. It was only for a few seconds that they looked at each other, for them, those few seconds were eternity. Blushing uncontrollably, she turned, only to stumble on a rock, then regained her balance, but not all of her composure. Without speaking she concentrated on walking to rejoin the path; by then she was fuming at herself, vowing, never to take the crossing route home, ever, and to detour by taking the high road which she occasionally used in winter when the stream was in flood.

Several weeks later she was on her way home and realised that she had, without thinking, walked towards the crossing. As she turned to retrace her steps, she saw a small blue book on the side of the path. She stood and looked at it, then looked around, although she sensed his presence he was nowhere to be seen, she crouched down and picked it up with both hands.

'COLLECTED VERSE' by William Butler Yeats.

3

THOMAS

was born in Liverpool to Irish parents, Conner and Agnes Finnegan who originated from County Donegal in Northern Ireland. After their marriage they moved to Dublin to expand Conner's building business. Hardworking and with sharp business acumen Conner was able to succeed in contracting ongoing work and before long was employing several tradesmen and laborers. After successfully constructing several houses, finishing on time and on budget, he successfully contracted to build an administration office for the English Government in the Dublin Merrion Street Quadrangle. The below ground construction work had been completed and the solid oak framing was well underway when late one night there was a knock on the door. Three burly guys barged in without being invited, although they didn't identify them-selves it was obvious to Conner that they were IRA. On no uncertain terms they expressed their displeasure of Conner, not only for working for the hated English but also that work contracted was to build an administration office in which to rule over the Irish. The only way they would allow Conner to continue the build was to pay them protection money, 'Protection from who?' Conner asked. 'From the IRA' they said, there was no point arguing the ambiguity of their mentality. There was no doubt that these were troubling times ahead for the Finnegans.

Conner and Agnes agreed to pay what was at first a moderate amount for 'Protection' but over a few months the demands increased. Conner told the 'bag man' that his business was having difficulty in paying wages therefore would only afford to pay a half of what they demanded. He suspected that the next knock on the door could be the boss-man with whom he could negotiate. It was 3.00 AM when their 'Protector' and a couple of heavies arrived. As far as they were concerned that anybody who worked for the English was a traitor and deserved to be punished. The boss introduced himself as 'Lugh', he had named himself after one of the prominent mythological Irish Gods who was the saviour of the Irish race. As they argued one of the heavies let it slip that Lugh's name was Seamus. His response to Conners objection was sharp increase in protection money which Conner told them that he could not afford to pay.

Conner recognised Seamus's Londonderry accent so employed a private detective to track him down successfully, 'Seamus Dillon, of Bogside, Londonderry, an officer of the IRA.

Several weeks later there was a mysterious fire in the Merrion St. Quadrangle and the new-build had burnt to the ground, by the end of the next week Connor and Agnes had boarded the ferry to Liverpool, never to return to their beloved Ireland.

Life in Liverpool was kind to the hardworking Conner and before long they became respected in the building industry that was recovering from the dark years of WW1. Inspite all the bad things that happened to them in Dublin they retained a deep longing for the green, green grass of their homeland. In their home they still spoke Gaelic which was taught to their children. Saturday nights they frequented an Irish pub in the Docklands where they would meet with fellow Irish compatriots, as the night wore on they would sing the songs of home. Who could not but shed a tear with an Irish lament.

'Romantic Irelands' dead and gone,

It's with O'Leary in the grave, in the grave, in the grave...'

What started off as a one-man enterprise quickly grew into the registered company, Finnegan Construction, no job too big, no job too small. Conner introduced an apprentice system to train his younger employees; also he found that he got better results from his employees with a five day working week rather than the normal six days. They built a grand family home in the affluent suburb Woolton and became respected citizens as much as this fine city of Liverpool would allow the Irish.

Thomas was a gentle lad and not inclined to follow his father's footsteps into the construction business. He was fascinated and influenced by his County Donegal ancestry. His mother told stories of ancient Ireland in their native tongue of which he became fluent. He enrolled in the University of Liverpool to study Humanities and Social Science. The more he learnt, the more he became disturbed by the English influence over Ireland and the plight of the Northern Irish people. He immersed himself in the Celtic heart and the great heroes of the ancient Celtic myths. On a more practical level, he studied the politics of the more recent times; with this background, his ambition was to return to his roots where his heart belonged.

He completed his degree with honors and found a way of fulfilling his dreams by successfully applying to the London based Home Office gaining a position as an Administrator in the Northwest of Ireland.

The English were softening their approach to the affairs in Ireland after realizing the disastrous effects of colonizing on the indigenous peoples of India, South Africa, the West Indies, Australia, New Zealand and the many other countries that formed the British Empire.

Thomas was posted to the small administrative office in the township of Delancey. His job was to liaise with locals who could not, or more likely would not, speak English. He was tasked to report back to the Home Office on how to create and build better relationships with local communities. Even with his ability to communicate in the Gaelic tongue and his Irish ancestry it was tough going to gain the confidence of the local population. Being England born and employed by the English he was not trusted.

As his time in the Delancy passed, The townspeople began to be recognized for what he was; a gentle soul with an Irish heart who continually fought the miserly Home Office for the well-being of the people, he liked to think that these were his people. Thomas, the dreamer had found a home. He became enchanted by the long hot summer that contrasted with a cool twilight that seemed to keep the night at bay. His pastime was long walks over the hilly and shallow lands, the still lakes and climbing the hill of Ben Bulben which often would drift in and out of the swirling mist. His wanderings often took him to sit in the sunny glade by the stream to read or just to dream. The waters of the stream were the color of weak tea caused by the tannin from the wooded hills above, a stream that was often shallow, in places bubbling, then deep parts that slowed to a seemingly bottomless calm.

The June afternoon was hot and still when Thomas was sitting in the dappled shade reading the passion of William Butler Yeats's poem of 'Aengus', the mythical god of love who had caught a little silver trout...

'When I laid it on the ground,
I went to blow the fire aflame,
But something rustled on the ground,
And somebody called me by my name.
It had become a glimmering girl,
With apple blossom in her hair,
Who called me by my name and ran,
And faded through the brightening air...
And kiss her lips and take her hands...'

Thomas looked up from his book, absorbing those wonderful words when a movement caught his eye, and there she was, the glimmering girl with apple blossom in her hair. Their eyes devoured each other for an eternity before she turned and ran. Cupid's arrow had pierced his heart.

He doubted the reality of this vision in this enchanted glade, was it just the power of Yeats's poem of love, or was she real? How do I find out where she has gone? Is she the frightened Doe? never to return to this enchanted glade.

At every opportunity, he returned to his glade awaiting this glimmering girl. Days passed and she did not appear so he placed his book of poems on the path near the steppingstones. His plan was to have Yeats to formally introduce them.

Unseen in the dapple light of the trees he saw her stop, look down at the book, then bend her knees while cautiously looking around, she picked up the book and thumbed the page's; stopping from time to time to read while still looking intently into the glade. She held the book to her breast as she faded into the brightening air, her body shimmering in slim adolescence.

4

I HAVE NOTHING TO GIVE YOU

but my dreams, tread softly, as you tread on my dreams.' Myfanwy went back to walking home by way of the stepping stones, each time, taking a hesitant look into the glade; he was not to be seen. It was on a Sunday, early afternoon after church, there he was, her heart leapt as she saw him standing over the stream gazing sightlessly into the deep.

She recalled Yeats's poem and thought to herself, 'He must be looking for that trout'. She took a deep breath and stepped into the unknown. He looked up, startled, there she was.

'I've come to return your book, that's if it is yours,' she said.

'It's mine, well, it was mine, but you can keep it if you like.'

She was taken back by his accent, 'You're English?'

'I was born in England, that's all, Ireland is my home,'

Myfanwy sniffed defiantly; turned and marched back to the path, when she got to the crossing she stopped, mid-stream, realizing she still had his book in her hand. She then held the book in both hands and spoke to it. 'What am I doing? This is the most wonderful gift I've have ever had, and I'm behaving like a child, the least I can do it thank him. With heart beating like a captured bird she slowly walked back to the glade.

17

'Thank you, I just love the poetry but, now that I've read it you can have it back,'

'It's yours to keep.'

'I can't take this from the…' she nearly said 'English', 'from a stranger,'

'If I introduce myself then we won't be strangers.'

She was trapped, it was wonderful; she looked across to the stream, thinking that she should have the freedom of the stream; not knowing or caring where she had come from or where she was going.

'My name is Thomas; I had no choice of where I was born. My parents are Irish, my soul is Irish, and Ireland is my home,'

'Well, if I had a choice of where I was born, it wouldn't be here, that's for sure,'

'Where would have liked to have been born then.'

'Arrr, maybe on a tropical island somewhere in the South Pacific, some place where we can be free, some place where tradition doesn't exist, a place where it doesn't matter who you are, a place where you are seen as what you are…' she was astonished what she had just said, she had never spoken of what she felt in her heart to anybody.

'At least we agree on something, for me, tradition is like being controlled by dead people.'

'My name is Myfanwy.'

'There we are, we are now not strangers. As he extended his open hand, she took it. as if her hand had a mind of its own. They touched, it was like a gentle electric current passing between them, their hands were a conduit of magic.

'Myfanwy, I love your name, Myfanwy', it just rolled off his tongue.

They both looked at their hands and slowly they pulled apart, 'I can't take your book.'

'Please do, it's my gift to you,'

'I have nothing to give to you, nothing.'

'For me, your friendship is my reward,'

She gave a slight curtsy, 'Can we share it? If you ever want it back, even it is just to read, it's yours, just ask.'

'Maybe we can read it together sometime, will you come back to our glade?'

She gave an ever so slight nod, turned and walked away. As she stepped on the first stone to cross the stream she looked back, knowing that he would be watching her, he lifted his hand in farewell but she just she concentrated on the stepping stones and hurried out of sight.

The next few days she was a blur of delirium, she recounted in her mind every word spoken, every gesture, every minute she had with Thomas. Sometimes she was afraid, not of him, but afraid of herself. Other times she felt the intense joy of her day an the glade, and an even greater joy of the unknown. She read the poems in the Blue Book over and over, exploring what was behind these wonderful words of William Butler Yeats. Her previous life of family, church, her garden, their poverty all seemed to dwell in a distant past. She could imagine, for the first time in her life she could dream.

Maureen noticed the changes within her daughter; one evening at the dinner table, when all the kids were their usual rowdy selves, she saw that her daughter was lost in another world, her own world. Myfanwy, who had been quiet suddenly burst out and said to nobody in particular, 'I know nothing, I know nothing of life.' She stood, pushed back her chair and walked outside, lost in tears.

The family quietened, looked at one another, 'What in Gods name has got into her this time?'

Maureen knew that something had changes, her daughter had become a woman, but there was more to it than that. She said out loud but to herself, 'She's just being a teenager,' and left it at that.

Maureen found an opportunity a couple of days later, 'Is everything alright at Church?'

'What do you mean?'

'You know, like, is Father O'Shaunasy... are you okay with Father?'

'Him, he's alright I suppose, but I'm just finding it as bit hard to believe in all this stuff he preaches about a God, and his opposite, the Devil. I don't understand why I should be made to feel guilty every time I walk into church, it wasn't me who nailed Jesus to the cross.'

'I think you'd better say a few Hail Mary's before you go to bed tonight.'

'Hail Mary's? You're as bad as he is, I've done nothing wrong. I am not going to hand over my life to a concept that a God, who may not even exist, can control my life.'

'I think you better go to confession next Sunday.'

'Confess to what? I have done nothing wrong, All I do is housekeep and mind children, I want to live my own life, I want to be me,'

'My beautiful child, I pray that you will not be punished for this blasphemy,'

'You may as well go and kiss the Blaney Stone as well,'

'For the love of God, my Rosery beads, where did I put my Rosery beads?'

'Gods not going to help you find them.' Myfanwy walked out the door to her garden, she spoke to her flowers, 'I get more sense out of you than anybody else.'

Maureen watched her go, 'I think my daughter has become a woman.'

Although to path via the crossing was the longer way home, she walked that way whenever she had the time, especially if there was a little sunshine hanging around. Those were the days when she thought that Thomas may be in the glade, but several weeks had passed without him being there. One Saturday, which was her day off from her church duties she went walking to the crossing, she took the Blue Book with her. From the crossing she followed the stream to the glade and leaned on the rock, feeling its warmth, imagining his warmth. She had her book open but wasn't reading, just closed her eyes and soaked up the sun. She wandered over to the still part of the stream and looked at her image reflected in the black water. She looked across to the other side of the stream at the reflection of the green trees that were hanging over the water. 'It was a river of green that was sliding unseen beneath the trees', (Pink Floyd). She looked back down at her own reflection imagining him standing next to her. When in love, 'everything is beautiful in its own way'. (Ray Stevens). She kissed the Blue Book and placed it under the rock, then floated home to her drab reality.

Sunday 16th May, Myfanwy turned 18, Maureen never failed to treat birthdays as a special day, and there were plenty of those days for the large Fitzgerald family. The luxury of meat would be added the often-daily fare of colcannon, which is mashed spuds, cabbage, sometimes with an onion thrown in. It was a Sunday so after Church the family headed home to prepare for the birthday dinner while Myfanwy had tea and cake baked by the nuns. She took the long way home vias the crossing, telling herself that she would pick the bluebells that grew alongside the stream. Of course, we know that the real reason to take the long way home; being a sunny Sunday he may be there, sure enough, there he was. He had picked up the book and was looking to the crossing where she was picking bluebells. He was stunned, there she was with basket in hand, apple blossom in her hair, a ribbon around her neck, a summer dress and face aglow.

She was the first to speak, 'You've found the book?'

'Yes, I have, but I want you to have it.'

'Which is your favorite poem?'

'All depends on the day, like today I've been reading about you,'

'Me? he writes of a world I know nothing about.'

'The world he writes about is the world in which we live, he writes of the beauty that exists in the mundane, we have but one life, therefore it is perfect.'

'Sometimes all I see is the bad, I would love to be able to create beauty out the mundane, I would love to do it with a paint brush.'

'For me, the poem of the day is about as glimmering girl, with apple blossom in her hair,who has entered my world, she called me by my name as she disappeared.'

'Do you think you will ever find her?'

'I found you.'

They sat close, their bodies touching as they read the poem together. Their first kiss.

Myfanwy was halfway home when she remembered her bluebells, she turned and again went back into the woods.

From then on, they met on prearranged days, reading and immersing themselves into Yeats and other Irish writers, James Joyce, Oscar Wilde and C S Lewis from Thomas's collection. Their love always took them back to Yeats...

'The silver apples of the moon,
The golden apples of the sun...'

Their world became an enchanted land of mystery, folklore and love, some days they would immerse themselves into just one poem, today was 'The Ragged Wood.'

'O hurry where by water among the trees
The delicate stepping stag and his lady sigh,
When they have but looked upon their images-
Would none have ever loved, but you and I.'

She asked Thomas what it meant.

Thomas stood, took her hands and drew her to her feet, they walked over to the stream where the water run deep and still, he said...

'The stag and the doe looked at their image in the pool, in doing so they became the only beings in their world. There was no other love but their own, nothing else exists except for their love.'

As Thomas and Myfanwy looked down at their image they became the only beings on this earth, they could see no other love but their own.

As the summer passed and the evenings cooled, a fear grew within them, it was only a matter of time before their love would be discovered. They were fully aware of the prejudice and the hatred between the Irish and English that could destroy them. Myfanwy was afraid that someday he could be posted to another town, city or even country. She was aware that her own people could destroy their love. As they parted late one afternoon, she recited...

'...but I being poor, have only my dreams;
I have spread my dreams under your feet,
Tread softly, because you tread on my dreams.'

5

THE TROUBLES

come to town. Even though the English were easing their firm hold on the Irish public, there was no avoiding the tensions that were building throughout Northern Ireland and as far south as Dublin. The Easter Rebellion in 1916 was an armed rebellion by the IRA against English rule intent on forming an independent Irish republic. This uprising was at a time when the British Empire was heavily engaged in WW1 and couldn't afford a lengthy fight against the Irish rebels. This armed resurrection cost many lives from both sides with the IRA being well equipped with weapons sourced from Irish expatriates from the USA.

The last stand of the Easter rebellion was a siege when the IRA were holed up in the Dublin General Post Office. The British Army and Irish constabulary gained control of the rebellion and their negotiation team offered the remaining IRA soldiers that if they surrendered their arms their lives would be spared. They laid down their arms and without trial their leaders were immediately hanged. The survivors were held in the notorious Kilmainham prison where many died of deprivation. There was condemnation throughout England and Europe of the English in regarding their handling of the people of Ireland who were just defending their homeland. The survivors, who included the aforementioned 'Lugh' were eventually released on the condition of the disbandment of the IRA. That agreement lasted until the minute they were released from Kilmainham and arrived back in Belfast and Londonderry.

The aftermath of the Easter Uprising gave birth to the political arm of the IRA was formed, Sinn Fein. The hard-liners of the IRA were never going to stop their fight against the colonial invaders. three lads from Londonderry, led by Seamus Dillon, aka, Lugh, were campaigning around the towns and villages of Donegal. They arrived in the peaceful town of Delancy, where they held a series of undercover meetings; to access these meetings needed the password, 'Revolution'. Lugh held forth…

'Brothers and sisters, revolution is not an act of war, it is an act of love, the love of people.' He paused to let that sink in, 'The invaders have stolen our land, we live in poverty, we are hungry, we are powerless, we live under the beck and call of these foreigners who have been delivered into our midst by the Devil.' He paused again,' God is with us, brothers and Sisters, but God cannot do this without our help,' he stopped and tried to look each of the audience in the eye, 'we all know that what God wants, God gets, but he needs our help to drive these invaders back into the sea where they came from.'

The people were stirring, growing from just a murmur to anger. 'Revolution' they shouted, standing and shaking their fists of defiance. 'Quiet my friends, these walls have ears,' the crowd hushed and looked around suspiciously, 'They now tell us that they are our friends and neighbors, but they despise us, this land is our land, and the time has come to take back what belongs to us, Revolution, my friends, revolution is the here and the now.'

Delancy was peaceful no more.

Thomas and Myfanwy began to live in fear, they took extreme caution to love in their own world. It was becoming dangerous to meet in daylight, sometimes the impassioned lovers joined at midnight in the room where Thomas lived above the Administration office; even that was high risk. Their times together were becoming infrequent therefore even more impassioned.

As we all know that on small towns, or islands, a touch of gossip spun into fact and spread like wildfire.

As the seemingly endless summer months passed and the autumn leaves drifted with the cooling winds they spent their last hours together in the glade, their paradise, where they found solace as tangled lovers in their troubled world. They found peace in their love triangle with William Butler Yeats...

'I would that we were, my beloved, white birds on the foam of the sea...

This had awakened in our hearts, my beloved, a sadness that may never die...

Where time would surely forget us, and sorrow come near us no more.

Soon far from the rose and the lily, the fret of the flames would we be...

Were we only white birds, my beloved, buoyed out on the foam of the sea.'

Thomas kissed their book of verse and passed it to his lover, she held it to her breast as they parted, this time, forever.

The gossip was rampant in the already fired up Delancy, where small town secret's do not stay hidden for long. For those in love, who are blind, as the stag and the doe discovered, 'only they exist'.

The Nuns told the Priest the gossip who tut-tutted as he knelt in front of Jesus nailed to the cross praying for guidance from above. Jesus must have answered his prayer, so he stood and walked across to the vestry where his choir boy was cutting grass with a scythe, he instructed him to follow Myfanwy home that afternoon. The boy returned and confirmed that the gossip was not gossip. The next Sunday the Priest told Maureen of his findings. She had instinctively known of the changes in her daughter for some time and suspected that she was up to no good. Maureen was horrified to find that her daughter was secretly meeting, heaven forbid, an Englishman. She dare not tell her husband because she knew that he would erupt into a pointin fueled rage.

When the townspeople had confirmation of this unspeakable affair a seething anger consumed common sense. The town informants on a moral high ground relayed this traitorous behavior to the IRA in 'Derry. Seamus, aka 'Lugh' along with a couple of his heavies were instructed to travel to Delancy and sort things out.

Thomas was out walking, but not to the glade, this time to climb the hill of Ben Bulben; it was a day of swirling mist with an autumn chill in the air. As he neared the summit, concentrating on the effort he was unaware of the three shadows following. He reached the summit he stopped and rested with the sense of satisfaction of achievement of climbing his Everest. He was above the mist in full, but weak sun. The Delancy church spire was above the layer of fog which obliterated the town. He turned around to see the green valley below, there was no mist, his eyes followed the stream which meandered through the fields and into the grove of light forest. He imagined Myfanwy in her summer dress with a woolen shawl over her shoulders, waiting for him. He looked up to the white birds, souring and dipping, sometimes motionless, being held aloft by the uplift of wind, they were watching, waiting, fully aware of what was unfolding. He then foresaw his death. Far below were the tops of the oak and birch, unmoving as they too watched on. The black rocks and boulders that were scattered down the steep face were also waiting. The sun, who had been playing hide and seek among the mist and clouds, hid its face, the wind dropped. In absolute silence he was quickly overpowered and plunged into the total eclipse of the sun, forever.

The only sound the three shadowy figures heard was the scream that echoed in the deep valley. 'Myfanwy.'

THOMAS FINNEGAN

b 1895 ----- d 1918

R I P

6

FERRY ACROSS THE MERSEY

The inquest into the death of Thomas Finnegan found that in all probability he had lost his footing while scaling the windy Ben Bulben and fallen to the rocks of the valley to die instantly. The Home Office refused to repatriate his body back to his home city of Liverpool.

Myfanwy plunged into a black hole of despair, she had nobody to turn to and was snubbed by the townspeople of Delancy. Her solace was to open her book of verse where she discovered a bookmark on embossed paper that he had created. It was a poem headed by a pencil drawn stylized rose, his beautifully handwritten words to her were...

'Those who love and know, live so most,

We may not reach the stars,

But at least, we have been up in a balloon.' (anon)

It was her mum who was the first to notice the bump in her belly, it wasn't long before the Nuns also suspected. She wore loose clothing to hide the growing seed of Thomas. After several months her secret was a secret no more, her dah, in a drunken rage screamed at her.

'You slattern bitch, I will not have an English bastard under my roof, you have brought great shame to my family, we will hang our heads before our Lord and beg forgiveness, that's if out Priest ever to allow us to enter the doors of our church. Get out of this house, get out of this town and never come back.'

Maureen tried to calm him down but that just angered him into further violence. She gathered up what few coins she had and told her daughter to go to the Church for sanctuary. The Nuns took her into their humble abode, praying for guidance from above. It didn't take long for the priest to realize Myfanwy's condition and that she was being protected by the Nuns who dedicate their lives to God and humanity. He too prayed for guidance but all he could think of was the fear of being ostracized by the Church's benefactors, he refused to have her under the roof of the house of God. He insisted that she leave and gave her a few coins to ease his conscience. The Nuns emptied the Church's purse and gave all the cash along with the address of an establishment in Dublin where Myfanwy could get help. The door closed with a resounding clunk behind her as she walked down the steps, turned around and took one last look at the Church, vowing never ever to set foot in the house of the Lord.

Myfanwy straightened her shoulders, stood tall and defiantly strode away from her people and a town that had no pity.

'I'll cry tomorrow.'

The damaged, but far from broken Myfanwy travelled by horse drawn carriage from Delancey to Belfast and then her first train ride to what she expected would be the fine city of Dublin. She was shocked at what she found on walking down the steps of the Dublin Connolly rail station. This fine city was of coal blackened stone buildings, streets dirty with uncollected garbage, a smog that felt like it was poisoning her lungs smell of urine had her wanting to vomit. She navigated these filthy streets having to continually avoid the horse shit when she had to step off the footpath. When she asked directions to the address given to her by the Nuns of Delancy she had difficulty in understanding the Dublin dialect. It was late afternoon when she eventually found the house of the Buckingham Street Women's Refuge. A sanctuary for the lost, the widowed, the unmarried, some barely teenage children, pregnant who lived under such terrible conditions that was regarded at that time the worst in the United Kingdom. The heavy door was opened by a woman who just looked at Myfanwy and nodded without speaking for her to enter.

Cooking was done in the basement over an open fire fueled by coal that was poured down a chute, it was the job of the fittest and strongest women to spend each day scavenging coal from around the neighborhood. Water had to be carried from a community tap situated several streets away. Food was scarce with very little option other than a huge pot that what food that could be scrounged then cooked in the basement and carried up to a communal dining room. The luxury of a breakfast did not exist, many women suffered from malnutrition.

The only income for this house of refuge was to take in laundry or sewing for other institutions like orphanages and the Kilmainham prison. There was the occasional donation from some guilty male or from an estate where a servant had been impregnated by the master of the household.

Myfanwy worked long hours as a seamstress which provided enough money for her dormitory bed and a contribution for food. In working these long hours in cold unventilated poorly lit conditions and the bad food took a toll on her heath. She lost weight, although the resident midwives agreed that her unborn baby was healthy enough considering her living conditions. These unfortunate, and sometimes wretched women, most of whom through no fault of their own and with no outside help were a very staunch family. The memory of these women remained with Myfanwy throughout her life. Often the screams of birth without professional medical help were heard throughout the whole of Buckingham St. Myfamwy realized that in her late pregnancy this situation had become untenable. She still had money remaining that was carefully sewn into her bodice which gave her the means to board the ferry to Liverpool to try and get help from the grandparents of her expected child.

During WW1 the passenger ship service between Ireland and the UK was practically non-existent; therefore, schedules between Dublin and Liverpool were not advertised except by word of mouth. 'Loose lips sink ships', was the call of the day. This meant that Myfanwy had to daily walk down to the Grand Canal dock. After several weeks she was advised that a ship which serviced the Irish outlying islands was due to dock and depart the next day for Liverpool.

She boarded the SS Thomas Currell and after promising the ships Purser that she would not have her baby en-route she secured a cheap passage in steerage to Liverpool. The voyage was a nightmare for Myfanwy who was violently seasick in the dank, airless, noisy and overcrowded steerage compartment. As the Thomas Currell entered the calmer waters of the Mersey her seasickness left her and for the first time on the voyage, which had been zigzagging across the Irish sea to lessen the chance of being hunted down by a German U-Boat. still recovering from seasickness and lack of nourishment she gained the composure to rise from the steerage hellhole and come out on deck breathe the cold fresh air.

The Purser watched her emerge and from the galley brought her a cup of scalding tea and a slice of lard covered stale bread, as disgusting that may sound it did the trick and settled her stomach. She pondered what fate would bring her in the coal blackened city. She watched the ferry cross the Mersey loaded with joyful families and a weekend ex-cursion to Birkenhead or Wallasey. There was loud music pumping out from the loudspeakers of the ferry which lifted her spirits, albeit, she was envious of these families enjoying life in these dark days of war.

As the Thomas Currell slowed to turn into the wharf, she watched the Dockers at work unloading grain and loading coal using horse driven drays while the winch driving sailors worked their steam pow-ered cranes. It was a hive of activity on the dock itself with the dockers in an endless line carrying sacks of coal, their faces and clothing black-ened with flashes of a white toothed smile, even the whites of their eyes stood out.

As Myfanwy was leaning on the rail taking in all this action a middle-aged couple struck up a conversation; she guardingly talked of her plight of not having any plan on arrival in their fine city. The couple introduced themselves as Marcia and Mort Tipper and said that they may be able to be of some assistance. They owned an old warehouse on the Docks which was rented out to a grain merchant which had a small room around the back that the Tippers themselves used as storage. They offered to rid their junk and the room could be converted into a flat for Myfanwy to lease.

At long last good fortune shines on Myfanwy, well, in the short term anyway.

On disembarking the Tippers walked her to the room at the back of the warehouse, it was just as they said, empty, cold, a small filthy window looking out on a bleak narrow street. For Myfanwy this was luxury compared to her dormitory in Buckingham St. Over the next few days Marcia was a great help in setting up the basics, a mattress on a wooden frame, a cast iron firebox for cooking and heating, a couple of buckets, one for carrying water and the other a toilet which was emptied into the harbor when darkness fell. It wasn't much but it was her own that offered some sort of independence, she still had a little cash to set up house and cover the rent. Little did she know that the crafty old Mort was grooming her.

Conner and Agnes Finnegan had two children younger than Thomas. The family had been informed by the Home Office of the death of their son several weeks after he had been buried in the Catholic Cemetery outside of Delancy. In their grief they talked about heading back to County Donegal, but their pain was too deeply imbedded. It was not only the death of their son but all the other bad stuff that they thought that they had left in their homeland. Agnes wore her grief in silence, unable to function except for the basics of running a household. She clung onto her grief refusing to leave her home, she shunned her friends who, one by one, gave up trying to console her other than the occasional letter or card. In those dark days there was little professional help available other than the clergy whose consolation she totally rejected. As far as she was concerned was that a loving God would allow her gentle son to be taken. Conner threw himself into his work as his way of coping.

Myfanwy tracked down the Finnegan's home address through the business directory at the Post Office; heavy with child she walked to Woolton in fear and shame. Yes, shame, shame of being with child out of wedlock and having to beg for help from strangers in this affluent neighborhood. She stood on the footpath and looked up at the imposing stone steps leading to a pillared porch and a heavy large door with a lionhead knocker. Conner was at work and the children at school, so the house was deathly quiet. She knocked using the brass ring, silence, she knocked again, this time louder and longer; there was a resounding click and the door partly opened to the head of Agnes.

'What do you want.' With curled lips and the emphasis on the word 'You'.

'I am Myfanwy.'

Agnes opened the door further and stared at this waif who was very pregnant. 'Who are you to come banging on my door? I don't know you.'

'I am from Delancy, your son Thomas is the father of my baby.'

'Thomas has never been married, he wrote to me from the town where he lived and never said that he had taken a wife.'

'We were never married, and Thomas never knew I was with child,' she hesitated, now unsure if the lady at the door was aware of the death of her son. 'Do you know that...'

'Do I know what?'

'That, that Thomas is, has...'

'Who are you, I don't believe you, how dare you come knocking on my door.'

'Our baby is soon to be born; I need help.'

'My son is dead, and that's all I care about,'

Blind grief and anger overrode Agnes's common sense, she looked at Myfanwy in the eye, sneered, and said slowly and deliberately...

'My Thomas would never marry some trollop like you, get out from my house and don't ever darken my doorstep again. You lie to get money from me. I'm not giving you a penny, get out, get out.' She stood back to close the door.

Myfanwy looked at Agnes disbelievingly, 'I don't want money, I just need help, we loved each other,'

'Loved, loved, what does a person like you know about love?'

The door slammed.

Stunned, she stood staring at the closed door, unable to think coherently, she turned and shuffled down the steps one by one. She couldn't think straight, and it was instinct that took her in an aimless downhill direction. It took hours to find herself back in her lonely cold room; she kept her sanity by concentrating on her baby, feeling that her time was close. Late that night she went into labor.

At daylight when life began to stir around the docks, she was able to walk to her door and signal one of the youths who always hung around in the hope of the odd job or two. She gave him the address of Marcia for her to fetch the midwife which had been prearranged.

Rose was born.

Rose was the most beautiful thing that Myfanwy had ever seen. Rose was hers, and hers alone, she had never had anything in her life that belonged to her. This beautiful child was her living link to Thomas, she could see him in their baby. When she held Rose, she held Thomas to her breast. The first time nursed her Rose, she told her of her vow to the dedication of her life to Rose and the memory of her first and what turned out to be her only, love.

As soon as she was up and about, she set to making a meager living by working around the docks, often with Rose on her back in a wrap carrier as her mum worked. She pushed barrows, mended sacks, made tea for the dockers on cold mornings, shoveling spilt coal and so on. Some of the work was unpaid but most of the time, the leading stevedores would find a way employing her so she could earn a few pennies. She gained the respect of these hardworking, head drinking, uneducated men and their employers who saw her has their responsibility to ensure her welfare. God help any male who tried to hit on Myfanwy.

The same could not be said for her landlord, the crafty old Mort. In the months that followed the birth of Rose he became the friendly uncle, occasionally dropping in bringing a baby toy for Rose and a small gift to Myfanwy. Before long he would appear at unusual times, like early evening, becoming over friendly and suggestive. Myfanwy was able to keep him at bay without putting him down, but she instinctively knew that his insistence would only increase to eventually she may have to physically fight him off. For the time being she felt that she was in control, also she suspected he may offer her some sort of financial help in exchange for favors. From the way he talked about his business dealings she knew that if she gave into him, she would just become another of his many assets and treat her as such. Eventually his wife, the doormat Marcia, would realize what was happening and Myfanwy would find herself living on the streets.

As Rose had her first birthday Myfanwy was able to extend her room into the warehouse by having a partition built with the luxury of a large window looking out into the street. She installed a Shacklock coal burning stove that had a flue directing the smoke outside. Another luxury was a cold water tap that she had piped up herself from the warehouse. She had electricity for the first time in her life by running a power lead into the warehouse. Rose had graduated to a backpack while her mother worked around the docks. Meaningful employment was near non-extent for women whose life in those times was a drudgery in the kitchen and the washhouse, bearing child after child while the male in the family was in full control, and especially in control of his pay packet.

Myfanwy was able earn enough to keep the wolf from the door and to keep herself safe from the crafty old Mort. Her nights were spent on schooling Rose and their pleasure time were the songs, poetry and stories of old Ireland. Warm weather took them to a picnic on the beach, sometimes window shopping on a Sunday when the shops were closed. They both loved the Charley Chaplin silent movies. Myfanwy afforded a second-hand Singer sewing machine from a junk shop and had them both looking very smartly dressed. Rose was ready for school.

Liverpool was the gateway between the many countries that the UK traded with, influences from the Americas, Europe and Asia filtered through Liverpool into England, Scotland and Wales.

This gateway brought the latest in technology, inventions, farming, manufactured goods, and produce along with culture, music and people. This gateway also introduced unwanted influences, sadly for both Myfanwy and Rose. This was in the form of an exotic virus later identified as a strain in influenza from which the population had no immunity and no treatment. Rose was seven when she succumbed and was quickly confined to bed needing constant attention to keep her breathing. She was unable to hold food or water and quickly wasted away to just a skeleton of her former self. Doctors reluctantly attended the sick, they, along with nurses included the many who succumbed to this dreaded virus. The medicine prescribed was expensive and mostly proved to be useless. Myfanwy was at Roses bedside for 24 hours a day, sometimes breathing for Rose by mouth-to-mouth as well as coaxing Rose's body to accept sugared water as some sort of sustenance. Her precious little life was ebbing. The do-gooders of the inner city walked the streets with a paint brush and whitewash, painting a cross on the doors of the homes of the sick. Two reasons, one was to isolate the sick and the other was that the cross of God may save the life of the dying. The docks had closed down and with no income Myfanwy became destitute.

Marcia did what she could for her tenants by leaving a little food or a few pennies on Myfanwy's doorstep. This was a cue for the cunning old Mort, unbeknown to Marcia he called around weekly and demanded his overdue rent and threatened to evict his tenants. That's when he came up with his cunning plan, he would forgo the rent if she was to become his lover. If she refused his generous offer, he would have her evicted and thrown out onto the streets.

'What about your wife Marcia, she wouldn't allow you to do this?'

'Marcia does what I tell her, you better think, and think hard, I'll be back tomorrow, and you keep that sick kid of yours in her room, I don't want her to be anywhere near me when I'm here.'

Myfanwy remembered her promise that she would, at all costs, do what it takes to keep her love of Thomas alive through the life of her daughter.

Rose clung onto life through the winter months with the 24/7 dedication of her mother, occasional visits from a doctor or nurse. All this cost money and Myfanwy's debts were mounting. Also, the Government coffers were running on empty from being still in recovery from the war, resulting in very little healthcare from that quarte, especially for the poor..

When Rose settled at night her mother had found a way to enter the large coal storage facility on the docks and steal coal. This kept her damp, draughty, uninsulated rooms from growing mold which caused breathing difficulties. The white cross painted on her door kept them well isolated, that was except for the occasional visit from the wily Mort. Finding sustainable food was near impossible. Myfanwy would write a note and with a few pennies she would leave it at the door of grocery shops who in turn would leave her order out for her. If she had no cash, that meant no food. She became aware of a wig maker up in Bold St, so she walked up the hill and sold her hair. It wasn't long after that she sold her front teeth to a dentist, with nothing else left, she then sold her body.

It took a year for the world to develop immunity and for Rose to recover, but recover she did and was eager to start school for the first time at St Columbia's. Mother and daughter went shopping for the very smart school uniform, it was Rose's first clothing she had that was not made by her mother. She told her mother now that she was old enough to be independent and walked herself to school. Myfanwy proudly stood at her door and watched her daughter walk away; she had painted the door green to cover over the white cross several months beforehand. It was time for a new beginning, or so she thought.

She went to make a cup of tea but was overwhelmed with exhaustion and emotionally drained, so she took to her bed. An excited Rose arrived home full of her first day at school she found her mum in bed asleep, she just put it down to tiredness. During the week Mort had arrived to collect his so-called rent, saw that she was not well but took his pound of flesh anyway. By the time the weekend arrived Rose could see that her mother's health had declined considerably.

When Rose had recovered, Myfanwy's immunity, which had remained strong in keeping her daughter alive, weakened and she too succumbed that virus that had been waiting for the opportunity to attack its host. Their roles reversed, against her mother's will Rose stopped going to school to become a fulltime nurse. As Myfanwy's health worsened Rose was continually having to pester all the health authorities for help, there was not a great deal they could do anyway. The Doctor had made several visits and prescribed medication, the best he could do was to write a note, addressed to the Mater Hospital that he strongly recommended that Myfanwy be urgently admitted. Rose's two-hour walk resulted in that the hospital would put her on their waiting list, they would contact the doctor when there was a bed available. That promise never eventuated, especially for the poor.

Myfanwy was having intermittent delirium, realizing that death was eminent, fearing that in her death Rose would be incarcerated in the infamous Nazareth House orphanage, this concept was totally unthinkable. Now completely bedridden she took from under her pillow and handed the eight-year-old Rose the 'Blue book of Verse' with Thomas's bookmark inserted.

'Take this book to the address written on the last page, knock on the door and give this book to the lady of the house, she is your grandmother, tell her your name is Rose and that your father is Thomas. Rose nodded apprehensively, Her mum added, 'Before you go, read this poem to me.'

Rose climbed into her bed alongside her mum, she opened the book and read the poem...

'The Lake Isle of Innisfree'.

'I will rise and go now, and go to Innisfree,
And a small cabin build there, of clay and wattles made;
Nine bean-rows will I have there, a hive for the honey-bee
And live alone in the bee-loud glade.
And I shall have some peace there, for peace comes dropping slow.
Dropping from the veils of the morning to where the cricket sings.
There midnight's all a glimmer, and the moon as purple glow,

And evening full of linnet's wings.'
I will rise and go now, for always night and day,
I hear the lake water lapping with low sounds by the shore.
While I stand on the roadway, or on the pavements grey,
I hear in the deep heart's core.'
'Go now,' said Myfanwy, 'take this to the family of your father.'
Myfanwy was at peace as her daughter stood straight, with her mission in mind, she gently closed the door quietly behind her.

William Butler Yeats wrote this poem while in London after hearing the tinkle of water from a fountain that was in a shop window in Fleet St. He was overcome with homesickness for his hometown of Sligo and his longing for the solitude of the Isle of Innisfree which lies close to the shore in Lough Gill under the watchful eye of Ben Bulben.

7

I HAVE A TERRIBLE STORY

that I've carried with me for nine years,' said Agnes when Conner returned from his day's work.

Earlier in the day Agnes had opened her front door to a timid knock. At the first sight of Rose she thought it was her son, Thomas, standing in front of her.

'I'm Rose.'

'I know who you are,' she fully opened the door and stood to one side, 'I've been waiting for you for such a long time, please come in.'

Rose had taken most of the day to find the Finnegan house in Woolton, she checked the number on the letterbox several times with the address that was written in her father's hand at the back of the blue book. She looked up at the house at the end of the freesia bordered path, she had never seen a house so grand. As she took the six steps up onto the fine graveled path as she desperately held back the tears that were welling. 'I must be brave, I must not cry,' she took a deep breath and counted the 25 paces to the start of the half circle of 15 steps leading to the front door. This is the same walk as her mother once did, 'I will not cry; I will not cry.'

Rose forced herself to lift the brass ring of the lion's head knocker, she hesidently knocked after a long minute she knocked a little louder and then again, this time a little louder. She heard the faint footsteps becoming louder and closer, then stop. The door opened.

Agnes led Rose into her lounge and said, 'your father, is my son, I'm your grandmother.' She crouched, sinking to her knees to be at the same height as her granddaughter, she opened her arms, 'Please hug me, I am sorry, I'm just so sorry.'

Rose didn't know what her grandmother was sorry about, but she too couldn't hold back the tears that she had bottled up for so long during her mother's illness. They sat together, on the chaise lounge as Agnes explained. 'When I opened the door, I saw your dad when he was about the same age as you, how old are you?'

'I've just turned nine,'

'Nine, yes, same eyes, I saw him in you when I first opened the door, I thought you were my son, I thought he'd come home. Your mother, where's your mother?'

'Can you please help, my mum is sick.'

'My husband Conner,' she stopped, a little confused, 'Of course he's your grandfather, isn't he? He'll be home soon.'

Agnes picked up the blue book from Rose's lap, she pulled out the bookmark, looked at the pencil drawing of the stylized rose, and said to her granddaughter, 'This is my son's handwriting, now I know now why your mum called you Rose, it's just like you, it's beautiful.' She read the poem to herself and then read again out loud, the poem her son had written in dedication of his love for Myfanwy...

'Those of us who love and know,

Live so most,

We may not reach the stars,

But, at least, we've been up in a balloon.' (anon)

Agnes had never told her husband the existence of Myfanwy all those years ago. When he arrived home and saw this child, with a glass of milk in front of her, he stopped in his tracks, and looked from one to the other. Agnes explained to him of the terrible thing she had done, she couldn't explain why she reacted as she did, she didn't know herself, why. It all began to make sense, she was ashamed of herself because of the grief and despair that had dominated her total existence. Rose had now entered her life, and this allowed her the opportunity to make amends, now, with a sense of purpose she was not going to let this chance for redemption escape. Her life depended on it.

Conner sat, with hands clasped and elbows on knees now understanding the anguish that his wife had been living with which had seeped through into their family. He looked at Rose, he looked at Agnes and an image of his son hovered back and forth between them. He went to stand to put his arms around his granddaughter, he held back, unsure of what her reaction would be if her were to hug her. He stood, offered his hands, which she grasped, and he gently pulled her to her feet.

'Shall we go and find your mother?'

They were shocked to see that the very ill Myfanwy had slipped into a coma. Conner took control of the situation, he organized an ambulance to take her to the best hospital that, 'money can buy' he said. Both mother and daughter were admitted into a suite in the Sefton Private Hospital. Rose was discharged several days later after being under observation and was picked up by Conner in his shining black Morris Cowley. Sitting in the back seat of an automobile, Rose felt like she was the Queen so she gave the royal wave to the poor unfortunate pedestrians who had to walk. This childish act was much to Conners delight.

Myfanwy was slow to recover, Conner and Agnes made sure she had every opportunity to get the best treatment money could buy. After two months at Sefton, she was discharged; Conner, Agnes and Rose picked her up, so mother and daughter sat in the back seat of the polished black Morris Cowley. Rose taught her mum the royal wave, several times pedestrians returned the wave, one even displayed his index finger.

'That was rude,' said Rose.

Mother and daughter became part of the Finnegan household; they had their own bedroom and shared the luxury of a hot water bath. Agnes regained her sense of purpose in life after finding redemption. Her own children were in their last years of secondary school doted on their newfound niece. The doctor from Sefton hospital visited regularly and arranged a dentist to rebuild Myfanwy's front teeth. The family employed a chef to ensure that they all had access to a nutritional diet. With the ladies of the house, Rose felt grownup, and with her Mum they made full use of the beautician, hairdresser and physical instructor who were all coming and going on a regular basis. They shopped at Compton House, then known as the most fashionable department store in Liverpool. Rose was enrolled at Calderstones School for Girls in which she struggled to be accepted because of her working-class accent and background. A year later she shifted to Liverpool Girls High where she was accepted for who she was rather than what she was. The Finnegan household was alive with visitors and they were part of the dinner circuit comprised of mostly Irish expatriates. Those were the nights that brought out the songs of Ireland fueled by the still illegal Pointin.

As Myfanwy regained her health, vitality and confidence she was able to take some of the load of managing the household from Agnes who was then able to spend more time in her garden and to dabble in watercolor painting. From a very young age Myfanwy had a flair for color and she too picked up a brush and played around with color on paper. Agnes soon came to recognize that her daughter-in-law, as she liked to call her, had an natural talent so she brought her a gift of brush's, paint and watercolor paper. This opened a whole new world for Myfanwy who at every opportunity was in the garden, just blending color without worrying too much about structure. This enthused Agnes to arrange night painting classes held at Knowsley Community College.

Myfanwy was feeling as little uncomfortable in not financially contributing to the household and the education of Rose. Agnes told her not to worry about it, 'We can afford it.' That was not the point of the matter as far as Myfanwy was concerned. Her confidence grew to where she would wander the streets and parks with sketch pad and pencil and then return home to paint. On Saturday mornings her and Agnes would go to the Farmers Market in front of the Lime St station where they came up with the concept of setting up a stall to try and sell her work. She was allotted a spot between a cheesemaker and a fish monger where she and Agnes set up their covered stall. Conner had his cabinetmaker construct a counter and easels to display her work. Her display of cityscapes and color impressions from the botanical Gardens created interest but failed to sell. People came to the markets to buy spuds and cabbages, not art. The were a couple of enquiries regarding portraits which were not in her vocabulary, however, those enquiries planted a seed in her brain.

The Market Day before Christmas traditionally was a fun day with music, clowns, pots of hot food, freshly baked bread, one could even buy as Christmas tree with decorations. Liverpool was well on the road to financial recovery after 'the war that was to end all wars.' We all know now that statement was a load of bullshit. However, a new middleclass arose from poverty giving strength to a more liberal government. The 'downtrodden' had had enough of being the 'downtrodden'.

Anyway, at the Xmas market, a well-heeled looking couple showed an interest in her painting of the Cunard building in light rain with blurred pedestrians hurrying with black umbrellas. The man's wife loved the painting, so he asked Myfanwy if she could wrap it up in brown paper. Her husband handed her two one-pound notes, desperately trying to look casual Myfanwy asked them to return in half an hour and she would have to painting ready. After they wandered off, she went around the back of the fishmonger's barrow, threw her arms in the air and yelled, 'Eureka'.

The well-heeled couple must have told friends because she made further sales to a class of people who normally would not frequent a Farmers Market. At last, financial independence, well, enough to pay Roses expenses and a little pocket money, occasional visits to the butcher and the greengrocer, and of course. canvas and paints. She was hungry to learn, to take risks and put her inner self on display through her art.

Myfanwy had learnt all she could from the Knowsley Community and enrolled in the very expensive Liverpool College of Art. She expected a creative, inspirational, innovational, imaginative attitude, but found just the opposite. She found the course was dominated by a bunch of old farts who could or would not break from the tradition of heavy oils and formality. Although she had to admit that she did learn about color and the technical side of basic drawing including the study of facial bone structure for portraiture. She was quite happy when she run out of money to pay for this sort of tuition, so, it was back to the drawing board, so to speak.

She found that the parks and botanical gardens of Liverpool restricted her lust for the countryside; when the opportunities arose she took to roaming the rural, often with Rose in tow. She would paint the simple scenes of country life, an old stone bridge over a stream, a farmer with scythe toiling in a field, often capturing a scene while sitting in a teahouse of a table with a pot of flowers looking out to a rural landscape. She would paint the same scene several times and blend colour in a changing atmosphere. One summer school holiday she and Rose caught the train north to Windermere in Cambria and the Lakes District. For mother and daughter this was a place of wonder and enchantment. This misty and mystical place oozed inspiration, not only the scenery but this was the home of story tellers and poets. It was a world of Beatrix Potter, William Wordsworth, knights in shiny armor, Camelot, imagining a long-haired maiden sitting side-saddle on a white horse, all this in contrast with the desolate Roman ruins atop of Hardknot. They fell in love with life.

In the winter months and confined by the weather she was able to concentrate on portraiture and still life, everyday objects like a simple bowl, a vase of flowers, a book lying open, her brushes in a row. She became totally immersed in all things art.

After a couple of years Myfanwy was emotionally strong enough to take the walk back down to Dockland, memories, good and bad flooded into her. There were some new faces, but basicly same people were there servicing the shipping industry, the workers, the boss's, the food sellers, the shady charactors looking for a score and so on, humanity with all its warts. She wandered around to the back of the warehouse where she once lived and cupped her hands to look through the dirty window. It was dingy, dark, but there it was as she had left it. Her old narrow street was changing, across the road there was a fish and chip shop and on the corner was and elegant looking sign offering Devonshire Teas. Wandering further she found that the whole area was being renovated, some of the old stone buildings that had been blackened by years of coal smog had been cleaned. She sat on a bench overlooking the Mersey letting her mind wander, where it will go.

Her stall at the markets had served its purpose and it was time to do things differently, a few scenarios came to mind and then discarded. Myfanwy soon formulated the concept of a studio where she could paint and also display her work on a permanent basis. Time for a nice cup of tea and a scone at the bright sparkling Devonshire teahouse. She opened the door which triggered a bell and a crisp white aproned waitress appeared and offered her a table, as she sat, she heard her name, 'Myfanwy'. Sitting at the table in the bay window, which invited a weak sun, was an elegantly dressed woman; it took her just a few seconds to recognise Marcia.

They were both genuine in their excitement of each other. Over English Breakfast tea with scones, jam and cream they were relaxed in their own company. After their initial exchanges Myfanwy began to feel queasy at the thought of the crafty old Mort, she dare not mention his name in fear of anger towards Marcia, whom she thought was probably unaware of his dirty deeds. It was Marcia who brought the subject. 'My husband,' she said, 'succumbed to the plague epidemic and has passed.'

'Oh, I'm so sorry of your loss, when did that happen?'

'Not long after you disappeared; he was always very careful about his health, always washing his hands and avoiding anybody who may have been in contact with the plague,' she thought for a minute, 'I just don't know where he got it from,'

'This is so sad for you, Marcia,'

'Oh, I'm okay, my Mort suffered so badly that it was a relief when he did pass, I know it's a horrible thing to say, but...'

'I understand what you are saying, Marcia, your Mort will rest peacefully until you join him.'

'That won't be for a while yet, actually, I have found a new life that I never knew existed, I now have friends of my own and I shop at Compton House,' she looked around as if conspiring, 'I even have a male friend,'

Myfanwy felt a sense of sadness for Marcia but also relief that she wouldn't have to front this evil man. It then dawned on her of the roll she had inadvertly played in the demise of the crafty old Mort, he probably contracted the plague from herself. She resisted her desire to stand, pump the air with both hands and yell 'Eureka'.

Instead, she just simply said, 'Good for you.'

As the afternoon cooled, they were warmed by an electric heater and drenched themselves with more hot tea and freshly baked gingernuts. The conversation had led to Myfanwy and her art; she asked Marcia if she still owned the warehouse.

'Yes, I do, the grain merchant still has the lease, your old flat is still as you left it, but I've done nothing about it since my Mort passed on, bless him, maybe I should sell it one day.'

'I walked past and had a look through the window, it occurred to me that it would make a good studio and maybe I could display some of my work.'

'I think that's a great idea, it needs major renivation,'

'My father-in-law, I suppose he's not really my father-in-law, because I never married, he's a building contractor and maybe he can help,'

'This is exciting, Mort had no brothers or sisters, so I was left with an excellent endowment, I never realized when Mort was alive how,' she looked for the right word, 'how, unhappy, I had been for the most of my life, I've always believed that everything happens for the best,' she put her forefinger to her lips, 'shush, don't tell Mort.'

'My lips are sealed, so, do you think we can make this work?'

'Sure, we can, I've got the money and you've got the talent'.

'We should be professional and have a formal lease,'

'Whatever, just tell me what you want, and we'll do it, by the way, this Devonshire Tea is on me, lovely scones.'

'The best cup of tea I've ever had.'

When Myfanwy got back to the Finnegans she told Agnes what had transpired, she too hopped onto the band wagon of enthusiasm. Conner arrive home from work and was told that they had a small job for him down at Dockland.

After they had explained to him their proposal he simply said, 'I thought you said small, this is a major.'

'Small compared to what you usually do.'

Conner and his team of tradesman got to work, the once high ceiling that caused the flat to freeze in the winter was now the perfect place for a gallery with a mezzanine for Myfanwy's studio. Agnes and Marcia went shopping at the importers of exotic goods of the international gateway of Liverpool. A large bay window from Persia, solid double doors from Tibet, a lacquered table from Shanghai, a spiral wrought iron staircase from Paris, no expense was spared, especially from the Merry Widow, Marcia.

Agnes and Marcia were planning a grand opening of French wine and Italian cheese until Myfanwy realized that she didn't have the quality and quantity to display. The three girls got their paint brushes to work, Myfanwy on canvas and the other two painted with gay colors, the interior walls of the gallery and studio.

Taking a break one afternoon Myfanwy wandered around the docks and came across three brown skinned children, unwashed with ragged clothing that offered little protection from the cold wind coming from the Mersey. They were huddled together sitting on cargo boxes. She asked them where their mother was, they looked at Myfanwy blankly, she realized that they could not speak English. The children had the features and skin colour that indicated they probably were refugees from some Middle Eastern country, fleeing war or famine. They wore the wide-open eyes of children suffering from cold and hunger. Myfanwy raised her arm with an open hand to signal one of the many message boys who hung around the docks to go get fish, chips and drinks, not only for the children but for himself as well. While waiting she pulled from her satchel, what were her best friends, her sketch pad and pencils, and went to work. Her sketching captured their fear and vulnerability that she too had experienced all those years ago. She felt their poverty and their intense loneliness at being left sitting, waiting, in this strange cold country and not having any understanding of the English language.

It didn't take long for the refuge children, the message boy and herself to polish off the fish and chips and, for possibly the first time in their lives, the sweet fizzy drinks. Myfanwy taught them to wipe their hands and faces with the newspaper wrapping. As she was gathering the scraps of newspaper their mother appeared from behind her, she looked at Myfanwy and the message boy, gathered her family and hurried off in the opposite direction from which she had come.

Myfanwy watched them hurry away, she then turned around to where the mother had come from. Leaning against the stone wall of a building was a shabbily dressed male rolling a cigarette while staring intently at the backs of the woman and her children as they disappeared around the corner.

She immediatly knew that the woman had sold her body to this man.

This whole episode shook Myfanwy to the bone and stayed with her for a very long time. This tragic experience filtered into her watercolor painting of the three refugee children sitting on the cargo box. She painted several versions of the children and displayed them on easels in her not yet opened gallery window. She felt that she needed to make an impact with the public on opening day and felt that she just didn't have the subject matter to capture the public interest. The refugees on the dock reminded her of the women of Buckingham St Dublin, whose similar vulnerability and desperation had played on her mind over the years. She had always felt that she had deserted these women with whom she had an affinity. Although reluctant to return to Ireland she was drawn to go back to Buckingham St to see if there was anything she could do to give the plight of these terribly unfortunate women some recognition through her art.

Myfanwy disembarked from the ferry at the Dublin Grand Canal Dock. This time travelling a lot more comfortable than her voyage while pregnant with Rose on the Thomas Currell. She retraced her steps from the Dock to Buckingham St imagining the same emotions she had when she had many years ago which just felt like yesterday. The Women's Refuge had not changed one iota, the same squalid conditions and although the women were of another generation, they wore the same look of fear and desperation. Several who had no choice except for prostitution had born several children and were shunned by society. All were in poor physical and mental health because of their diet and lack of professional medical care. They were shut behind closed doors, they were unseen and ignored. The Nuns were over-worked and often in the same poor health as the ones they cared for in this place of so-called refuge.

The Mother Superior, actually she wasn't, but that's what she was called, of the Sisters of Mercy remembered Myfanwy and accepted her offer of help; she was given a bed in the lower floor and did what she could. In volunteering as she did, she was able to think beyond just the day to day struggle, she thought that there must be a better way. She had the courage to knock on doors, the City Council, the different reli-gious denominations, Government agencies, volunteer organizations, but got nowhere. They all said that, yes, they were aware of the plight of the Refuge and were doing all they could do to help as they showed her the door. The males of these entities were not interested. Myfanwy did what she could to talk to the few women in a position to recognise the issues but just didn't want to get their hands dirty. It was the women of Buckingham St who got the blame for their own predicament.

All through this she was sketching their portraits, adding a little watercolour here and there She asked the sitter to tell her story which she recorded on the back of the sketch, most did, some could not, some would not. There was a suicide, this was not rare, but it shook Myfanwy to the core.

The girl was hardly a teenager, she arrived at the door at about six months into her pregnancy, she never spoke a word, not even her name; the women called her Meg. The way she worked alongside the women showed that she must have worked as a servant in a large estate. When she felt the first movement of her baby she took to her bed in depression. She was found dead, smothered in blood in her bed, she had run a razor down both forearms. Myfanwy was shocked with her own morbid fascination, she felt compelled to sketch the face of the dead girl, such a young face that, in death was so innocently beautiful.

Myfanwy eventually ran out of money so had no choice but to depart for home. Walking back down Buckingham St, she, with guilt and shame could not look back and in a blur of tears returned to her home in Woolton.

She lived with anger and frustration of not being able to do anything about Buckingham St. Her release was to paint from the sketches that she had brought back with her. She set up a camp stretcher on her Mezzanine studio and isolated herself, working with intensity while the raw emotions that she had brought back from Dublin were foremost in her head and heart. Her only release from her torment was to transfer this raw emotion to canvas.

Agnes and Marcia became informal partners with Myfanwy in the soon to be opened gallery cum studio. The two things they had, which they put to good use, was time and money, while Myfanwy concentrated on the women of Buckingham St. The art world was shifting from the elaborate Art Noveaux to the new age of Art Deco with an emerging new wave of artists, sculptors and potters who were always looking for space to introduce their craft to the public. One problem they had was the naming of the gallery which they had bandied about and argued about. Conner stepped in and created a sign in accordance to the Art Deco style.

'Art and Object'

It had taken Myfanwy three months to complete her series which she entitled.

'The Women of Buckingham Street'

Agnes and Marcia oversaw the grand opening and had spent a small fortune on the French wine and Italian cheese. Myfanwy had designed a poster which they had printed and employed the Dockland lay-abouts to nail these posters on lampposts around the area. The day arrived with mixed results, the 'old-rich' wouldn't lower themselves to be seen in the working-class dockland area, the new-rich were keen to look but couldn't understand Myfanwy's style, which at that time was unnamed until in later years as 'modern impressionist'. Most were more interested in the freeby wine and cheese than what was hanging on the walls. Several of her cityscapes and one landscape of the Lakes District were red stickered. Her portraits of the Buckingham St, women created comment, but none sold. Once the wine ran dry the show was over Myfanwy was very happy to have finished early. She had run out of patience with what she called, pointless conversations. She wanted time to herself so when Conner, Rose, Agnes and Marcia departed leaving Myfanwy to sleep on her camp stretcher. She knew in herself that she had created something uniquely special that gave her an immense satisfaction. Sitting on the overstuffed lounge, which Agnes had insisted, correctly, that would give customers time to think and spend money, Myfanwy's brain flashed back on her life which engulfed her in a wave of tearful emotion. Before sleep she put the past back to where it belonged, thinking about her art, said out loud to herself...

'England is not quite ready for me just yet, one day...'

Art and Object struggled to make any money, but between them, Marcia and Agnes had become close friends and took great joy in opening the doors every morning while Myfanwy was at work upstairs with brushes or out and about with sketchpad. In walking the streets of Liverpool and Manchester she was always on the lookout for new ideas around the modern concept of Art Deco. She discovered the pottery of the New Zealand architect Keith Murray and the porcelain painting of Claris Cliff and others who were all too willing to display their stuff at Art and Object. However, just as with Myfanwy's work, the general monied public were a little slow to catch on.

Once again, the fickle fingers of fate found Myfanwy, this time in a more positive manner. The Liverpool to Dublin ferry had been delayed until a squally weather front had passed. Saroise La Nouse had travelled by express train from an exhibition at the London Portrait Gallery to Liverpool and became bored while waiting in the overheated ferry building. Bundled up in her mackintosh, galoshes and tweed scarf she braved the gusty NE winds to blow the cobwebs of her brain. To get some relief from the wind she turned into a narrow street and saw the sign… Art & Object.

Saroise lost track of time as she studied, with intense scrutiny, the faces and the stories of the Women of Buckingham Street. Like many Dubliners she had some vague knowledge of the Refuge but, with unintended snobbery avoided its existence; 'out of sight, out of mind.' She was shocked by the raw fear and desperation of these women, she was morbidly captivated by the stories of each and every face. The last portrait was of a young girl, a child, with closed eyes, was she asleep or was she…' Her provenance simple.

MEG

d. Buckingham Street 16/05/1926

Brimming with tears, Saroise, could do nothing but turn away. She forced herself to turn back and read the name and the date of her death again. Who was this Meg? Where is her family? How did her life end in that forsaken house? Did anybody love her?

Agnes was waiting behind the counter, pretending to read a magazine while watching Saoirse's emotional response as she walked back and once again closely looking at each painting and their own personal story.

'Who is the artist?'

'Myfanwy, she should be in tomorrow morning,'

'Myfanwy, would it be possible to meet her? What's her second name?'

'Fitzgerald, whom shall I tell her is enquiring?'

She withdrew a card from her purse and handed it to Agnes.

Saroise La Nouse

Curator

Dublin City Gallery

'I'll make sure she gets it.'

Saroise walked to exit and got as far as the large Tibetan doors, stopped, turned and went back to Meg and said to her.'

'I will be back in the morning my sweetness,' she cleared her throat, 'Yes, I for one, love you.'

The fine city of Dublin was not ready for the exhibition of the 'Women of Buckingham St'. The Dublin Gazette and the Dublin Voice reporters had a field day. The house of Buckingham Street headlined the front pages. Reporters with camera crews camped outside at the bottom of the steps of the Council owned Dublin City Gallery waiting for somebody, anybody to appear; even the cleaners who exited a side door were confronted. The front doors remained locked tight as were the lips of the bureaucrats who were responsible for the welfare of all Dubliners.

Saroise was interviewed by the media in her capacity as the Curator of the Gallery. she was bombarded with questions regarding the artist.

'Yes, she is Irish. No, she will not be attending the exhibition. Yes, her name is just Myfanwy. No, she does not live in Dublin. Yes, she chooses to remain anonymous. No, Myfanwy did not have permission from Meg to paint her portrait. Yes, the paintings will be sold. Yes, the proceeds will be going to the Buckingham women's refuge. Yes, the Dublin City Gallery will purchase one painting only. No, I do not intend to answer any more questions.'

It didn't take long for the media to stir up the blame game. Social Services blamed the Council, Council blamed the Government, Government blamed the Mayor, the Mayor blamed the Prime Minister, The Prime Minister blamed Sinn Fein, Sinn Fein blamed the Bishop, The Bishop blamed all wanton women, The IRA blamed the Nationalists, the suffragettes blamed all men, the Protestants blamed the Catholics, the Pope blamed the Devil. The following enquiry found fault everywhere they investigated, and the many public funded agencies did not get off lightly; except of course the Devil, he's a cunning bugger, that one.

Saroise had a letter of introduction from the Bishop for the Sister in charge of Buckingham St who in turn gave her permission to interview the women who were there at the time of Meg's death. Nobody knew anything about her, Meg never spoke a word, not even her name. The women called her Meg after the grandmother of the mid-wife. She worked in the laundry prior to confinement, she took her life when her baby was taken away at birth. Megs body was taken away under a canvas in a horse driven open cart by the man employed to deliver and collect the laundry. Saroise interviewed the driver who said he delivered the body to Glasnevin Cemetery for paupers.

The Dublin city Gallery announced that they had purchased the painting 'Meg' on behalf of the people of Dublin. Saroise created the 'Meg Charitable Trust' with the initial funds from the sale of Myfanwy's series 'Women of Buckingham.' This endowment led to the creation of a modern maternity hospital and women's refuge situated adjacent to Phoenix Park. This facility, which is still known as 'Buckingham Women's,' came back into the public eye because of their stand on the controversial question on abortion in Catholic dominated Ireland, but that's another story for another day.

Saroise and Myfanwy designed an Art Deco stylized headstone for Meg which was unveiled under a yew tree in a secluded spot in Glasnevin Cemetery. At the unveiling Meg's story was told to all of Dublin who gave her the love, that she so much needed but never received in her tragic life. Seek and ye shall find.

'OUR BEAUTIFUL MEG,
WE CRY FOR YOU
WE LOVE YOU'
d. Buckingham Street 16/05/1926

8

ART IS LIFE, LIFE IS ART

Never in her wildest imagination would Myfanwy have thought that her art, well, art in general could have such a powerful impact on the lives of people. There were times when she thought that her art was just a meaningless and frivolous pastime. She had no desire for the notoriety that her exhibition in Dublin and, in turn, Art & Object had earned. She went to great lengths to avoid the public and media scrutiny that went with controversy. Her passion was to hunt for the subject matter whether it be countryside, cityside, seaside or the unheralded people who were at the base of the pyramid of humanity. The finished article on the canvas was just the result of her observation of humanity's roll in nature. The Gallery was being well managed by Agnes and Marcia who kept close scrutiny on finances. The base income came from the sale of Myfanwy's art but also the Gallery had become a desirable outlet for emerging artistes with whom the partners who had developed a keen eye for what would open the purses of those who had disposable income in the short boom years after the war.

Life took a change of direction for Myfanwy while Rose was in her last year of college and had a successful interview to enroll for a degree in Education at the University of Manchester. This meant that Rose would live in the University Halls of Residence. Myfanwy had become restless in the confines of Liverpool and saw this as a chance to expand her horizons into the big wide world.

Marcia and Agnes had emerged from being destined, like most women of their era, to fade into old age as they continued to be a doormat for the bread winner of the family. They became envied by their neighborhood peers as being successful women in a world of male dominated enterprises. Their vision was to drag Liverpool from its reputation of being a hellhole into the center of art in the UK. In fact that was not to happen until the 21st century. They both dressed accordingly for the late 1920s and early 1930s, lower waistlines and higher hemlines. Less formality in favor of simplicity and comfort; they both practiced smoking factory-made cigarettes with a long thin holder, that didn't last long because of the coughing and Conner complained that kissing Agnes was like licking an ashtray.

Myfanwy's decision was to go and follow wherever her art would take her. Her partners wanted to throw a farewell party at Art & Object, Myfanwy objected to the fanfare, and they settled on Devonshire Teas, including Rose and Conner, at the Teahouse where all this started.

"Where are you going? What are you going to do? How are you going to live? Who's going to carry your bags? It's a dangerous world out there, take care, don't forget to write, are you going to send us paintings?'

Myfanwy had no answer for these questions, simply because she didn't know. The only concrete answer she gave was that she had heard of an artist collective in St. Ives that may be a good place to start.

Marcia didn't know where St, Ives was, could have been on the other side of the world as far as she was concerned. 'How you going to get there?'

'By train for most of the way, after that, maybe I'll have to walk'.

'What about your clothes and painting stuff?'

'I have a backpack,'

'Backpack, what's that?'

'I've just bought one from Cotswold's, it has a wooden frame that holds a canvas bag with compartments, it's got leather straps that go over your shoulders and you tie it around your waist, then your arms are free.

'Heaven forbid. I suppose you'll be wearing short pants and boots like a man'.

'Thanks for the tip.'

'That's my mum,' said Rose.

It took Myfanwy several days and several trains to arrive in Plymouth; she stood on the rise were Sir Francis Drake finished his game of bowls as the Spanish Armada appeared on the horizon. She stood on the stone steps where the Pilgrims and departed to sail the Atlantic and settle in America in the 1600s. Myfanwy too began her own pilgrimage from Plymouth to St Ives by way of walking the coastal trail of Cornwell via those magical seaside villages and avoiding the larger towns. She often found shelter in a B&B cottage, sometimes a soft bed in a hay barn for a few pennies to a subsistence farming family. Weather permitting, she would sleep rough; sometimes it was the luxury of a hot bath and a hearty stew at a pub. The coastal trail meandered inland through misty moors where the farmers were obliged to allow 'right of way' to travelers. On arriving in a village, she would seek out the best Cornish pastie and who could not say no to the fish-n-chips in Penzance.

Standing on the cliffs of Lands End watching the seabirds soaring and dipping she opened her arms as if she too was a white bird in the foam of the sea. (W.B. Yeats).

'Freedom', she shouted into the SW wind.

She had estimated that her journey would take several weeks but in the end it took several months, several sketchpads, a new pair of boots and minus half a stone in weight. Every day there was an abundance of sea and sky which was at the mercy of the forces of ever changing light.

As the coastal trail slowly turned to the north her sense of excitement grew as she neared St. Ives. The last day of her trek was lunch with the tin miners who guided her down into the mine in a mechanical lift and then leveled into the mine that went hundreds of yards under the sea-bed. What brave men they be. That afternoon was spent sketching the hard faces of these men with the mine workings in the background. They respectfully invited her to camp with them for the night.

The next morning, she climbed the steady rise and there, spread out before her, was the small town of St Ives. Celebration was a nice cup of tea in the beachfront cafe. By word of mouth, she found a room in an old rambling house with shared bath, kitchen and lounge. There was a notice on the hallway wall.

HOUSE RULES

Rule No 1 ---- 'One bath only, per person, per week.'

Rule No 2 ---- 'Leaving dirty dishes in the sink is forbidden.'

Rule No 3 ---- 'No Parties'.

Rule No 4 ---- 'Male visitors are forbidden.'

Rule No 5 ---- 'Do not flush sanitary pads down the toilet.'

Rule No 6 ---- 'Smalls must not be washed in the kitchen sink.'

Rule No 7 ---- 'Rent must be paid every Friday, no exceptions.'

'Any breech of the rules immediate eviction will follow.'

'All rules are made to be broken, except for number seven, I'm Barbara,' came a voice from behind her.

'I'm Myfanwy and I think I need more than one bath a week,'

'Sometimes the hot water is not all that hot, it's all in the timing, you're Irish?'

'That I am, hope it doesn't count against me,'

'I just love the way you talk; do you drink wine?'

'Is the Pope a Catholic?'

'Well, I'm not sure about that sometimes, we all pool our money, 5 shillings a week or whatever you can afford, we always seem to be able to rake up enough money by the time Friday comes, if there is any left-over, we head down to the winery.'

'Does the Landlady live in?'

'Old Ma Seaton, no, the only day we see her is on a Friday. It's Friday tomorrow so we'll have a count up and see how much cash is left after the rent and spend it on wine, once the word gets around that we have a new addition to the house we can do some intro's, seeing we're not allowed to call it a party so we call it our weekly House Rules meeting.'

There was an old two storied building in disrepair, one block back from the beach that nobody seemed to own. This building was used by the art fraternity as a workshop. Council turned a blind eye to it because this was a source of attracting artists and art lovers to their otherwise sleepy town.

Myfanwy loved her life of art, working with other like-minded people sharing knowledge and experience. This creative place attracted not only painters but sculptors, potters, musicians who would come and go at all hours of the day or the night or the week or the month, no matter of age, color of skin, sex or, heaven forbid, sexual orientation, which was illegal. This freedom attracted the good and the not so good alike, it didn't take long to sort the misfits who were quickly given their marching orders.

Frivolous things like money were not all that important in those gay times. Myfanwy, along with her housemates lived a meager existence, sometimes not knowing where their next meal was coming from. The word 'money' was only mentioned on a Friday. If one had money, all had money, if one was broke, all were broke. Canvas, paints, brushes and all tools connected to producing art were shared.

Thursday was Farmers Market Day when the Art Dealers, collectors and bargain hunters would come from as far away as London on the lookout for the next Picasso, Turner or Georgia O'Keeffe. Barbara was a sculptor who was attracted to St Ives because her favored stone of alabaster was mined there. Her work was well sort after, as was the art of the New Zealander Francis Hodgkins. Myfanwy found it difficult to sell her work, she wasn't perturbed by this simply because she believed in what was doing and just being in St Ives at that time provided the courage the keep trying. To keep the wolf from the door she sometimes worked along with other struggling artists at menial tasks, sometimes a waitress, house cleaner, laundry, washing, ironing for the many hotels of the area. The St Ives beach attracted many summer and weekend visitors whose scant regard for rubbish disposal gave Myfanwy a job with the council a couple of days a week. She walked the streets with a pointed stick and bag, the pay was meagre at best but she loved every minute of this paid job.

Barbara's sculptures were in demand commanding a price high enough for her to afford to buy an old rambling house with an extensive rundown garden. She called her property Hepworth House and transformed it into a place of living art. There was always something happening that attracted collaborators like the sculptor Henry Moore, the eccentric writer Virginia Wolfe, Ben Nicolson and his fellow writer, the volatile Vita Sackville-West. Also, from New Zealand, the painters Maude Burge and Francis Hodgkins, the latter becoming a lifelong friend of Myfanwy's.

Weekends were party time, dancing the Charleston fueled by copious amounts of cheap wine and honey mead. The occasional Royal would take a break from the pomp and pargetry of London to slum it in St Ives, they certainly knew how to let their hair down and party. Often the day would arrive when a chauffeur driven Daimler would be parked outside Hepworth House waiting for the errant hung-over Royal to stagger out.

'Those were the days, my friend; we thought they'd never end.

We'd sing and dance, forever and a day.' (Mary Hopkin)

But end they did.

Myfanwy continued to find it difficult to gain recognition, as did Francis. There were many other clever artists to compete with. They both decided that the party was over and that it was time to find out what the city of London could offer. After arriving at Kings Cross Station they found an apartment in Hammersmith. First and foremost they did the rounds of the galleries in London which gave them some idea what would sell to pay the rent. The city was enjoying an increasing tourist trade from the cashed-up Americans who were fascinated by royalty and all that went with it. Francis and Myfanwy with set up canvas on easels and paint for the tourist trade. They held a stall at Portobello Rd and slowly gained recognition from the smaller galleries who sold on behalf. This was not the type of art that they were passionate about, but it was a great money spinner.

Over the Channel to Paris, the City of Light, and for the next couple of years they wandered Western Europe. They painted the simple things of life, the people of the streets, farmers toiling in the fields, a housewife hanging washing on a windy day, a vase of flowers on a veranda, the soft colors of Marrakesh, the autumn colors of Tuscany, the canals of France, the snow on the Alps, villages dotted along the Rhine. Winters on the Mediterranean, summer across the Baltic and beyond to Scandinavia. Life was hard, but simple, they lived their dream. All their possessions they owned were carried on their backs stuffed in their Cotswold backpacks as they wandered and wondered along the country roads and into the teeming cities.

Most of their work was sold on the street corners or weekend farmers markets, anything they thought was of gallery quality the posted to Art & Object. Both Agnes and Marcia were aging and slowly withdrew from the day-to-day operations of Art & Object. They employed the young and the enthusiastic who had studied art or art history at the universities of Liverpool or Manchester. The Dockland area was emerging as the new public space of downtown Liverpool developed. Sadly the area was a target of the German Luftwaffe bombers at the start of WW11 and it took until the early 21st century to restore the Dockland as a public destination.

The dark clouds of war had been building in Europe for several years with Hitler flexing his muscles. When the Nazi's invaded Poland it was time for Myfanwy and Francis to get the hell out of Europe and return to the UK before they too became collateral damage of this upcoming war.

Over the years after she left Liverpool for St Ives and then Europe there had been several causal men in her life, however if things got too serious she would wander off to another town, city or country. While exploring Lake Como in Northern Italy they had been the guests in the estate of a flamboyant woman who somewhat flattered Myfanwy by crouching on one knee and offered her hand in marriage. The bemused

Francis suggested that she should have accepted because there were a lot worse things in the world than life on an estate on Lake Como and all the rich's that went with it. For Myfanwy her life was her art, her freedom, her Rose and her grandchildren whom she only knew by photographs.

Agnes and Conner had passed just before the war and on Myfanwy s return from Europe lived in the Finnegan house with her stepbrother and sister until it was destroyed by an errant bomb while they were safely in an underground bomb shelter. Myfanwy then lived with Rose and her grandchildren for the duration of the war as her health began to fail.

Bedridden with her time on this earth coming to an end she received a visit from the Curator of the Tate Gallery in St Ives. The gallery had been collecting her English and European work over several years which included the Buckingham St women and the Dockland Refugee Children. The Gallery requested her permission to stage a solo exhibition in St Ives and if successful to the Tate Modern in London.

Myfanwy never got to see her exhibition.

MYFANWY FITZGERALD

B 1888 ---- d 1953

'England, at last, has given me recognition.'

R.I.P.

PART TWO

9

DANNY BOY

was the third son of Seamus and Kathleen Daymon. When Seamus, who referred to himself as 'Lugh' after the Irish mythical God, was released from Dublin's Kilmainham prison, he returned home to his family in Londonderry who lived the confined and overcrowded slum of Bogside just outside the Londonderry wall. This wall was built by the Protestant rulers was set on the high ground overlooking the Catholics of Bogside.

By then Seamus was the shadowy leader of a faction of the IRA that was hell bent on the violent disruption of anything Protestant or anything pertaining to British rule. He operated not only in the city of 'Derry but often travelled the county of Donegal as an enforcer. he became a ruthless soldier for the IRA and had no qualms of committing murder as was the case in Delancy and the death of Thomas Finnegan.

Dan's two elder brothers had followed their father's footsteps into the IRA. They had no choice but to be involved in petty crime as jobs for non-educated Catholic youths rarely existed. If work did become available, the wages paid to Catholics were pitiful. They had inherited their father's bitterness of the downtrodden.

As a youth Dan was of lean build, above average height, soft blue eyes and a face that easily creased into a smile. His sisters teased him

64

with the name of 'Skinny Minnie' in comparison to his sturdy brothers who also gave their young brother a hard, sometimes violent time.

'Just to toughen him up,' they said.

'Hey, Dan, what are those two bits of string hanging from your shorts? Ooops, they must be your legs'.

Dan inherited his mother's easy-going nature rather than the humorless, resentful disposition of his father who'd never recovered from his time in Kilmainham prison. His erratic schooling was basic, due to the prejudice towards Catholics in the education system so most of his learning came from his mother who was always on there hunt for books that may be of interest to him.

Unlike his brothers, Dan had a yearning for tales of adventure and travels of the great explorers like Marco Polo, James Cook, Vasco de Gama and Robert Falcon Scott. He devoured and got lost in the fiction of writers like Jules Verne, Daniel De Foe, and the likes of Robert Louis Stevenson. His father and older brothers taught him insurgence with violence.

He liked to tinker, find out how things worked; the first motor vehicles in the city fascinated him. He could often be found hanging around the local vehicle repair shop, peering under the bonnet of the early automobiles.

Like most Irish, Dan had music in his heart and soul which came from their ancient Celtic chants and laments. In Dan's era this music had developed into something lively like a polka put to the tune of a flute or accordion. He could listener hours to he old laments that remained of Irish folk-law and blended with romantic and political poetry enhanced by the best musical instrument of all - the human voice.

As a young teenager Dan would hunt out music by sitting outside or sneaking inside the many pubs and taverns, listening to the rousing drinking songs that would develop into nostalgia as the Guinness freely flowed into the night.

Such was the life of Dan in his early teenage years. Little did he know what fate had in store for him because of the sins of his father that was thrust upon his innocent soul.

10

VIOLENCE

found Dan in 'Derry. The long history of unrest in Northern Ireland involved the 'Siege of 'Derry' in 1689 when the Protestants of William of Orange held out the Catholic's of James the 2nd for over three months. This siege is the icon of Protestant culture in 'Derry and celebrated what is now known as the 'March of the Apprentice Boys'.

The parade by the Protestants had, and still is, regarded as a triumphant sectarian victory. To the Irish Catholics, these Marches of the Apprentice Boys are an insult, often resulting in violent clashes. These marches, which the British Government has tried to outlaw, continue to this day much to the ire of the Catholics of Northern Ireland.

When Dan was seventeen, Seamus decided it was about time he became a man. The annual Orange Order 'March of the Apprentice Boys' was due and Dan was told to join in with the neighborhood protesters. This sector was led by Seamus and his sons who relished the opportunity to publicly demonstrate their disgust of the blatant insult. Often, much to their delight, their protest often ended up in an all-up donnybrook.

Dan, for as long as he could remember, had always felt uneasy with his father's shadowy disappearances from home without any explanation of where he'd been or what he was up to. It was never discussed in their household. All Dan knew, was that it was something sinister connected with the IRA. He never knew it was his father and brothers who had murdered his future wife's father, Thomas.

On the fateful day of the 'March of the Apprentice Boys', the men of Seamus' family armed themselves with concealed batons. They made their way, with male neighbors, to a prearranged street corner on the route of the march. They had gathered missiles; stones, bricks and lumps of coal ready to hurl at the Orange Marchers. Dan's face whitened when he saw a handgun tucked into the belt, and hidden by the jacket of his next-door neighbor. That gun confirmed the extent of his family's hatred and violence towards anything British. They were prepared to kill for their cause. A spasm of fear shook Dan to the core when he realized what was about to unfold.

From a distance, the beat of the base drums could be heard. Other than that, silence. Anger simmering in the crowd as bottles of pointin were passed round, each man taking a swig, some gulping the whiskey. When the bottle was passed to Dan he pretended to swig and handed it on. The drumming moved closer. He could hear boots hitting the ground in unison with the base drum.

As the marchers rounded the corner into sight, Dan saw, for the first time, the hated uniforms of red with a gold sash and flamboyant hats. The lead marcher was carrying the purple and orange banner which commemorated their victory - the 'Siege of 'Derry'. The sight inflamed the Catholic crowd, and the rumble of voices built to yells of abuse. The 'Apprentice Boys' advanced to the location of Seamus and his seething band of men.

The mounted police attempted to keep the crowd at bay with reasonable success. But, as the marchers closed in, the crowd surged onto the road to disrupt the march. Police on horseback rammed into the crowd, knocking a few men down. A hail of missiles descended on the police.

The marching Orangemen were physically confronted by the baton-wielding mob. Many were knocked to the ground, bleeding, then stomped without mercy as they lay on the road.

A gunshot cracked the air, Dan froze. He was trapped in a cauldron of hate. Another gunshot, then several more more. In horror he saw a policeman fall from his horse. The drums ceased their infernal beat and the long line of marchers followed by Protestant civilians, came to a halt. Flames licked the burning banner which was held aloft by Seamus's next-door neighbour. The Catholics cheered.

Dan tried to escape the chaos. Impossible; he was carried to and fro by the surging mass, then everything went black. It was as if somebody turned a switch from day to night. He was knocked down by a police baton and was stunned for a few seconds. He raised his arms and hands to protect his head as the policeman laid into him. The beating stopped when the policeman fell to the ground. Through the blood in his eyes, Dan saw his brother flaying his baton onto the policeman who lay on the ground where he was stomped on by Dan's brothers.

When Dan staggered to his feet, looking for a way out of the danger zone, to his horror, he heard boots pounding in unison. A platoon of British Army soldiers arrived on the scene, double quick marching with rifles pointed towards the seething mass on the streets. They fired over the heads of the protesters who were scattering in all directions. A rifle butt connected with the back of Dan's head. He stumbled, then turned to face the rifle barrel that was held to his forehead, put his hands up in surrender. Dan was shoved to the ground, kicked until he rolled over. Face down, the soldiers forced his hands behind his back and Dan was cuffed in cast-iron shackles.

'One move, you're dead meat'.

Dan, and 25 other shackled prisoners were force-marched to the infamous Derry Gaol. His father and brothers escaped by sliding down a coal cellar chute and hid there for a day and night before the coast was clear. They made their way home in Bogside.

'Derry Gaol was built in the late 17th century, then rebuilt in the 1860s to incarnate serious criminals and political prisoners. In the early 1900s it was filled with IRA dissidents. The prison was notable for its executions, with the gallows being a permanent installation because of its regular use. The recently arrested were held as political prisoners, therefore the law was that they could be held indefinitely without being charged with any offence. When the constabulary eventually got around to interviewing Dan who had been held in solitary confinement for two weeks. His cell was below ground level without bed or blankets, a toilet bucket that was not emptied until full, and fed when the guards felt like it. The first interrogation was for 15 hours and the second 24 hours. Both were undertaken without food or water, and he had no indication of the time of day or night.

Dan was eventually charged with the murder of the mounted policeman and sent back to his cell to await trial. After several weeks he was interrogated further. This time the police interviewer said that if he revealed the involvement of his father and brothers, along with their collaborators of the IRA, they would reduce his charges to 'Disturbing the Peace'. Dan was just as afraid of the IRA as of the law of the British, so he stuck to his defense of being just a spectator.

Seamus and his sons were arrested, then released due to a lack of evidence. Their alibi was that they had not attended the march but were celebrating the holiday of the 'Apprentice Boys' by attending a picnic at St. Coloms Park. Their alibi was substantiated by 60 witnesses. Dan's Mother tried to visit her son and waited for hours before being told that visiting time was over; to come back in a week. She left food parcels which he never received. He shivered and starved for three months. Sometimes in solitary confinement, sometimes in a crowded yard without protection from the icy 'Derry winter.

There is a folksong called 'Derry Gaol' with lyrics lamenting that the only release was in a wooden box. The song played continually in Dan's imagination.

Dan was eventually charged with 'Disturbing the Peace' and for being a member of the outlawed IRA. His day in court arrived, and without representation he fronted the British appointed judge Harold Pilkington who went by the name of 'Hanging Harry'. The first prisoner to be sentenced was his neighbor from Bogside, an IRA member, who was found guilty on the statement of witnesses who said he fired the handgun. His fate was to be 'hung by the neck until dead'. The so-called witnesses were the Protestant marchers whose evidence was accepted by the court so their sentence to be hung was symbolic rather than factual.

As far as the British were concerned, they were all guilty of insurrection. The other protestors arrested that day were sentenced for periods of five to 15 years in 'Derry goal. Some died before their sentence was fulfilled which meant they were buried in the prison cemetery. These men weighed so lightly what they gave.

Dan was terrified, as was his mother who was in the public gallery. However, when he stood in the dock he found that the Judge's nickname, Hanging Harry, was a misnomer, for Dan anyway. There was no evidence to prove he was part of the violence inflicted on the lawful 'Orange Marchers.' Dan, being a minor, who had already been imprisoned for three months was punishment enough. He was convicted and discharged. His criminal record states that he is a member of the illegal IRA.

Dan, with his mother Kathleen alongside him, walked out of the courtroom a free man, He turned at the bottom of the steps, and looked up at the stone engraving of the woman holding a perfectly balanced set of scales, symbolizing justice.

He said to the engraving. 'What a load of shite'. He turned to his mother and added, 'never, never again, will you find me back in a courthouse.'

As they walked through the town gates and down the hill to Bogside she said. 'Dan, I thank the Good Lord that you are not like your father and brothers. I understand what drives them to the hate that's now buried deep in their souls. I fear that one day this hatred will destroy our family.'

'Mother, this has nothing to do with the so-called Good Lord. I've always tried to be like them, but I can't, I just don't know what else I can do?'

'The Good Lord has already blessed you. I have been living in terror that prison would turn you to bitterness, like so many of our own people. This hatred destroys those who remain in Ireland. When you look around, you see that the wise ones have left these troubles behind and are scattered all around the globe, they never come back.'

'The one thing I do know is that I will never be going back to that prison, ever. I just can't see the point of it all. We are not going to change the past'. Dan was lost in thought. The only answer he had was, 'yesterday is history.'

'And tomorrow is a mystery,' said his Mum. 'What's the opposite of hate'?

He thought about that one, it was simple. Dan realized that what kept him alive in prison, wasn't hate, it was love. He had a mother who loved him, he loved music, he loved open spaces, he loved life.

'The Good Lord teaches us to forgive and forgive we must.'

'Mother, you make me mad at times - forgiveness? I'll leave that to you and the Pope to sort that one out.'

'A baby is born with love and learns to hate along the way. We could be as children at play if we want to.'

'There you go again, just a minute, I'll go get a violin.'

They both walked for home, lost in their thoughts.

For Kathleen it dawned on her that prison had taught her son of love. She felt that love had walked out of her life a long, long time ago.

All Dan could think was, 'I gotta get out of this place, if it's there last thing I ever do.'

Shoulders touching, their shadows as one, they turned and walked the stony path to their front door.

11

I GOTTA GET OUT OF THIS PLACE

if it's the last thing I ever do.' This was foremost on Dans brain when his 18th birthday arrived. The Damon family organised his birthday celebration at St. Colms Park. Not only for his birthday party but to welcome him home after his release from 'Derry Gaol. The Bogside Irish, never missing a chance to party turned up bringing 'Potluck'. Traditional Irish fare, a large pot of boiled bacon and cabbage. Simmering on the open fire was another pot of spuds, black pudding on the grill, soda bread and lard. Not to forget that a party was not a party without the bubbling cast iron pot of coddle. A stew made up of leftovers of anything laying around the kitchen that was added to the brew. As for the men, it was their job was to supply the poiton. There were no complaints about that tradition which always involved an argument about who was most skilled in the art of the illegal distillation of spuds.

The game of the day was 'road bowling'. Starting in the park and often extending onto the streets, using a stick, shaped by training a young willow branch, the ball was fashioned from a round piece of pumice. This was probably a fore runner to hockey or another game that the Scots claim they invented which they played on a coastal field called St. Andrews.

It goes without saying that the most important ingredient at an Irish shindig was music, music and more music. The old folks brought their accordions and fiddles that got people on their feet dancing the Irish jig. When exhaustion and Poiton took charge, the songs of sadness and loss meandered into the evening.

As the oldies and children drifted off to their beds the young ones came alive. One of Dan's friends who recently returned from Liverpool brought a guitar and with it music that had originated in America. For Dan this was life changing. He realized there was a wonderful world out there just waiting for him to explore. The strum of the guitar and the beat of a drum was the rhythm of his heart. Late in the night somebody put the guitar into his lap and said,

'See what you can do with this.'

The guitar slipped naturally under his arm, fitting like a glove. He strummed, he picked, it was like coming home, he knew from that day on that he was born to make music.

It was in the early hours of the morning Dan arrived home to find Seamus, his brothers and a few neighbors sitting around the kitchen table chewing on a bottle of poiton. They were talking a little above a whisper, he knew instantly that trouble was brewing.

'Take a seat son', said Seamus. Dan sat at the end of the bench seat, declining the bottle that was offered.

'Dan my boy, you have made us proud by keeping your mouth shut in prison. You are now 18 and old enough to be a soldier of the revolution, welcome my son, to the IRA.'

Dan was silent.

'You are now one of us and now is the time for revenge, and that revenge will be oh so sweet. Nobody treats us Damons like they have and gets off lightly.'

Dan stood without thinking, not knowing what to do next he walked over to the coal fired stove and turned his back to it pretending to be warming himself. His heart was ice.

'We are going to hit them hard. Hit them where it hurts and hurt those bastards it will.'

They all looked at Dan as Seamus continued,

'Michael and James have picked up the dynamite from our lads in Belfast. Spud here, used to work in the Delancey quarry for those Pommy bastards. They were too dumb to know they were teaching him how to blow things up.'

'Lugh, you're the man', said Spud. 'Can't wait for action, we've been sitting on our arses for too long. I've made up eight sets of six sticks of dynamite and the Foyle bridge will be no more, just a pile of rubble.'

Michael, with an evil smile said 'More importantly, tied up alongside the fucking bridge is that fucking Pommy, fucking Navy ship, with its fucking guns pointed at our homes in Bogside. That's going up as fucking well, fucking good job.'

They all thought that it was hilarious, even Dan managed a smile, not at the bridge and ship blowing up but all the 'fucking' that was going on.

The bottle did another round as Seamus looked Dan in the eye and said, 'Danny boy, we need you to run the fuse-wire under the bridge to the wharf. I will be unwinding the reel and Spud will be connecting the packs of dynamite under the wharf where that, what did you say Michael? 'Fucking ship' is parked. Your brothers will be getting wet doing their bit. My estimate - this will take about two hours to set up and then we will be ready for Guy Fawkes.'

'What's our escape plan or do we just wander down the road with our fingers in our ears?' joked James.

Seamus grinned, 'I'm surrounded by idiots.' They all looked at one another, pointing. 'We will meld into the night, give it about half an hour before one of us sets off the big bang, all we need is a volunteer to plunge the plunger.'

Nine hands shot up and Spud was chosen because he put up two hands. Dan gave a false yawn and left the room.

'Better watch that boy,'

'Leave him to me, I can handle him,' said Seamus quietly.

When Dan's brothers came to bed, they asked if he was okay, and he pretended he was asleep.

After the household quieted Dan crept out of bed. He was fully dressed and gathering what belongings he had and stuffed them all into a shoulder pouch. He put the strap over his head, he stood for a few seconds in sadness. In the gloom of a half moon, he watched his brothers sleep, they looked vulnerable and innocent, yet, oh so dangerous. His eyes were wet with tears as he quietly closed the bedroom door carrying his shoes he walked down the hallway into the kitchen.

Dan opened the pantry door and stuffed some unleavened bread, a cooked pig's trotter and some raw sugar into his bag. He reached to the top cupboard for the small box that his mother secreted what few trinkets and jewellery she had. Dan took out a few coins, then hesitated when he saw the stub of a pencil; there was no paper in the house. Licking the lead of the indelible pencil to make it work, he wrote a message on the inside of the cupboard door knowing his dad would never be guilty of opening a kitchen cupboard. The workings of a kitchen were woman's work.

As Dan strode into the night, a frost was falling. He shivered and pulled his jacket collar tighter around his neck. Peering into the moonlit night, feeling that thousands of stars were quietly observing his departure from the ones he loved, his home, his boyhood and all things familiar, he was pierced by a stab of solitude. A deep breath gave way to a wave of emotion that invited his soul to adventure. Without looking back, he strode into a future of whatever life may hold. He knew then he was a man.

At dawn Kathleen started her day as usual, lighting dry straw to fire up the peat fueled stove. She soaked bran for porridge, kneaded dough, for her this was the best part of the day. She was at peace while her family slept. Sitting at the table with the stove warming her back and silently praying, she remembered she'd forgotten to mix the baking soda in with the bread dough. Kathleen opened the cupboard door.

'Dear mother, don't cry for me, I am blessed. I thank you for my life.'

'My baby's gone.' Kathleen whispered through tears. These were tears of not of only deep sorrow but also of joy. Relieved that she'd given her children all she could, she could give no more. Her son had made his choice, and that choice was the right choice. She dreamed of a day when the troubles were done, a day of peace, a day when her son would come back home. That day never came.

'Partings sweet sorrow'. (thanks to the Bard for that one)

12

RUN, RUN, RUN

Dan had never travelled outside 'Derry, in fact he'd never seen the sea. He'd been told stories about the tides that snuck up beaches and claimed lives, giant octopus that would stretch a tentacle and pluck a sailor off the deck 'bugger that', he said to himself, he thought he would keep well clear of that lot. The priority was to put as many miles as possible between him and 'Derry. Belfast was too close and full of IRA, so Dublin it had to be.. He had a rough idea that it was to the south and east, so every morning he would face the sun and walk in that direction.

Keeping clear of railway stations and main roads by taking the country lanes, avoiding towns by crossing fields at night were a necessity for Dan. He knew all too well a search would be mounted for him because he was aware of the plan to bomb the Foyle bridge. Seamus would probably lead a separate search party to try to get to him before the IRA, who were based in Belfast, tracked him down with their long tentacles of informers.

He walked for several days avoiding farmhouses and the small villages, sleeping rough and surviving on the little food he had. At night Dan would creep into farm sheds in search of food. Sneak into a chook house for eggs or raid the potato pit, although raw spuds were not very high on his list of favorite foods. Oh, for a pot of coddle bubbling on the stove. His boots quickly disintegrated so he crept onto a porch and stole a pair and had to run like hell while being chased by a barking dog.

Dan rested for a day in a narrow gorge with a creek meandering and spent several hours lighting a fire using flintstone he'd found. It was worth the effort. Along with the boots he also had stolen a skinny old hen to go with the spuds. Food fit for a king, he thought. He'd thrown the worn boots into the stream, then retrieved them to remove the leather bootlaces just in case. The laces reminded him of a silent movie called 'Gold Rush' where the starving Charlie Chaplin cooked up his bootlaces pretending it was spaghetti. 'I'll keep that in mind' he said to himself, realizing he'd been talking to himself ever since he left home.

The freedom was exhilarating, 'Derry, the troubles and his family seemed as if they were from another planet. Often, he would rest during the day when it was warmer and walk during the cool of the night, warmed by the exercise rather than trying to sleep in the cool nights.

One night he walked past a window of a farmhouse that was close to the road, he stopped and looked through the window into a candle lit front room where a family had just finished their evening meal. They were casually interacting with each other before bedtime, he felt a pang of envy and a longed to become a part of this simple domestic scene. He quickly backed off not wanting to disturb this contented family. He imagined himself being invisible in the room with the family. He could see the remains of the evening meal on the table, plates and pots stacked on the bench. Father drowsing in front of the fire, the youngest yawing on her Mother's lap, the oldest girl, of slim adolescence drawing on a slate, the youngest boy with his small hands struggling to catch the knuckle bones he was throwing in the air. The two middle boys playing knights in shining armor, another boy, with an open book gazing into the fire imagining he was sailing the seven seas fighting off pirates or in a far-off jungle, or on top of a snow-covered mountain. Mother, looking at each of her flesh and blood in wonder of what life had in store for them, will this one be rich, will this one be pretty, will this one be a leader, will this one fall by the wayside?

Father woke and said, 'Story time', and the family scrambled around his feet.

Dan's loneliness caused deep pain as he lost himself to the dark looking for somewhere safe and somewhere warm to sleep.

'One day, I shall have a family, a family, just like that one,'

Mid-morning, he plucked up enough courage to knock on a farmhouse door which was opened by a large stern looking woman with sleeves rolled up, wearing a blood-stained apron, he gulped.

'I am on the lookout for some work, do you need help with anything, anything will do.'

'Are you any good at cutting up a mutton?'

'I think so,'

'You think so? Well, I can't pay you, but I've got wood to cut, spuds to be dug, mouths to feed. Arrr, do you think you can dig a dunny hole?'

'Yep, I can do that, but I don't need money, just food will do,'

'Well, you better start digging then, these useless men around here always find an excuse, pack of lazy buggers, come and I'll get you started.'

As they walked past the old outhouse Dan took one sniff and said, 'I think smells like it's about time you had another hole dug.'

The menfolk arrived back from the fields to where Dan was digging,

One said to the other, 'That was supposed to be your job,'

'No, you were supposed to do it.'

'I got a sore back.'

Father was behind them, and said 'You'll both will have a sore arse by the time I've finished with you', he looked at Dan. 'Who are you'?

'I'm Dan the dunny digger,'

'Well Dan the dunny digger, don't let me stop you.'

It was just on dark when the back door opened and one of the sons called out. 'It's dinner for Dan the dunny digger.'

'I'm all but finished.'

'Finish it in the morning, you can wash up at the tank-stand, make sure you're clean otherwise you'll have to eat out on the porch.'

Mutton and spuds topped off with soda-bread and butter pudding, the butter was a little rancid but what the hell thought Dan, best feed since his birthday, even though that was just a few weeks back, for Dan, that was a lifetime away.

Dan had a soft bed in the hayshed accompanied by a few rats. He was woken while it was still dark by a noisy rooster who obviously couldn't tell the time. Hole dug and the dunny towed over by the old draft horse from the old and very full hole to the fresh sweet smelling new one. Dan had the pleasure of breaking in the new dunny. The rest of the day was sawing and splitting hawthorn for the morning wood before the slow burning peat was added to the stove.

After another night's sleep with the rats, it was time to hit the road with enough bread, lard and salted mutton in his pouch to keep him going for the next few days.

Dan had been taking care to avoid the towns and villages and as the distance away from the Troubles increased, he became more confident that the risk of being hunted down by the IRA or his father was becoming remote. Looking down from a rise he could see a church spire of a village. Because of the terrain he could see that it was difficult to circumnavigate so he felt it was safe enough to walk up the main road into the village. He passed a few shops and the inevitable tavern, he smelt the bakery before he saw it. Following his nose to a side street he stopped outside the town bakery peering into the window display. He drooled over the loaves of bread, pastries and was salivating over the Irish apple cake with cream and topped with a dried sugared cherry. Transfixed it took an effort to take his eyes off the cake, when he turned to go it was then he saw the notice on the closed door.

'PEAT DIGGER WANTED

APPLY WITHIN'.

As he opened the door, the bell, that was attached to the door rang, and a very round cook came in from out the back wiping her hands with a towel that was tucked in his apron string.

'You look like you're here for one of my pies?'

The penniless Dan replied, 'I'm applying within.'

Along with directions the baker gave Dan a half a loaf of bread, as he walked out the door he said,

'I'll be back sometime for a piece of that apple cake.'

A fair way out of the village he came to the house that was down a long narrow track well off the main road. After knocking, the front door was opened by woman, tall, strong looking with brushed auburn hair, an outdoor ruddy complexion, unlined, belying her 40 years on this earth.

'Looks like you're here for the peat digging job,'

Her accent was not one he had heard previous, so Dan guessed that she came from the counties of the south.

'Yes, I have, I've done it before.' he lied.

She looked him over. 'It's tough work and my husband is a hard taskmaster, you look young enough and strong enough so I guess you will harden up in time. What's your name?' she asked

'Dan, Dan …' he realized that he should give an alias. He'd stopped off at a cemetery on the other side of town and the only name he could remember from a headstone was Paddy Ryan,

'Ryan, Dan Ryan.'

'Well Dan Ryan, the job is yours, you will eat with us at night, and I will supply you with bread and meat for the day. By the way my name is Meg, and my husband is Fergus. Do your work and you shouldn't have a problem with him, if you don't, well…' she left it at that.

Dan nodded.

'I'll get Irene to show you where you sleep, it's not much but you should be comfortable enough. There's a bucket over there for washing and you are to wash up and change out of your work clothes before you come to my kitchen for dinner, you'll find some sandsoap over there as well.' She looked him up and down. 'Certainly looks like you need a bit of a scrub up.'

Irene, who was from the same town in Limerick as Meg, had a four-year-old daughter born out of wedlock. She worked as a housekeeper and cook for Meg and laboured in the peat-brick drying shed for the taciturn Fergus who paid her a few pennies, when he felt like it. Irene had escaped an abusive home-life in Limerick and in pregnancy Meg had provided a haven for her and her daughter. She was wary of Fergus and his unpredictable spasms of temper, especially when he was hung-over from the Guinness stout. In her late teens, Irene bore the look of good health of being raised in the countryside on basic food. Irish green eyes and a face that was emotionless which showed a deep sadness of the life that she had been dealt. Like her distant relation Meg, she was of strong build and able to work hard under the iron hand of Fergus.

When Irene came out from the scullery, she looked at Dan, flushed and nodded indicating that he should follow her. He tried to catch up with her to walk alongside but she just walked faster, she led him into the shed where there was a straw mattress covered by a coarse but a clean wool cover. There was a large, crudely built set of shelves using hand hewn poplar for a table with a carbide lamp on top, to the side was a wooden bucket with a cake of homemade sand-soap. He glanced around to a partition and could see another bed. There was neatly folded clothing on shelves fastened to one wall, on a table there was an extensive row of well bound books held up by two hand carved sandstone sphinxes as bookends. Dan's curiosity got the better of him and he took another step into the room, there was another shelf with a razor and strop, he put his hand to his own chin and rubbed his thin straggly whiskers. Alongside there was a neat row of pencils, notebook, pocket-watch, framed photo of an attractive woman and a few other odds and ends. Irene said.

'Is your name Mr. Nosey Parker?'

'I'm Dan, you must be Irene,'

She indicated his compartment. 'It's not much but better than sleeping out in the mist and the rain,' she said. Looking at his shoulder pouch, she added, 'you travel light.'

'This is all I need, for now anyway,'

'What are you running away from?'

'Running away,' he repeated, 'I guess I'm running away from bad times and a bad place. Anyway, that's all behind me, now I have the freedom to wander to... well I don't know really know where I'm heading and probably will still not know when I get there. For now, I need to make some money.'

'Money's not everything.'

'Tis when you aint got none.'

'So, what are you going to do with all this money that you hope to make?'

'I hope to head back to town and buy a piece of apple cake from the baker, what about you?'

'Me? I can't go far but one day I'd like to go to the city and live. But, for now, this will have to do and Meg's good to me.'

Dan nodded towards the partition and asked, 'Who lives in there?'

'Pieter, he doesn't say much, he has an accent and been here about half a year but keeps to himself and his books. I suppose he's from Europe or somewhere,'

'Well, there's no doubt I'll meet him before long. Where's the boss?'

'He's around the back of the peat shed, I got to go.'

'Thanks for the tour.'

She didn't answer.

Dan wandered around the hedge protected yard over to a hand pump which was connected to a clay pipe that went down to an underground well. The water tasted good, alongside the pump was a wooden washing board, scrubbing brush and soap, what luxury thought Dan. The long drop was scrubbed clean with a small stack of fresh green furry leaves on a shelf, this time he said out loud,

'Fit for a king.'

He walked around the back of what looked like the peat storage shed that was well ventilated to allow a constant draft to dry the peat. He entered the shed where he saw Fergus grunting with effort as he stacked peat bricks on slats which kept each brick separate for drying. He looked a lot older than his wife, a big man, barrel chested, long powerful arms muscled by hard work, unruly dark hair and a heavy grey speckled beard, eyes set close together, he wore a bulbous nose and the red veined face of a heaver drinker. He looked up and stared at Dan for a few long seconds,

'I suppose you are here for the job?'

'Yes, I am,' and held out his hand.

Fergus looked at the extended hand, ignored it, and stared Dan in the eye and spoke. 'You look soft, but I'll soon knock that out of you,'

Dan held his gaze and said, 'Tell me what to do and I'll do it.'

'Don't just stand there, look lively and let's get you working, then we'll see if you can handle it.'

Fergus set a cracking pace stacking the peat bricks from a flat decked dray, they both broke into a sweat as the stack got higher to where they had to throw each brick into place. Dan's shoulders and arms were screaming out for relief but there was no way he was going to give into the pain which went beyond the physical to become a mental battle. The only thing that saved Dan was the late afternoon gloom when Fergus called it a day, by then Dan was buggered but there was no way he was going to show it. Each were determined to be the one who threw that last brick up, the only thing that saved Dan again was that they run out of bricks. For Dan, that summed up Fergus's personality, he realised then that he was a man never to be crossed.

'Wash up and come up to the house for dinner, and smartly does it,'

'Good to meet you Fergus.'

'Mr. Higgins to you and don't you forget it.'

Dan went over to the hand pump and managed a full body wash with coldwater and sandsoap. He then washed his underclothes and put them back on wet. Goose pimpled he walked over to the sleeping quarters which was a walled off part of a hay barn that also sheltered the house cow. On hearing noises of human activity on the other side of the partition he poked his head around to see his future workmate. Pieter had just returned from the peat bog and was dressing for their evening meal. He flashed a smile at Dan and introduced himself with an unfathomable Eastern European ascent.

'Looks like I've got a workmate, I'm Pieter, we had better get moving or we'll get a rark–up for being late for dinner,'

He looked Dan up and down and asked, 'You got any clean clothes?'

Dan had put his grubby clothes back on and said, 'This is all I have, by the way I'm Dan,'

'Dan, it looks like you travel light,'

'People keep telling me that, everything I own I carry on my back.'

Pieter rummaged around handed Dan clean shirt and trousers, 'Probably a bit big for you but, will have to do for now.'

Dan and Pieter sat at the dining table with Meg, while Irene served steaming hot coddle and the inevitable spuds. Stilted conversation flowed on everyday stuff starting with the age-old subject of the weather. Irene was still in the scullery and as they finished Meg stood and gathered the plates and left the men at the table, Dan asked Pieter where the master of the house was.

'He goes to the Tavern most nights and often doesn't come home till late; I think there is a demon in the bottle for our Fergus. He's not a nice man at the best of times so take extra care around him, especially when he's hung-over. He pays well enough and expects us to work as hard as he does, all you have to do is keep up to his expectations and you will do well enough.'

When they got back to their digs Pieter asked Dan if he had anything to read,

'Not since I was a teenager.'

'Come and have a look at what I've got, you're most welcome to take what you want, nights can be pretty long, lonely and boring without the company of a woman or the magic of a good book.'

'If I had the choice, I would pick the magic of a woman rather than the company of a boring old book.'

He didn't mention that he wouldn't have a clue what to do with the magic of a woman, instead he said 'I wouldn't mind getting to know Irene a little better,'

'Dan, my boy, that one is a block of ice.'

'Ice melts in the hot sun, in the meantime a book will have to do.'

Dan looked along the two rows of books, taking his time to choose. Some were in German or French, the ones written in English were of authors he had never heard of. In fact, he had only read one book in his life which was Marco Polo's travels to China which installed his desire to travel the world. Other than that, he knew nothing about a world outside of Londonderry.

'Tough to choose.' he said.

'Maybe I can help you', he pulled an ornately bound book off the shelf by the spine and added, 'How about this, it's a translation from a German writer.'

'Hope it's not a war story.'

'Just the opposite.' and handed the book to Dan.

Dan took the fine leather-bound book that was embossed with a stylized star-studded universe and imprinted with gold lettering.

'Siddhartha' by Herman Hess

'He was a German who spent a great part of his life in India, as I have done. What we both took from away from India is imbedded in our hearts, you should go there sometime,'

Dan's body hardened up to the heavy work and was bronzed by the hot summer sun, along with the plain sustainable country food from Irene's scullery he began to look forward to each day's challenge. The harder Dan worked the more Fergus expected from him, as Meg said, 'he's a hard taskmaster,' Pieter and Dan worked well as a team and Fergus, in his gruff manner respected his workers.

In the long summer evenings Dan devoured Pieter's books of which they would discuss and dissect late into the night. Pieter would be out of bed well before daylight practicing meditation and yoga before starting his day. Dan thought that this was weird as this sort of stuff was unheard of in the backwaters if rural Ireland. As Dan slowly got to know him, he began to understand that behind Pieter's hardworking exterior there was a delicate interior. Pieter wore a calmness that seemed to surround him and this calmness would enter those with whom he came in contact. Dan had never heard of meditation and yoga until one Sunday, their day off from work, Pieter convinced him to do some breathing exercises which led to meditation and yoga.

For a while Dan didn't notice any changes within; after time he began to look forward to rolling out of bed at 4.00 and then with

Pieter's guidance start their day in meditation and yoga. After a couple of months, it dawned on him that there were incremental changes to his body and mind happening, so slow, that he just didn't notice until he looked back to before he started these morning rituals.

Pieter was mysterious regarding his background and avoided any direct questions, Dan knew that there was a lot going on behind those gentle eyes that he would rather not talk about. Over time Dan was able to piece together snippets of general conversation of how he ended up in Ireland digging peat. Even though Pieter's hands were roughened up from hard work with a spade he had the fine fingers of a concert pianist. A face that was bronzed by the summer sun that failed to hide the refinement of a genteel upbringing and an intellect that belied the fact that he had previously worked in a copper mine somewhere in Europe.

As Pieter's life unfolded, Dan's imagination saw him as an aristocrat from some exotic east European country with the word '-stan' behind it. It turned out that he was not wrong about that one, over the course of many months his story revealed and put together the content of character within this mysterious man.

He was involved in WW1, not as a soldier but had something to do with infiltration and surveillance because of his fluency in many European languages. Dan was unsure of which side he was on but towards the end of the war he was captured. He was able to convince his captors that he was on their side and was a double agent so was released. Pieter hinted that in fact he was on both sides and was in it for the money rather than idealism. He survived the war still in one piece and wandered around Europe working for various governments, liaising with the occupying forces for several years. In Vienna he had an affair with a married woman of aristocracy that resulted in him being challenged to a duel by her aggrieved husband. This tradition had been outlawed many years prior but was still, although rare, used in cases of an insult or, as in Pieter's case, matters of the heart. At a formal function the aggrieved husband walked up to Pieter and with his glove slapped his face, this insult was to challenge Pieter to a duel as a matter of honour that Pieter could not refuse.

The duel was carried out in secret in a clearing of a secluded forest, using single shot dueling pistols with each man having a 'Second'. A referee was appointed, a doctor in attendance and half a dozen witness from each side. The duelers stood back-to-back, each with pistol in his hand, the referee counted the required 20 paces when both turned and simultaneously fired. Pieter, who showed Dan his scar, was shoulder wounded. His opponent took Pieter's bullet in the chest and died several days later. There were no secrets in the aristocracy of Vienna, and it didn't take long before this fatal duel was on everybody's lips in and around the city. The family of the deceased was seriously aggrieved and began the search for perpetrator, intent on revenge. The Bundespolizie were officially informed and were hot on Pieter's trail in Austria and before long they surmised that he had left the country so requested Interpol to join the hunt.

Europe became too small for Pieter, so he disappeared into the Eastern Bloc countries and then south through Afghanistan to India where he spent several years under the tutelage in a yoga and meditation Ashram in Rishakesh. On returning to Europe, he kept a low profile working on menial jobs including the copper mine in the Ukraine. He had to keep on the move, ending up digging peat for Fergus Higgins in Ireland.

Pieter, if that was his real name, opened a world that Dan had never known existed, his once dormant mind became like a dry sponge that absorbed anything and everything from Pieter's books along with stories of adventure and philosophies of the human mind which stayed with Dan throughout his short life.

After a month of toil in the peat bog, Fergus handed Dan the first wage in his life, he gazed in awe at the coins in his hand, at first with disbelief then with pride in that he had earned every penny of it. His body had developed and hardened, his past was surly behind him, and his mind had ventured far beyond the horizon. Sunday was a day off work and at dinner the night before Meg had told him it was about time he kept in touch with God and to attend church in the village, about an hours walk away.

With money burning a hole in his pocket he hit the road early and walked straight past the church and directly to the bakery, the meat pie was followed by a piece of that Irish apple cake smothered in cream and that was followed by the same, a meat pie and again another slice of sugar loaded cake. The drapery 'Isaac and Son' opened on a Sunday to catch the out-of-town church goers before the 10 o'clock bell sounded. Isaac measured Dan up for some basic work clothing and an Irish linen shirt to wear at the dinner table. While Isaac's son Isaac was treading on the Singer sewing machine Dan sorted out a razor and strop, scissors and would you believe it, a comb. He headed back to the farm carrying a brown paper parcel tied with string with his old clothes inside. He walked awkwardly, breaking in a new pair of boots that were like most of the new boots of the day, squeaked until worn in.

With shining shaved face, clipped hair from the deft scissor hand of Pieter and linen shirt Dan was fussed and teased by both Meg and Irene, Fergus had headed to the Tavern on horseback late afternoon and had not returned for dinner.

Dan was soundly asleep, at first, he thought he was dreaming that his bed covers were being lifted by an outside hand. This was not a dream. A whispering female voice, 'Shhhhh', as a woman's body slipped in beside him. 'Irene', he whispered as soft fingers were placed on his lips. He turned on his side as she was kissing him, gently at first while guiding his hand, he was blurred by passion as she held him with arms and legs and then rolled on her back, she kept one hand over his mouth.

As the first traces of dawn lighted the sky he heard the deep breathing of Pieter settling into a yoga pose, he was in limbo for quite a few seconds as his brain unraveled what had happened during the night. Still in a sleepy trance his hand searched the bed alongside, cold. Dan sat up and smelt her presence, yes, it was real, it really happened.

For the first time in his life, he believed in the power of prayer.

'Dear Lord, thank you, thank you, thank you,'

'Who are you talking to?' Called Pieter from the other side of the partition.

At dinner that night he tried to catch Irene's eye as she served dinner, she wore her usual impassive face and said nothing out of the ordinary. After dinner he poked his head into the scullery and said,

'Thank you, it was wonderful, arrrm, the dinner I mean.'

She looked up from what she was doing and just nodded without expression. The next Sunday he walked over to the clothesline where she was hanging Fergus's work clothes. She had her back to him with arm's up fastening clothesline pegs, his imagination undressed her; by the time he was within earshot he was close on drooling. She sensed him and turned and looked at him, quizzically, he stuttered as he asked if she would like to go for a walk. Emotionless, she just shook her head and carried on working; he was taken back by this. He thought about it later, that if thems the rules, so be it.

A few days after that they had another night of silent passion to the thankful sound of Pieter snoring, again she slipped away into the night. Dan couldn't understand that the few times he searched her out during the day and found her totally unresponsive, however he had no complaints in that she had become a regular nocturnal visitor.

As the autumn approached the pressure was on to get as much peat in the drying sheds before the winter rains set in that made it impossible to work in the fields. As the days shortened and the weather cooled, they spent more and more time in the shed shaping and restacking peat bricks ready for Fergus to deliver to the Saturday morning market. This was a big day for Fergus, being cashed up he would head straight for the Tavern for the afternoon. His horse had done this many times and would, while he slept in the drivers seat, take him home in the dark.

When working with Fergus, Dan and Pieter learnt that the mood of the day depended on the state of his hangover, still the three men worked as a team and Fergus paid his workers fairly and on a regular basis. Dan fed off Pieter's intelligence, which wasn't arrogant or overbearing. He would always give Dan an opportunity to form his own opinion even if that contradicted Pieter's theories. They would talk about the workings of the internal combustion engine through to the meaning of life and the never-ending philosophies of politics. Dan looked forward to their early morning meditation and yoga.

Life was pretty good for the Dan, but as we all know that the good times don't stick around forever. One Saturday night he was on his back being ravaged when, with eyes closed, he sensed a light, it was a light of a candle that was moving closer, partly obscured by the body that straddled him, he froze but his lover was unaware of the intrusion was totally absorbed in passion.

'Bloody hell! Bloody hell! Sorry, sorry, I didn't know what the noise was, I thought…'

The voice belonged to Pieter who was retreating backwards out of the room, As the candlelight faded, Dan eyes adjusted to the light, he looked up and to his shock and horror, he was looking at the face of Meg!

'Meg, Meg, it's you, I thought…' his voice trailed off as his brain was struggled at this turn of events.

Her body faded as the light left the room as she once again became invisible, he felt a gentle hand on his face as she whispered 'Dan', she quickly slipped out of the bed then Dan heard the door click shut.

'Holy, fucking Moly', he said out loud, then it sunk in that she had just said 'Goodby'.

'Dan, my boy, you are the one,' came the voice of Pieter from the other side of the partition.

'I'll be up Shitters Creek without a paddle if Fergus fucking Higgins finds out, I think I'll take her advice and make myself scarce.'

'Yes Dan, I can just see you hanging from a tree with your testicles stuffed in your mouth.'

His decision was made for him, he heard loud voices coming from the house, getting louder, there was a smash of broken glass and he heard Fergus's voice roaring. Pieter came into his room with his candle while Dan threw everything that he could fit into his pack and slung it over his shoulder.

Pieter was standing between him and the door. Hugging a man was never a practice way back then but with Pieter it was the natural thing to do with a true friend, with a tear in his eye Dan bade farewell to this unforgettable man. A man who had such an enormous influence that never left in his heart or brain during his short time on this earth.

On the road again but not before he opened the gate of the horse paddock to allow the horse to go find the best grass on the farm. In the faint moonlight he could see the outline of remote and uninviting craggy mountain range on the horizon.

'There's safety in them their hills,' he said to himself.

He quickened his pace as he imagined those fierce bulging eyes of Fergus catching up with him, he couldn't help but to keep looking behind as he occasionally broke into a trot. Come daylight he found shelter well off the road where he stayed until dark.

Hit the road Dan, don't look back and run, run, run

13

SPUD LA NOUZE

was the first connection that Dan had with the Chathams, although he had no knowledge of the islands existence, actually he had never heard of New Zealand other than a rugby team called the 'All Blacks' which he surmised was a team made up of indigenous men dressed in grass skirts.

The road petered out into a winding track climbing into the dark purple hills, the temperature dropped as the cloud thickened. He passed the odd empty house or shack of subsistence farmers who probably wintered at lower altitudes. The land was becoming steeper with deep valleys on either side of the track, sparsely vegetated, rocky and exposed to the icy NE winds, he was above the snowline.

Dan found a few odds and ends to eat in the vacant shepherds' huts which also gave him shelter at night. Late afternoon on the third day light snow began to fall so he kept walking in hope of finding shelter for the night, the countryside was bare. The snow got heavier, and the track got steeper as darkness fell, desperate to find some sort of protection he kept on walking with the wind and snow at his back, he couldn't stop in fear of freezing to death.

The track had leveled off for a few hundred yards then he felt that he was walking downhill. As the wind and snow eased, he realised he had passed over a summit and was descending, he said a prayer in thanks to the God that he didn't believe in. The dark was light enough for him to search out shelter in a rocky outcrop where he curled up into a fetal position and exhaustion sent him to sleep.

Hunger woke him to a full sun overlooking a deep valley that widened into an expanse of flat farmland that was sectioned off by stone fences. Far below him a stream meandered down the valley, his eyes followed the stream as it widened to pass alongside a village. With the mid-morning sun on his face and legs pumping blood through his veins he soon warmed. He recalled the ancient Greek poem that Pieter used to recite..

'Brave Phealus, wake up your steeds, and bring the warmth the countryside needs'.

Similar as to the effects of fasting he had overcome the hunger pains that had dominated the last 36 hours he found himself striding down-hill feeling strong, lean and mean. The track that followed the fast-flowing stream turned into a road winding through the ruminates of an oak forest and then to the occasional clearing where sheep and cattle grazed. There were increasing signs of human presence with stone and gorse fenced paddocks and a Borie, which is a round stone shelter built by bored shepherds many hundreds of years ago. In the distance, smoke spiraled into a windless noon sky, warmth, beautiful warmth.

Still no sign of another human being, Dan sited a secluded clearing about 100 yards off the side of the road next to the stream, which meant water, free flowing water which was an improvement from eating snow or slurping muddy water from a puddle. Within an hour he had found a fruiting crabapple tree, yuk, wild strawberries, yum, Quince, yuk, blackberries, yum. He stood on the top of a stone fence for a better view and in the paddock was his favorite, wild turnips, a feast for a king.

The cool flowing water of the stream invited him to strip off and wash, his face stinging after a cold-water shave. He took the opportunity to wash his clothes with the luxury of soap that was in the bottom of his backpack. He lay and slept in the soft grass while his clothes lay drying on a hot rock in the sun. The new man was back on the road once again walking with a purpose of the expectation of something completely different.

The valley had flattened out as he made his way into the village, passing tidy whitewashed cottages, neat gardens with flowers lining cobbled paths which invited visitors to the front door that was adorned with a fresh flowered and leafed wreath. It was as if each householder was competing with their neighbor for a 'Home and Garden of the Year' competition.

The King James hotel had a warm fire and a cold Guinness with the offer of Irish Stew that was written on a blackboard at the bar. When Dan walked in there was about a dozen patrons who eyed Dan suspiciously and stopped talking for about 20 seconds, nobody greeted him, and the conversations restarted intermittently as if Dan didn't exist. He walked up to the bar where the lady of the house was pouring him a Guinness.

'Welcome to my establishment, I'm Molly'.

Molly O'Leary was a diminutive but fiery woman in total control of not only the house, but her clientele as well. The Guinness was drawn up from a wooden keg in a cold dank cellar, Dan tried not to drink too fast, not only to savor this nectar of the Gods but also due to his very limited cash-flow. Molly's friendly manner, along with the alcohol on a very empty stomach put Dan at ease, despite the unfriendly locals. She slowly drew out of him a story that he concocted that he was a fisherman who had a near death experience at sea and wanted to find a new land-based life as far away from the sea as he could get. Molly intuitively knew his story was a load of bullshit but that didn't bother her too much as she just took people as they came and as far as she was concerned, he was just another lost soul.

'So, you'd be on the look-out for some work.'

'Sure am, anything will do, I've been digging peat for the last 6 months, but winter closed in, so that was the end of that lot.'

'There's no peat around here anyway, well, except for that bugger over there by the fire, Pete, Pete Saunders is his name.'

As the other patrons in the bar were conversing amongst themselves, the usual stuff, moaning about the disgusting weather, the poor returns from farm produce, the price of goods in the general store and so on, they were also following the conversation between Dan and Molly.

She said out loud, 'Well, you all heard, can anybody here offer work for young Dan here?'

Their silence was deafening.

'Cat got your tongue, are you just a bunch of old farts who do not accept anybody of anything that's new and different? No wonder we are losing our young people who leave this town and we don't see them back again, how about letting go and give somebody else a chance.'

A few grumbles came from around the bar.

'His name is Dan and he's looking for work, he's a good keen man and able to do anything, anybody got any ideas?'

Eventually a lone voice piped up,

'I think Spud La Nouze needs some help to dig his potatoes before the weather packs up.'

Molly said quietly to Dan, 'These are good people, but sometimes they need a stick of dynamite under their arse, you can stay here the night and go see Spud in the morning, you hungry.'

'Starving.'

'So, looks like you got a pocket full of dreams and a belly full of nothing,'

'I guess that's me all over.'

'I'll go and rustle up a plate of stew, should warm the cockles of your heart.'

'And some lead in your pencil,' came from the farmer's table.

Pete couldn't resist 'And put muscles in your shite.'

'It's about time you grizzly lot livened up a bit.' Said Molly as she went into the scullery.

Dan had a dreamless sleep in a bed for a change aided by a couple of helpings of stew and a couple of pints of Guinness. He had no money to pay for the bed so the next morning he did a few chores around the pub, including a repair job on the hydraulic water pump that had clogged up with weed in the stream.

The village of Clancy in this deep lush valley was isolated, there was no road out other than the road in, so there were no travelers passing through. Clancy was the end of the road in more ways than one. If the winter was exceptionally brutal Clancy was often snowed in for weeks on end. This was a blessing, as the British didn't bother interfering in such a small insignificant part of their colonial rule. Perfect refuge for Dan who felt as if half of all Ireland were on his tail. He thought to himself that the only thing he was good at was making enemies.

Molly told him that La Nouze family were originally Huguenots who had immigrated from religious persecution in France. They had subsistency worked their 50-acre farm for many generations.

As the Dan walked down the long track towards the house, he could see the man who he thought must be Spud with a scythe cutting barley. He had the help of three children who were spreading the seed laden stalks to dry in the late autumn sun. The children stopped working when they saw Dan walking across the field, it wasn't often they had a visitor, their dad had his head down concentrating on the rhythm of his scythe. Spud had the fine features of his French heritage, thinning brown hair and clean-shaven, his face was sun-bronzed and ruddy with the effort of the hard work, his torso was bare with rivulets of sweat tracking down his dust-laden body.

The eldest of the children, a boy of about 13 called out to his dad who was so deep in concentration on the flow of his razor-sharp scythe that the call of his son didn't register. When there was just a couple of yards separating them, he suddenly stopped in surprise to see Dan standing in front of him.

'Looks like you can do with some help around here, I'm looking for some work, that's if you want me to,'

Breathing heavy, Spud leaned his scythe on his chest, and flexed his fingers and shoulders to give himself time to think while appraising this young man in front of him. Dan was refreshed, bathed, shaved with his linen shirt underneath his calfskin jacket. For something to do while

Spud made up his mind Dan swung his backpack off his shoulders onto the ground.

'Well, I certainly could do with some help, but I can't pay you until I sell this stuff,' gesturing towards the field of barley.

'That's alright by me,'

'We can make up a bed in the hay barn, its warm and dry and you won't be sleeping with any animals, they have their own barn. Sorry, I just remembered the dog sleeps in there as well, he supposed to be a guard dog but if thieves came he would probably lick them to death.'

'Yeah, we had a dog like that once, what's his name'?

'Suni, Suni by name and Suni by nature,'

'You don't have to pay me. Just food and a bed will do.'

Spud held out his hand, Dan took it and felt something like dry hard leather, through that rough skin Dan felt a warmth, it was the same warmth that was in his eyes. He then handed over the scythe and spoke.

'We'd better get you started then, see what you can do with this?'

Dan awkwardly started swinging the blade in the direction of the barley, Spud laughed and said, 'looks like to me that you need a bit of practice,'

Late afternoon Spud called it a day and they made their way back to the house, as they walked past a field of potatoes with their tops brown and dying, Spud said that their next job after the barley had been cut was to start lifting the spud crop.

'Looks like I won't have time to get bored.'

'Bored? you won't even have time to scratch yourself, I harness up the old Clydesdale to tow a single furrow plow, that's the easy bit, then it's all hands-on, kids and all, picking up, sorting, drying and the bagging is the hard bit. It's seven days a week till we get this season's stuff to the market'.

'The market, where's that at?'

'Dublin, we load the dray to the hilt with all that we can sell, spuds, barley, oats, turnips and cheese, if we get a spell of good weather it takes about four or five days, bit slow going through the gorge as there is a couple of river crossings, if there's been heavy rain we have to wait for the river to drop, but normally its pretty good. There are some bog flats before Dublin which can slow us down a bit.'

'Sounds like Murphy's law to me.'

'So true, so true, what can go wrong, will,'

'The good thing is that my eldest boy Fionn is a good horseman and the horses have been to Dublin and back many times, they could probably find their own way.'

'You said you make cheese?'[

Spud went quiet and didn't answer, Dan waited for him to continue as they neared the homestead. The house was built of the ancient Clochan stone using clay mortar, the roof was of thatch with a spiral of smoke from a weather worn brick chimney. The cottage was framed by oak, walnut and elm trees which presented a warm and safe family haven.

Spud stopped walking and turned to Dan. 'My wife used to make the cheese', he hesitated, 'she died.' Dan didn't or couldn't say anything. 'She died last winter, I forgot we don't make cheese anymore, well, we do, but my eldest, Saorise is just learning, she hasn't quite got it right yet so it's quite not good enough to take to Dublin, this year anyway.'

'What happened to your wife?'

As soon as Dan asked the question he regretted it, the pain and grief inside Spud poured out, he rarely talked of Maeve and the devastating affect her passing had on the family. Dan could feel Spud's devastation like an aurora that that hovered over him.

'We don't know, probably consumption, she had been sick for some time, but she hid it, by the time the doctor came all the way from Howth it was too late and...'

Dan went over to his sleeping quarters that used to be a harness room but now turned into a spare bedroom, he felt the mattress, kapok, luxury; when sorted he walked over to the house and knocked on the door.

'Come in, come in, you don't need to knock, come in and join us at the table.'

The family must have been waiting for him as they were already seated, Spud was at the head of the table and indicated that Dan sit at the other end. The six children sat on a hand-hewn bench seats on either side of the long oak table, which, to Dan, looked as if it had been in place for generations of the family. The children sat in shy silence, the two youngest sat with heads down with the occasional furtive look at Dan while trying not to giggle. Fionn sat next to his dad and although he was just an early teenager, he had the confidence of his roll of being part of the families wellbeing, both him and his sister had left school when their Mother died.

The 15-year-old Saorise flushed with embarrassment as she carried over an iron pot of Irish mutton and potato stew and placed it on the table in front of her dad, to have meat was a treat. She went back to the stove and opened the oven door, the smell of the unleavened soda bread arrived at the table before the bread did. The family's pride and joy was the lidded china bowl that contained the lard to spread on the bread. The children were drooling but had to sit still and suffer as their dad asked the youngest to say grace.

When she finished, Spud then said a few words, at first Dan thought it was a prayer, but it was as if his wife Maeve was sitting at the table and he was having a conversation with her. Dan then realized that his place at the table had always been kept empty as if one day their wife and mother would return and dine with the family.

As the meal progressed the family got used to Dan, who didn't say much, It didn't take long for them to overcome their shyness and become their normal rowdy selves. Dan could see that even though the family was relaxed each of them were grieving in their own way, they just missed their mum.

Saorise was the quiet one, her grief was a lot deeper by having to carry the responsibility of the welfare of her siblings. She had the burden to ensure they were fed well, to comfort them when they were hurt, to encourage them when they were down. How can she teach them of life that she herself didn't know or understand, she was not equipped to give them a mother's love, when she herself, was just a child desperately in need of a mother to guide her through her difficult teenage years. She was trapped with what life had dumped on her and was robbed of her childhood.

At times when the burden of responsibility overwhelmed her, she would inadvertently lapse back into childhood thoughts and speech as a way of coping. Then reality would shock her back into the enormity of her responsibilities. She desperately strived for adulthood and was soon to fall in love with Dan.

Spud, Dan and Fionn worked daylight to dark to finish the barley harvest to be stored into jute sacks ready for the trek to Dublin. The potato crop was overdue for the arduous job of lifting, then washed in the stream, dried and graded. The pick of the crop was bagged to be sold and the second grade was stored into bins layered with bracken for air circulation for their own use. The family was financially desperate after paying off by installments of the Doctors fee in attending the terminally ill Mauve. Education for the children was spasmodic at best as teachers had to be paid; the family income came from the annual trip to Dublin.

One cold wet Sunday afternoon after church the family huddled around the fire, Spud produced his guitar, after a few minutes tuning he asked Dan if he could play, Dan shook his head.

'It's about time you learnt.'

That day was the beginning of a lifetime, well, in Dan's case, a short lifetime, the sound of the guitar was to take him to many strange places in this world.

Back when he first arrived in Clancy and spent the night at Molly's tavern, he saw that she had a bookshelf of the classics of that time. On one of his rare visits to town he asked Molly if he could borrow books from her library in exchange for odd job around the pub, deal done. Besides the books she would always include a sweet treat for the children. As the autumn nights lengthened into winter he would, after dinner, take the family, including Spud who couldn't read or write to the world of Robinson Crusoe, to the Great Expectations of Mr. Pip, of Blackbeard the pirate, the Wonderland of Alice and the heartbreak of Black Beauty.

Dan had found the family that he had longed for.

Most of his spare time was spent with the guitar which sat comfortably on his lap and under his arm while his voice and the instrument came alive to connect and become one. Spud could teach Dan no more, his final instruction to Dan was that to become proficient at anything, or in this case the guitar, there were three simple rules, practice, practice and, yes, you guessed it, practice. One evening Dan asked Spud,

'The name La Nouze, it sounds French, where does that come from?'

'I don't know much except that my ancestors were Huguenots from Le Vigon, a town in France where they were persecuted by the Catholics. They were originaly Celts so they must have followed the Celts of hundreds of years ago and fled to many parts of the world including Ireland. How they got to Clancy I don't know but they were accepted by the people of this town and given land to farm. Over the years we adopted Catholicism and are buried in the Catholic cemetery,'

'So, you must have many relations around here'.

'No, I don't, my grandpa told me that during the potato famine most of the men deserted Ireland, some went to South Africa and the women stayed and married Irishmen. I remember my grandpa telling me that his long-lost uncle who had returned here for a visit, he had worked on a whaling ship in the South Pacific before becoming a magistrate on some far-flung island called Chatman or Pitts or something like that.'

Late autumn and it was time to make the annual pilgrimage for Spud and Fionn to the market in Dublin, with excitement the family loaded the high-sided dray with the produce of their years toil. Saorise had made a successful block of cheese that she sliced and neatly arranged in the lidded china bowl. She placed dried wildflowers around the cheese in the bowl and instructed Fionn that it was his job to sell the cheese in the Dublin farmers market-day.

When loaded and before being covered by a tarpaulin the family stood back with pride, their wellbeing for the coming year relied on what was on that dray. Even the old draft-horse's, Ringo and St.

Lennard became skittish with excitement as they were being harnessed. Spud reckoned that both horses were old enough to vote and had done this trek many times previous. It was if both horses were aware of their important role within the family. For the kids it was the treats, trinkets and treasures that came back from the fair city of Dublin.

The trek was at times arduous, having to navigate the sometimes-boggy road from the autumn rains, potholes, there were potholes in the potholes and a broken axel would be a disaster. They slept under canvas, each taking turns guarding their precious cargo from the threat of highwaymen. On arrival at the Dublin Market his agent, Willy Mc-Bride, greeted them with the same vigor that Spud and his father before him had dealt with. This pipe smoking, rotund man was welcomingly warm-hearted, Spud had always suspected that his enthusiasm was generated by profit. He always thought that someday he would try another agent, but he never did. His Father always told him that a long-term business relationship was far better than a short-term gain. There were times of a glut in the marketplace and produce became difficult to sell, Willy would still buy his produce, which was always reassuring, as with most primary producers, supply and demand determines price, not what it costs to produce their product. While in Dublin they were hosted by Spuds brother, Bobby, who was a Merchantman, shovelling coal down below deck of the trader, SS Thomas Currell which served Dublin, Liverpool and the outlying Islands off the west coast of Ireland.

Dan was not yet ready for Dublin and decided to keep out of sight for the time being, there was plenty for him to do on the farm. He always found an excuse to play around with the forge and anvil repairing and creating. Night time was guitar-time, as he gained confidence to use his voice to accompany his guitar; he had a couple of ardent fans. Their neighbor's daughter Sinead was about the same age as Saorise, who stayed with the family for three or four weeks to help out while Spud and Fionn were in Dublin.

Both girls fell in love with Dan. As for Dan he was completely oblivious to this, which was probably a good thing because teenage hormones, being what they are, may have caused a problem or two and then made worse by the eternal triangle.

The men arrived back from a very successful trip in Dublin, cashed up and with presents for all. Dan was presented with several sets of guitar strings and a song book. Fionn handed Saorise the lidded china bowl she lifted the lid and inside were copper and silver coins in amongst the dried flowers that was all that was left, she meticulously counted the coins. Two shillings and sixpence halfpenny, she looked up at her dad who told her that the money was hers to keep.

The winter project for Spud and Dan was to cut down the old elm tree that had been part of the family for several generations. They got to work using Spuds old crosscut saw, axe and wedges and then after digging a pit under the trunk and cut planks using a long double handled rip saw. This project took most of the winter and the planks was sold locally. It was a good year for the farm and Dan earned a bit of cash which some of it went into the coffers of the King James tavern on a Saturday night. Dan became confident enough to join up with a fiddler and an accordionist to turn on music for the entertainment starved and mostly drunk crowd.

Spring, then summer came and went, by then Dan had itchy feet and although his life in Clancy was the best he ever had, it was time to move on. The dray was loaded and with the horses pawing the ground, tears were shed, promises made that were never to be kept. Spuds gift to Dan was his guitar telling him that guitars were made to be shared. Saorise was missing, Dan knew that when she wanted some space, she would isolate herself in the garden shed that she had decorated and furnished as her private refuge, he told Fionn to make a start and he would catch up. He had never been into the shed before but there she was, broken, he then realised, for the first time, what was up with her. He had always treated her as a child and not seen her as she was, a beautiful young woman. He too cried with her as they both made vows that he was never to keep.

When Saorise turned 18 she claimed independence of her family and the small town of Clancy to travel to Dublin with the hope of finding the love of her life, Dan was well gone by then. She eventually became the Art Director of the Dublin City Council to become the initiator of the 'Women of Buckingham Street' exhibition.

On arrival in Dublin their produce sold well to a buoyant market much to the delight of Willy McBride who handed out cigars. They spent a few days with Fionn's uncle Bobby and his wife Marlene exploring the city by day and at night the many pubs around the docklands of the Nanican River. The many musicians and bands of Dublin did the pub circuits, playing for pennies or sometime just a glass or two of the Guinness that was congruent with their music.

Bobby's ship, the Thomas Currell was in dry-dock and he was able to secure Dan a job of chipping rust and painting the hull. As Fionn trundled off back to Clancy, Dan, saddened by understanding the finality of his past life in Northern Ireland was ready for whatever fate had in store for him. The Thomas Currell was due to go back to sea so Dan asked the Chief Boiler-man for a job down below deck shovelling coal,.

'The jobs yours if you're tough enough, those boilers with their insatiable hunger for coal will knock out that soft lifestyle of your past.

'The truth is often told in jest.'

14

DOWN TO THE SEA IN SHIPS

was the name of the game for Dan over the next few years. It all started with feeding coal into the insatiable boilers down in the heart of the Thomas Currell. The intense heat and the physicality with a bent back using a short-handled square mouthed shovel built strength, resilience and the mental toughness that takes over when the body is pleading to stop the pain. That shovel became his friend in that it toughened his body and mind, and when the going got tough that same shovel became a hated enemy.

The Thomas Currell was built on the Clyde for the Liverpool based Cunard Line and Dan signed off when she was sold to a North Sea fishing company. After some arduous years fishing for halibut and cod the Thomas Currell was sold to a NZ, Cook Strait, fishing company led by Albert Meo.

At the start of WW11, she was commandeered by the then fledging RNZ Navy who had her boilers removed and replaced with diesel engines. The weight of the boilers was compensated by several tonns of concrete and large diesel tanks used as ballast. She served as a minesweeper, hunting the North and West of NZ. This mission was likened to putting out a fire with gasoline in that the mines laid by the German

Raider 'Aquarius' were magnetic and of course the brave Thomas Currell was built of steel.

The crew, including the Chatham Island fisherman, Bruce Kyle, sighted a mine off the Three Kings Islands and detonated it using a .303 rifle. At the end of the war, she was repatriated back to Albert Meo and resumed fishing in Cook Strait targeting grouper. Her next adventure was to lead a convoy of small fishing vessels to the Chathams to support the short-lived crayfish boom in the late 1960s. One night while on anchor in Port Hutt she started taking in water so the man on watch, Eric Dix, lifted her anchor and steered her onto the rocks where she still sits, pride of place to this day. At that time in Port Hutt there was a cray processing plant and a row of huts for workers that were supplied with electric power from the engine of the Thomas Currell.

Our Dan never got to see the Thomas Currell at Port Hutt.

Dan always looked forward to his time between voyages on the Liverpool leg of the Irish trade where he could follow his expanding passion for music, frequenting the many bars, clubs and dance halls. When the Thomas Currell was sold to go fishing in the North Sea he registered with his employers, the Cunard Line, for a place on one their many diesel-powered international cargo ships. During this lengthy time ashore he said goodbye to his old friend, Spud's guitar, making sure it went to a good home. He replaced it with an American made Gibson L-5 Sunburst which cost him several months wages. He paid for lessons and learned to read music from a teacher who introduced him to the Merseyside music of that time.

Through his teacher he got to know members of a band who called themselves 'Creeping Jesus', they mixed Irish folk with American country. He would go and listen to the band in their home base, the Cavern was a dark, dingy, and smoky bar with a stage. With the help of his music teacher, he was invited to join in with the band's jam sessions, for Dan, this wasguitar heaven.

Cash flow was looking a little grim, so he hounded the office of the Cunard line and eventually found a place down below deck of a heavy diesel-powered coastal trader. After several voyages he proved his worth and signed up on the MV Liverbird trading between the U.K. and the Eastern seaboard of America. After many voyages to the ports of New York, Boston and Montreal the Cunard line contracted a trade for the Liverbird to ship British steel to New Orleans then return to the U.K. with bales of cotton to feed the dark satanic mills of Manchester.

While ashore in New Orleans Dan frequented the bars and clubs of the French Quarter. Gospel music was at the time moving from the Church into the bars of Frenchmans Rd and morphing into the early days of Soul which in turn gave birth to the Blues. He fell in love with the streets of the French Quarter which were filled with the music of black America from the swamps of the bayou to the guitar pickers of Nashville. He signed off the Liverbird and with knapsack and guitar strapped on his back he walked down the gangway into a brave new world with the words from Molly of Clancy, echoing in his brain.

'A stomach full of empty and a pocket full of dreams.'

15

THE BIG EASY

is the melting pot of the Deep South, concentrating in the French Quarter where diversity reigned with Black, White, Hispanic, Cajun, Creole, French and everything else in between. This is where hot food, cool music, language, the rich, the poor, the ugly, the beautiful all mingled on the streets, in the bars and the clubs. These few streets around Jackson Park, Bourbon St and Frenchmans Rd were alive with buskers and there was always an excuse for a parade. On Sundays atheist Dan would join the Black gospel singers praising the Lord with his guitar.

Work was impossible to find so all that was left was to do was to join the buskers on the streets, he became known as 'Dan the Irish' finding a place on the concrete of Jackson Square where the statue of the General 'Stonewall' Jackson was mounted on his horse with seagulls taking turns to sit and shit on his plumed hat. Dan the Irish concentrated on his versions of his homeland ballads mixed in with some of the music of Creeping Jesus, this attracted the occasional coin thrown into his guitar case. The one thing about busking was that it was a way of testing his music to a critical public, also it can be soul destroying if one didn't get it right, busking has the power to make or break. The competition around the Square was inspirational for the Dan as these people were in the same situation as he. As the nights wore on and the often-generous tourists trundled off to bed leaving only the drunks and dopers. He would call it as night in the hope that there were enough coins for a doss house bed and a bowl of gumbo.

Dan's place on the Square was shared with the fortune tellers, Creole Voodoo women, card tricksters, dope dealers, hookers on the lookout for a trick, idlers of all sorts, guitar and guitar pickers. The prime spot in the square is where the brass band performed surrounded with large tip buckets. The various musicians would join in, play for a while before wandering off, so the makeup of the band was continued to change. As each musician departed, they would take a share of the coins from the tip buckets. Dan became friendly with a busker, Robert, who had a permanent place in the Square, he strummed guitar and blew harmonica. Dan liked his music so would set up as close to him as possible. When one would play something the other knew they would join together, their music often attracted a crowd, so they informally teamed up on a permanent basis.

Dan found the Blues and the Blues found Dan.

Robert Johnson had worked his passage on a Mississippi paddle steamer from Memphis. Eventually he became recognized as the father of the Blues. Like many great artists his fame came well after his death, so be it with Robert. One hot night while Robert and Dan were making music a guy stepped out of the crowd with a set of wooden buckets and a couple of sticks and without saying a word he set himself up behind Robert and Dan and gave them the beat.

And the beat went on with the locals getting into their music that was named by the Preacher of the St Louis Baptist Church in the square as the 'The Devil's Music'. He would gather up his congregation, arm them with placards and march around the Square in protest. Eventually they too got into this 'Devils Music', leaned their placards on the wrought iron fence that surrounded the inner part of the flower gardens of the square. They too boogied with the white northern tourists from New York, Chicago and Boston.

A large rotund man had been hanging around at the back of the onlookers for a few nights, Robert asked him if he liked the music, the guy hesitated and struggling to get his words out said,

'Needs b-b-b-b-base,"
'You slap base?'
The guy nodded.
'Where's your music come from?'
'J-J-J-J-J, be fucked if I can say Jackson.'
The next evening the guy arrived back with a black painted tea chest with cat gut strings and started plucking with rubber like fingers, he didn't stutter when he sang Blues.
'What name do you go by?' asked Robert
'F-f-f-f-f, fucking Fats.'
'Well, Fats, you're in.'
The, yet to be named band attracted a following that often was waiting for them to crank up their music. Late one evening an ostentatiously dressed and plumed Cajun woman with two muscled minders in tow arrived on the scene. She seemed to be well known by the bystanders and approached Robert speaking in French before she realized that Robert had no idea what she was talking about, so she repeated in accented English.
'So you better come and play for me at my establishment,'
This was not a question but a command.
'Which is your establishment?'
She ignored that question and asked,
'What do you lot call yourselves?'
'Arrrr. Crossroads.'
'You better cross the road and come up a see me.' she turned with a flourish and walked away leaving the minders scowling at the band that was now known as the 'Crossroads'.
'Crossroads?' asked Dan.
'It was the first thing that came into my mind, I'm writing a song called Crossroads, I think we need to put it to music before we go on stage, who the hell was that lady?'
'Isadora,' said Remy the drummer, 'everybody in the 'hood knows who she is, she's the Madame of the bordello in Decatur St. you know the one, its called 'The House of the Rising Sun'. The story goes is that

if you cross her you end up on the bottom of the Mississippi wearing concrete gumboots.'

'Isadora's, that's a step up from the streets, hey, Remy, you better go find a set of drums from somewhere, you know, real drums.'

'And Fats, it's about time you retired your old tea chest for something a bit more modern.'

Once set up at 'The House of the Rising Sun' they initially played for tips that was hardly enough to keep them bedded and fed. The Devils music loosened the inhibitions of the mainly male crowd much to Isadora's delight, her girls were kept very busy in the upstairs rooms. It took a while for her to get around to paying the band a reasonable fee congruent to the business they brought into her Bordello. Even the Preacher was happy not to have the threat of the Devil on the streets, although unbeknown to him it was his his congregation who churched on Sunday after a night of debauchery at Isadora's. The word was getting around the French Quarter of this mixture of gospel and soul with a beat with jaw-dropping songs like 'Crossroads' and 'Kindhearted Woman Blues', which was on everybody's lips. The House of the Rising Sun was a rocking. These blues took a long time to venture out from the French Quarter and cross Canal St into mainstream America. The band were completely unaware of all this and just went to work every night with Robert always on the lookout for new material. The birth of the Blues meandered up the Mississippi to Baton Rouge bringing customers by paddle steamer that kept the smile on Isadora's face.

Their Mississippi delta fame was not without problems, Robert had an eye for women, more often than not, somebody else's woman. He would just concentrate on one woman in the audience, flattering her with things like 'she was the one who gave him the inspiration' or 'this song is dedicated to you'. Isadora's minders were instructed to protect Robert from jealous husbands. Remy was just as bad, he hit on a Cajun woman to the annoyance of her husband who loosened his front teeth which put an end to his vocals for a while.

Dan also was not immune to women troubles, he met Anna, one of Isadora's girls. She was a little older than Dan, her Russian mother,

Natasha, was closely related to the Romanov's in St Petersburg and had escaped the revolution after the Bolsheviks had murdered her husband. Europe was in turmoil after the war, so she made her way to the USA and down to New Orleans. Natasha found it difficult to master the English language but from her Romanov education she was fluent in French which was the first language of the Creole. Life was hard for a refugee in the Big Easy in those days, she had no choice but to work in the Bordello's. After her death, her daughter Anna followed her footsteps.

Dan became infatuated with Anna, her Creole father, who had disappeared before she was born, had passed onto his daughter a sultry light brown complexion, her soft brown eyes, fine European face and a slim beauty she inherited from her Mother, she certainly didn't have the busty flamboyance of the other Isadora girls; her first language was French and her education was Creole.

The House of the Rising Sun often lived up to its name and sometimes it was the first glimmer of light when the band finished up. Dan would still be pumped up by the Devils music so he would seek her out and have a drink in the bar as the last stragglers called it a night. At that time, she would be available and if he had a little cash they would head upstairs to one of the plush rooms. Sometimes they would just lay on the bed and talk, Anna was vague about her mother's past and her own life, she did say she shared an apartment with an elderly man whom she thought of as an uncle. Her main ambition in life had been to return to her roots of St Petersburg, which was recognised as the Venice of the north but was now named as Leningrad. She shuddered at the name of Leningrad which put fear into anybody connected with the Romanovs.

They had a lot in common, both being lost souls; she loved Dan's accent and his tales of ancient Ireland, of Irish folk-law, of faeries, of leprechauns and the laments of tragedy, sometimes he would sing to her in Gaelic.

Isadora's was becoming notorious from both sides of Canal St which is the unofficial border between the French Quarter and the rest of

America. Most of the slave owning Mississippi planters had built town mansions in the French Quarter which eventually became the 'House of the Rising Sun'. Back in the plantation owners days the inner court-yard housed the stables and slave quarters. The grand staircase led to a gold painted ballroom and above that were the guest rooms. Several floors and on top of all that was the plantation owner's apartments with a magnificent view of the Mississippi Delta. This mansion had about thirty slaves working full time, even when the owners were upriver overseeing their plantations.

That was until Isadora got hold of it and converted the stables into bars, a stage and general party area. The first-floor ballroom was very exclusive, attended by invitation only and with Isadora's best girls mingled with the rich and famous who gambled at the tables. The Devils music was only allowed on the bottom floor where there was a back staircase leading up to where the girls traded their ware in themed rooms. For those who could afford it, these themed rooms of lush drapery, a shower, music was performed by a string quartet. This is where Anna worked.

These days those wonderful old mansions have now been converted into boring old tourist hotels.

'Bring back the Bordello',

Isadora's was earning notoriety for both good and the not so good, the police tolerated it because it brought all the underworld in one place where they could just keep an eye on who was who. Isadora increased her security staff who would often have to turn customers away be-cause of a full house, some came just for the music but most others to party with all the fringe benefits thrown in. She was making good money and a little of it trickled down to the band. She herself travelled the neighborhood in a plume fringed, wrought iron two horse carriage with a livered horseman and a gorgeous black footman.

This lady had class to burn.

For Dan, being a professional musician was like being on top of the world, for a while anyway. His attraction towards Anna became overpowering, he desired not only her body but her presence, she was constantly on his mind, he became obsessed, was this love?, or was this just passion, was it blind love where one can only see what was in the mind which was not reality. Somerset Maugham had written about blind love in his book 'Of Human Bondage'. Dan didn't give a damm, the only thing he wanted was more of the same. He didn't, or wouldn't, ever think that to her he was just another trick, she was just very skilled on what she did for a living.

Late one night as he was packing his gear, he saw Anna leaving, transfixed, his eyes followed her as she crossed the road, a man stepped out of the shadows and she took his arm. Dan had no control over what he did next, he followed them around the corner into Bayou Rd. As they passed under a street lamp, he could see that the man was dapperly dressed in a stylish fedora, double breasted coat, sharply creased trousers, lacquered shoes and swinging a brass knobbed cane, he looked at about 60 years. They stopped outside a two storied apartment adorned with flowers overflowing from hanging baskets, he opened the wrought iron gate, stepped aside as she walked on a slated path, they stopped on the porch while he unlocked the door, he stepped aside and allowed her to enter first, a light flicked on as the door closed. Obsession now controlled our Dan.

Several days later he found himself in the café that was opposite Anna's apartment, watching. About mid-afternoon Anna's 'uncle' stepped out and walked along the paved footpath, swinging his cane, as dapper as ever. Dan stood, leaving a few coins for his many cups of coffee that he had drunk and walked out to follow the dapper man. Dan stopped suddenly and turned away, it was then that it felt like being hit on the head with a sledge hammer.

He stopped in his tracks and cried out,

'What the fuck am I doing, am I loosing my mind?'

With him standing in the middle of the footpath, he attracted the attention of a few wanderers, including the Dapper man. A person yelling on the street in the French Quarter wasn't unusual and the locals just carried on with their day. Dan was in a blur for the rest of the afternoon and that night after the band had been playing for about half an hour Robert told Dan that he was just a waste of space on the stage.

He sent a message to Anna who was upstairs to meet him in the usual room they used which was without the knowledge of Isadora, it was a Cowboy themed room.

'Roy Rogers is riding tonight.' (Elton John)

He was quiet as she undressed herself and lay on the bed, Anna sensed that all was not right with Dan. She held out an arm to him, unmoving, he just stared at her body, she stood and slowly undressed him, she coaxed him onto the bed and as they lay, she gently kissed him.

'You can hurt me if you want,' she spoke softly.

'What, what do you mean?'

'Only if you want to.'

'I never, ever want to hurt you, I...' he was about to say "I love you" but thankfully the words never came out, 'I couldn't do that, oh sweet Jesus,' he cried out.

He rolled on his back, his mind went into turmoil, he couldn't look at her and it wasn't long before he tumbled into a troubled sleep.

Dan's obsession became depression as once again he found himself drinking Cuban coffee at the café, The Dapper man was a man of habit and appeared on his porch at the same time as usual, he walked down his short path and through the gate. This time instead of turning right he stepped off the curb and crossed the road and entered the café. Dan froze as he sat down in the booth opposite him and ordered coffee with liqueur, Dan shrunk, terrified, he hid his face by looking out the window. It was then he felt that he was on the edge of insanity. He looked at his own reflection in the windowpane, eyes that were drawn into their sockets, jaw tight and tense, the normal creases of his easy smile did not exist, he looked at the face of an insane stranger. Dan stood, turned, looked at the gentle face of 'Uncle' and spoke quietly.

'Have a good day sir,'

'And same to you too, my good man.'

Dan walked out of the café for the last time.

Dan was aware that he could not trust himself if he encountered Anna so went to great lengths to avoid her, one night the band were on the first verse of 'Kindhearted Woman' he looked up to see her standing, expressionless, motionless.

'But these evil hearted women, man, they will not let me be'. (sang R.J.)

Dan concentrated on his guitar and while on the last verse he looked for her, she was gone.

'She's a kind hearted woman, she studies evil all the time'. (R.J.)

It was time to talk, first he tried the Voodoo Creole fortune-teller he had got to know while he was on the streets; all she said was that the only thing she could see was cold, cold black water.

'Cold black water', he repeated. 'Where do I find cold water around here, what else do you see?'

She frowned, 'Nothing, there's nothing else, just cold black water.'

He turned around to walk away and mumbled, 'What a load of bullshit.'

'Hey Dan, you owe me a dime.'

'I'm not paying just for some 'black water.'

They both laughed, as he walked away, she frowned and shook her head.

'Hey man, you look good, what's up?' asked Robert late one night over a drink or two after they finished for the night.

Dan told them his story, Remy, through his loose front teeth said, 'Man, looks like you got the blues alright.'

Fats, the gambler picked up Robert's guitar and started strumming and as we know that when he sang, he did not stutter.

'I see that worried look upon you face,
You got your troubles, I got mine'.

'Fats, I never knew you could play guitar,'
'Th, th, ths, there's a lot you, d, d, d don't know about me.'

What they didn't know was that Fats was not only a gambler but a gambling addict and the 'Heavies' were pressuring him for debt's that he had accumulated.

Robert, who was still having major women problems said, 'Hey guys, things are getting a bit hot around here, looks like we need to get our arses outta town for a while, I think we need some fresh air to clear the head'.

That conversation was the breakup of the band 'Crossroads'.

Well, not quite, he reached over and took his guitar from Fats and said,

'I hafta' write a song about this,'

'Me and the Devil Blues' was the last song they performed in the House of the Rising Sun'.

'Early this morning
When you knocked upon my door
Early this morning
When you knocked upon my door
And I say, "Hello Satan."
I believe it's time to go'. (R.J.)

16

CROSSROADS

are on Highway 61 just a stones-throw from the subsistence cotton farm where Robert Johnson was raised. When the band gave notice to Isadora, she said that if it was because of money that she may be able to rake up a bit more even though they were overpaid as it was.

'Too late for that,' said Robert, 'We gotta get out of this place, if it's the last thing we ever do.'

'Humph,' her minders scowled as she spoke, 'is this is how you repay my generosity after me getting you off the streets,' both her minders took a threatening step towards Dan and Robert, 'Down boys,' she told them and carried on, 'don't expect me to give you another job in my establishment, there are 100s of guitar pickers around this place who would give their balls to come and work for me,'

As Dan and Robert were walking down Decatur St with their knapsacks and guitars strapped on their backs, Isadora's minders were nailing up a sign on the rise of the levee overlooking the Mississippi so it could be easily seen by the public,

MUDDY WATERS
PLAYING SAT NIGHT
THE HOUSE OF THE RISING SUN

'Who's this band?' Robert asked the Minders.

'The guy calls himself Muddy Waters, Isadora recons that they better be bloody good, or they'll find themselves rotting in the muddy waters of the delta wearing concrete gumboots.'

Dan didn't trust himself to see Anna before they headed north, he kept telling himself that as far as she was concerned, he was just another trick, one of many. That was what hurt the most, especially when it dawned on him that she was very proficient at what she did best.

The paddle-steamer 'Laura Belle', was named after the infamous cotton plantation owner and slave trader Laura La Robertie, headed north towards Baton Rouge and beyond. Dan's delusional insanity drifted like the morning mist on the Mississippi that burnt away as the shimmering heat of the day took control. The Laura Belle, like the many river steamers that plied the towns and cities of the deep south was a floating den of gambling, music, sex and bourbon whisky. Robert and Dan were given a slot on the main ballroom stage early one evening but their Devils music didn't go down very well with the white passengers. Added to that there was the issue of a black man and a white man doing music together. Blacks were not allowed in the ballroom. The partying passengers preferred the big band music of the likes of the Dorsey Brothers, Benny Goodman and the Glen Millar Orchestra etc., especially if they had large breasted blonds on vocals. In the early hours of the morning a local band would finish off the night with the old Confederate songs that came out of the woodwork.

Blacks were not allowed anywhere below deck so had to sleep in an uncovered partitioned area with no cooking or toilet facilities. Dan was not allowed to mix with the blacks so had to sleep in third-class steerage, along with the other white trash.

Their upstream voyage to Lafayette was slow due to the river being in flood from heavy rains in the mid-west. After they disembarked, they wandered around for a few days checking out the old bars, speak-easies and haunts where Robert had once played his Devils Music before he tried his hand down river in the Big Easy.

When they encountered any of Roberts's friends and acquaintances the first question asked was...

'What you doin, running round with a white-boy?'

'Why, he aint white, he's Irish.'

Mornings would find them on a bench in Moncus Park shooting the breeze with whoever wandered past; and there were plenty who had the time to shoot the breeze, paid employment for blacks in this town was rare. They sat smoking their homemade cigars from tobacco that grew wild on the outskirts of town, much to the annoyance of the tobacco plantation owners and the Federal Excise Tax collectors who would arrest anybody they caught smoking tobacco that wasn't produced in a licensed premises.

Late one morning a group of guys wandered in their direction, Robert's face lit up.

'It's ole Leadbelly,'

After many handshakes and high-fives Robert introduced Dan.

'What you doin with a white boy tagging along?'

'He aint white, he's Irish.'

'I guess that explains it.' laughed the guy called Leadbelly.

'He's going to be a heavy load to carry round in these parts,' said one mean looking guy who had prison written all over his face.

'He aint heavy, he's my brother,' (sang the Hollies)

'Arrr', said Leadbelly, 'That sounds like those words could make a good song, some day.'

'That day aint gonna happen too soon,'

Robert looked Leadbelly up and down, 'I thought you was still on the chain-gang?'

'Nah, they let me out on good behavior.'

'You! Good behavior, the guards must have been sleeping, hope you brought out more of those songs with you this time,'

'I always do, don't I? if you want to hear some, we will be at the picnic right here in this very park next week, what's it called?'

'Independence Day.'

'Independence! my fat black arse.'

After they had done the rounds of Lafayette, they loaded their packs with food and treats for Roberts's family, Robert thought he had about 11 or 12 siblings. They hit the road, occasionally hitching a ride on sharecropper's horse drawn carts but mostly just walking in the shimmering heat. The land was flat, bare and featureless. By late afternoon when the day was at its hottest, they came to a set of crossroads. Wiping the sweat that was dripping off their bodies they stopped for a drink of water from their canvas waterbags. There it was, the dilapidated sign that was on a lean with two boards that were nailed onto a post resembling the letter X. Each board had the word, CROSS-ROADS painted with both words sharing the letter S, the black paint was bleached to a muddy grey colour.

'This', said Robert, 'This is where I made my decision,' he pointed,

'Go down that way and you will rot, you'll bust ya gut for the rest of your life, you will live hungry, and you will die hungry, owing more money than when you started.'

He pointed the way they had come from, 'I went this way and got the chance to be somebody, life is full of crossroads and each time we arrive at our own crossroads we have to choose, I got lucky.'

They continued walking, 'Ya know Dan, there are many around here who are far better guitar pickers than me, I was the one that got lucky.'

'Robert, I guess you and I come from the same place, we made our own luck.'

The road had dwindled to a track with a scattering of broken clapboard houses dotting the bare landscape. There was a hot steady wind blowing the dry dust that covered everything, the rocks, the weeds, the scrawny bent dry trees, a land that was devoid of anything green, nothing rotted in this dry heat. They themselves became covered in the dust and to Dan it was as if the whole world was just the colour of light brown. They stopped for a drink and Robert nodded at the landscape.

'The topsoil has blown in the wind, nothing will grow, when I was a boy my dad and our neighbors grew cotton. We worked together, we planted cotton together, we picked cotton together, even us kids picked cotton, we had competition to see who could pick the most in one day. Then the big dry came and we starved. Now, sometimes the rains come back but we aint got no money to buy seed, no money to buy fertiliser, no money to put down a well, simply because the banks in Lafayette won't lend money to us Blacks,' he stopped for a few minutes and then carried on as they walked,

'The Clan is still alive and kicking round these parts, they own the banks and the business's, they look after their own anyway, they call us their po-boys.'

'Sounds to me like Black lives don't matter.' (In memory of Tranon Marton)

The house that Robert spent his childhood was built of clapboard to the common design of the deep South. This concept was called 'shotgun' because if one fired a shotgun through the front door the shot would go straight through the house and out the back door. The house was patched up here and there with scraps of wood and flatiron. The sky could be seen through the lounge ceiling and the two back rooms of the house was of no use in the wet simply because there was no roof. Robert's sharecropper father was long gone after fathering about ten of Roberts siblings. His mother had two more children by a go-good man who disappeared out the backdoor when Robert arrived with Dan.

The first words his mother said when they walked up the rickety steps were,

'What you doin with a white boy?'

The stayed for a few days of boredom and tried to fix a few things around the house without much success, simply because there was nothing to work with. It took Robert half a day to find a hammer which was useless as there were no nails to be found. On a previous visit Robert had organized and paid for a cartload of timber, flat iron, a handsaw and nails for the no-good man to do repairs. He asked his mother why the work wasn't done, she said that she never even saw the stuff and that the no-good man had swapped it for corn-liquor.

Robert showed Dan his first guitar that was on the front porch. As a boy he had hammered six nails into the wall and another six nails about two feet apart, the strings, he said were made of catgut.

'Catgut, did you make strings from the guts of a cat?'

'No. I tried that, but they kept breaking, an old guy down the road showed me how to use sheep guts,'

'You made your own?'

'Yep, you gotta get em while they are hot, wash em, soak em in oil and then stretch em out to the right thickness,'

'I'm impressed,'

'The hard part was in stealing the white man's sheep, I got shot at a couple of times, I used to sell the strings in Lafayette.'

With guitar's strapped on their backs, they hit the dusty road and headed back to Lafayette for the 4th of July picnic. When they got to the park, Ole Leadbelly was on stage which was a packed dirt mound originally created as an auction block for the trading of slaves. Late in the afternoon, Leadbelly finished off with his signature song 'Irene, goodnight Irene' and the white crowd began to pack up and head to their homes.

Dan looked around to see that besides himself there were just a few whites scattered around in small groups still drinking bourbon and finishing off the last of the fried chicken.

The band were just sitting around smoking and shooting the breeze while swigging corn-liquor from an earthen-ware jug.

'Is that it?' asked Dan.

'No, no, we're just getting warmed up, when I sing 'Irene', it sends the white folk to sleep so they all pack-up and go home, now we can have some real music.'

As they were talking people started arriving, seemingly from no-where, just appearing from the trees and the scrub, whole families were turning up ready to party with help of corn liquor and the devil's music.

Leadbelly and the band, including Robert climbed back up onto the mound, did a bit of tuning, harmonizing and the party started rocking. A bit of Gospel, 'Shine a Light on me', then into the old songs that

Leadbelly picked during his stints in prison. It was the music that the long termers sang as they toiled on the chain gang, 'Cotton fields', 'Bo Weevil', and then there was the 'Rock Island Line', and let's not forget 'Working on the Chain Gang'.

'Hey, Robert', Leadbelly called out, 'This one is for you and the white boy.'

'There is a house way down in New Orleans
They call the Rising Sun
And it's been the ruin of many a poor boy.
And God, I know I'm one'.

They parted company at the Lafayette dock, Robert headed south back to Nawlins and Dan said that he wasn't ready for that town just yet, so he caught the next tramp-steamer north to Nashville. It has been said there was 5,000 guitar pickers in Nashville, now there was 5,001, so there was very little space on the pavement for the likes of Dan. Times were tough and it took Dan all his guile and cunning to stay alive in this 'university of hard knocks'. He spent a couple of hours a day standing with tin cup in hand in line at the soup kitchen. This was the most entertaining and sometimes tragic part of every day, everybody had a story to tell of the road that delivered them to this long line for the hungry and the lost, waiting for food.

Nights Dan would hang round the bars and speakeasies with guitar on his back soaking up the music. In the several weeks he was there he felt a creeping uneasiness, he couldn't pin-point what this was about but what he did know was that he had to get out of this town, not an easy task without money. Whenever a southbound paddle-steamer tied up at the dock he would line up offering to work a passage shoveling coal. The response he got every time was the same,

'Only Blacks do that kinda work.'

There was a buzz of excitement happening around Music City's Honky Tonk Ave. There were notices being pasted around town advertising a Country and Western guy was coming to town for a concert at the 'Grand Ole Opery' music hall. Although Dan had never heard of the guy the buzz was that this was a show not to be missed. His cash flow was somewhere between grim and empty, so he was going to have to give it a miss. He was busking without much luck outside an upmarket bar when a well-dressed drunk staggered out the door, trying to walk, bumping into everything he could find, he then fell on a step and flaked out in a darkened doorway. While Dan was watching this guy's antics the doorman of the bar told Dan to take his music somewhere else, so he packed up and went over to the sleeping drunk to see if he was O.K., he was out to the monk. Dan looked around to find the coast was clear and said to the guy.

'Times are tough my friend.' and relieved him of his wallet.

Woody Guthrie's 'This Land is Your Land' brought down the house with each encore, Dan quipped that this guy must have Irish ancestry, Dan was to eventually carry Woody's and Robert Johnsons music back to Liverpool. The proceeds from his new life of crime gave him a chance to high-tail out of this town before things got out of hand, he got a cheap fare on a Kentucky based coal-carrying paddle steamer heading down-river to a coal fired power station just north of New Orleans.

Back in the big Easy he asked around for Robert and was told that he had taken off for San Antonio where there was a recording studio, this was the only time Robert recorded and these sessions resulted in the music of Robert Leroy Johnson being covered by the many hundreds of musicians and bands to this day. He mysteriously died from an unknown cause at the age of 27, which also turned out to be the start of another trend which includes...

Jim Hendrix, Jim Morrison, Janis Joplin. Amy Winehouse, Kurt Cobain, Brian Jones and so on, there is a 27 Club in Tel Aviv.

There is a prize of 'Chocolate Fish' to the reader who can guess the music that is covered there.

Although he had no desire to see Anna, he just couldn't help himself from knocking on the door of Isadora's one afternoon before the House was due to starts it's day. The door opened a crack and a female voice lied that Anna had not been seen for a long time. The door clicked shut, along with that chapter of his life.

The was nothing left in New Orleans, so he sold his Gibson and found passage in steerage onboard a Trader that eventually took him back to Liverpool. From his first day at sea, it dawned on him that the uneasiness and sense of longing he had felt while in Nashville was because of his time and distance away from the sea. He then realised that it wasn't blood that flowed through his veins, it was salt water.

17

THE DOGS OF WAR

were hovering over Europe as Dan, once again sailed up the Mersey. He was welcomed to his homeport by the two bronze Liver birds on top of the Cunard building. Once ashore he was interviewed by Captain Walker for a job back in the Cunard Line, the Captain had been in the past a Junior Officer aboard the Liverbird and was awaiting a post with the Royal Navy. There was no immediate work available for Dan but at least he was registered on the waiting list on one of the Companies many ships that plied the seven seas. In the meantime to survive he had to do a bit of couch surfing and the occasional job seagulling on the Docks. Most nights he would head up to Mathew St and the Cavern and join his old cronies of 'Creeping Jesus' who were eager to get a handle on the music of New Orleans and Nashville that Dan played on a borrowed guitar.

Captain Walker soon signed him up to work back down below deck on the Liverbird, which was at that time shipping iron ore from Pittsburg to Liverpool that was destined for the Sheffield steel mills in preparation for the probable war in Europe. It was predicted that if war did break out the British Merchant Marine shipping would play a major role in the war effort. The Liverbird was dry-docked for hull strengthening and the upgrading of her powertrain to gain several more knots. This time ashore the cashed-up Dan with his new Gibson Archtop guitar was offered a fulltime place with Creeping Jesus. He was back being a part of a band that was congruent to the Devils Music that Dan had discovered in the US of A. The blues proved to be something new for the Scousie teenagers that was alien to their parents, also this new music was a distraction from a possible war in which they were bound to be conscripted. Here Son, give me that guitar and take this rifle.

During a band break at the Cavern one night Dan and Kodie, the percussionist walked across the road to the Rubber Soul bar for a bit of peace from the rowdy Cavern. They were having a quiet beer at the bar with a mate, known as Lucky Jim. Just across from them was a table of five girls, with guys being guys, their eyes kept wandering in that general direction. The girls were having what looked like a serious conversation and then all burst out laughing, one stood up and encouraged by her friends walked over to Dan and his mates. She hesitated when she got to the table, looked around at her friends who nodded in encouragement.

'We were across the road the other night and heard your music, we thought it was great,' she looked over to her friends, who again nodded in encouragement, 'Well, I've been elected to invite you over to have a drink with us. Arr, at our table.'

'Who can say no to a bunch of pretty girls?'

The guys picked up extra chairs and drinks as the university girls made space for them. The girls, being the hosts took charge of the conversation and pumped the guys on the origins their music, have they ever cut any records and so forth. Soon the guys were rescued by a message from across the road, the band was waiting for them.

The next Saturday night while on stage Dan missed a beat when he saw the girls take a table next to the stage, he nodded to Kodie, the drummer, who hit his drums with a flourish. It was the best cover of Crossroads they had ever done. At the break Kodie nearly tripped over his drumsticks on his way from the stage to the girls table, Dan wasn't so confident so he went to the loo and on returning he saw an empty seat and one of the girls tapping the seat with her hand. The seat tapping girl introduced herself as Gabriel, just call me Gabby she said, and chatted on and on that they were about to graduate from Manchester University and were over for the weekend, especially for the band and their music.

Creeping Jesus was gaining a reputation when a Cockney accented Sharpie arrived at the Cavern one evening and offered them a one-off gig in a London dance hall. The next Friday they arrived in old London town and fronted up at the dancehall. That was a failure, simply because the Londoners wanted to jitterbug and just couldn't get their heads around the beat of this new music.

The Sharpie got them another slot on the Saturday night in a rowdy pub, the audience response was just the opposite of the dance hall. The drunken crowd wanted more and by the early hours the band had had enough and called it a night. The Sharpie told them how fantastic they were and that if they played their cards right, he would make them famous. He set up a meeting the next day in his Hammersmith office where he would have a contract drawn up by lunchtime, they never showed up for the meeting and headed back on the Express train to the Lime St Station in Liverpool

Back at the Cave the Manchester Uni girls were a regular fixture on Saturday nights and Dan would join their table after the band finished for the night. He found himself drawn to the girl Rose, and she to him, their eyes would meet, lock for several seconds and both would look away. Rose must have had a word with Gabby because, when he went to sit at their table the chair next to Rose was empty, Gabby, never one to beat around the bush, said…

'Looks like you two need to sit together,' she leaned over a patted the empty seat.

The best Dan could do was to say, 'Hi,'

'Hi to you too,'

'I'm Dan, I know you are Rose, so, hi Rose.'

'Are we just going to sit here and say hi to one another all night.'

They both laughed, it was then his hand, with a mind of its own, reached over and touched her bare forearm, the skin on his hand tingled, it was like a vibration of electricity that travelled up his arm, filled his body into his brain. Suddenly, nothing else existed except her face, their eyes locked, she didn't move, he looked down at his hand on her arm and realised what he had done, he quickly pulled his arm back and mumbled,

'Sorry, I'm sorry, I didn't mean...'

'No, no, don't be sorry,'

'Did you feel that?'

Rose nodded, from that moment on only they existed.

The dogs of war in Europe began to growl.

The then P.M. Neville Chamberlain, after having fought in the horrors WW1 was doing all he could to avoid armed conflict by making all sorts of concessions to the German war machine. He spent a year dithering around with Hitler who had sensed a weakness in him and the British. With increasing confidence, Hitler increased the Nazi strategy of his 'Final Solution' in exterminating the Jewish race, firstly in Germany and then looking further afield, intent to wipe out of the Jewish population throughout Europe.

Hitler invades Poland and concentrates his formidable war machine on the border of the Fatherland and the totally unprepared France.

Chamberlain declares war on Germany and is replaced by Winston Churchill.

The USA remained a neutral ally and heeded Churchills call...

'Give us the tools and we will do the job,' announced Churchill.

The British armed forces had been in preparation for war for several years and had gained momentum, introduced conscription and Dan was manpowered back into the Merchant Navy and back onboard the Liverbird. His ship had been fitted out for the transport of the machinery of war requested by Churchill from the East Coast USA to the UK via Liverpool.

The steel and arms manufacturers of the USA supplied both Germany and the UK until Japan bombed Pearl Harbor.

Both Germany and the British claimed to have God on their side and as has we all know, 'What God wants, God gets.' The world was in a war that delivered 20 million souls to their grave.

18

ROSE

enrolled at the University of Manchester for a degree in teaching. Education at that time did little for women after their primary schooling. If they happened to be fortunate or rich enough they graduated into a secondary school. Good fortune blessed Rose, Agnes convinced Conner that she had the intelligence and ambition to train for a career. Normally there was little choice for women other than the subject of Home Science in preparation for marriage and a hoard of kids. University education was practically non-existent but with the help from her family, she was determined not to succumb to the male privilege of those times.

Prior to enrollment she was required to be interviewed by the Vice-Chancellor. She stood on the pavement outside the main hall and looked up at this formidable building, a lone female in this male dominated institute. She took a deep breath and entered the lobby after having to push with all her strength to open the heavy doors, she thought that these doors were designed to make it even more difficult for a female to enter. Facing her was a wide ornate marble staircase, her heart thumping and brain racing, 'I can do this.'

Rose first concentrated on her posture, pushing her shoulder-blades together which opened her chest for deep breathing, chin in, head up, she looked without seeing she deliberately placed her foot on the first step, She soon calmed and with a wave of confidence she purposefully strode up the well-worn staircase. By the time she got to the first floor she was totally relaxed, breathing as normal she confronted a set of double doors with large ornately scrolled handles, above, in gold leafed lettering was...

VICE CHANCELLOR

At the desk was a prim woman with hair in a severe bun, half lensed glasses perched on her nose while noisily tapping a typewriter. Rose, with feet together stood in front of her and waited to be acknowledged. Miss Prim and Proper kept on typing until she finished the page, without looking up she pointed across the room and said 'Wait.' The large room was without chairs so Rose was kept standing for about 20 minutes. For 20 minutes she stood straight, with shoes firmly and evenly anchored to the bare marble floor, she concentrated on breathing and nothing else but breathing, counting her breaths, she counted to a 100 and then went back to one and counted another 100. There was no way she was going to be intimidated by this bullshit.

A buzzer sounded on Miss Prim and Proper's desk and without looking at Rose she pointed to the closed door behind her. The Vice Chancellor, wearing a cherub looking round and ruddy face with pork shop whiskers was reading Rose's C.V. She stood in front of his enormous desk, he looked up and waved towards a chair and said,

'So, you want to be a teacher, why?'

She had prepared for this one and replied,

'I have learned that ignorance breeds poverty and poverty breeds ignorance, as a child I experienced both, my ambition is to take part in giving everybody an equal opportunity, no matter who they are, what they are or where they come from.'

'You think so, do you? Somebody must work the mills and the factories of Manchester and Birmingham, that type of work doesn't require an education, what all these people need is to learn to do what they are told.' he stopped and studied Rose's reaction, then carried on. 'Education costs money so why waste money on an education they don't need, would it not be better putting our effort into educating our future leaders?'

Rose took time to think and chose her words carefully.

'Theoretically we are all born equal, some are born more equal than others and most of those who are less equal are women. We, as women, make up 50% of the population, so by denying 50% of people an equal opportunity this country is losing 50% of its potential.'

'What a load of poppycock,' he bristled, 'How can a person like yourself, a mere woman, control a classroom of ignorant brutes who need the rod to keep them in line?'

Although her brain was racing, she had total control of herself by imagining this bully, this pudgy man, standing shirtless, away from the protection of his desk, he would be insignificant.

'There are other ways of doing things, we need to learn new ways of teaching that does not take the power away from the student but gives them the chance to express their individuality as human beings. Our future doesn't have to be these dark and satanic mills or life in a kitchen surrounded by unwanted children. We need to provide the best education we can to give everybody the choice of their future rather than just writing a script that they are stuck with for the rest of their lives. Those who have absolute power all too often, tend to become toxic, unless challenged.'

His cherub face slowly creased into a shy smile, he stood and walked around to her side of the desk and offered his hand,

'Well done, Rose, is it? this is what I want to hear from you, so true, so true. women make up 50% of our population but about 1% of our leaders, what a waste of talent'.

Rose was gob-smacked, she thought she had blown it.

'Welcome to the University of Manchester', he handed over her C.V. 'I don't need to look at this, you're going to make a great teacher.'

Rose shared rooms with five other University girls, who, had to work harder than their male counterparts by having to wade through the constant sexism that prevailed. On top of all that, tertiary education was normally for the financially well to do. Rose's grandparents had agreed to pay her fees, but it was left to her to finance her living expenses, her Mum occasionally sent her some cash, but that wasn't consistent, money was just not in Myfamwy's vocabulary. Rose took whatever work she could find, like household help, waitressing and so on, when Conner and then not long after Agnes died, she had to take a gap year to finance her degree.

When not wandering around Europe Myfamwy would stay with her daughter in Manchester, their mother-daughter relationship developed into a strong friendship during their infrequent times together. As Rose matured her interest in her Irish roots grew but her mum had no desire to return to her place of birth and bitterness, it wasn't until her later years while living in Canada that Rose searched her Irish roots. Mother and daughter often returned to the Lakes district by train to Windermere and walk the hilly lands with backpacks sleeping rough in the old stone shepherds' shelters or sometimes in a pub for a hot meal and the luxury of a bathtub. While Conner and Agnes were still alive, they would stay with them in Liverpool, they were family. Those Liverpool days took them back to the Dockland factories and warehouses in this dirty old town, they didn't see the shambles or the coal blackened buildings, they saw humanity with all its warts and scars. Although Myfamwy rarely talked of her bitter youth, she would reminisce of romantic Ireland and her love in the times of Rose's father, Thomas

It was on one of these visits to Liverpool that Rose first heard of the music coming from the Cavern in Mathew St, both her and her Mum were captivated by the music of Creeping Jesus. Back in her rooms in Manchester Rose convinced her flat mates to have a weekend trip to Liverpool and the Cavern. Money was scarce so after the music died and the Cavern closed the girls walked up to the Lime St rail station, flutter their eyelashes at the station inspectors to turn a blind eye and allow them to sleep with safety on the hard wooden benches. They would catch the early morning train back to Piccadilly Station in Manchester. It was on one of these weekend trips that romance found her,

her first kiss with Dan was by a factory wall, in this dirty old town. (Ewan McCall)

Before graduating Rose and friends spent their summer break together in the council owned camping ground of Strawberry Fields Forever, the summer stayed with them, days of lazing and nights of music. One night they were sitting at their usual table in the Cavern, slowly sipping the one drink that their budget allowed. Two guys of the band were on a break having a beer at the bar, Gabby was elected to invite them over to make their acquaintance. Dan sat across from her as the conversation drifted around the music of Creeping Jesus, where did this stuff they called the 'blues' come from, are they going to cut any records and so on. Rose was captivated at first by Dan's quiet Irish American drawl. Although, from a distance she wasn't all that attracted by his appearance but when he was at the table and talked about the music of the American deep south, he was unassuming and without ego. She hung onto every word he spoke and when he did speak the table listened. Rose didn't trust herself to be gushy as were her friends, she left it to them to do the flirting. Several nights later during a break he walked over to their table, Gabby, sitting next to Rose could sense their interest in the other, stood and patted her chair. Dan couldn't get to the empty chair quick enough, there was an aurora that enveloped them both, although the bar was noisy, they were oblivious to anything but themselves, nothing else existed. Through their small talk Dan reached over and accidentally on purpose brushed Rose's forearm, he pulled back and apologised, it was as if a magician was standing over casting a spell with a magic wand. She said quietly, 'You don't need to apologise'.

Without speaking they got up from the table and walked outside, she felt her hand in his, magic, in the alleyway they stopped. She felt every piece of his body become part of her body, she had an overwhelming desire to go into his body, to be inside him, to lay with him. Their first kiss never ended, it was as if the Northern Lights had engulfed them, forever.

The brutal rumblings of war could be heard across the English Channel.

After Rose graduated her first teaching job was at Derby Collage in Liverpool where she taught Geography and History on the effects of English discovery and colonization had on indigenous peoples. She lived with two of her university friends in a cold water flat in Penny Lane.

Dans accommodation was a lot more fluid, living with the band in a converted warehouse with a constant stream of couch surfers where their amplified jam sessions were not a problem, the only problem was in find enough money to pay for food and rent. One of the couch surfers who was responsible for their sound systems was a guy from Manchester called Lucky Jim who had become a close friend of Dan and the band, he eventually went on to become a permanent fixture on a stool in the bar of the Rubber Soul.

Time together was precious for Dan and Rose, one worked day and the other worked night, so at every opportunity like school breaks or holidays of they would pack a pup tent, some food, warm gear for the often-foul weather to tramp the dunes of Crosby beach and beyond. In those prewar days sex was mostly within the realms of marriage, Dan and Rose broke that rule, as regular as possible.

Little did they both know that it was Dan's father Seamus was responsible for the death of Roses father, Thomas.

Rose, at times, questioned her overriding desire for Dan, when together all that existed was themselves. When apart, she became afraid for her career that she loved and worked so hard for. Several times she tried to distance their relationship. She no intention of abandoning her dreams for a guitar playing male, a man with a mysterious past who was just living in the here and now without any regard for a future. As she got to know him, she learnt that underneath he was vulnerable and insecure. At times she found that she didn't really know him, it was if he was wearing a mask to hide the person that even he didn't understand, he was a lost soul.

To Rose's increasing consternation she couldn't control the fire that was burning inside, was it love or was it just lust. What will remain when lust just simmers, will love also just simmer and die a lonely death. Can lust, love and a career co-exist with this man who is just a boy at heart. What about the word 'pregnant', she shuddered at the thought, sometimes lust overrules common sense as it does so often, with her and Dan that risk was growing by the day. As the weeks turned into months Rose concluded to call the whole thing off, she carefully chose the time and place. Ferry across the Mersey to Birkenhead and a long walk down the river to the solitude of the Wirral Peninsular where they sat on a bench looking East across the Mersey to the haze of the city. Rose had brought up the subject of the cooling of their relationship in the past but each time she let it slide, her mind made up that today was the day to move on with her life as a teacher.

Dan had suspected what was coming, he still was totally unprepared and just couldn't get his head round what was happening, his love was blind. They sat, apart, on the bench, afraid to be within touching distance, slowly he went from disbelief to anger, anger toward himself for once again falling so fast, and once again, to hit rock bottom. He didn't trust himself to look at this woman who looked so beautiful in her grief, he stood, and without speaking and began the long walk back to the ferry building. The broken-hearted Rose gathered her strength and with brain in a turmoil she followed Dan along the boardwalk, looking without seeing into the shop windows, she watched him board the ferry and waited the hour before it returned.

Their parting lasted about two weeks, there was no way that Dan was going to knock on the door of Rose's flat in Derby, nor was Rose going to anywhere near the Cavern. They were both too proud for that, this false pride didn't last for long as they both began to frequent the likely places that they may accidently on purpose run into each other. Sure enough, it was in Sefton Park where, on a Sunday they would go and watch the Liverpool Brass band performing in the rotunda and treat themselves the luxury of an ice-cream in a cone. This fateful Sunday the Armed Forces Military Band were strutting their stuff in the square performing the marches of the American composer John Phillip Sousa. The very rotund bandleader provided the entertainment with his skill in twirling, with precision, his long brass baton. Several times he dropped his baton which would bring a round of good natured applause from the spectators.

Dan felt the presence of Rose before he saw her, she had seen him before he found her, they both stopped in their tracks, oblivious to anything else other than themselves. They collided heavily with arms, legs and bodies entangled as if they were trying to get inside one another. A passerby quipped,

'Hey, you two, looks like you need to go somewhere private.'

Although they had a million things to talk about when they come up for air the best Rose could come up with was,

'What do you think about the Army band?'

Caught off guard Dan repeated the question.

'What do I think of the band? Rose, all I can think of is you, I thought I had lost you.'

'These last weeks have been my most miserable time, ever, I couldn't think of anything else but you,'

'Me to, I don't think we can stop this, I thought of going away somewhere but I just can't,'

'I just feel as if I'm trapped, but, but I can't escape, I don't want to escape, maybe you should have gone away, I don't know, I don't know what to do,'

'You asked what I thought of the Army band, they were funny, but underneath they scared me.'

'Me too, I think the Government is telling us that we are going to go to war.'

'The world is going crazy once again, we haven't got over the last one yet and now it's 'de ja viue' all over again,'

'There is not much we can do about it, actually we've got more important things to think about, like, what's going to happen with us?'

While the dogs of war hovered, Myfamwy escaped from her wanderings of Europe back to Liverpool. It didn't take her long to understand what was happening with Rose and Dan, she herself had lost love so she wasn't going to let that happen with her daughter so went to the local bakery and ordered a cake. The next Sunday she invited Dan over for dinner at Rose's flat, after the main course she said that she had a special treat for pudding, with fanfare she presented the iced cake that had a miniature Bride and Groom and 'Just Married' piped onto the icing. She asked Dan and Rose when they were going to set the date.

They duly married and honeymooned in Wray Castle in the Lakes district where they warmed the cockles of their hearts in the Wedding Chamber with a fireplace and the veiled four posted bed. After a pheasant dinner they retired to the games room where Rose defeated Dan in a game of snooker, the concierge remarked that...

'When girl beats boy, girl loses boy.'

They settled into a flat in Derby close to where Rose taught, Dan worked the docks during the day and several nights a week at the Cavern where Creeping Jesus were making a name for themselves. Prior to Dan's return from the Deep South their music was mostly covers of the popular songs of the time like 'Happy Days' and 'Minnie the Moocher', with Dan's influence they began creating their own material like 'Going Down Town', Rattle those Chains' and the very popular 'Everton Blues'. For a while they were joined by an Irish fiddler for their excursion into Country & Western 'Lonesome Girl' which became a hit, albeit a hit just in Liverpool. They returned for a stint in London which didn't attract a wide audience, London was not yet ready for their music. Many of their followers were the Liverpool Irishmen working in the mills of Manchester and Sheffield in preparation of the probable invasion of the Hun, these young Irish likened the bands Blues version cover of the song 'In London's fair city, where the girls are so pretty...'

Oh, no! Rose is pregnant, she is shattered by this unplanned turn of events, this was not supposed to happen, at first, she became depressed that all her hopes and dreams that she had worked so hard for were gone, like a candle in the wind. All she could think of was of 20 years of an unrewarding existence of motherhood, of household toil and the poverty of being the wife of a lowly paid Dockworker. She had been cheated by lust and passion. As her time became closer, she took a year's leave from teaching. She was determined to go back to work as soon as possible. Dan agreed to shared parenthood that would fit in with his casual work on the Docks. Also, he had a somewhat small income from music that he was confident that would in time, develop into recording. The changes within Rose began to take an effect to where her depression lifted and was replaced by the joy of motherhood that she began to suspect may enhance her life as being a woman, even with all his shortcomings, she could not but love the man of her life.

Hitler invades Poland, Great Briton declares war on Germany, Creeping Jesus is conscripted, and Dan is manpowered back into the engine-room of the Liverbird.

The first causality in war is the truth and the second causality as far as Creeping Jesus was concerned was that two of the band were reported missing and presumed dead at Dunkirk, one was killed fighting Rommel's Desert Rats alongside the Kiwi's and Aussie's. Kodie, the drummer was wounded alongside 10,000 deaths of the allied soldiers on D-Day. We all recall in the first chapter of this book of what happed to Dan when the Liverbird was torpedoed in the North Sea.

The music of Creeping Jesus's had never been recorded and was lost, forever.

Tony, James and Ellen were born just before and at the beginning of the war, Rose was left mostly to fend for herself while Dan was at sea, his port calls into Liverpool were very short-lived because of the vulnerability of shipping being attacked by the Luftwaffe while docked. Rose, as with the people of Liverpool, lived with the fear of nighttime air-raids, food rationing, poverty and the unknown survival of their brave men at sea.

There was a knock on her door, she froze, she knew as she opened the door, that the uniformed Naval Officer who was standing to attention holding his cap under his arm, was going to announce, he saluted.

'The Liverbird has succumbed to a torpedo attack in the North Sea'.

19

'Where have all the flowers gone?
Long time passing
Where have all the flowers gone?
Long time ago
Where have all the flowers gone?
The girls have picked them every one.
Oh, when will you ever learn?
Oh, when will you ever learn.' (thanks to Pete Seager for that one)

19

THE CRUEL SEA

and the icy water of the North Atlantic shocked Dan to his senses, he had no memory of why or how he got there, his body was numb, his brain in shock, there was no sound, his first reality was that he was screaming, but without sound, there was nothing but blackness, he thought that he must be blind, he had no body or limbs, it was if he was in some sort of limbo of death.

Then the pain started, pain, glorious pain telling him that he was alive, think, man, think. His first rational thought was to keep breathing, he gagged and vomited, it was oil, the sea surface was covered in oil, it was his lifejacket that kept his head up out of the water. Concentrate, breathe in, breathe out, push everything out of the brain, breathe in, breathe out, concentrate, he closed his eyes in concentration, don't breathe in oil, nothing else exists except to breathe. His numbness shielded him from the intense pain of cold, he cursed the oil and then blessed the oil in the way that it flattened the sea into a glassy surface, just don't swallow the stuff. Then the oil had a glassy light reflecting surface, it was a flashing light coming from behind him, he turned but the light turned with him, the light was coming from the inflated collar of his lifejacket. Time was impossible to measure except by counting his breaths, then he would lose count and have to start back at number one again. As his thoughts became more rational, he talked out loud to himself, the silence frightened him, deaf but still alive. He had no idea how long he had been in the water but knew that he had a lifespan of about 20 minutes or so. Don't think about it, one second could be a minute, one minute could be ten, ten minutes could be sixty minutes, he had no idea, breathe in, breathe out, breathe in, breathe out. In the blackness Dan saw a shimmer of light, it was Rose, he called out, the light became stronger, her face radiated into a gentle smile as she held out both arms as if to embrace him. He swam towards her, silently sobbing.

'Rose'

The bright light overpowered her image as the light of a torch blinded him, a pole reached out towards him, he ignored it and pushed it away as he turned in panic looking for Rose, he called out again.

'Rose'

He felt himself being lifted and heard male voices,

'We gotcha mate, don't fight, we gotcha.'

The launch was from a Royal Navy Corvette that was part of the convoy, Dan looked at the men realizing that they were talking to him, he shook his head indicating he couldn't hear. As he came to his senses, he felt the throb, throb, throb vibration of the Lister diesel motor of the lifeboat, he looked around to see that the launch was overcrowded with his shipmates of the Liverbird. The lifeboat crew were pulling the rescued on board, the dead had their lifejackets removed and were silently slipped back into the cruel sea, the dead made way for the living. The Corvette was nervously circling the flotsam in fear of a German U-Boat or Raider that could be lurking around, hunting for another soft target in the dark.

After seven days Dan woke in hospital from an induced coma, he moved his fingers, then toes, shoulders and head from side to side, everything seemed to be working, Rose was at his bedside, although hesitant she held him gentle as if he might break, he felt the warmth of her breath on his face and her breasts on his chest, while still holding him she lifted her head and saw that his eyes were glazed, it was if he was looking but not seeing. Dan could see that her mouth working but without sound, she mouthed the words,

'I love you.'

He didn't speak, she held him close again as he softly cried.

After another week of physical rehabilitation, he was walking, a little unsteady as if his balance was affected. There was no damage to his eardrum so there was no reason he couldn't communicate. The doctors diagnosed his condition as 'shell shock', the modern version is now known as PTSD and he was transferred to the Clock View Mental Hospital.

This institution was overwhelmed with soldiers suffering from shell shock, treatment was practically non-existent as the average number of patients per Psychiatrist was about 100 to 1. Most inmates, after a short period were deemed fit enough to be discharged and sent back to the front-line to face their demons, alone. The penalty for cowardice in the face of the enemy was prison, a slight improvement from WW1 when the penalty for cowardice was to face a firing squad.

Dan's recovery was slow and tormented, but recover he did without a great deal of treatment. The best help he got was from within, where he put into practice the teachings of Pieter from way back in his peat digging days. Meditation and yoga calmed him enough for the heavily pregnant Rose to bring him back to some sort of normality. His hearing returned, then Rose taught him to have the confidence to start speaking again, it was like teaching a child to form words. Nighttime brought the nightmares when he would wake screaming, the Psychiatrist said that the only cure for him, time.

Rose brought him back to some sort of mental state where he could be discharged, the birth of their son Tony brought some sort of normality to them both, as husband and wife.

And the nightmares continued.

Soon after he was discharged from Clock View, Dan was deemed fit to go back to sea and was required to sign up once again with the Cunard Line. The company's manpower officer interviewed Dan and recognized his fragile mental state, so kept him on standby until such time when he was forced to send Dan back to sea because of the major shortage of merchant sailors.

At that time the German Navel war machine was in command of the North Sea, resulting in the lifespan of a merchant seaman averaging about six months. Dan was assigned to the passenger liner 'Mariposa' which had been commissioned by the Royal Navy as a troop carrier transporting conscripts and volunteers from the colonies of New Zealand, Australia and the Indian sub-continent to the war zones of Europe.

While on standby Dan ventured back to the Cavern, which was at most times deserted because of the war effort and the almost nightly blackouts. Liverpool prayed for adverse weather which hampered the Luftwaffe bombers. Creeping Jesus had disbanded, so Dan, after a few beers of encouragement, picked up his guitar and played solo, this two pronged self medication gave him confidence that had been shattered by his mental state after being torpedoed. The music part of his recovery worked okay but the few beers increased to more than just a few and quickly became a monkey on his back. There was a demon in the bottle for Dan and it didn't take long before he had to go to bed drunk to keep the nightmares at bay. Alcohol being the depressant it is, just made his life and his family's life a misery. He was terrified of going back to sea but was ashamed at the thought of himself being a gutless coward while thousands of men were dying.

After one late night at the Cave, he staggered outside only to fall asleep in a bus shelter and was picked up by the police to spend the night in a cell. He was charged with being drunk in a public place, kept in a cell till that afternoon when, hungover, ashamed and dishevelled, fronted the Judge to be convicted and discharged. This incident gave both Dan and Rose a big fright and he stopped drinking, for a while anyway. About a week later he was back in the Cavern strumming guitar to his solo version of Crossroads. Crossroads he thought, just one cold beer won't hurt, but in Dan's state of mind one drink was too many and a thousand would not be enough. It didn't take long before he was back drinking and back to the mental place he was at prior to spending the night in the prison cell.

And the nightmares continued.

The Mariposa docked at Portsmouth to discharge the conscripts from the sub-continent to lay down their lives for dear old Mother England. Dan departed Liverpool by train to Portsmouth to crew on her next voyage transporting poorly trained troops from Auckland and then to Perth to pick up the Auzzies. The Mariposa shipped several thousand young men and women to North Africa to fight Rommel's Desert Rats in Egypt. These soldiers from the colonies chased Rommel out of Africa and then went on to battle with victory over the Germans in Italy.

After discharging troops, the Mariposa then crossed the Atlantic to the USA. Dan's terror of being torpedoed mounted to breaking point as his ship re-entered the north Atlantic, his only solace was from the alcohol that was smuggled on board. The Mariposa, heading to Liverpool was overflowing with the expatriate British citizens of America who were enlisting in the armed forces for the possible invasion of the UK by the Germans. Although the Mariposa was heavily guarded by the Royal Navy, Dan spent most of his non-working hours on deck on the look-out for any indication of the German U-Boats that were surely prowling. It wasn't until they were in the relative safety of the Mersey that he began to relax from the immediate danger.

He still suffered the terrifying sleepless nights that continued when he was back with his family. Rose organized an appointment with the Psychiatrist who said that there was little he could do other than Dan with the help of Rose needed to do something about the demon in the bottle.

The next voyage of the Mariposa was back to Australasia as a troopship, although at that time her destination was created by rumors, 'loose lips, sink ships' was the call of the day. Prior to departure the ship had to go into the heavily defended Liverpool dry-dock for some urgent repairs and maintenance. Those next few weeks were the last, ever, that Dan, Rose and their children were to be together. Back home with family Dan stopped drinking and was sleeping better and on the road to recovery, this period was the happiest ever for the family. For Rose and Dan their love had been rekindled and was aflame with passion and desire. In the warm weather the family would bus and walk to Boyles Beach and picnic, dig in the sand for cockles and open them over a fire. They huddled close together in their small tent for the night. Boyles beach was well away from the danger of being bombed although their fire caused the Air Raid Warden to give them a telling off, he quietened down after a feed of cockles. In their tent the family sang along with Dan and his guitar and were mesmerized by Rose's stories that she had learned from her mother of an ancient Ireland. They were a family again. Back in the city when the air-raid sirens sounded Dan would make a fun-game of running to the shelters and then entertaining everybody with music which somewhat drowned out the noise of the enemy bombers. When bad weather grounded the Luftwaffe in France Dan would play at the Cavern to earn a few pennies for the luxury of a piece of meat or something sweet for his family.

The Mariposa was refloated from dry-dock and was bunkering in preparation for sailing, Dan was ordered to be back on board the next day to sail in the dark of night to who knows where. For Dan this was to be his last day with his family, his last day with Rose and his last night, ever, at the Cavern. The fickle fingers of fate took control once again.

20

TWO OF ENGLAND'S FINEST

were in the Cavern along with a reasonably sized crowd of regulars, some were dock workers and others were the ones unfit or too old to put on a uniform. Also, there were half a dozen of Dan's shipmates from the Mariposa having their last fling before many dangerous months at sea. There was drizzly fog that had been around for a few days so Liverpool was relaxed without the interruption of the dreaded air-raid sirens. The two men in their mid 20s, were not locals, although dressed in civilian clothing they had a military bearing and with their upper-class London accents identified them as probably Army Officers on leave. They had been in the bar since midafternoon and were becoming a little boisterous drinking the local Cains beer that had a fair kick in it compared to the London beer that they were accustomed to. Dan was onstage strumming some blues before calling it an early night, he was signing off with his signature 'Crossroad Blues' when one of the English officers called out loudly.

'Hey, Scousie, you're useless, ya can't play for shite.'

When Dan had finished playing he said into his mike,

'So, fucking, what!'

He stepped off the stage and went over to the bar to farewell his mate Jimmy Nuts, while they were yarning the two guys staggered over to them and one spoke.

'You fucking useless Scousie, look at yourself, boring us to tears with that black American music with a guitar that you can't even play.'

Dan, ignoring them, turned his back and carried on talking to Jimmy.

'Hey, don't you turn your back on me, I put my life on the line defending the likes of you, you Scousie bastard, I'm the one that's out there getting shot at and saving you're arse from the Hun! Fuck you, you gutless coward.'

Dan turned around, stared at them with the best stone face he could conjure up and then insulted him by laughing in the guy's face.

The officer stepped forward and raised his fist and took a wild swing at Dan which was easily avoided by a quick step backwards, the guy lunged forward again but his mate held his arm and spoke.

'Not in here,' He stared at Dan with hatred, 'You'll keep,' after a few long seconds he turned and said to his colleague.

'Let's get out of this dump.'

Jim turned back to the bar and said to the barman,

'I'd expect nothing less from those arrogant Pommy bastards,'

Jim, from Manchester, had no tolerance whatsoever for anybody south of Liverpool, especially if they were aristocracy or the like.

The aggressive officer had to have the last word as they exited.

'Fuck you lot.'

Dan gave the guys about 10 minutes to get out of Mathew St, his planned early night that he was going to have had disintegrated, he said his goodbye's and walked out into the street. In the dark he was met by a fist that smashed into the side of his head, he staggered back, and was able to ward off another couple of blows. He regained his balance as the drunk officer, swaying, lined up another punch, he was an easy target for Dan to hit, the guy's eyes glazed, and Dan pushed him over and his legs buckled, falling to the ground. The other guy charged Dan with a rugby tackle, he easily rolled out of the tackle and punched his assailant on the back of his head. The guy, propelled by the punch, fell heavily, face down hitting his forehead on the stone curb. Dan regained his balance and saw blood pouring into the gutter, he bent down and rolled the guy onto his back, there was a split and large dent in his forehead with blood oozing from his ear and nose. The other soldier was on his feet looking down at his comrade while Dan was bending over him. they both saw his eyes sightlessly wide open as his life slipped away.

By then, Jim, along with a couple of Dan's shipmates had, on hearing the kerfuffle, burst out of the bar just as the officer pointed at Dan and yelled.

'You bastard, you killed him, I saw you do it, you punched him, you murdering bastard.'

Dan was numbed, speechless as he looked in horror at the man on the ground, by then a few more people had arrived in the scene, some from the Rubber Soul across the road, all looking the soldier on the ground who was obviously very dead.

'What happened?'

'It was him.' the man said pointing at Dan.

'What happened?'

'We were standing outside, having a smoke, this bastard,' pointing at Dan again, 'He came out of the bar abusing us and then punched my friend here', he pointed to the dead man. 'We were just standing and minding our own business and this fucking Scousie hit him, for no reason.'

'You right Dan?' asked Jim.

Dan, in shock couldn't speak.

'What happened?' asked somebody, as his shipmates gathered.

Dan, still in shock but recovering, 'They were waiting for me, he's bullshitting,' he looked down again at the dead man, 'What the fuck have I done? No, no, no.' He had his face in his hands.

The man was retelling his bullshit story to whoever would listen and added.

'Has anybody called the Police yet?'

'They're on their way.'

One of Dan's shipmates said, 'I think we'd better get you the hell out of here mate, quick smart, looks like it's your word against his, you won't stand a chance once the Coppers arrive, what do you reckon?'

Dan's brain was racing, he couldn't think let alone speak. His shipmates bundled him into the Morris 8 that one of them had parked further up Mathew St and they drove down towards the Docks and the Mariposa.

'Where are you taking me?'

'Down to the ship mate, we'll be out of here by this time tomorrow night?'

'Take me home first.'

Dan gently shook Rose to wake her, one look at his face and she knew something was wrong, he told her, including the version of the officer, horrified, she said that he had to give himself up. He said that the only witness was an Officer of the British Army and that it was his word against Dan's. Rose's argument was that justice would prevail. His shipmates knocked on the door telling him to get a move on because it wouldn't be long before the Coppers arrived. Dan told them of Rose's opinion. Jim had entered the bedroom and said,

'Who are they going to believe? You or the words of an Officer of the British army, this is the time of war, you would probably be found guilty of and be hung for murder.'

'Give us five minutes', said Dan.

Rose was still adamant that he should trust the system, Dan made his decision, this decision was based on his life as a lad in Londonderry and his time in the Deep South of the USA in that there were two laws in this world, one for the privileged and one for the downtrodden. As Dan walked backwards out the door, they were looking at each other in shocked horror, he said one word.

'Mariposa.'

The next day Liverpool's newspaper the 'Echo' headlined.

'MURDERED, ONE OF ENGLAND'S FINEST'.

The Chief Constable of Liverpool held a press conference…

'The Liverpool Police have mounted a search for the fugitive named Daniel Seamus Dillon, this man is a person of interest regarding the murder of Major Reginald Montgomery DSO the eldest son of Sir Watford and Lady Eleanor Montgomery, Sir Watford was knighted for his distinguished service in the Boer War. The victim's grandfather, General Humphrey Montgomery was honored for bravery in the 'Siege of Lucknow' in India and was responsible for the quelling of the Māori uprising in New Zealand. Major Montgomery with his colleague and friend Lieutenant Adam Crookshank were on leave awaiting a post in the war against Nazi Germany.'

The Chief Constable hesitated for effect and then carried on…

'This murder was the consequence of an unprovoked attack on the Major by the previously named perpetrator witnessed by Lieutenant Crookshank. Dan Seamus Damon is a member of the outlawed IRA. The fugitive, had, in his murky past, been arrested and charged with the murder of a Police Officer in Londonderry. This charge was withdrawn on the grounds of insufficient evidence. The Londonderry Police have not made any further arrests regarding this murder. Recently, in Liverpool, he was arrested, convicted then discharged for being 'Drunk and Disorderly in a Public Place.'

Once again, he paused to let this sink in to his captive audience.

'This fugitive, when apprehended will face the full force of the law.'

He pulled back his shoulders into a military stance…

'We all mourn the tragic loss of 'One of England's Finest.'

21

GO ASK A RAT

if you're looking for a place to hide on a ship. The police questioned Rose extensively on Dan's whereabouts. Her lie came easily in that she hadn't seen him since he had departed their flat in Derby to go to work at the Cavern at about 7.00 the previous evening. She said that he had never arrived home and was most concerned of his whereabouts, had he done something wrong?

They ignored the question and stated that to withhold evidence of the whereabouts of a fugitive was an offence that would lead to a term in prison.

At the same time a large contingent of police with sniffer dogs boarded the Mariposa and carried out a search for the day, without success. There was a Police watch shipside throughout the night while Dan hid in the funnel. That night the German Junker Du88 bombers protected by the Messerschmidt fighters made their biggest full moon attack on Liverpool to date. The artillery defenses surrounding Liverpool, assisted by the newly invented radar, caused severe damage to the Luftwaffe attack. Captain Walker believed that the enemy was targeting the Mariposa that had been provisioning and bunkering for the long voyage downunder. He gave the order to his officers to prepare for an immediate departure and the police were ordered off his ship. They were compliant as they felt like sitting ducks onboard the

155

targeted ship and were very happy to head to the nearest air-raid shelter. In the darkness the tugs escorted the Liner into the middle of the Mersey and once under her own steam was well gone by daylight.

Dan spent a freezing day in the false funnel and come darkness was taken to one of the Staterooms where he spent the rest of the voyage in relative comfort, well physical comfort anyway, bound for the colonies downunder.

There were a few other passengers on board, military personal to advise on the training of NZ conscripts, a man from the Bank of England who was responsible for the gold that was to be paid to the NZ government for lamb and dairy products. The ship's crew spent the whole voyage on scheming how to steal some of the gold, every day somebody would come up with a cunning plan and what they were going to spend their good fortune on, dreams are free. Also, on board there were expatriates returning home to escape the carnage of the possible invasion of the U.K. Dan never got to meet any of his fellow passengers, so he was relatively safe. As far as the crew went, the word very quickly got around of the events leading to Dan being on board. His shipmates, well unofficial shipmates, of both crew and officers were aware the reasoning of Dan being on board. They has sailed with Dan on many voyages and knew that violence was not part of Dan's character. The crew who were at the Cave on that fateful night were emphatic that it was not Dan who had provoked the fight that had landed him in the mess he was in. Captain Walker sniffed that something was amiss on board his ship and eventually got the full story, which was quite different from what he had been told by the Police. He agreed with his officers that Dan's evidence in the courtroom would not hold water against the word of a respected and decorated Regimental Officer. Captain Walker turned a blind eye to Dan being aboard but told his Bosun that he wanted Dan to be off his ship on arrival in Auckland.

Several weeks later the Mariposa was in the relatively safety of the South Atlantic well below the Falklands heading west towards the south of Chile, the distance slowly widened from the dangerous German Navy that riddled the Atlantic. Dans nightmares were receding and was, on occasion, able to get a full night's sleep in the luxury of his stateroom and the fine food delivered from the Master chefs of the Cunard Line. He often went to work below deck in the engine-room to give his shipmates a break. Keeping a low profile, he would spend the midnight hours on the upper deck in his usual stance of leaning with forearms on the gunnel, hands clasped together with one foot on the lower rail with a self-rolled cigarette between his lips while looking into the foreboding gloom. He was coming to terms that the life he had left behind was a life that he may never see or feel again, maybe he should have fronted the justice of the courtroom to trust that justice was not blind. For a thousand times he argued with himself, what would the hangman's noose do to Rose and their children or was his absconding, however painful that may be, was the better option. He spent the rest of his short life battling with this dilemma. The pain that he carried was physical as well as mental, he had a sadness that would never die. As the ship steamed westward, he resolved that he would not look back over the stern rail and dwell on his past, he walked the deck to the bow as the ship plunged head-on into the Southern Pacific Ocean and a new life. Sometime, somewhere, somehow, he would once again hold her close; the ghost of Rose would be with him forever.

The Mariposa kept well south punching into the never-ending S.W. gales until reaching the 180 deg meridian then veering north to pass the Chatham Islands and then well off the East Coast of N.Z. to the Port of Auckland. While passing west of the Chathams he could make out the lay of the land and the comforting light of Soanes Point blinking brighter as darkness fell. He wondered of the land and of the people who inhabited this isolated outpost of civilization.

A few days out from Auckland the ships Purser put together I.D. papers and a forged passport with a vague photo and a new name, Robert Dan O'Shaunasy, he could still call himself Dan. The Purser, who, Dan thought, had plenty of experience in somewhat shady activities organised a cash collection from the crew. To top up his fund raising, the Purser tickled some petty cash from the ships stronghold that was used for provisioning, fuel and other port expenses which was covered up by forging invoices from shore based Providor's

The Mariposa, with Pilot on board made her way into the vast Hauraki Gulf weaving her way between Great and Little Barrier Islands, Kawau and the recent volcano of Rangitoto Island, where she was picked up by the tugs to be guided to dock at the Jellicoe wharf.

Over the previous weeks there had been a steady build-up of poorly trained troops from all over N.Z. For training purposes they carried wooden rifles, for target practice they shared one .303 rifle per platoon of about 20 men. The most important part of training was to learn to take orders without question, very difficult task for these wild colonial boys. Although they didn't know it, they were headed for North Africa to fight Rommel's Desert Rats. Victory in Egypt that was followed by defeat in Crete with an extensive loss of life. By the time they got across the Aegean Sea to Italy their numbers had dwindled significantly. As they prepared for their big O.E. here was an excitement in the air as if they were all going on a pleasure cruise to exotic countries that they had only read about in books. Dan was on deck and witnessed the 28th Māori Battalion deliver a haka on the wharf, farewelling their people, Dan felt confident that the Germans were in for a spot of bother when they mixed it with these NZ Māori.

The expectation of the Kiwi's was that it was only take a couple of months before Hitler surrendered. The fighting would be over, the battle would be won and that they would all return home as heroes. These brave men and women were totally ill prepared for a very unpleasant surprise.

Dan correctly surmised that the Liverpool police would have contacted their counterparts on the probability of a person of interest wanted for questioning regarding a serious crime in Liverpool being on board the Mariposa. The purser had gathered up all the passports of the crew and had them stamped by NZ customs. In the melee of soldiers with families and the loading of produce for the war effort Dan was not challenged and made it ashore without issue. He thought it wise to head south away from cosmopolitan Auckland via the overnight Express to Wellington and cross Cook Strait by ferry to Lyttelton.

Dan was on the top deck as the ferry docked in Lyttleton. The harbour was rimmed by a near complete circle of steep but negotiable cliffs indicating that the harbour and surrounds was created by an ancient volcano blowing a huge hole leaving a deep-water harbour, he imagined it as once being a 'Ring of Fire'. The small village looked to have a couple of pubs, a shipping providor, the inevitable church, a time-ball on a hillock, a street of half a dozen varied shops and what looked like a theatre. My kind of town thought Dan. Ashore, the first building he arrived at was a pub, which turned out to be the infamous British Hotel, yes, it still is today what it was then, rough and drunk proof. A place where one would be asked no questions and told many lies, where a man was judged on face value. The pub serviced the port workers and sailors and to greet them were the painted ladies on the lookout for a trick. He checked in, my kind of pub, thought Dan, easy to keep a low profile while he looked for a job.

The M.V. Rangatira was a coastal trader built in the shipyards of Esbjerg in Denmark and was trading on the coast of N.Z. and infrequently to the Chatham Islands. It didn't take Dan long to become friendly the Chief Engineer, Harry Styles in the bar of the British, who talked about his upcoming voyage to the Chatham Islands. Dan's interest in these Islands had already been kindled so he asked Harry if he could have a look around the engine-room. When back on deck he asked Harry for a job. Harry asked Dan if he had a 'ticket', Dan didn't but said that he had extensive experience with her Kelvyn marine engine, as far as Harry was concerned Dan had asked and answered all the right questions so he threw him a pair of overalls and leather gloves.

'Show us what you can do, Danny boy,' he said.

That evening Dan signed up, checked out of the British, boarded the Rangatira, once again to become a slave to the fickle fingers of fate.

PART THREE

22

WELCOME TO THE CHATHAMS

offered Bosun to Dan when the mighty Rangatira tied up at the Waitangi wharf after her three-day voyage from Lyttelton. When Dan first sighted the coast, he was leaning on the portside rail looking into a murky dawn to a vague outline of land. On the port bow the Soanes light came into view, the same light that he had seen from the Mariposa. He crossed the deck to starboard to see the Durham light in the distance, both these lights beckoned the Rangatira into the safety of Petrie Bay and into the lee of the stiff southerly that had been buffeting the ship, beam on, since Lyttelton.

As the dawn lightened the wind dropped, he could make out the South Coast which was undulating with bush that followed the many creeks running down to the sea. Each line of bush gave away to green pastures dotted with sheep, there were spirals of smoke coming from wooded sections indicating a foliage protected homestead surrounded by the stone fence of a home garden.

The soft morning light belied the crisp air, Dan fastened the top button of his pea jacket, cupped his hands over his mouth and nose and blew the air to warm his hands and fingers. For the first time in a long time, he felt good. This early morning scene, along with the slow comforting throb of the engine reminded him of the ancient Greek poem that Pieter had recited back in his days of another past life of digging peat, a lot of water had flowed under the bridge since then.

'Brave Phileas, wake up your steeds, and bring the morning warmth, that the countryside needs.'

As the Rangatira steamed further into the protected bay facing the early morning sunrise, a long, white-sanded beach came into view. Steep dunes rose to wooded slopes on the horizon, which was interrupted by high red clay cliffs, known as Red Bluff. The vivid colors that were emerging contrasted with the deep blue sea, the white foam of breaking waves, white sand and the intense blue flower of the Chatham Island Forget Me Not that mingled with the white fluff of the flowering Sow Thistle.

On the north coast of Petrie Bay there was a series of five inlets that likened to looking at an outstretched hand with each finger representing an inlet and each fingernail representing a white sandy beach: a haven for any ocean-going vessel. On each of the wooded headlands there were signs of habitation, a spiral of smoke, the white paint of a modest home, the black creosoted shed that was surrounded by green pastures with lean but hardy cattle grazing on what grass there was available which gave way to bracken as the land rose from the sea. The large expanse of peat-land area, known as the 'Clears' rose to meet a soft blue sky that was interrupted by a string of perfectly formed extinct volcanos. Dan imagined that this land had not changed in millions of years when molten lava spewed out from the volcanos and run down to meet the ocean where the molten basalt froze, creating a buffer to protect the land from the rolling swells of the great Southern Ocean. Dan thought that if an artist was to paint the perfect volcanos this would be the perfect subject.

The anchorage and village of Waitangi are in the sheltered center of a horseshoe shaped bay within the larger Petrie Bay. The long beach, known as Long Beach, was interrupted by the Red Bluff which slopes down to the beach once again, then to end at the tannin-stained Nairn River. A bridge crosses the river then the land rises to a plateau on which the village sits above another small beach. Down on this beach is the Hotel and Post office.

As the Rangatira rounded Tiki Tiki, the village came into view and Dan guessed that the centrally gabled building was the Mungautu Hotel, he was soon to learn that it was simply known as the Pub. Next to that was a small unadorned building of solid sandstone with a corrugated iron roof. Further on was a rusticated wooded planked building with the N.Z. flag at full mast indicating that it was the Post Office and today was ship day. From the front of the pub there was a crushed lime road that was carved out of the cliff of Tiki Tiki leading to the solid timber-built wharf shed leading to the T shaped wooden wharf. From the other side of the pub, the road ascended from the beach to the CBD which consisted of another single gabled building called the 'Travelers Rest' which was a general store with hotel accommodation. On the South Road corner there were several milking cows grazing in what was known at the 'pub paddock'. Adjoining that was the Chatham Island County Council offices and Community Hall. Across the road was the Police station and Court house and winding up the hill was the Daymond Farm homestead and a scattering of houses; motor vehicles were rare. On the north edge of town was the Hospital with a resident doctor and nursing done by the Nuns of the Catholic order of the 'Sisters of Mercy of the Society of Mary'. Next to the hospital is the morgue, then a bottle store, and next to that is the Catholic church and vestry for the Priest, then a track leading up to the Ngati Mutunga Urapa. Hospital Road was known as the Dead-End Street where life started and finished and one could get drunk along the way, all of this within a few hundred yards. Like all roads on the Chathams it was dust in the summer and mud in the winter, it's either one or the other.

The Rangatira skirted the large patch of kelp and turned into the protection of Tiki Tiki, where there were about half a dozen narrow-beamed Cod boats moored in the lee of the wharf. As she maneuvered, avoiding the moored fishing boats, the helmsman lined up the wharf T allowing for the swells that pushed his ship away from the wharf. The Able Seaman threw a light line that was attached to the heavy mooring rope to the docker who looped it over the wharf bollard. The first mate messaged the engine-room to increase revolutions which swung the bow to gently nudge the wharf at the top of the T. A perfect landing. The main engine remained idling with the propeller slowly turning to keep the ship steady to counteract the rolling swells.

Dan had been told by the Chief that his job was to work the winches on deck, a job he had experience with on the Thomas Currell many years before. It didn't take him long to get the gist of which of the eight levers were used simultaneously to remove each of the hatches to open the cargo hold. Lined up on the wharf T was a row of flat-decked drays, each hitched to a horse of mixed breed but dominantly Clydesdale. The horses were as excited as the drivers, snorting and pawing the wooded deck of the wharf, all ready to go to work. Motorized transport was few and far between. Lined up along the wharf was a rusty old Bedford truck, a few tractors, some with trailers, these tractors often were the only form of motorised transport for a farmer. The Government was the only entity able to afford the luxury of the two Land Rovers on the Island. They were parked outside the wharf shed, one was driven by the Policeman and the other driven by the Resident Commissioner's wife. Gossip had it that the Commissioner was once again nursing a hangover. Against the cliff there were more that a dozen horses tied to a hitching rail, several were saddled but most just had a split-sack for a saddle and a rope bridle.

The Island stopped work on boat-day, shearers stopped shearing, farmers stopped farming, Teachers stopped teaching, the Nuns stopped nursing because nobody got sick on boatday, businesss closed, including the pub which was recently known as the 'The pub with no Beer', (thanks to Slim Dusty for that one), wives stopped housewifing, idlers got busy, fishermen had a bath for their day off, the oldies and infirm came to town for the action, kids kept on being kids, and generally speaking, differences were put aside, well, for one day anyway. The whole Island was in town, handshaking and hugging as if they hadn't seen one another for years.

The women workers gathered in the wharf shed over large pots of milky tea, gossip was rife, anybody who wasn't present had their content of character assassinated. All were patiently waiting to see what the other women were getting off the ship, jealously ruled.

The menfolk were in the yard, standing around in circles according to their status, fishermen mingled together, farmers, South Coasters, Te One, family groups, Government employees, Owenga, Tama, Mutunga, misfits, residents from Kaingaroa (they're a weird lot that lot). Somebody would pull out a pouch of tobacco and papers, roll his smoke and offer his pouch to anybody who had run out of tobacco, matches were scarce so once one was struck it would light as many cigarettes as possible. This simple act, often without words, cemented an unspoken bond of a people who lived hard, worked hard and played hard on this isolated land. Boat-day, weddings and funerals were times of goodwill, as for all the other times, well, let's put it this way, each and everyone has their own opinion on all subjects, gossip gathers momentum from mouth to mouth, gossip becomes truth, truth becomes fact and fact is followed by a pack-hunt, the enemy of my enemy becomes my friend, in saying that, enemies are only temporary because tomorrow we may need that enemy for a friend. All Islanders are related in one way or another, and as Tom Tuuta used to say…

'You can pick ya fuckin friends, but ya can't pick ya fuckin 'lations'

School is closed for a couple of days so there are kids everywhere, doing what kids do, jumping, climbing, playing bull-rush, tag, cowboys, jumping off the wharf, mischief reigns.

The adults do what adults do when kids are having fun, telling them to shut up, bugger off, you'll get a boot up the bum, wait till you get home, no more lollies for you, you won't be going to the pictures on Saturday night, all those empty threats that kids take no notice of.

As for the teenagers and their never-ending struggle between raging hormones and common sense, well, nothing has changed for thousands of years.

And everybody must eat, on the seaside edge of the yard there was the smell of grilled meat with fat dripping over the red-hot embers of a Matipo log. On the flat rocks at low tide the hunters and gatherers probed the fissures for crayfish with sharpened ake ake spears, one old guy, using a shovel so he didn't get his feet wet, was prizing the paua that were clinging onto the shallow underwater rocks. Several kids were told by adults to jump into the deeper water to harvest the fat kina, known these days as Chatham Island Viagra.

Dan, using the ships winches lowered the gangplank for the first person to board was Bosun, who was responsible for the wharf administration. He saw the new man on the winches and with that friendly smile of his he walked around the deck and offered his hand.

'Welcome to the Chathams.'

He walked aft and up the laddered steps to the bridge to collect the pages and pages of handwritten manifests from the ships Master, Captain Ward Waitere, a Chatham Islander who was the first N.Z. Māori to achieve an 'Ocean Going Master' ticket. Ironically, Capt Ward's ancestors had been navigating the vast Pacific Ocean for hundreds of years without compass, sextant, charts, motor or an 'Ocean Going Masters' ticket.

Unloading began, anything and everything a modern society needs to function was being winched from deep inside the Rangatira. 44-gallon drums of diesel, Harry's garage had run out of diesel several weeks beforehand so most of the household generator sets had been shut down. Bundles of milled timber, household goods, a corrugated iron water tank, flour, sugar, pallets for the General Store, tobacco, six rams for a farmer, two thoroughbred mares, and so on. The pub had been out of beer for several weeks, the Cop was very happy to see the ship arrive simply because the homemade moonshine that had taken the place of beer had been making his life a misery. The second most important item to come ashore was the mail. When the mailbags started to be winched up from the hold all the wharf traffic made way for Uncle Ned and his Bedford truck, by the time the last bag was loaded, his high-sided Bedford was bulging at the seams. There was one more bag that had been stored in the ships safe and was being carried down the gangplank by the ships Second Mate who was being escorted by the First Mate, the bag was placed on the front seat of the Bedford. Ned and the Mate both had to sign an official document in receipt of the mailbag. Dan was a little mystified by this one, he asked around and was told that the Island had run out of cash and the bag contained banknotes and coins to go to the Post Office.

There was no room in the cab of the Bedford so Ned's worker, Albie, so he had to sit on top of the pile of mail, as he was rolling a smoke with tobacco that had just come off the ship, he looked down at the bag he was sitting on to see a tag 'FRAGILE'.

'Oooops.' he said to nobody in particular. 'Too late now.'

As Uncle Ned was driving up the hill, he too was rolling his first smoke for a while. He was using both hands to roll his smoke, steering his truck with his knees while singing 'Pearly Shells'. By the time the Bedford had trundled up the hill, past the store and back down the hill, then past the Pub and the derelict jailhouse to park outside the Post Office, a large crowd had gathered for the mail to be unloaded and sorted.

All communication between N.Z. and the Chathams were done by mail and carried by the ship, when the ordered goods eventually arrived, the invoice, the statement, the reminder for payment and the final demand for payment would all arrive on the same ship.

The ship's crew, aided and abetted by locals worked like Trojans to unload cargo as quickly as possible, their incentive was the crates of bottled beer that was stowed, to reduce breakage, in the most stable part of the ship which was at the bottom of the hold. The workers all agreed to work late into the evening to get some of the beer to the pub, they first had to stack each crate of beer onto a pallet which was lifted out of the hold by signaling Dan, the winch operator. When the first pallet appeared and was lowered onto the back of Ned's truck a big cheer verberated around the wharf and could be heard all around Waitangi. The women in the wharf shed were having their first cup of Ceylon tea, the store had run out of tea, so they had been drinking Kawakawa fused tea prior to the ship arriving, they looked at one another, rolled their eyes...

'Looks like we are not going to see our useless menfolk for a couple of days.'

Meanwhile back in the ships hold strange things were happening, mysteriously the caps of a few bottles of Wards beer fell off.

'Oooops, we'd better drink the beer before it goes flat, and we can't have that can we?' This wise observation came from one of the workers who had the dubious ability to be able to pick up anything that was left lying around. Like for instance, food from the ship's galley, a hammer laying on the deck, a pouch of tobacco left on a table, coal from a torn coal sack and so on. He was renowned for wheeling and dealing with the ship's crew, reselling contraband around the Island; actually, nothing was safe or secure while Hydraulic Jack was around, he earned that name because he could and would lift anything.

Dan had a great day on the winches, there was always somebody on board for a yarn, he was soon to learn that most Chatham Islanders had an opinion on any subject that came up in conversation although some of these opinions were farfetched, but at least it was an opinion. The most common subject was of Dan's news of the war in Europe, there were several Chatham Islanders to volunteer and from the few letters received their whereabouts were often blackened out by the army Security Intelligence. One letter that had got through unedited was written in Māori from Bunty Preece describing the fighting in Egypt against Rommel's Desert Rats. Bunty had left the Chathams at the age of 17 to enlist, lying about his age. He did his boot camp training in Burnham Military camp as a store-man. Private Preece quickly rose through the ranks to become an Officer in the 28th Māori Battalion serving in North Africa, Crete, the battle of Monte Cristo in Italy and was part of the peacekeeping J-Force in Japan.

The women, who worked in the wharf-shed, unpacking and sorting, invited Dan into the smoko-room to share their potluck lunch,

'Lunch,' said Dan when he saw the laden table, 'This is more than lunch, it's an orgy, an orgy of food I mean.'

All the single girls and half the married ones fell in love the Dan and his lyrical accent. It was if each woman had tried to outdo the other in the quality and quantity of food. All Islanders were hunters and gatherers which took priority over their day job and the results appeared on the lunch table. There were several items that Dan found it hard to acquire a taste for, there was one food item that he found near impossible to get past his nose let alone into his stomach, not wanting to offend his hostess's he concealed his desire to retch while swallowing, Much to the delight of the ladies, he had passed their test with flying colors.

'The way to a man's heart is through his stomach.' he said.

'And what hangs below it.' a voice piped up to raucous laughter.

The fickle fingers of fate had found Dan a place in this world, but unseen by Dan, the ghost of Rose hovered from above.

23

PITT ISLAND BLUES

would make an interesting song thought Dan after his first trip to this lonely outpost of the planet, Pitt Island must have some sort of Irish ancestry because 'Murphy's Law' rules.

'What can go wrong, will.'

After the unloading was done and dusted in Waitangi the mighty Rangatira prepared for her annual service to Pitt and then to the outlying sheep stations and settlements around the Chathams. The surfboat was winched onboard and along with a few passengers and a battered landrover she dropped her Waitangi moorings at midnight to anchor at Flowerpot at daybreak.

The moderate SW swell made unloading difficult as the ship rolled from side to side and the surfboat rode up and down with the swells. Timing it right the winch-man would skilfully lower the cargo to land in place on the surfboat. The crew would then quickly remove the strop from the solid steel hook that would be swinging wildly with the rolling of the ship and surfboat. If the winchman didn't time it perfectly the cargo could be swinging midair over the surfboat, then possibly dip into the sea. The surfboat's Perkins motor was giving trouble, so Dan was given the job of helmsman to keep an eye on it, he soon had it running smoothly.

The first surfboat load to arrive at the jetty brought the passengers, their bags loaded with goodies for the school kids who had been waiting on the wharf since daybreak. Also, and much appreciated, was tobacco with papers and a half gallon jar of whisky. There were about ten guys standing round in a circle rolling cigarettes in between passing the whisky-jar. Within 10 minutes all were pretty pissed and spent the day staggering around very happily unloading each surfboat as it tied up to the jetty, much to their own amusement, and before long to the annoyance of their womenfolk.

Pitt Island's first short wheel-based Land Rover was winched over the side of the Rangatira onto the surfboat which caused it to become dangerously overloaded and top heavy. Several times the surfboat rolled with the swell and seemed to take forever to right herself before the next swell arrived. Once clear of the ship Dan, at the helm, rode the swells and then straitened up before the next swell arrived. It was touch and go whether he would be able to turn between the swells towards the jetty or to end up on the rocks that seemed to be inviting him to come on in.

As the Land Rover was being lifted from the surfboat onto the wharf the weight of it caused the diesel winch motor to conk out, leaving the vehicle swinging in the breeze. The new owner, old Tom G-H, had a dizzy spell and passed out on the wharf. Chippy poured a shot of whisky down Tom's throat, and when he came to the Rover was sitting safely on the wharf. He suddenly stood, puffed his chest in pride as he waved his arms around to make his way through the crowd who were milling about admiring his somewhat ancient, dented and batted vehicle. Tom clambered into the driver's seat, spat on both hands, rubbed them together, straitened his shoulders, leaned forward and turned the key, nothing happened, he turned it again, again, nothing happened. His brother Willy found the crank handle and the men took turns cranking, still nothing happened. The crowd stood around giving their expert advice.

'How about checking the air in the tires?' everybody roared with laughter.

'Try the window wipers,' came the next bit of expert advice.

'It's got a sprained fetlock,'

'How about calling a vet?'

'Looks like the Rover took one look at Pitt and went on strike.'

'It's just like it's owner, hard to start.'

'Pour some whisky in the tank,'

'Don't do that, might make it fart,'

'Fart? You're the expert on farting,'

'You can go and get stuffed,'

The only good idea suggested was to get Dan to have a look, Hydraulic Jack took the helm of the surfboat while Dan lifted the bonnet of the Rover. Tom was still sitting in the driver's seat, red faced with anger, puffing on a hand rolled cigarette that was in his mouth. Dan gave him the thumbs up, Tom turned the key and the engine roared into life with a large cloud of blue smoke coming from the exhaust, the engine was screaming. Tom who had never driven a vehicle before, had his foot flat down on the accelerator. He tooted his horn, and everybody scattered, make way for Tom. A loud graunch of gears and somebody yelled out,

'Clutch,' then louder, 'Clutch, you stupid old bastard.'

Tom showed him his index finger. While this was happening a team of kids were fighting to climb onto the flat deck which wasn't big enough for them all, so some climbed onto the bonnet and roof. Dan winced at the graunching of the gearbox until Tom pushed his foot on the clutch, the Rover gave a shudder, then jumping and jerking, trundled off the wharf.

'Hey Tom, what you got in the tank, kangaroo juice?'

While still in first gear and engine screaming, Tom didn't know how to change gears, the Rover jerked up the greasy clay road, which had never seen a motor vehicle before and was more suitable for horses. The road steepened and narrowed to a track and the Rover gracefully slid off the greasy clay and gently lay on its side in the creek. Giggling, all the kids slid off the tray into the creek. Tom abused the kids, blaming them for causing his pride and joy, which he had been waiting for over a year, to fall over. Ranting and raving he stormed up the hill to his horse paddock to harness his two draft horses and was able to tow the 'Bitch', as he now called it, out of the creek. For the next few weeks, he would drive around in his Rover with his horses in tow in case he got stuck in the mud again.

Hydraulic Jack was employed by the Chatham Island Council to work the surfboat with Dan, not that Dan saw much of him. While the others worked on the unloading of goods and loading of bales of wool Jack spent a most of his time fishing for cod and grouper over the side of the ship. He had a deal with the crew, swapping fish for anything that he could sell to somebody else. He got bored with fishing so went ashore with a back-pack loaded with stuff he had lifted from the ship's galley, a couple of frozen chickens, ice-cream, a bottle of rum, a spanner, leather gloves a couple of pencils and so on. He arrived back on board later in the day with a wooden box of cray-tails, live paua and half a dozen mutton birds. He had not done a drop of work since he left Waitangi, that's our Jack.

The weather was pretty good enabling the Rangatira to discharge all cargo and take on bales of wool, this was the only income for Pitt Islanders for the year. In the early days of Pakeha settlement their common ancestor, Francis Hunt added to his farming income by dabbling in a bit of bootlegging of alcohol plus a few somewhat illegal escapades, this trait of scallywaging had trickled down through the generations. The only physicle contact with the outside world was a cod boat, the 'Franklin' based on Pitt and skippered by Ken Lanauze who landed his catch at the processing plant in Owenga. Other than that, it was just the annual visits of the Rangatira. Old Jim Moffat had a SSB radio and was in contact with ZLC Chatham Island radio.

Dan made a connection with the Pitt Islanders who were fascinated by his Liverpool Irish accent, they kept him in conversation just to hear him talk. They were interested in his background and how he ended up on the Chathams; Dan had rehearsed a fictional background, so the lie's easily flowed off his tongue. He talked of the war in Europe, international politics and a little of the Chathams Island gossip he got from Hydraulic Jack, like most gossip, was totally inaccurate. Dan had always been a teller of tales and had the ability to improvise fiction into fact which is congruent with the Island physic.

The weather held, with a light Easterly breeze veering to the north that was to increase in strength before backing round to a strong SW, time to up anchor and get out of Flowerpot and head to Owenga. The SW was perfect for working the northern sheep stations and settlements of the main Chatham Island which were often inaccessible, except by horseback. The last of the wool was loaded along with empty 44-gal fuel drums. Prior to the ship arriving the Pitt farmers had slaughtered steers and prime lambs which had hung in trees to mature. There was no refrigeration on Pitt, so the meat was processed and packed and along with blue cod fillets were frozen on board the Rangatira. These products were highly sort after in Christchurch because of their unique flavor.

Ship day was also a very emotional time when secondary school children departed for Christchurch and not return for another 10 months, these were tough times for both parents and their children. The ship was delayed for half a day when a young boy went bush and couldn't be found, the ship departed without him. When these secondary school children did return, they had matured into young adults in the cusp of puberty, with their parents having to adjust from having a child leave home and to return as an adult.

As the last of the passengers clambered into the surfboat Dan was asked if he had ever the inclination to return to Pitt, he would be most welcome, Dan asked,

'Is this offer based on my personality or is it that you want some mechanical work done around the place?'

'A bit of both.'

With the surfboat back aboard, Dan went down below to help get the main engine up and running while the deck crew closed the hatches and secure the ship. Capt Ward, using the internal phone system ordered the Chief engineer, Harry, to put the ship ahead, which was in the direction of the rocky coast. The anchor was raised from the seabed, as it came out of the water Capt Ward phoned the engine room to go astern. To do this, Harry and Dan had to stop the main engine, engage the gearbox and then restart the engine using a compressor to pump air into one cylinder. When that cylinder fired up the other cylinders would be brought into line one by one. As the compressed air was being pumped a coupling parted and the compressor decompressed. Harry and Dan hurriedly went to work on the twisted coupling while Capt Ward could be heard on the loudspeaker phone, ordering the engine be put astern. As the frantic work was happening in the engine room the officers and helmsman on the bridge watched in horror as the Rangatira drifted towards the rocky cliff. Thinking that there must have been a communication breakdown Capt Ward sent his 1st Mate down below to verbally order the engineers to put the ship astern. When the Mate had climbed down he took one look to see Harry and Dan franticly working on the coupling. His face drained of blood, and he thought it was better not to interrupt them by asking what the problem was. As he climbed the ladder to the bridge he heard and felt the scraping sound of the keel on the sandy bottom. Then there was a loud screeching and scraping as the bow encountered the basalt rock of the seabed, bringing the ship to a sudden halt. Capt Ward, with tight lips asked his Mate in a slow, quiet, deliberate voice.

'What, is, the problem?'

'I, I, I don't know,'

'When do you think you will you know?'

'I, I don't know when I think I will know'.

'Well, get your skinny arse backdown below and fucking well find out.'

'Y-y-yes Sir.'

As he took the first step down the steep ladder his feet went from under him and he bumped his bum on each step to the engine-room deck landing in an untidy heap.

Harry and Dan, working franticly, didn't look up, the disheveled Mate got to his feet and asked,

'Captain wants to know how long you will be?'

No response.

'How, how long will you be?' he stuttered.

'Fuck off.'

He clambered back up the ladder and back on the bridge.

'Well?' asked Capt Ward.

'They told me to fuck off,'

'Well then, you can fuck off from here and go and give the crew a hand to launch the surfboat.'

'Aye, aye Captain,' as he saluted then scurried from the bridge, happy to get away from the wrath of his Captain.

Capt Ward let out a deep breath and shook his head from side to side,

'Some Mothers do have them.'

He had already instructed the 'Bosun to run a line using the surfboat to hold the stern into the wind. As the surfboat was swinging over the side hanging from the derricks there was a puff of black smoke from the funnel. The first cylinder started firing unevenly and then into a smooth rhythm as each cylinder came into line. He ordered an increase in revolutions and the Rangatira slowly backed off from under the cliff. When well clear he signaled to go ahead and set a course to clear Motapu, and then to round Manakau reef into Owenga, about three hours away.

The somewhat drained Chief Harry felt it was safer to keep a low profile by staying down below for a couple of days. The Mate developed a headache and confined himself to his cabin for the day.

As for Captain Ward, for him it was all in a day's work on the briny.

24

TURN THE WORLD

on its side, give it a good shake and anything loose will land on the Chathams, these were Dan's thoughts as he began to understand the Islands and the diversity of her people.

The Rangatira anchored in a slight SW breeze well out of the exposed bay of Owenga and well clear of Old Man Reef. There were several small double ended cod boats moored in the harbor close to the shore where they could be hauled up the beach in adverse weather. Their catch of Blue Cod was processed and frozen by a family of Shetland Islanders in their modest processing shed situated by the stream running into the bay. These ingenious people installed a wood fired boiler, which not only ran the freezers but produced electricity that was circulated around the Owenga community; also, they distilled great whisky. There were three major farming properties who shore about 12,000 sheep annually. One of the properties, Manakau, was home to the Moriori Solomon family. There was a general store, a Māori Pah and an Anglican Church with an extensive cemetery dating back to the whaling days of the 1860s.

The wind was perfect for the ship to work, the surfboat was lowered to allow the passengers to climb down the rope ladder to be ferried ashore. Once again Dan was on the tiller of the surfboat. He was supposed to have as his crewman the light-fingered Hydraulic Jack,

178

who ostentatiously saluted when he had climbed down the ladder. It had been said that Jack, with a smile, would take the sugar out of your cup of tea. Once ashore Jack disappeared inland not to be seen until late afternoon, a little under the weather, with a live goat in tow and a mysterious looking sack strapped with a rope on his back. When back on board he tied the goat to the ships rail and wandered off. Capt. Ward, looking from the bridge shook his head at the folly of his fellow Chatham Islanders.

The next day Dan handed the tiller of the surfboat over to Jack who was annoyed by having to stay in one place and work for a change. Dan walked up the hill to check out the Church and cemetery with its many unmarked graves dating back to the days of the whalers. As he was trying to decipher one of the headstones the Rev. Rewai came from the inside of his Church. Introducing himself, he escorted Dan around and giving a commentary on the residents. There certainly was a melting pot of race, creeds and colors, all buried together for their long cold rest. Who were these sons and daughters of mothers who were never to know the fate of their children who had disappeared forever. These strangers would lay together for eternity.

As they wandered around the Rev. Rewai told Dan that he once walked out from the Church to see six pall bearers carrying a coffin. They were followed by black dressed mourners, they walked around the Cemetery several times, so the Rev. asked them what they were they up to, their response was…

'We've lost the plot.'

On parting the Rev. Rewai, encouraged by Dan's laughter, told him that nobody currently living in Waitangi was allowed to be interred in the Owenga cemetery,

'What's that all about?' asked Dan

'They have to be dead first.'

The next port of call was Kaingaroa where Dan's boss Harry, took some time out to go ashore for a break to stay with his old mate Bollen Goomes, leaving Dan down in the engine-room. The SW wind was dying which meant that in a couple of days the wind would swing around to the north which would make the next port of call at Waitangi West difficult to work. There was an urgency to work the ship before the wind change. Poor old Jack had to man the surfboat, although that didn't seem to hinder his wheeling and dealing. He arrived back on board with two kerosene tins, each containing albatross preserved in their own fat; this deal was done in exchange for the goat. A quick turnaround, up anchor to set course to Waitangi West under the imposing peaks of the volcanic Maunganui.

To shelter from the increasing Northerly, the Rangatira anchored in the NE part of the bay behind the protection of Tuparunga point. The landowner, Mike Cannon, had loaded his flat-decked two horse dray with bales of wool. The Homestead and woolshed were on the other side of the bay, so it was a long haul of about two miles along the beach at low tide. At high tide the sand was too soft to navigate so the horses had to walk in the surf. At the end of the beach he drove the horses into deeper water where the surfboat would pull up alongside the dray to roll the 400lb bales of wool into the boat.

The neighbouring farmers also had wool to move so there was a steady procession along the beach, into the water, onto the surfboat and out to the anchored ship. This backbreaking work lasted all day and throughout the night. Dan and Mike were in the surfboat and worked for 36 hours straight under a full moon with only a few breaks for a quick cuppa, rancid buttered scones and a few cold mutton chops. They both were very competitive and thrived on the backbreaking work, one was never going to show the other any sign of tiredness. In the distance a figure could be seen in knee-deep water digging for tuatua's, sure enough it was Hydraulic Jack. True to form he had abandoned his post in the surfboat, claiming that his bad back would be aggravated by tossing the bales of wool around. He had taken with him one of the kerosene tins of preserved albatross and arrived back with 4 smoked eels, 10 swan eggs and a clock that had been brought to the Island by the German Lutheran Missionaries back in the 1860's. The clock eventually took pride of place on his mantlepiece, although, it was of no matter to him that the clock hadn't worked for years.

The Rangatira clewed up about 3 AM, up anchored and set a course for Cuba Channel on the inside of Western Reef, guided by the full moon and Soanes light. Once through the notorious tide affected Cuba Channel which was named after the sailing vessel that came to grief there, doing just what the Rangatira was doing, albeit, having the advantage of having diesel power. Once clear of the channel they skirted the confused waters of Bumsucker Reef, Capt Ward set a course direct for Waitangi.

'Bumsucker', asked Dan, 'how did it get that name?'

'Think about it,' replied his Captain.

25

PUT A BOOT ON IT

and send it to work, was the call from the netball girls while crossing the Nairn river bridge on their way to the pub.

The Rangatira had tied up at the wharf at 8.00 AM Saturday and was readied to begin loading. There was frozen cod, wool and several hundred prime lambs that were to be loaded into pens on deck destined for the Riccarton sale-yards. Winches were manned, wharf and shed crew ready, excited passengers, destined for Christchurch had arrived waiting in the wharf shed. Hydraulic Jack and others were doing their last deals with the crew, there was a buzz of excitement around, however that wasn't to last. The 4X4 Bedford truck carrying a sheep crate full of lambs had broken down on the South Coast Road at Te Ngaio. The wool had been loaded, hatches fastened with just to lambs to go. It looked like that by the time the Bedford was up and going it would be too dark to finish loading so Capt. Ward decided to delay sailing until the next day. The delighted crew knocked off work at lunchtime and headed down to the Ngati Mutunga reserve to watch the netball and rugby, followed by a beer or three at the pub. The policeman arrived at the wharf in his Landrover to pick up Dan and drive him out to Te Ngaio to see if he could get the Bedford truck going. Dan's prognosis was grim, parts were needed that were not available on the Island, so the truck was towed to the Durham woolshed to be kept out of the weather until such time as the Rangatira, with Dan, returned from Lyttelton with replacement parts or another motor.

The netball had started by the time Dan had arrived at the reserve where the Northern team was playing against Waitangi. No quarter was given or taken by these competitive uniformed females, their ages ranging from correspondence school teenagers through to Grandmothers. The older women made up for their lesser agility, by cunning, guile and aggression. Dan, from his Londonderry days, always thought that netball was a non-contact sport, on the Chathams he was dead wrong about that one.

Being a home game, the Waitangi men's rugby team kitted up in the small changing shed while the visiting Northern team had to change under the Macrocarpa trees. As the teams trotted out onto the field a black cloud came over and dropped a heavy shower of rain, both teams turned around and trotted back off the field. The Waitangi side took shelter in their changing shed while the visitors huddled under the trees. The rain didn't deter the netball girls who kept on playing, a mere shower wasn't going to interrupt their battle for supremacy. While the Northern rugby team was trying to keep warm by sheltering under the trees, somebody produced a bottle of whisky. That not only warded off the cold but certainly livened up the game once they got started. The men were no different from their women, no quarter was given or asked for, bodies were put online without a thought of self-preservation.

Included in the contest of rugby was the usual intergenerational past and present conflicts that were reignited on the field, for instance, a late tackle, a sneaky punch, a bit of stomping in the ruck, a knee in the back, a coat-hanger tackle, (oops, sorry matey), an elbow here, an eye gouge there. If the referee, who was the local Cop, blew his whistle for any infringement whatsoever he would be good naturedly booed by the spectators.

And let's not forget the sledging which went something like this...

'You useless bastard, you're nothing but a thief, get your eyes of my girlfriend, you put your earmark on my lambs, I know it was you who cut my fence, go and find your own fishing spot, and so on…

Dan had played rugby at school in 'Derry but he was quite happy to be standing on the sideline watching the on-field antics as the game unfolded. Well, he was happy until the Northern winger was flattened in a heavy tackle and carried off the field. Coach Alby took the guys boots off and handed them, along with a clean jersey, to Dan, told him to gear up and get on the field. There was nowhere for Dan to run, so, feeling sick to the stomach he trotted onto the field. The Waitangi Capt, Henry, put his hand over his mouth and said to his teammates,

'Let's soften this guy up a bit.'

When Floyd took the pass from his half-back, he kicked an up and under directly to Dan, as he took the ball, Floyd nailed him with a shoulder charge. This was followed up by two big loose forwards who crunched Dan into the ground, then proceeded to ruck both the ball and the unprotected Dan. The Waitangi team cleared the ball and sent it along the backline as Dan staggered to his feet to watch Geoff dive over to score an unconverted try in the corner. Dan felt like pulp, he was bleeding from sprig marks that ran down his back, one bruised eye was closing, and his right arm wouldn't work properly.

'You all right Matey?' asked his teammate Patch.

'Who would want to be an All Black,' said Dan through a fat lip as he limped back out to the relative safety of his position on the wing.

He was able to keep out of trouble until two minutes to to the full time whistle and two points down when his teammate big Joe, wrestled the ball free from a ruck and with three or four would be tacklers hanging off him he unloaded the ball out to his halfback who was able to spin the ball to his standoff, who fired a cutout pass to Brendon at center. He stepped around his opposite, and with Dan trying to keep up and outside him, Brendon took the tackle of the fullback Alex and was able to get the pass away to the terrified Dan. He momentarily took his eye off the midair ball to see if there was a defender in front of him, all he saw was a clear passage to the try-line. The ball hit him in the chest and while running at full pace he reached out as the ball hit his fingers out of his grasp. A huge groan came from his teammates and sideline supporters which was drowned out by a cheer from the Waitangi team. The ball was in the air floating in front of Dan who lunged forward and caught it on the tips of his fingers as he was hit by the flying tackle of Floyd. For Dan, all this was happening is slow motion, dropping the ball was not going to happen; when the ball hit the white line he was in full control with downward pressure. The ball was left sitting on the white line as Dan rolled away with momentum landing him back on his feet, he held one arm up in the air, claiming the try.

His battered body felt no pain as he realized that his future on the Chathams was secured in that split second.

'Nice try.' said Floyd.

The Ref. blew his whistle for full time, the Waitangi coach took off his hand knitted beanie, slammed it onto the grass and ground it into the mud with his Red Band gumboot, and there it stayed.

With game over the bottle of whisky was emptied and some of the players walked across the road to the Nairn River to take off their rugby gear and wash up in the icy tannin-stained water. Hot running showers were not invented in those times. Although they didn't know it at that time the ice cold water was great for repairing battered and bruised bodies. The Tube and his mate Rubberlegs, oversaw the building of a fire alongside of the river for the players of both teams to dry and warm after every game, when they got to the pub their reward was a bottle or three of Wards beer.

The netball girls, walking across the bridge on their way to the pub, stopped to lean on the bridge rail to watch the guys standing, unclothed in the river washing off the mud and sweat; they could not resist an opportunity like this one that didn't come often.

'What's that thing waving in the breeze?' one called.

'Wish I had a telescope,'

'Need a microscope for that one,'

'Without his clothes he looks like a bomb,' said another, pointing to the short and barrel-chested hooker.

'His fuse isn't very big,'
He showed the girls his index finger and said,
'Big enough to blow you to the maternity hospital,'
That one brought raucous laughter from all.
'Why don't you put a boot on it and send it to work?' quipped one of the grandmothers.

Dan didn't have to pay for a beer that night, he was, the man. For once in his life, he was in the right place at the right time. As the night wore on, the bar was becoming a little boisterous, Happy Jack, the publican thought it wise to shut the bar, all he had to do was to turn the lights out and the bar emptied. Nobody argued with Happy Jack, if one did. one would spend the next six months sitting in the little hollow half-way up the hill along with other naughty drinkers. To be allowed back into the bar one had to do penance by stacking beer crates or splitting wood for the fireplace in the bar.

As the bar emptied the patrons carried on drinking around a fire that was blazing on the beach. A steel grill appeared with a large grouper that was split open, laden with butter which was melting into the flesh as it cooked over the embers. When the grouper was done a heap of very fatty chops appeared while tuatua's were opening on a hot flat iron. Henry was on guitar with his wardrobe of songs in both Māori and English. There were a few loud voices being bandied about that had stemmed from the game of rugby, this time there was no Ref to blow the whistle. When a couple of preliminary skirmishes started Dan thought it wise to return to the ship before the main bout of of the night got under way.

Once back on board Dan settled into his hammock for the night feeling a sense of belonging that he had not felt for a long, long time.

The Ghost of Rose hovered from above.

26

THE SHALLOW END OF THE GENE POOL

The Rangatira, heading to Lyttelton set a course well south of the Chathams to lessen any chance of a German Raider lurking around looking for a soft target, once well south of the Chathams, a coarse change to the NW and Lyttelton. On siting the east coast OF THE South IslandcDan had made up his mind that he would sign off the Rangatira on her next voyage to Waitangi. He thought that the Chathams was about as far away from the long arm of the law as could be. He never lost his intention that he would eventually be back with his Rose, unsure of how or when, he always felt she was with him in his current life as a fugitive.

When on the bridge he talked to Capt. Ward of his plans to sign off on the next voyage to the Chathams.

Capt. Ward was enthusiastic. 'We are always looking for new blood on the Island, especially after the rugby game last week and with you being a fix-it man you won't have time to scratch yourself,'

'For me there's something familiar about the place, I don't know what it is, it's as if I have been there sometime in the past,'

'Something tells me that there is something in your past you want to leave behind, whatever it is, put it behind you and start again,

Chathams is made up by people like yourself, the lost, the lonely, the wanderers of this world.'

They were both lost in their own thoughts.

'When they put me out to pasture, I'll be heading home. Just like yourself, there's salt water in my veins so I can never be far from the sea,'

'I'm a bit like that as well, I never saw the sea until I was about 19, I guess it was a bit like the Chathams, I felt as if I had arrived home.'

Dan, my boy, your skills and your basic character will strengthen the gene pool, that's if you find someone to help you with that, our Islands are the last frontier so make the most of it,'

'Skills, I hope these so-called skills are not needed on the rugby field,'

Capt, Ward's eyes lit, the closest Dan had seen him get to a smile,

'You'll get on OK, the genes that you have inherited will suit island life'.

'As far as the genes go, if you knew me you would know that I was born in the shallow end of the gene pool.'

Back in Lyttelton the cashed-up Dan hitched a ride over the Port Hills to Christchurch, hunted out the music store of Sydney Eadies and blew his budget on a Gibson E175 guitar.

The Rangatira was three months away from her return to the Chathams so in the meantime, with Dan down below in the engine-room she was trading around the NZ coast. Some of her time was spent in the Lyttelton dry-dock having steel plates replaced on her hull that had been damaged by the wear and tear on the Waitangi wharf piles. That suited Dan fine, he would wander around the Garden City where its forefathers had recreated an old England in the stone architecture and public places. He lazed on the banks of the Avon which was dug to drain the swamp on which the city was built. Dan had heard a lot about the earthquakes of N.Z. which often was called the 'Shakey Isles', he was assured not to fear because there were no tectonic plates any-where in the Canterbury province, so the event of an earthquake was highly unlikely.

He was able to find part time work as a fitter and turner's laborer at Lyttelton Engineering where the Rangatira had been in dry-dock. On the weekends he was able to access the workshop to rebuild the Bedford truck motor with the help of the boss man Stephan. He had a room at the British Hotel in exchange for putting on some late-night music in the often-unruly bar. This was another test of character although compared with Isadora's 'House of the Rising Sun' the British could be likened to a kindergarten.

He got to know his way around Lyttelton and was a frequent customer of the Volcano eatery and getting to know some of the very talented Lyttelton musicians. Dan was wary of playing in public while trying to keep a low profile so kept on the fringe of the local music scene. He was invited to perform in a variety concert at the Lighthouse theatre raising money for food parcels for the Kiwi prisoners of war. Sadly, both the Lighthouse and the Volcano with the murals on the walls and toilet door of Bill Hammond, were destroyed in the 2011 earthquake. Ironically, the beer gods smiled on the British where she is still serving thirsty seafarers and wayfarers to this day. Dans mixture of music of the Crossroads, Creeping Jesus and the country and western style of Woody Guthrie created a lot of interest in the Lyttelton community, just what Dan did not want in his attempts to keep anything Irish and his music in a low profile.

When Capt. Ward sited the Chathams south coast twin volcanic cones known as the Horns in a swirling mist he called the engine-room for Dan to come up to the bridge.

'Dan, take a look at your new home, the Moriori people call these lands Rekohu, which translates to 'Misty Land'. There is a warm current that descends from the north to Rekohu around mid-spring, these warm waters mingle with the cold waters of the Great Southern Ocean creating this mist. It's this mist that has created havoc for seafarers for the last 150 years leaving the islands littered with shipwrecks.'

'They tell me that the fishing' is pretty good.'

'You can say that again.'

'They tell me that the fishing's pretty good.'

'So true, so true, this mingling of the oceans has created wonderfully rich fisheries and a benign climate, although it can get a little windy at times.'

'I see a few bent trees around,'

'The trees don't lie, I may tell lies about the weather, but the trees don't.'

Dan walked out on the deck and absorbed the damp salty mist that intermittently revealed then shrouded the many steep outcrops and cliffs that seemed to form a circle encompassing both Pitt and the Chatham Islands.

'Not only misty but mysterious.' he said to himself.

Capt. Ward was standing alongside Dan,

'Yes, it looks like it from here but no doubt, that in time, all will be revealed, warts and all.'

He thought for a minute.

'Take a look at the sea, Dan, now turn around and look at the hills, they were here long before we came and will still be here long after we've gone, they are completely indifferent of our presence.'

Dan felt a chill in the damp mist, but it was deeper than that, the chill came from within, it was an uneasy chill, he stared into the mist to see or feel, he wasn't sure what it was, but it was there, it was Rose. He shrunk back against the bulkhead feeling as if he had been pushed by an unseen force, his knees gave way, he knew then that he had a sadness that would never die. He regained his composure and was enveloped with the warmth of her love; he closed his eyes and thanked the God that he didn't believe in. He was ready to face whatever life had in store for him. Bring it on.

Little did he know that the bloodhounds of Liverpool had his scent.

27

THE LIFE AND TIMES

in the 'Devils Paradise' a visiting Bishop once called the Chathams. Dan was back working the winches before signing off the Rangatira after the unloading was done. Capt Ward was keen to get the unloading done and to get his ship away to shelter before a strong SW gale arrived bringing with it a heavy swell making it impossible to remain tied up to the wharf. Once out of the bay the Rangatira would seek shelter around the Northern part of the island; when the weather came right then return to Waitangi to load wool, fish and prime lambs.

When the crew had battened down the hatches Dan went to the bridge to sign off and collect his wages.

'Just to get you started,' said the Capt as he handed Dan a bonus. 'Good luck, Dan, I have organized a humble abode for you, it's not much and needs a bit of work but it will get you started. Actually, you are going to live in a jail, a mate of mine, Ben, will meet you in the wharf-shed and set you up.'

Dan and Ben walked along the wharf road and down onto the beach, Dan asked where the name, Goomes came from.

'In actual fact the name is derived from my Great-Grandfather Gomez who was a Portuguese whaler from the Azores who married my Great-Grandmother, she was of the Ngati Mutunga people from Taranaki,'

He pointed to the sandstone building on the foreshore between the Post Office and the Pub.

'This is your new home; it was a jail built by a guy called Te Kooti to imprison himself,'

'That was very generous of him,' said Dan as he looked at the hand-hewn sandstone hut that had stood in place for about 80 years, although it was a single roomed cell it was quite large, Ben reckoned that Te Kooti must have been expecting visitors.

The door was hanging off its rusted hinges as Ben lifted and pushed it open to a room full of what looked like junk. To a Chatham Islander it was a treasure trove of stuff that may be of use sometime in the future, like most of the other junk that's scattered around the Island.

'Who was this guy, Te Kooti?'

'It's a long story but I'll give you the short version, well, my understanding of it anyway.'

'Te Kooti and his band of warriors known as the Hau Hau's had, in the 1860s rebelled against the settlers encroaching on Māori land in the Heretonga. Initially what they did was to peacefully round up the would-be farmers off Māori land and escort them to a camp on the beaches. The Colonial Office retaliated by confiscating more Māori land for the Crown. Te Kooti was an astute leader with a sense of humor which infuriated the English. It has been said that he once seduced the wife of one of the colonial officers he was at war with. After Te Kooti's hit and run tactics destroying buildings and fences the English put together a contigent of soldiers, mercenary's and militia and the outnumbered Hau Hau's were eventually captured and banished to the Chathams which was then designated as a penal colony. Along with their wives and children the Hau Hau's were transported here on several voyages with provisions, building materials, tools and so on. They were escorted by several platoons of professional soldiers. When they arrived in Waitangi they were welcomed ashore by Mutunga and Tama, who sympathized with them because they too had been dispossessed of their lands in Taranaki. The Hau Hau's were regarded as heroes and their hosts provided several days of welcome ceromanies and feasting. The guards who had been standing off with rifles primed were invited to join the festivities.

The Hau Hau's then went to work diligently and built a compound for their guards and themselves, they grew potatoes, kumi kumi and corn. They worked on community projects like building roads and draining swamps for farmland. Being their leader and seen as a possible threat Te Kooti had to build his own jail here which is your home, for the time being anyway.'

'What happened to them?'

'Te Kooti was a wily chap, his people were so compliant that the guards relaxed and not having much to do spent their time fishing and, of course, in the pub. There was a Māori land court sitting and Te Kooti applied for an allocation of land which gave the colonial office the confidence that they had quelled the insurrection, so over time the government recalled most of the guards back to NZ.'

'Te Kooti had other plans, while he was here he had a vision led to the creation of the Ringatu religion. With the help of a few locals he commandeered a ship and escaped back to his homeland where he was regarded as a Prophet. To this day his followers make a pilgrimage back to the Chathams as a mark of respect to Ringatu and the Te Kooti's Hau Hau's.'

'What a story', said Dan, 'It is an honor to be a guest in this house of a good man,'

'It's all yours, just get rid of the junk.'

Dans first job was to drop in the motor into the Bedford which was still parked in the Durham woolshed. After a couple of days the Bedford was ready for action and Dan was packing his tools to get a ride to town. Doug, who farmed the Durham sheep station was in the process of mustering his wethers and ewes ready for shearing.

'Dan, can you shear a sheep?'

'Nope,'

'Can you operate a wool-press?'

'Nope,'

'Well, it's about time you learnt,'

'I think I've got a sore foot,'

'Bugger your sore foot, your old buddy Hydraulic Jack is on his way out here so you and him can work together on the board and wool pressing.'

'Looks like I got no choice,'

'It's that or walk back to town.'

The two weeks shearing went fast for Dan, he would have a quick lunch and then pick up as handpiece and shear a few wethers while being coached by the shearing contractor, Terry. The days were long and hard, 5 AM start then 7 AM breakfast of mutton chops, fried spuds and eggs. Morning tea of scones and gooseberry jam with rancid butter, or sometimes a treat of doughnuts fried in albatross fat. Dinner of boiled or roasted mutton, spuds and cabbage.

He slept well in the woolshed in a jute woolpack lined with freshly shorn greasy wool to keep in the warmth.

When the last sheep was shorn, the last bale was pressed, the last mutton chop was eaten Dan announced that he would be very happy never to see another sheep in his life. He stank of sheep shit and sweat so it was about time for a shower. The system was a bucket suspended on a swivel that was filled with warmish, if you were lucky, water, and the cake of home-made soap was a luxury. Doug put on the usual cutout shout of a few dozen Wards beer before the shearing gang went onto his next door neighbour.

Jack, as per usual form, had arrived was few days late, perfect timing for just several days work and more importantly for him, the cutout shout.

'Hey Jack, watcha been up to?'

'Gainfully employed,'

'Bullshit.'

'I've just enrolled in a correspondence course,'

'Bullshit,'

'No shit, it's fair-dinkum, I'm doing a course on 'Time and Motion', I find it very, very very interesting,'

'Yeah right, plenty of time and bugger all motion.'

Dan, hung-over, said that he needed some fresh air for a few days so decided to walk the uninhabited south coast to Owenga and then hitch a ride back to Waitangi. The walk took four easy days, a half loaf of bread and some cold mutton, handlining for a feed of cod and a few paua's kept him going to Owenga. The first sign of civilization was the home of the Solomon family who farmed their 5,000-acre block called Manakau. This Moriori family had heard on the bush telegraph that an Irishman would soon be knocking on their door. Dan didn't need to knock, the door was already opened, and the large teapot was simmering on the stove. The cup of tea lasted all afternoon as the menfolk trickled in from what supposed to have been, a hard day's farm work. But as normal, a hard day's work consisted of hunting and gathering as they had done for many hundreds of years. The cups of tea were followed by what Dan described as a banquet, but he guessed this was normal fare for his hosts.

The patriarch, Benji, was fascinated by Dan's accent and his stories of old Irish mystery and mythology that went well into the night, as we well know that Dan could tell a good story. He recognized the knowledge and intelligence with the underlying humor of these people, this surprised him because of their isolation. They had a primary education at the Owenga school and in their home they spoke what Dan worked out to be a pigeon language of Moriori, Māori and English. In Dan's presence they would converse in a more English version of the improvised language which Dan could understand.

Dan, at that time was unaware of the series of events of when Pakeha then Māori first came to Rekohu, innocently asked the question. Ole Benji, in his wisdom, described in the Latin phrase,

'Veni, Vidi, Veci'. (They came, they saw, they conquered).

He went on to describe the warrior nation of Māori custom that clashed with the pacifist first nation people of Moriori. Then the Māori tradition of walking the land therefore the vanquished did not exist.

'When the English arrived our land of Rekohu was then renamed the Chatham Islands, then after Māori invaded it became Wharekauri.'

Dan could see into the eyes of Benji that there was a lot more to this story that Benji kept to himself. The Admiral, as his son Gary was known, said with a twinkle in his eye that overshadowed something far deeper than Dan could imagine.

'Take a look at me, I exist and I'm not going anywhere soon.'

Dan lived, ate and slept with the extended family for a couple of days, rested till he was ready to head off to Waitangi, the Admiral offered his young gelding called Dusty, to ride the fifteen miles back to Waitangi.

'Hey, Bones,' as he nicknamed Dan, 'you can keep Dusty but I want my saddle back.'

He bade farewell, humbled by his host's warmth and unpretentious generosity and by late afternoon was back in Waitangi with his home fire heating a kettle of water. He stepped outside and looked across the bay as he was watched by the full moon rising over Red Bluff.

'The sound of absolute silence.' He was joined by the ghost of Rose.

Dan settled into a simple existence as he converted his jailhouse from junk storage into a livable home. A bit of fishing from the wharf, the odd job or two for Happy Jack around the pub, or giving a helping hand here and there to be paid in kind. Evenings he spent getting his fingers mobile again with his Gibson. He wasn't ready yet to play for an audience, keeping a low profile, living a simple and peaceful life.

Well, the peace didn't last long, he got a message from the pub that the Kaingaroa School's power generator had packed a sad. The engine parts were still in the wharf shed waiting to be picked up, could he ride out to Kaingaroa and rebuild the Lister. 'No sweat', was the message he sent back to the Kaingaroa school principal. The next message he received from the school was for him to pick up stores from the Travellers Rest and a bit of cowboy juice from the pub to take with him to Kaingaroa.

There was a knock on the door and Ned introduced himself as his guide to Kaingaroa. Uncle Ned was a big man with a shy smile, thick black hair under a battered hat, alert brown eyes of his mixed race, his Pakeha ancestor was sent to the Chathams as a magistrate in the 1860s to try and enforce some sort of law and order into a lawless population, a near impossible task, even to this day.

Leaning on the doorframe he rolled a smoke then passed his pouch to Dan who shook his head,

'Trying to give it up,' he said, 'How long will we be away?'

'About as long as a piece of string.'

Uncle Ned had three horses nibbling on the few patches of grass behind the pub, the two pack horses were packed with goods for Kaingaroa including parts for the Genset from the wharf shed.

When Dan saw the horses, he said to Ned that he thought they were going on Ned's truck.

'Impossible,' said Ned, 'With all the rain we've had, the truck would get stuck in the mud, we have to take a step back to the old days, for now we're on horseback.'

'In that case I'd better go and catch Dusty, like me, he will be keen for an adventure.'

In the wet the best route to Kaingaroa was to ford the Te Waanga lagoon, following a shallow sand bank from Kawera Point across the lagoon to Wainui, a distance of about 4 miles. Before they departed Waitangi, they had a ZLC radio message sent to Laurie Smiley at Kaingaroa Station that if by chance they had not crossed the lagoon by nightfall could he arrange for a fire be lit on the beach to guide them.

About half-way across the lagoon, they lost track of the sandbar and no matter which direction they took, they rode into deeper water. In the failing light Ned saw a swan's nest which guided them back onto the shallow sandbar. By then darkness had fallen and they lost sight of the shoreline of Wainui. The darker it got the harder it was to follow the sandbank and they kept walking into deeper water and loosing the safety of the sandbank. Ned decided to stop and wait for the fire to be lit. An hour or so later and still no fire, with no moon, the darkness was that heavy that they could not even see each other. It was a long night sitting in the saddle, swapping yarns, their stories grew taller, sang a few songs, told a few jokes.

'Hey Ned, what's your favorite sport?'

Uncle Ned was lighting a smoke before he answered with a twinkle in his eyes as his face rounded into a smile.

'Hide the sausage.'

As the cold seeped into their bones, they dismounted into thigh deep water and rearranged their load so they could lean back in the saddle and maybe get some sleep. 'Yeah,' Ned remembered the bottle of Scotch that he had brough for his mate, Laurie, 'Sorry Laurie' he said as he took a swig and passed it to Dan. This kept the cold at bay and shortened the night which included a few intermittent dozes.

As the first streaks of dawn crept in, they could just make out a figure on a horse on the distant shore, a couple of kicks got their exhausted horses moving along the sandbank to Wainui.

'Hey Uncle Ned, you guys are a bit late,' called out Pete who lived at Wainui.

'It's better that uncle Ned is late than the late uncle Ned, where the hell were you?'

'You wouldn't believe it, I was here stacking wood for the fire, stopped to roll a smoke and dropped my box of matches,'

'Is that right?'

'Into a puddle,'

'No wonder they call you Boof.'

The horses were exhausted, so it was a long slow walk to Laurie's homestead. They arrived around lunchtime to the smell of boiling weka, spuds and watercress. Laurie, a bachelor, opened the oven door as the smell of baking bread drifted around his house,

'Hope you got plenty of butter.'

Both Ned and Dan slept the afternoon and through the night, waking at sunrise, the first question asked was.

'Got any of that boilup left?'

Pete had unloaded the packhorses and fed them some hard feed, Ned's gelding refused to eat, and sadly, died during the night, as for Dusty, just another day in the office.

Dan soon got to work on the rebuild of the Kaingaroa school Lister genset, being a simple low revving motor, he soon had it ticking along nicely. Most of the people of both Kaingaroa and Waitangi had Listers so the chug, chug, chug could be heard at night until shutdown at bedtime. Everybody knew what time their neighbor went to bed, If a chug, chug, chug could be heard late into the night there was probably a party happening. In later years there is the story of the school kids flying on the Sunderland into Christchurch in the evening for their first trip to N.Z. On seeing there city lights one of them commented that Christchurch must be a very noisy place with all the generators chug, chug, a chugging.

After the job was done, the guys wandered down the hill to the local watering hole called the 'Sports and Social Club', a few beersies, swapping a few yarns and by the time the evening ended Dan had a heap of fixit jobs lined up. Next to the club was a small fish processing plant where one could find the occasional carcass of meat hanging in the freezer amongst the wooden boxes of grouper and cod. On the rise overlooking the harbor there were a smattering of houses of the permanent residents like the Goomes and Grennell families. Along the shoreline were the huts of the transients who went fishing when they felt like it, shore sheep with they needed shearing, mustered the stock when they needed to be mustered, hunting weka when they were fat, swan egging when they were laying and telling lies at the Club. that's if they were cashed up. The women worked in the fish processing plant and grumbled at their good for nothing men, Island life is much the same the world over.

As they walked along the beach to Kaiwhata Ranch Laurie pointed out to where Capt, Broughton of HMS the Chatham who, while on his way from Port Phillip to Tahiti stumbled across these islands of Rekohu. The Capt. with some of his crew went ashore in their longboat and were inspecting a washout canoe on the beach above the high-water mark. Toro Toro, a Moriori, who was the master of his treasured canoe, had been watching these strange people and their antics. His race had believed they were the only people of this earth. When the intruders were poking around his canoe he walked out of the bush and challenged them in the belief that they were interfering with his fishing gear. In the melee that followed Toro Toro was shot and killed. Capt. Broughton, named the island after his ship, nailed a lead plaque onto a large Kopi tree claiming the Island on behalf of the King of England.

'Mmmmm'. Said Ned, 'That bit of lead would have made a good sinker for a fishing line.'

Time for a cuppa at the Kaiwhata Ranch, homestead of Ray and Alfie Wiesner and Ray's American wife Katey who had arrived on the Island before the start of the war. While walking across the paddock and through the Nikau's Laurie related of how Katey arrived on the Chathams.

'The brothers had subscribed to a magazine that had a Lonely-Hearts column, unbeknown to each other they both corresponded with the same woman, each describing their life on the Chathams and an offer of marriage. Katey eventually arrived on the Island and chose Ray, whom she said, wrote the most poetic letter.

Sitting around the kitchen table Katey prattled on and on about how great and advanced America was in compared with the rest of the world. After an hour or so, during which had the men gazing at the ceiling hoping she would have a case of lockjaw or for a tsunami to roll in for some relief from her constant prattle. Laurie cleared his throat and announced that he had to go fix something.

Ned said later, 'I wonder which brother got the best deal.'

Alfie was getting his horse ready to head to Waitangi via the east coast which meant crossing the dangerous channel of Te Awapartiki which linked the lagoon to the open sea and then on to Owenga for a Saturday game of rugby. A night in Owenga and then to Waitangi to pick up the mail and stores, the round trip taking about four or five days.

Ned also played in the Northern rugby team and said he would do the trek with Alfie to Owenga. He asked Dan if he was going with them to play rugby.

'I think I've got a sore foot.' he lied.

In fact he didn't have anything wrong with his foot and had agreed to service some of the machinery in the village. He spent a couple of weeks doing a few odd jobs, a bit of time on a cod boat, a bit of weka hunting, a bit of this, a bit of that with each day ending with a beer or three at the Club. Paid work was drying up so it was time to head back to Waitangi, the weather had been reasonably dry for a few weeks so the track on the west coast was passable and a lot safer than the lagoon crossing.

He called in to see Bolen at Matarakau whom he had met while he was on the Rangatira anchored at Kaingaroa. One cannot visit Bolen without staying for a feed of whatever was in season at that time. This time it was home cured bacon and swan egg pie with the pastry being made of rancid butter for which most Chatham Islanders had an acquired taste. This was a bit of a struggle for Dan who certainly appreciated the cups of black tea to wash down the pie.

On the advice of his host, he rode through the coastal bush onto the beach of Ocean Mail, named after the wool clipper that was wrecked on French Reef on her voyage from Port Phillip loaded with wool destined for the dark satanic mills of Manchester. The margins of the low-lying dunes were covered by the deep rich blue and the shiny green leaf of the coastal herb of the Chathams Island Forget-me-not. Scattered amongst the blue and green was the brown Pingau and the light green and the fluffy white flowered Sow Thistle. These colors contrasted with the Mediterranean blue of Hanson Bay. Perfection. Dan was seized by a wave of homesickness of the Ireland that he was never to see again, he dismounted and walked describing out loud this perfect scene to the ghost of his Rose.

He set up camp at the end of the beach at the flat basalt rocks of Taupeka that was littered with the flotsam and jetsam of the Southern Ocean. Scattered amongst this litter were the sun-bleached bones of ancient Moriori whose souls had long ago departed into the northern mist.

A slow morning had him crossing the scrubby peatland which was dotted with the tiny red berry hanging from the uninvited resident, the Chilean Guava. The track took him to shore of the lagoon where his passage was ignored by the craggy Mt. Chudley who was totally indifferent to his existence, Chudley was more intent on reaching for the sky. Riding through the Nikau Forest which lined the lagoon shore at Kaingapakeha a wild boar bolted out from a thicket directly in front of Dan. Dusty reared and lurched sideways to avoid the tusks, his saddle slipped and Dan found himself sitting on the wet ground. He watched Dusty bolting in the direction they were travelling while the boar crashed through the undergrowth heading in the opposite direction.

Mmmm, these boots were made for walking that's just what they do, one of these days... (with thanks to Nancy Sinatra for that one).

28

CUPID, DRAW BACK YOUR BOW

and let your arrow go, (said Marvin Gaye) which was on Dan's brain when he eventually arrived back in Waitangi.

After being dumped by Dusty he walked down to the grassed shore of the lagoon where he thought Dusty may be grazing, it was a warm, still sunny day. It looked as if he had a long walk in front of him so there was point in hurrying. Just on the rise before what he guessed was Blind Jim's Creek he was startled by the bright yellow flowers of the Kowhai which were being attacked by excited chattering Tuis. In the grassed clearing by the creek Dusty, with another four horses were calmly grazing amongst old remnants of an Ake Ake forest. The sound of bleating ewes with lambs took his attention inland to rising pastures pocketed with native bush that was dominated by the tall red berried Nikau palms that competed with the shiny green leafed Kopi that were displaying bunches of yellow berries that were being eaten by the Kereru (native pigeon).

All this action was being observed by the volcanic cone of Korika that Dan imagined was inviting his soul to adventure, to climb its summit and share their domain spread below. Dan absorbed nature at its best, he said to Korika,

'You must have looked magnificent back in the days when you were an angry volcano, hopefully, may you rest in peace.' Dan had heard of the eruptions and earthquakes of the region. 'hope you don't blow up while I'm around.'

He had felt before he realized the sound of excited children who were knee deep in the lagoon with spears poised to strike. About 15 yards from the children was a woman with the long dark hair of her race, she was intently concentrating into the still water. As he got closer to the water's edge he became aware of her light brown complexion, face freckled by the sun, a fine nose that indicated some European ancestry. She looked up, startled to see this male who appeared from nowhere, then quickly looked back down trying to look as if she was concentrating on the sandy bottom of the lagoon . He caught a flash of her eyes, a change of color from maybe green to light brown, later that night he decided on the word hazel. She wore a simple modest flowery dress tied up above her knees, In one hand she held an Ake Ake spear, polished with use with carved barbs, poised, ready to strike. In her other hand was a length of No. 8 wire with speared flounders threaded through their gills, trailing in the water behind her. She held back a smile,

'Lost something?'

'My horse,'

'How did you do that?'

'For me, very easy,'

He had taken his boots off and rolled his trousers to wade closer to where she was. He stared intently through the glassy surface, vaguely making out the shape of a flounder, which was the same color as the seabed.

'I see one,' he whispered.

'Don't move,' as she handed him her spear.

He carefully held the barbed point just above the still flounder laying on the seabed, plunged the spear through the flounder and into the seabed, he held it there as a flounder wriggled in death, 'Yeah! got it,'

He passed the spear over to her with the fish still flapping, she threaded it onto the wire and then removed the spear.

'Just call me the flounder whisperer,'

'You don't need to whisper; the flounder can't hear you,'

'That was a buzz.'

In actual fact the buzz he felt was being on the same wavelength as this young woman, in her natural environment. When he first saw her she didn't strike him as a thing of beauty but in this act of food gathering he felt not only her strength but beauty as well. He didn't think it, it was more of an emotion rather than thought. His brain was racing trying to absorb this time and this place, the glassy lagoon reflecting flashes of sun, the spring flowers behind him, close to him the huntress, concentrating on her prey, all under the watchful eye of Korika.

The children were giggling in the background and were being shushed, unsuccessfully by the oldest boy. In return he was being splashed by his cheeky siblings. They were acting the goat by pushing one another into the water, successfully scaring away any lurking flounder. All this added to magic, and, as we all know that if one believes in magic, then magic will happen.

'What's your name?' he asked.

'Don't be nosey?'

'Hey, kids, what's your sisters name?'

'Don't you dare tell him,'

The kids all looked at one another, then called out in unison. 'Molly'.

'Hi Molly, I'm Dan, you know, the man who lost his horse,'

One of the kids handed Dan a spear so he turned his attention to floundering. Molly and Dan kept about 5 yards apart, each acutely aware of the other while pretending to concentrate on the seabed. If they found themselves closer that that they would both deliberately change direction, they avoided looking directly at one another, just a sneaky look out the corner of the eye was enough.

Molly eventually called out, 'Home time,' and said to Dan. 'We've got enough flounder to feed half the island,'

By then, kids being kids were soaking wet, shivering and complaining about the cold.

'Stop your moaning and run up the beach and back, and if you're still cold, do it again, you'll soon warm up.'

Out of the water Molly and Dan, without talking, unthreaded the flounder from the wire and packed them into a split sack that was to be tied onto one of the horses. They gathered the spears and wire and stood them up against a tree ready for the next person looking for a feed of flounder.

As they walked over to catch their horses their shoulders inadvertently touched, they quickly parted, Dan looked down, the sun had cast their shadows as one.

The kids all piled onto three horses, Dan climbed into the saddle of Dusty and Molly barebacked on Fern, as they crossed the creek she said.

'Looks like we are heading in the same direction, that's if you don't fall off your horse on the way,'

'I'll do my best.'

As they headed up the hill towards Marakarpia, which was about 5 miles away, Dan asked who was Blind Jim.

'He was African from the West Indies who crewed on an American whaler, but, I suppose, because of his color he was treated badly. Anyway, he jumped ship and was taken in by our people at Te Roto Pah, which was then known as a haven for anybody who needed a safe place. My Great Grandfather, who was Portuguese, lived there at the time told me that Ngati Mutunga had given Jim some land to farm on the lagoon shore, the creek used to be called Te Kaito. Jim lost his sight while fencing with barbed wire. He lived by himself and when he wanted to go to town all the farmers would leave their gates open for him, his horse, knowing the way to town and back was his guide, it's always been known as Blind Jims since then.'

The road, or the be more accurate, the track, rose gently to the North to crossroads then down to Lake Marakarpia where Molly's family lived. There they parted, Molly pointed out to the lowest part of the sand dunes,

'That'll take you down to the beach.'

'I saw you playing Netball.'

'I watched you play rugby.'

Back in his humble abode, humble may it be, it was home, a cold-water wash while standing in a galvanized iron tub. Dan decided that he would have to improve on that one, as far as a flush toilet went, that was a luxury for some time in the future. His day ended with a steaming mug of tea while sitting on his ancient stuffed couch on the porch, watching the fat old sun lowering to hide beyond the dunes. His brain wandered around to 'his day of the flounder', he felt a chill as the ghost of Rose engulfed him.

A troubled sleep had him up well before dawn planning how to store his violent past in a box with a closed lid, but without a lock.

The Mungautu Hotel is where Chatham Islanders go to conduct business, gossip, news and views, and of course entertainment. Islanders from out of town would come in for days at a time, especially ship day or Christmas and New Year's horse racing and all the entertainment that went with it. Some would stay with friends or relations around town; others would camp on the Ngati Mutunga reserve set aside for that purpose. Potatoes and turnips were grown in this reserve for the use of anybody in need.

Step into the bar and one could find the Doctor yarning with a fisherman, the magistrate joking with the man he once fined for some now forgotten minor offence, the policeman trying to pretend he wasn't drunk, the county clerk staggering around like a one-legged man with a rubber crutch, Bill Miller cutting hair for beersies, the ladies sitting at a round table cunningly playing cards for coins. A word of warning, don't mess with these ladies, they will annihilate you with a razor sharp tongue, and, of course let's not forget Hydraulic Jack wheeling and dealing where there is only one winner.

The bar was run with the iron hand of the ever-grumpy Happy Jack, don't upset Happy Jack or your punishment will be severe. Gossip had it that the pub would run out of beer before the next ship was due to arrive, Dan mentioned this to the whisky drinking Happy Jack.

'I don't give a stuff; I don't drink that shit,' said Jack

The pub also was the local employment agency, somebody's looking for a broken window to be replaced, Shep needs a shed hand, Charlie's deckhand decided to go for a walkabout, Council is looking for a couple of workers to fill in some potholes. Are you coming to rugby practice? (Dan had a sore foot). George Black oversaw the coast-watch and was always on the lookout for volunteers, once signed up, one was bestowed a rank in what became known as 'Georges Army'.

Dan did all those things and sometimes he even got paid, some evenings, especially after rugby and netball Dan would shake the dust of his Gibson and put on a show. The people were entertainment starved, radio reception was sparse except for the NZ National station, which, during wartime, played the most boring music along with the war propaganda. Dan injected a whole new world of music which was soaked up by the love of music that is imbedded in the Polynesian ancestry of the Chathams. Dan's background of Irish, blues and country slipped in nicely with the Polynesian rhythm and beat, all Māori can sing, and most can strum guitar. The Māori language seemed to flow off his tongue so once again, his music evolved. Dan often thought that the Māori language flowed like an Italian opera which took him back to his days of Pieter who would often burst into something that Dan thought was operatic with his tenor voice.

'Maybe someday there will be a Māori opera.' he often said.

Wedding bells would soon be chiming on the Chathams, the tying of the knot had been the expectation of two families for many years, not that the couple were all that perturbed about this arranged union, it had been imbedded within them for many years. Their happiness was secondary to the happiness of the matriarchs and patriarchs, anyway, as long as everyone was happy, what the hell. The ceremony was to be held at the Te One Hall of Memories which in later years, when somebody decided that the Island should have a marae, became the Whakatunata Marae. There were local musicians but they had not played as a band for some time so Dan was asked to help them get back together. The word was out that there was going to be a band practice on Thursdays at the Waitangi Hall in preparation for the wedding. After a few sessions they had sorted themselves out and were ready to go.

Pita and Dan on guitar, Rick on base if he remembered to turn up, Floyd on percussion, George with his squeezebox and Sister Ig pounding piano. George and Liz on vocals with Molly and Linda on harmony, that's if Molly could get away from being Mother to her eight siblings and the 10 miles on horseback to town and back.

The Thursday night band practice was soon to become a night of entertainment, and many would turn up just to have a listen. One of the songs they practiced was a Waiata that Dan struggled to get his Irish tongue around. The Waiata was a lament, and we all know how the Irish love to lament. Eventually this waiata was to become one of the band's signature tunes.

On these practice nights Dan and Molly would acknowledge one another, but kept their distance, Dan held back because he didn't trust his own emotions of desire to be near a woman, especially this woman. Often, he would find himself looking at Molly and this frightened him to where he had to deliberately concentrate to keep Rose and his family close to his being.

For Molly, she was frightened of an intense desire that she had never had in all of her 18 years. After her mother had died. Molly, being the eldest female, was expected to take on the role of being caregiver to her siblings and homemaker to a father who had given up on life after the death of his wife. There was a demon in the bottle for Totara that had taken charge of his life. This lead Molly having to feed, clothe and manage a household on what she could forage from around their farm and the income she had from being a teacher's aide at Te Karakau School.

After band practice one night Dan and Molly found themselves sitting together over a cup of tea, a power far stronger than they could control had brought them together.

'What brought you to the Chathams?'

To avoid the question he said, 'The mighty Rangatira,'

'Yeah, I know that, but why have you come here to live,'

'I don't know really, it was just a decision that made itself, I suppose you could call it fate,'

'It must be something more than that.'

Dan didn't like the way the conversation was going.

'That waiata we sing, I think I have it sorted, but I don't understand what it's all about, when we play it I see tears in the eyes of some of the old people,'

'Yeah, I love it, it was made up by the women when their men returned home from prison,'

'From prison? What was that all about?'

'Some time ago the Government found that they couldn't tax Māori land so they introduced a 'Dog Tax' on those who farmed Māori land. The farmers refused to pay this tax. The main reason was that they just didn't have any money because the farms were communal and the produce went to feed their extended families. The government was sneaky in those days, still are. Anyway, the men who refused to pay this tax went to court and each were given a three-month jail sentence to be served in N.Z. They all got a free trip to Wellington but had to find their own passage back home, thanks to the very generous Captain Ward. We didn't have a wharf in those days so they came close to the beach as the surfboat could get and then waded ashore, The women also waded out to welcome their menfolk by singing the waiata that they had composed for the occasion.

'Ena rakau tenei ra,
ko hui ake nei
Nana mahi au to au
Tatou hurihuri mai
No reira te kupu i anei
Hamei ra heare mai…

While Dan listened this story of her people his hand reached over and rested on her forearm, he didn't realize he had done this, he looked down and saw what he had done and went to pull his hand away, but Molly had put her hand on his. They each looked at the other, completely oblivious to their surroundings, for them nothing else existed.

'It's a beautiful song,' he said.

The old Kuia's seated around the hall were watching, remembering their own lives and the beauty of youth; intuition telling them of troubled waters that lay ahead.

Time to tie the knot for the forever engaged couple, the men had been hunting and gathering for several days; the women, doing what women loved to do, decorating the hall, scrubbing, cleaning windows and so on. (Women look at a window and see dirt, men look at a window and see what's on the other side). There were no invitations sent, all Chatham islanders would turn up invited or not, even enemies put aside their differences, for the time being anyway.

The Paddock across the road of the hall was owned by the Remi family who had shifted their cattle except for one fat steer that was destined for the pot. Also it became the camping ground for the outlying families that was on the edge of Lake Huro where the men had set their hinakes (eel traps) for the eels to be smoked.

Dan's job with the help of Hydraulic Jack, was to relocate the Lister genset from the Lanauze woolshed to the hall for the big occasion. As they were loading the Lister onto a dray there was a large cloud of dust coming from the direction of town, from around the corner came a long line of traffic that drove straight past the wedding venue and up the hill towards Rapanui. Leading the pack was a couple of guys on horseback so Jack waved them down.

'What's up?'

One pointed up the hill, Jack and Dan turned around to see clouds of smoke,

'Bob's fern paddock is on fire and the winds' blowing it towards his house?'

They cantered off.

Dan looked back down the road to see the procession heading up to the fire. in the lead was the Bedford truck with an empty water tank on the back. Following was the Resident Commissioner and his wife in their Landrover, next was old Bob Jacobs on his Fordson tractor with a crate of beer securely fastened on the tray, then a pair of horses towing a cart which stopped at the Te One hall calling for volunteers who were in the process of erecting the wedding marquee. Last of all, with bells ringing, was the hand painted red fire engine with the uniformed fire brigade volunteers. The pub had emptied and the patrons had been picked up by the fire truck and were all swaying to and fro, grimly hanging onto the back of the fire truck.

Hydraulic Jack, forever thinking of his stomach, cut down a mutton that had been hanging from a tree at the back of the hall for the wedding feast. He threw it onto the dray and told Dan that they were heading to the fire. They passed the fire truck which was parked on the side of the road with a cloud of steam coming from the radiator. Jack set up his grill fairly close to the fire where he reckoned there should be enough embers to grill a few chops and set to cutting up the mutton.

The wedding was postponed for a day.

'You are now man and wife.' Stammered the Rev. Riwai who had imbibed a tipple or three before his big day out, he was more nervous than the Bride and Groom.

All Chatham Island events include copious amounts of food and this wedding was no exception, wild pork (it was wild then they shot it anyway), weka with watercress to neutralize the fat, paua patties, kina (regarded in later years as Chatham Island Viagra), boring old crayfish (which was the favorite of many a household cat), smoked eel dripping with its oil, delicious bannocks fried in albatross fat and so on. Dan looked at the spread the thought that salads must have not yet been invented on the Chathams. Pudding was of many concoctions involving sugar, cream, chocolate and the usual swan egg sponges.

Speech time, the old Kamatua took the floor, carved stick in hand as he paced the floor, after each sentence he would turn around and pace back for another sentence, any interfering noise he would thump his stick loudly on the wooden floor. This was his day in the sun, and nobody was going to take that away from him. His speech was, word for word, the same speech he had made at weddings for the last 50 years, the crowd rolled their eyes and expressed false yawns.

'The Groom', he said, 'has been well educated by a size 12 boot in the bum', he then complimented the bride of, 'her beauty and intelligence that came from the Kamatua's side of the family and that behind every successful man was a working wife and that all their problems would be little ones.'

The hall groaned.

Gary Solomon, a fisherman known as the Admiral congratulated the Bride and Groom on this auspicious occasion when Venus aligned with Mars bringing peace and goodwill to us all. The Admiral, as a man of reputation of the appreciation of good food gave homage to the cooks and stated he was going on a diet straight after the wedding, that one brought the house down. On a more serious note, he apologized on behalf of his Moriori people that their aging Kamatua, was unable to attend because of ill-health. His time on this earth was coming to an end. The people hushed and murmured condolences.

Somebody asked the newly-weds where they were going for their honeymoon? The groom replied that he was going to be too busy crutching. This statement brought on a huge round of laughter in thinking that the word, crutching, was to some sort of romantic inter-lude. The embarrassed bride nudged her husband several times before he realized what he had said. He stammered, stuttered and said that the ship was due and that he had to crutch his sheep that were booked to go to N.Z. That statement brought on an even bigger round of laughter. The comments started flowing thick and fast,

'I always thought that you were a bit of a ram.'

'Take care with the handpiece'.

'If we hear, Baaaa, Baaaa into the night we know what's happening.'

Eventually the band called it a night and joined the party which by then was becoming a little rowdy, teenagers flirted, enemies had arms around one another, the oldies sat around the hall trying to stay awake. Dan gravitated towards Molly as she stood talking to friends, they saw Dan coming so backed away saying that they were going to leave them to it. It was too noisy to talk, his lips moved but she couldn't hear what he was saying. He took her elbow and nodded towards the door at the back and said into her ear.

'Maybe we should get some fresh air.'

Molly nodded, not finding her voice, without trying to be too obvious they made their way through the door and outside where peace reigned.

'What were you saying?' she asked.

'Hazel, your eyes are hazel.'

The found each other's hands as they drifted into the night under a waning moon, they didn't speak as they picked their way through the dunes and down onto the beach, leaving the noise and the lights of the party behind. On the beach they stopped, looking into the dark ocean, a breaking white wave appeared, and stretched out from both sides of the break, growing longer until it was swallowed in the gloom, another white wave appeared behind it, then, as was the first wave it melded into nothing. There was no sound from the sea as the waves were rolling rather than breaking. The cry of a weka calling to its mate, then silence. Only they existed. Both turned and faced, holding both hands as their lips touched, first kiss, each breathed the other's air, paradise in the dark as their bodies explored the other. Their hands let go to wrap and crush the other, their second kiss lasted forever as their tongues gently tasted. Dan took her shoulders, gently pushed their bodies apart.

'Let's get back to the party or tongues will be wagging,'

'Oh them, let them wag as much as they like, I don't really care,'

Back in the hall they were met by a barrage of wolf whistles and the tut, tut, tutting of the old Kuia's and the wink, wink, nudge, nudge of some of the guys.

The ghost of Rose faded into the night.

29

GEORGE'S ARMY

was the nick-name of his volunteer Coast Watchers who were in charge the keeping a vigilant lookout for German invaders. George knocked on Dan's door and asked him if he would like to join his team to attend his weekly briefing at the Pub. This meeting was always well attended aided by the funding George received from the Defense Force that went across the bar. Dan said that he was a starter.

At the meeting a team of 4 were selected to spend the next week, on horseback, combing the steep uninhabited thickly wooded cliffs on the South Coast for any sight of the enemy.

'Which enemy is that?' asked Golly.

'Don't you know?' replied George. 'Germany, we are at war with Germany, you know, the Huns,'

'First time I've heard of that.'

After a few beers George selected his next week's team consisting of Dan, Hydraulic Jack, Golly, (named because of his hair style) who was on the run from authorities from Lyttelton, rumor had it that it was something to do with girls on ships. Also, there was Southwest Sam, a semi-retired fisherman. George, who bestowed himself the rank of Major appointed S.W. Sam as his Sargent. Departure from the pub was set at midday Saturday where they loaded two pack horses with provisions and a couple of bottles of rum to keep the cold at bay.

Sargent Sam brought his two excited pig dogs who knew that there was some sort of action ahead. It took about an hour to load the horses and about three hours for the George to extract his team from the pub. Because of their late start they only got a far as the Durham woolshed where they camped for the night. An early start had them at the Tuku gully where they met the relieved Coast Watchers who were returning to civilization after a week or so of doing nothing. A fire was lit and a good old gossip over a billy of tea and scones provided by George's wife Betty. The relieved team handed over their 303 caliber rifles to George who asked where the ammunition was. They shrug their shoulders indicating that they had none left.

'If that's the case,' said George, 'I expect to see the bodies of the German invaders laying on the beach.'

'Good luck with that one mate,' was the response as they rode off in the direction in town, more importantly, to the Pub.

George handed each of his soldiers a rifle and five cartridges each that he had in his saddle-pack. Now that they were armed George took on the role of Major Black, straightened his shoulders and said in a military tone.

'Don't load them into the breach otherwise, knowing you men, you'll end up firing at anything that moves and then we won't have any ammunition left when the enemy attacks.'

'What'll we do with the bullets then?' asked Sargent Sam.

Major George shook his head, 'Didn't your mother teach you anything? Put them in your top pocket, and I must add, that they are called cartridges, not bullets, the bullet in the bit of lead at the front,'

Corporal Golly couldn't help himself, so he added his bit to the conversation by asking.

'What am I supposed to do with this here gun?' he held his rifle up.

'Whew!' exclaimed the Major, 'Think about it, do you want to be throwing stones at any Germans lurking around or do you want to shoot them,'

'I'd probably shit my pants,'

'By the way,' said the Major, 'it's a rifle, not a gun,'

'Oops, sorry, what's a gun then?'

Major George shook his head in exasperation and held up his rifle and said,

'This is a rifle,' Then, with his other hand he pointed down to his crutch, 'and that is your gun,'

'One's for shooting and the others for fun,' said Jack.

They all cracked up, except for the Major of course.

'So, you could say that with one it would be an advantage to be quick on the trigger and with the other it would be a disadvantage to be quick on the trigger.' quipped Private Jack.

Private Dan had to throw in his bit, 'Don't get them muddled up.'

In disgust the Major George dug his heels into his mount, slapped the reigns and cantered off.

When they caught up to George, Jack asked

'Major Sir, you said that we shoot any Germans on sight, what about Ray and Alfie Wiesner? their ancestors came from Germany.'

George ignored that one.

Corporal Golly reckoned, 'We had better not shoot them otherwise their American wife would be on the loose,'

Sargant Sam said, 'Hey Dan, you're a bachelor, this would be an opportunity for you to play Uncle Ned's game,'

'What game's that?' asked Major George.

'Hide the sausage.'

'She's right mate, she'd never stop talking,' Wise words from Golly.

Once again George cantered off in disgust.

When they eventually caught up with him, Jack asked. 'More importantly Sir, what are we having for dinner?'

'Whatever you can shoot.' said the Major.

It was just on dark when they arrived at the very well-organized hut at the Horns owned by a farmer known as Zambesi because his father came from that same place. He lived on a farm in Waitangi, but also run a few hundred sheep on this very remote part of the Chathams. Under the light of carbide lamps Major George organized a roster for each in turn to climb to the top of one of the twin volcanic Horns to keep a daily watch for the enemy. The other three were to scout along the cliffs in case there had been a landing in the night. Well, that plan lasted for about 10 minutes as off they went hunting for the wild cattle that roamed the uninhabited expanse of the South Coast. Dan was leading his horse along a winding animal track when he came to a grassy clearing, unknowingly to Dan he had cornered a young bull who had backed into a tangle of undergrowth. There was only one escape for the bull who was snorting and pawing dust ready to charge. Dan's rifle was in a pouch which was buckled to his saddle, Dusty reared and pulled away from Dan as the bull dug his back hooves into the ground and leapt towards Dan, there was nowhere to hide. The gunshot from just off Dan's shoulder just about deafened him, a squirt of blood from between the bull's eyes dropped him stone dead about 10 yards in front of Dan.

'Bullseye! What do you think of that shot?' said Sargeant Sam.

'Not bad for an old fella,'

They cut off the hind legs to feed the dogs for the next week. Back at camp Sam said that they would return to the clearing after letting the carcass rot for three or four days, then the wild pigs would turn up for a feed. Sure enough, a few days later they had two young barrows hanging from the Ake Ake tree outside the hut.

It was Dan's turn to climb one of the horns on lookout for the day, his guitar kept boredom at bay, he could see his mates far below fishing for cod off the rocks. It was late afternoon and he had packed up his gear and took one last look at the horizon before scaling back down to the hut. The sky was grey, the sea was grey, the ship was grey, in the distance he could make out the shape of the ship well to the south, it seemed to shimmer and then just dissolve into the haze.

'Was it or wasn't it?' was the question asked by the Major, Dan said that he couldn't be 100% sure, it may have been just a smudge on the horizon. Deep down he knew it was a ship, he knew because he had seen the same sight in the North Sea, seeing it again was like a stab in the gut. He had been running, hiding on this far-flung post of civilization and still his past clung on, was there no escape from his murky past? After a feed of boiled pork-belly he walked outside the hut into darkness as the mist swam and curled in the wind, the ghost of Rose joined him.

S.W. Sam and Dan were scaling the cliffs hunting for seagull eggs when they came across a cave high enough to stand with a length that diminished into darkness. Inside were the remnants of an old habitation, a fireplace, paua shells, bird bones, seal skins, adze's of various sizes, bone fishhooks fastened to platted flax fibers. They followed a precarious cliffside track that led to a cleft in which were three perfectly preserved human remains in a sitting position, facing out to sea. The bodies were mummified by a constant cold dry draft of air that came from a funnel shaped basalt formation at sea-level. Their skin was intact so that facial recognition could have been possible, hair and fingernails were long indicating that they had continued growing after death, such was the preservation. Sam's take on it was that they were Moriori who may have been hiding on these cliffs from the Māori about 100 years previous. Dan and Sam agreed to respect these sites and backed out of the cave to leave them in peace. They agreed to take the knowledge of their discovery of this ancient memorial to their own graves.

A week later saw Georges Army heading back to the big smoke of Waitangi with Jack and Sam each leading a packhorse fully loaded with stuff that Jack had intended to sell. He told his mates that he was going to share the proceeds, but they all knew that was a load of bullshit. On the packhorses were four legs of pork, two rumps and back-steaks of a steer, two prime lambs stolen from old Zambezi, (what he don't know won't hurt him was Jacks philosophy), salted and dried cod fillets and six Taiko (Magenta Petrel) preserved in their own fat. What he didn't tell his mates was that he had found on the small beach at the bottom of the cliff what he thought was the very valuable ambergris. He was non-communitive on the journey back imagining himself as a millionaire in some tropical paradise smoking a cigar with one hand and a drink with an umbrella in the other, surrounded by pretty girls. That was until he had it analyzed by Doctor Moss who told him it was a ball of mutton fat, that didn't deter Jack who still tried but failed to hock it off as ambergris anyway.

Dan was kept on his toes with casual work and was able to generate enough cash to convert Te Kooti's jail into a warm, dry home. Happy Jack allowed him to run a power cable from the Pub's genset to his home in exchange for a bit of maintaince around the pub. Dan had a plan to try burning the peat from the Port Hutt clears in his wood fired Shacklock stove. A boat trip across the bay in Sam's old fishing boat, the 'Lyndor', to Whangamoe where there was a layer of peat on the beach that had dried through being exposed to the wind. There was so much heat using the peat that he burnt out the grate in his stove after a couple of weeks. He contacted Lyttelton Engineering to make 10 robust grates as part of his plan of harvesting peat bricks for sale around Waitangi, hopefully, his best customer would be the pub.

His jail was too small for a bathroom, so he built a cubicle attached to back of his jail for a toilet, yes, the luxury of a flush toilet which he connected to the Hotel septic tank. The shower he set up was the first on the Chathams and was the talk of the town, he had many visitors knock on his door to see how this new-fangled thing worked. The advantage of having electricity from the pub was that he installed a small electric pump that was connected to a wetback on his stove. Another of his jobs was to look after the Hotel's vegetable garden in exchange for electricity, water and drainage, there was no such thing as a free lunch as far as Happy Jack was concerned.

While all this was happening, Dan was constantly tormented by the night of the wedding, he tried to push Molly from his brain by keeping himself continually occupied, he failed miserably. They did come across one another several times and Dan's attempt to distance himself lasted about five seconds until he melted. He would make a weak excuse and back off, then beat himself up for a day or so later.

Some say the 'distance makes the heart to grow fonder', others say 'out of sight, out of mind', this was Dan's dilemma. There was only one way to find out.

'The heart wants what it wants' wise words from Selena Gomez.

30

EMERALD AND GREENSTONE

thought Dan after he made his decision that he was not going to hold back from courting Molly any longer. What was needed was a bold plan, he didn't have the courage to just go and knock on her door, however, opportunity knocked on his door, well, the Post Office door anyway. The public notice was advertising an upcoming movie which Dan had not seen but heard about back in his Liverpool days.

A faint heart never won a fair lady, so he painstakingly wrote an invitation to Molly.

'You are accordingly invited to attend the movie "Gone with the Wind" accompanied by myself, being shown at the Waitangi Hall at 8.00 PM on the 10/02/1944. Your host will escort you from the Post Office at 7.45 on said date.

'Yours…?'

He had a dilemma on the next word, he tried "faithfully", but didn't like that one, he wrote "sincerely" but screwed the letter up again, he didn't want to scare her away. He eventually settled on…

'Yours truly, Dan.'

He knew that Molly rarely came to town thinking that the movie may come and go before she received her invitation. He sealed the letter in an envelope and gave it to Pete Saunders, known as the 'Commodore' of his non-existent yacht club to deliver Dans invitation to Molly at Marakarpia on his way home to Port Hutt. The Commodore being the Commodore, couldn't resist the temptation so called in to one of his mates, Mutu, on his way up the road and they steamed the letter open over the boiling kettle. There are no secrets on the Chathams.

When he arrived at Marakarpia, the Commodore, with a leering grin, ostentatiously bowed as he handed the letter to the bewildered Molly and spoke.

'I hope you enjoy the movie.'

A few days later the Postmaster Bob, knocked on Dan's door and without saying anything but with a guilty look on his face handed Dan a letter. Bob stood for a full minute waiting for Dan to open his letter. Dan studied the envelope, looked at Bob and said…

'Have a nice day.'

Bob abruptly turned and stomped his way back to work.

The single page had pencil drawings of some of the elements of the Chathams, a weka, a bunch of Kopi berries and the range of volcanic peaks. There was but just a single word on the page…

'Delighted.'

Dan looked up from the page at the diminishing Bob and said to himself.

'This Island's full of Cupids.'

At 7.30 on said date, Dan, who had been shopping at the Waitangi Store was waiting at the Post Office dressed in a new pair light grey trousers, a white shirt that had been pressed by Ollie, she lent Dan one of her husband's ties. Dan didn't have a clue how to do the knot so Ollie had tied a Winsor knot that he could just slip over his head. Over his shirt he wore a black and grey flecked jacket that had been for sale for about a year at the Store. It had been tried on by most guys who had deemed it too expensive and too flash for Island life. Slicked down hair was the fashion of the day, Dan didn't have any hair-oil so used a couple of drops of engine oil which did the trick.

The Post Office clock slowly clicked from 8.00 to 8.01 and still no Molly, thinking that she must have got cold feet and that he was going to be stood up he left the apple blossom that he had picked for her on the P.O. bench seat.

'That's it,' he said to himself as he loosened his tie in disappointment, then from behind him he heard her speak, he turned, his jaw dropped as he gaped, she was stunning, face firm with a quizzical smile, her brown skin was flawless.

'Wait for me.' she said.

Dan still hadn't recovered, her black hair was parted in the middle and was resting gently on her shoulders, she stood tall dressed in a flower print green dress with a light shawl over her shoulders and upper arms. On her left wrist she held a small finely woven flax kete, she reached out to greet him with a white gloved hand, that small gesture was of graceful, supple youth. Still speechless he took her hand and felt her femineity that he not experienced for a long, long time.

His mind was struggling to say what he was thinking, the best he could come up with was...

'I didn't think you were coming,'

'Girls are allowed to be late on their first date, although I don't know what I would have done if you weren't here,'

'You are worth waiting for so as far as I'm concerned you can be as late as you like,' he stopped and looked at her directly in the eye.

'Do you know that you are a beautiful woman,' Those words just came out of his mouth, he nodded in the direction of the hall and said,

'Shall we?'

'We shall, actually you are looking pretty cool yourself.'

He had forgotten to give her the apple blossom which was left forlornly alone on the bench.

Saturday night at the movies was always well supported by most, except for the thirsty males who would use Saturday night at the movies as an excuse to head to the pub. We all should know by now that there are no secrets on the Chathams. All the movie goers were waiting for the couple to arrive. Merle, the projectionist, delayed the start of the movie until Dan and Molly arrived. Their original plan was to arrive at the hall after the movie started and to take their seats at the back and in the dark, this cunning plan was doomed to fail from the outset. The whole theatre hushed as they all turned their heads to watch the couple take their seats in the back row.

'Let her rip Merle.' came from the front seats who had been waiting the longest.

The long movie was in three reels, so after each reel Merle would turn on the lights as she changed the reel while her sister, Shirley, would open the lolly shop. Dan stood up and joined the queue for a paper-bag of soft jubes and a bottle of lemonade, the kids in the line would look at him a giggle, the guys would give him a wink and a nudge while Molly's friends rushed over to her for a quick gossip. The older women in the hall would think back to their younger days of innocence before they succumbed to the script that had been written for them at birth. This script was to burden them by having multiple kids and the drudgery of the life of a woman living on the Chathams. Their men, of course were down the pub.

Molly had rode horseback to town that afternoon and dressed at Jed and Lynn's and to stay the night. After the sad ending that was appropriate to the name of the film 'Gone with the Wind' Molly took Dan's arm, as they walked towards Jed's place Dan remembered the apple blossom.

'I brought you a present, but I left it at the Post Office, it's not much but I think you'll like it, maybe,'

'You brought me a present?'

'Yes, I did, well, I didn't actually buy it, maybe we can walk along the beach, that is, if you want to,'

'Hey Dan, I really, really want to.'

The pub was closed, and all was quiet as they walked down the steps onto the beach, Molly held onto Dan's shoulder for balance while she took off her shoes. With her free hand she guided him onto the damp hard sand and water's edge,

'That's better,' she said, 'my shoes were hurting.' what she didn't say was that she had borrowed them from Lynn and had spent the afternoon learning to walk in high-heels.

As they strolled shoulder to shoulder, they talked of the film which was set in the American Civil war; they talked of the slavery of the Negro and of the personalities of Rhett Butler and Scarlet O'Hara.

The apple blossom spray looked lonely on the bench but came to life as he wove it into her hair above her right ear, he kissed her forehead.

'I'll make us a hot drink.'

Sipping scalding hot tea, they sat on the ancient stuffed couch that Dan had rescued from the rubbish dump and had installed it on his porch. They shared a blanket, without speaking, they both held onto this moment in time. May this night last forever.

Molly broke the silence,

'I wonder why Rhett never told Scarlet he loved her, it was obvious he did, he would arrive from who knows where, they would spend passionate time together, then they would disagree on something minor, argue and the next thing he would just mysteriously disappear, I don't get it,'

'Yes, he was a bit of a mystery, I suppose he had to because of what he was up to in the Civil war,'

'What was he doing?'

'He was a gun runner dealing with both the Yankee's and the Confederates, which was a pretty dangerous game to play. My guess is that he was also a spy for both sides, selling information to the highest bidder, a dangerous game in which he had to protect himself,'

'So, you think he was just using her,'

'No, no, I think he did love her in his own way but kept his distance, he knew that if he did commit himself to her, he would just become another one of her possessions, she would use him, become bored and then discard him,'

Molly had to think about that for a while.'

'Scarlet was portrayed as a petulant, spoiled little brat, maybe she had to be like she was to protect herself, especially after her parents were murdered by the Yankees,'

'Protect herself from what?' although he knew the answer to that as he asked the question.

'I think she had plenty to be wary of, loneliness, for one, then there was the Yankee's who were making their way south, also, she probably never realized that her maid was probably her wet nurse when she was a baby,'

'Yes, you could be right because she was more than just a maid to her, pity Scarlet never realized that but there is no way she would accept having a surrogate mother who was black,'

'As for her father who was the plantation owner, who traded by the buying and selling of slaves, did you notice the slaves of mixed blood working in the fields, maybe he fathered them, I don't think he was a nice man,'

'Mulatto, they used to be called, they often took on the name of their white father, the mixed blood slaves were worth more on the auction block.'

They were quiet for a while, Dan broke their silence,

'What about you, are you lonely?'

'Well, I shouldn't be, I've got my sisters and brothers around me,' she stopped and looked down, 'My Mum died when I was fourteen and I'm the oldest, lonely? I guess I am, I shouldn't be but I am. I'm expected to take the place of being a mother, but I can't do that, I live on a day-to-day basis', she hesitated. 'With no future,'

'Do you dream?'

'Yes, I do, in-between keeping myself safe'.

Dan could relate to that, his life was spent in keeping himself safe, but he could see that Molly in keeping herself safe was far different than him, they both, in their different situations lived in a dangerous world.

They were quiet again; this time Molly broke the silence.

'You are a stranger in this land, so, what about you?'

'Me?' Dan retreated to the defensive, 'me? well, I'm not lonely now,' he lied.

She could see that she touched a nerve with that one and raised her eyebrows waiting for him to carry on.

He concentrated on looking out to the dark sea where his answer lay, he swallowed, 'Yes, I have a story to tell and tell it I will, but not tonight, for me, tonight has, is, great. I like being with you, do you think we can do this again, that's if you want?'

She was stepping into unknown territory that may be fraught with danger, exciting danger, she took a hesitant step telling herself she could always step back. What Molly didn't understand was that her heart was more powerful than her brain.

"Yes, yes I want, that's if I can trust you,'

'You can, shall I walk you home?'

Dan floated back down the hill totally unaware of the ghost of Rose was fading into oblivion.

The next few days was spent thinking of an excuse to ride out to Marakarpia and Molly. What could be better than mixing business with pleasure. Dan's concept of supplying peat bricks to not only the pub and a few households but to supply the government entities in Waitangi who were supplied coal that was imported from N.Z. for cooking and heating by their respective agencies. There were the police, teachers, hospital, Met and radio stations, resident commissioner and so on, but this was going to take a bit of organizing. First, was to inspect the Whangaroa clears on the quantity, quality, accessibility of the peat and of course this inspection would take him past Molly's home at Marakarpia.

Prior to Captain Broughton nailing his bit of lead on a Kopi tree Rekohu was heavily forested and populated by the hunter gather Moriori for many hundreds of years. With the arrival of the Pakeha deforestation quickly decimated the Island to render whale oil, to fire the boilers of fish processers and to clear the land to make way for sheep and cattle that fed a modern economy. The destruction of these large tracts of woodland caused a climate change on these very fragile

Islands. The forests that had attracted rain slowly disappeared and as the protective bush opened, the drying winds entered every nook and cranny causing the erosion of the topsoil. Overall, the fertility of the land diminished and was not being replaced, wetlands and waterways have dried up. To reverse this decimation is simple, all it takes is a fence.

Anyway, let's get back to Dan, he could see that the burning of peat may reverse this deforestation an opportunity for him to make a living. His plan was to call in on Molly on his way to check out the peatland that ran from the end of long beach to the NW and Soanes light. From there to follow the coastline to Mike Gunns farm at Waitangi West. He sent a message to Molly, this time in a wax sealed envelope to keep out prying eyes. He wrote that he would be calling in at Marakarpia on his way around the north western coast.

Several days before he was ready to depart, he received a message from Mike that there was a mechanical problem with the Soanes navigation light and that he would meet Dan there on an agreed date to assist with repairs and maintenance.

Dan, riding Dusty with packhorse Ngaromi loaded with tools, spare parts, mail and stores for his hosts at Waitangi West, headed along the inland beach track, up and over Red Bluff and onto Long Beach. The highest point in the dunes was a basalt outcrop called Lilly Rock that had once been a significant place where Moriori souls departed to their mystic homeland.

The track branched off about half a mile past Lilly Rock up and over the dunes to Lake Marakarpia where, on the north side was a grove protected by the dominant Kopi and Ake Ake Forest. When Dan got to what he guessed was the Marakarpia farm he dismounted and tied his horses to a rail. He entered the house section through a punga gate to reveal a rundown homestead which was sorely in need of repairs and a coat of paint. On the front door there was a note from Molly inviting him up to the Te Karakau school and to bring his guitar with him. He left Ngaromi quietly grazing, strapped his guitar on his back and headed up the hill to the school that was protected by a Macrocarpa grove. Te

Karakau school was at that time the main school on the Island catering for the large families of the area that was generally known as Te Roto.

Molly was employed as a Teacher's Aid and was taking class when there was a knock on the door. She nodded to the eldest boy to open the door, surprised, the last thing he expected was a Pakeha guy with a guitar on his back.

Molly, blushing said to the boy, 'Don't just stand there, invite our guest in and offer him a seat.'

Dan looked around, there were only two chairs in the classroom, the Headmaster Michael O'Connell was sitting on one behind a desk, so Dan was offered the other, in the front, facing the class. The giggling class all sat cross-legged on cushions as Dan opened his knapsack and produced a few goodies he had put together for the class. A bundle of pencils, a ream of lined writing paper and several books on fictional adventure. The brown paper bag he pulled out was full of sweets that caused a stir, anything sugar was a rare treat.

Dan's presence ended any sort of concentration from the class, there was only one thing to do which was for Dan to do a bit of strumming on his guitar. He dredged up from memory, the children's songs he had learnt from way back on the La Nouse farm in Ireland. How about…

'Teddy bears picnic,' 'Yankee Doodle,'Frog went a Courtin.'

Brings back a few memories, don't it?'

Schools out and the younger Remi's piled into the back of Dusty while the older ones skylarked around, pumped up by the unaccustomed injection of the sugar laden lollies; all trying to impress the Dan, who was secretly flattered. They took the long way home down past the lake, where, kids being kids. were soon soaking wet. Unlike many of the tannin-stained waters of the Chathams the Lake Marakarpia waters are clear and potable. Due to inadequate water storage at their house that during the summer months the family had to cart water from the lake to the house for household use. During the warmer months it was easier for the kids to bathe and hair wash in the lake. Back at her house Molly had to cook dinner, which was mostly a one pot affair, she suggested that Dan go for a wander around the garden, he asked her,

'Where's your dad?'

'There is a party happening down the road which has been going for a few days, he'll be back when they run out of booze, if you want to stay the night there is a bed in the sleepout, I'll make it up for you, that's if you want to stay,'

'Mmmm,' he pretended to think, 'Well, seeing you have twisted my arm I guess I'll have to,'

'Not only are you the best in town but you're the easiest,' she stopped for a few seconds realizing what she had said, 'easiest to convince I mean.'

With a grin he wandered out of the kitchen to check the sleepout before it got dark. When he first saw the garden, he was taken by color, after the dunes, then the multiple greens of the forest that opened up to the brown-green fern paddocks, the colorful house garden was a contrast. It reminded him of the house garden of the La Nouse family back in the Emerald Isles, he shuddered, 'What am I getting myself into here?'

The house was nestled in amongst this color that was dominated by the blues and the forget-me-not and bluebells that were scattered in and around a kitchen garden of mainly silverbeet, cabbages and turnips. In a clearing protected by Ake Ake's and towering Kopi was the early spring stages of a spud patch. Close to the main house there were several out-houses built of punga with haphazard corrugated and flat iron roofs fastened to Matipo poles. The doorless long drop toilet gave a view of the lake to the sitter, alongside the toilet was a small grove of Rangiora, known as the 'bushman's friend', which provided a ready supply of paper. Dan had a look into one of the outhouses which had a wood fired copper alongside a rinsing tub that sat on a wooden stand. On one side of the shed was a bath cleverly built of Ake Ake, using metal strips constructed similar to a barrel built by a Cooper. He looked around for plumbing, that drew a blank, so it looked like the hot water had to be heated in the copper and bucketed into the bath. As he wandered around it began to dawn on him the enormous task that Molly had to endure the script that fate had written for her.

During the night Dan heard a commotion from inside the main house dominated by a loud male voice, their dad must have arrived home. As usual Dan's body clock had him up and about before dawn, the morning was windless as he wandered down towards the lake, he didn't get far in finding a dry place to sit and watch the morning unfold. The lake was like glass with the surface broken by the occasional duck or a swan with buried head searching for breakfast, the perfect place for meditation.

On his way back to the house he headed for the woodpile, picked up the axe that was buried in the chopping block, he run his fingers along the blade, 'you need sharpening' he said to the axe. His body soon loosened and warmed as he rhythmically split Ake Ake for morning wood and Matipo into larger pieces for when the fire was up and going. The Matipo had long lasting embers that kept a large kettle bubbling slowly during the day. The household was still asleep when he got into the kitchen, so he quietly cleaned the grate of the Shacklock stove and lay dried cabbage tree leaves, topped with Ake Ake kindling and got the fire going. The main kitchen, dining and living room was sparsely furnished, the oblong wooden table was surrounded by rickety bench seats, the floor was of a mixture of lime and fine schist that had packed down smooth and level and hardened by many years of use. Kitchen utensils were hung from No. 8 wire tightened above the stove; walls were bare with clay mortar filling the gaps between the wall planks. The only bit of color was a vase of arranged flowers sitting on the middle of the table. Up against one wall was a magnificent long, sturdy benched set of drawers that was built in place with aged, yellowed Ake Ake. This piece of furniture was very cleverly built that combined beauty, form and function that housed all the household items and the few family treasures. Although the door to the rest of the house was closed it looked to Dan that there was 2 bedrooms on each side of a hallway. Adjacent to the stove was a doorless pantry and sink, on the bench sat bags of flour and sugar and what he guessed was condiments behind a closed cupboard door. On the outside wall was a fine netted perishable food safe that protruded out onto the porch to catch any cooling breeze that wandered by.

These very basic living conditions reminded him of his homeland, he stood with his back to the warming stove as the household began to stir.

A sleepy Molly slowly walked into the warming kitchen, his heart melted as her face creased into a smile, she took in surroundings that was so different from her normal start to the day, the kitchen was warmed by the heat of the stove, there was steam rising from the kettle and a gorgeous man dominating her space.

'My sleepy beauty', he said, 'you O.K. this morning?'

'All the better for seeing you,'

Molly walked over to face him, they both held the others hand, bodies close but not quite touching.

'This the first time I've walked into a warm kitchen since my mum died, I think we should keep you on.'

It took all Dan's strength to stop himself from wrapping his arms around her, instead, he stood back and watched her start her day, his brain raced.

'Is there anything I can do?'

Molly felt a little exposed of Dan being in the kitchen watching her start her day, so she said.

'Yes, you could make useful outside with the axe and chopping block.'

Glad to have something physical to quell what was happening within has body and brain, again he attacked the woodpile with vigor.

(It's just us guys being guys, we can't help it, we see the world as a huge paddock in which to spread our seed)

School time for Molly and the kids, Dan saddled Dusty and Molly's mare Treacle and rode with them to school. Michael the headmaster, suggested to Molly that seeing she had a guest she should have a few days off and come back after the weekend. Molly lifted her eyebrows, so Michael, realizing the gesture added.

'With full pay of course.'

They rode around the farm and down to the lake, over the dunes and onto the beach. Dan could see that the farm was in a poor state, partly because of neglect but mainly because of just 200 acres was uneconomical and was another subsistence farm on the Chathams. Sheep wandered through boundary fences as if they didn't exist and internal fences were ineffective except for the house paddock, Molly made sure of that. Sheep had not been dipped, drenched or shorn, lambs not marked and in poor condition, the wild horses off the dunes and the neighbors' cattle wandered in and out as they pleased.

They dismounted and sat on the hill overlooking the lake, Dan understated.

'Looks like the farm needs a bit of work, does your dad own the land?'

'No, he doesn't, it's owned by the women of the family, my mum and her three sisters, their dad died and left all his land to all his children. Then the men shut the women out, so they took their brothers to the Māori Land Court and the judge allocated this farm to the women'.

'I guess that was rare in those days,'

'Sure was, the males still haven't got over that one yet, now my mum's gone, me, and my sisters have succeeded.'

'So, one day you'll be a farmer,'

'Not too sure about that one, my dad's heart is not into the land he used to be a fisherman and I think that the salt water still runs through his veins, along with all the beer he drinks,'

'Yeah, I understand that, I'm lost if I can't see the sea.'

'Before my mum died, he built his own boat so he could go fishing, he has lots of abilities but they have all gone by the wayside,'

'Did he build that cabinet with the drawers that's in your kitchen?'

'He built all the furniture in the house, but now, for him, there's a demon in the bottle that he just doesn't have the strength or will to chase away.'

A sense of anger passed over her, she continued,

'See all this land here,' she indicated the paddocks on the rise to the peat lands which included her neighbors on each side, 'In the past produced wheat and potatoes for export, sadly those days are well and truly gone.'

'What happened?'

'The war, when the first world war started shipping became near non-existent and has been erratic since then, for several years the farmers planted acres and acres of spuds, but they just couldn't get them to the markets and when they did, they got paid bugger all, so it was just not worth it. Most of the crop just rotted in the ground for several years. I wouldn't care if I never saw another spud in my life, we had them boiled, roasted, chipped, fried, hangi'd, mashed, pied, soup and even with milk for pudding.'

Sounds a bit like Ireland, except that we got blight which led to a famine,'

'Mmmm, tell me about Ireland, is it an island?'

He laughed, 'Yes, I suppose it is an island,'

'Are there emeralds there?'

'I wish, no, I think it is because of the green, green grass of home, what I remember most is poverty.'

'I've heard a few Irish jokes,'

'Yes, that's us, and they are all true.'

When she laughed it was like seeing a darkened room suddenly blink into life with a thousand lights, that was something he didn't want to change. He wanted to tell her of every sorrow he knew. He didn't want to tell her the lies of a romantic Ireland, that the fairies, the Leprechauns were just tales of a past that may have existed a long time ago. The truth lay in a haunting story that his mother told him of the potato famine, that she, as a child with her old grandmother holding her hand, walked through a devastated land, clasping a penny in her palm. She remembers her mother biting her trembling lip as they wandered the Irish countryside looking for shelter, warmth and food. His mother, orphaned by the famine had taught him a poem of those times of poverty and the suffering of the people in death. Every time she told the poem her tears would flow.

'The grass waves green above them,
Soft sleep is theirs.
The hunt is over, and the cold.
The hunger has passed away.'(anon)

Most of all, he was afraid of his own truth. Instead, he simply said, 'It wasn't so nice.'

'If I didn't have a heap of kids to look after and was in control of the land, I would get rid of the sheep, they bring out the worst in me, and graze a few cattle. I find it frustrating that the bush is disappearing before my eyes and am powerless to do stop it. I would fence off the wetlands and the lake and what areas of bush that are left. The island is always short on fresh vegetables and with the land being so fertile I could probably scratch out a living, but...'

'There is always a but, but what?'

'That's not going to happen, it's going to take money and that's a rare item around here, and as for the tribe of kids I have to look after, well, they are not going to go anywhere soon.'

'There is more to life than the Chathams, and, we have but one life, so, in your wildest dreams what would you like to achieve.'

'Me? A teacher? I would love to teach. But, yes, another but, I've thought a lot about it. Getting off this island and going to teachers' training college is my dream.'

'The good thing about teaching is, come 3.00 in the afternoon they all go home.'

She laughed, 'I wish.'

'Somebody once said to me that we can have everything that we work for.'

'Maybe so, but, oops, another but, but there are times when I see myself doing what I'm doing for the rest of my life, this island is dominated by male privilege who treat women as if we were born without a voice. It is common here for women not to have a choice in a marriage that may have been arranged many years beforehand. There are tragic stories of women who have followed their hearts over the demands of their elders, that won't be happening to me, well, unless a Rhett Butler comes along.'

She suddenly stood up in anger and swung herself on the back of Fern and said to Dan.

'Nobody, nobody is going to tell me what to do with my life.' she gave a flick of her reigns and cantered back to the house paddock with Dan struggling to catch up.

Molly's father was sitting at the table with a cup of tea when they walked in, he scowled at Dan,

'Who are you?'

'This is my dad, Totara,'

'I'm Dan,' offering his hand.

Totara ignored it, 'You must be the man I'm hearing about around town,'

'All good, I hope.'

Totara scowled again, 'Are all these stories about the Irish being thick, true stories?'

Dan laughed, 'Every word you hear about the Irish is true, give or take a little, did you hear the one about the Irishman who...'

'I don't want to hear it, you better sit down and have a cuppa, daughter, make this man a cuppa,'

'That's my dad, as welcoming as ever,'

'I'm Irish and used to it, water off a duck's back,'

'Water on the brain, what brings you to this god-forsaken place.'

'Everything that's here has flown or floated, I floated,'

'Smartarse, what are you doing hanging around my house and my daughter?'

'Sir, I have come here to listen to your fine words of wisdom and I'm not disappointed, it's my pleasure to make your acquaintance,'

Taken back a little, Totara softened, 'You'll do, just mind your manners and keep your hands off' 'a my daughter or I'll knock your block off, anyway,' he looked at Molly, 'I've got something to tell you,'

Dan stood, 'I think I will go for a wander,' and wandered out to the woodshed.'

'You've got a new mum,'

Molly paled in shock, 'What do you mean, a new mum?'

'Your auntie is coming here to live with us,'

She stood in anger, 'Auntie Marama, is she bringing her kids with her?'

He nodded; her anger turned to fury. 'Where is everybody going to sleep? How we going to feed them all? This place is crowded already, and I don't want this woman living in my house.'

'This is my decision, I have decided, and you have no say in this matter, anyway, she will be able to take some of your workload off you,'

'She's fat and she's lazy, and she's not my mother, and will never be,'

'Your brothers and sisters will be stoked to have their cousins to play with, and...' He was trying to think of something else. 'And I'm going to get a job with Tim Brown to build his new house.'

'You, get a job? next thing, pigs will fly.'

'And it will increase the school roll and you might get paid a bit more from that miserable headmaster of yours,'

'I am not a child anymore and have the right to have a say in this,'

'No, you don't', he put his head in his hands, 'go away, I've got a headache.'

'A headache, you are going to have more than a headache when that lot move in.' she slammed the door on her way out.

Dan was back on the woodpile stacking, he had heard the door slam, 'What's up?'

Molly couldn't speak as she marched in fury down to the back garden, Dan followed, she picked up a hoe and was vigorously attacking weeds. When he caught up her she stormed off and went over to the spud patch and needlessly mounded the rows, he caught up again and pulled at a few weeds, feeling helpless, her frantic hoeing slowed, then stopped.

'I'll cry tomorrow.'

'Let's walk.' he said.

Molly dropped the hoe, and they wandered up the gully to the wetland as Molly, on the brink of tears told him what Totara had said.

'I'm on my way to meet Mike Gunn at the Soanes light for a couple of days work, come with me?'

'But, I can't, I've got to...'

'Molly, think about it and this time no more buts.'

She was silent as it dawned on her that, if she wanted, a huge load could be lifted from her shoulders. She stopped and lifted her head and looked Dan directly in the eye.

'Maybe, just maybe I'm free, I'm twenty years old and for the first time in my life I'm free, you're right, no more buts, I don't have to do this anymore.'

A wave of emotion engulfed her as, without thinking she wrapped her arms around him, she could hear and feel his heart beating before realizing what she had done, she pulled back and spoke.

'Yes, yes, yes, I'm coming with you, good things happen when you are around.'

Holding her at arm's length, he couldn't find the right words as he felt a stab of anguish, 'I'm living a lie he thought, 'what the hell am I doing to this girl?' all he could say was.

'You don't know me yet.'

'Well, I like what I've found so far, I'm coming with you.'

When they got back to the house, she left Dan to get the horses ready and went inside to tell her dad what was happening, he was still at the table nursing his hangover.

'I've had time to think about Auntie coming here to live, I now know that for the first time in my life I have a choice. I'm going to Waitangi West for a few days with Dan, in the meantime you'll just have to manage the best you can until that woman and her tribe get here.'

He sat there still with elbows on the table and head in his hands, he looked up and made one of his longest speech's he had ever made in his life to his daughter.

'I think that's the best way out, we both have been grieving in our own way for too long and that is not going to change itself, it's been, how long? 10 years now. In many ways you are your mother and I have always blamed her for dying on us, I blame myself because of the way she died, it wasn't her fault she got sick. I just never thought she would die. I've realized lately that my anger towards you is because you are so much like her, and...' he had run out of words,

Molly's anger left her, he added.

'I'm not the father I should be, I just...'

He sat up straight and put his hands on the table.

'I'm not sure if this will work out, your Aunt Marama is pretty fiery but since her old man buggered off to NZ she has nowhere else to live; she can cook and is good with kids, it should work out okay.'

'Well, you are going to find out soon enough, it's up to you to make it work and it will work if you want it to. I guess it is an opportunity for both of us, for you the party is over and for me, I'm off to Waitangi West in the morning,'

'Where you gonna sleep?'

'Mind your own business.'

After dinner that night and the house was quiet with the family in bed, Dan and Molly were sitting in front of the stove which had the oven door open so they could warm their feet, Dan asked,

'What happened to your mum?'

'She died in the kitchen here, the Doctor was too late, and, and she just died.'

'That must have been absolutely terrible.' Molly quickly stood and walked out of the kitchen, she returned a few minutes later with a book, she thumbed through the pages until she found her place, she couldn't read through her watering eyes so just stared sightlessly into the oven.

'What are you reading?'

She recovered, 'Short stories by Somerset Maughan, have you heard of him?'

'I have, but never read his stuff, I once had a friend, Pieter, who always talked of him but it sounded a bit deep for me, how did you get to know him?'

'My boss at school, he gets all these books sent to him from the Education Department which is my job to read to the class but most of the time it is way over their heads. They'd prefer comics but that's not what gets sent to us, Michael calls comics 'penny horribles'. How do they expect Chatham Island kids to relate to something like, like that poem, 'Host of Golden Daffodils'.

'Something tells me that they would be more into something like 'Blackbeard the Pirate.'

'The good thing is that Michael passes these books on to me after he has read them, are you a reader?'

'Off and on, I like stories of explorers, you know, books about men who go out looking for adventure on a white horse and fall in love with a beautiful maiden.'

'You have landed in the wrong place for that,'

'Don't agree with you on that one, although, the best I can find around here are cowboy comics or something like the Classic Comics, one of my favorites is 'Twenty Thousand Leagues under the Sea'.

'That sounds pretty deep,'

It took him about 10 seconds to pick up on that one.

'The quality of the writing or do you mean the depth of the sea?'

They both laughed.

'Have you got anything I can read?'

She got up and walked out of the kitchen to come back and hand him a book.

'To Kill a Mockingbird', he read the title out loud, 'I wonder why you'd want to kill a mockingbird, what's it all about?'

'Well, it's about the wisdom of Atticus who says that we should walk a mile in the other persons shoes.'

'That don't tell me much, what's your favourite?'

'I've got lots of favourites, there is one that saved my life, 'Anne of Green Gables.'

He waited for her to explain.

'Anne taught me how to be me, from her I learnt how to be strong, brave, how to be patient'. She stopped for a while, 'When my mum died, I didn't think that there was any way to overcome the pain and grief that would be with me forever. How could a God do this to me?

After reading Anne's story Iearned that this is the reality of life and that in my heart and soul never to give up. Like Anne, I never gave up and I will succeed because I am me and at the end of it all, it will only be me.'

As Dan was trying to absorb all this she carried on,

'Maybe sometime in the future I will be able to trust, the one thing I do know is that I will never trust a god, especially a male god.'

'As for me,' he said, 'I don't think I will ever meet this guy Atticus or Anne for that matter, but they sound like wise people, even though they never existed in real life.'

'The sad thing I find with fictional characters is that sometimes they die, or the book ends and we are left with just a memory.'

'I've been thinking about you in the fact that, in the end, everything will be OK, if it's not OK, then it is not the end.' (Thanks to John Lennon for that one).

'A bit of deep thinking going on here, how deep can you go?'

'About twenty thousand leagues deep.'

'In Ireland, are all people born equal?'

'The politicians and the church tell us that we are all born equal, if that is the case then some are born more equal than others. In saying that, I see life is like a game of cards, some, through no fault of their own, are dealt a bad hand, I think that it is what you do with the cards you are dealt with that counts in the long run.'

'You could be right; I have always wondered what that song by Kenny Rogers meant when he sings about the gambler...'

'Every hand's a winner, every hand's a looser
You got to know when to hold 'em, know when to fold 'em
Know when to walk away, know when to run.'

'So, you and I had better put a lot of thought in how we play our cards.' She said thoughtfully.

'So, if I play an ace will I win a Queen?'

'I have a feeling you are a bit like Rhett Butler, the ace of spades,'

'And you Molly, are my Queen of hearts.'

'I think we both need to watch out for the most dangerous card in the pack. 'The Joker.'

After Molly got the kids off to school, they saddled Dusty and Treacle, tied a split sack to Ngaromi and loaded Dans tools, bed rolls, a canvas fly in case of rain, flour, tea etc. Their main hunter, gatherer, was Molly's dog, Drive, who was jumping up and down ready for adventure,

'What's the breed of your dog?'

'He's a bitza, bitz of everything, he can do anything, OK with sheep, loves herding cattle, a soft mouth for catching weka's, he thinks the whole farm is his dinner plate, he even eats paua's, loves crayfish, I call him Drive because he drives me crazy, keeps bringing me weka's and swan eggs from the lake.'

'We won't go short of food then,'

'If it was up to him, we would have to employ a full-time chef.'

They rode over the dunes and onto the beach and headed north and west on the beach track, about halfway towards the end of the beach they climbed the dunes to the Dix Urapa at Te Roto. Molly had been walking for a while silently picking flowers which she placed on a mound in the Urapa which was identified by a oil polished 'heart of Ake Ake' cross with the name 'Te Hau' imbedded. Molly wandered, pulling a few weeds here and there, straitened a fence post while she talked to her ancestors. She had told Dan that most Chatham Islanders relate back to this Urapa and that her mum rested in a peace that she had never found while alive. The day had warmed, so they both stretched out in the sun, with hats on faces, snoozing alongside the dead.

A mile or so further on they rode through sparse bush to the site of Te Roto Pah, this where Molly's great-grandfather was taken in by Ngati Mutunga after he had jumped the Portuguese whaler he was indentured to. They fossicked around the remains of the once populated village finding interesting objects of a daily existence of past generations. Dan found three adze's that had been partially buried under a tree, must had been a hiding place of the owner, he put them back where that had lain for 100 years or more. 'Probably Moriori', said Molly. She showed Dan the cannonball made of marble that she had found as a child then reburied it in a fissure in the craggy limestone where it had lain since the 1830s.

'Marble,' said Dan, 'That's interesting, how did that get here?'

'It's a long story, this Pah was attacked when the Chathams was at war with France, I'll tell you about it sometime,'

'Yes please, I'm interested, I wonder what life was like for your ancestors in those days,'

'There was a lot of bad stuff happening back then, Te Roto Pah was regarded as a haven for any lost souls, like my ancestor Joe Diaz. He changed his name to Dix. Moriori were often persecuted so they came here for protection. As I said, there were a lot of bad things going on, no law enforcement, one good thing was that when the missionaries came, they taught us that our old ways were not the ways of a Christian.'

'What old ways?'

'Slavery and eating one another for a start,'

'Well, I don't suppose we can judge history by contemporary standards.'

With that they mounted their steeds and rode over the clears to Port Hutt, each lost in their own thoughts.

They arrived in the small settlement of Whangaroa, known as Port Hutt, nestled in a deep narrow bay which is protected from all wind directions and was the safest anchorage on the Chathams. Being so narrow and the sometimes-boggy track to Waitangi its use for larger vessels is limited. There was a collection of huts in line along the beach, hence the name Port Hutt. Seated on the porch was the Commodore and his mate Bun Bun Poki chewing on a bottle of homemade firewater while shooting the breeze. The Commodore was also known as the 'Walking Newspaper' because of his knowledge and opinion of current affairs, what he didn't know, he invented. Dan and Molly were naturally expected to stay the night and share Bun Bun's bubbling pot of weka's, spuds and watercress. The bottle of firewater had the conversation travelling along lively with the main subject being the sanity of Hitler and the war in Europe and that some time in the future they may be having to speak the German language.

The Commodore had just received a letter from his fisherman mate, Bruce Kyle, who had signed up with the fledgling RNZ Navy and was currently serving on a minesweeper patrolling the waters around northern N.Z. Bruce wrote them about the mine they had detected, and the Minesweeper's marksman had detonated the mine with a .303 rifle. The Commodore reconned that the minesweeper, being built of steel and hunting for magnetic mines was likened to pouring petrol onto a fire to extinguish it.

What Dan didn't know was that the minesweeper was the Thomas Currall on which he had shoveled coal out of Dublin. After her life of cod and halibut fishing in the North Sea she was sold to a Wellington based fishing company owned by Albert Meo. While grouper fishing in Cook Strait the war broke out and she was commandeered by the Navy who had her boilers replaced by a diesel motor and gen-set to become a minesweeper. The mine described by Bruce had been set by the German Raider 'Aquarius' which was responsible for the sinking of the Niagara out off Whangarei Heads.

Just in case it has slipped your mind it was the Aquarius that had sunk the Liverbird in the North Sea which caused Dan so much grief throughout his life.

After the war the Thomas Currell went back fishing Cook Strait till the crayfish boom started on the Chathams when she was sent to Port Hutt to support what became known as the 'last gold rush'. While on anchor one night she began to take in water and was run up on the beach by the nightwatchman, Eric Dix, where she still sits today: for several years her generator-set powered Port Hutt.

They all slept well, lulled by the Commodore's firewater and Bun Bun's boilup, Totarawould have been pleased to know that Molly slept in Bun Bun's spare bed and Dan spent the night on the couch on the Commadore's porch.

The next day they stopped off to rest the horses and a cuppa along-side the creek on the small beach at the end of the long inlet of Ocean Bay. As they gathered twigs and dried fern to start a fire, they both became acutely aware of the other, avoiding contact, conversation was stilted as they concentrated on getting the fire going. The horses were grazing quietly drinking from the tannin-stained creek of which makes a great cup of tea. Dan wandered along the beach picking up the odd piece of barnacle covered sawn timber, he found a short plank that had bent and tarnished copper nails imbedded, when he got back to the fire he asked Molly if she knew anything about his find.

'It's connected to the canon-ball we looked at yesterday, there was a French whaler that was sunk in the bay here and the canon-ball was fired by French Naval ship, which had been on its way to Akaroa to claim the South Island for France, but instead it diverted to the Chathams.'

'So if the French had claimed Akaroa before the English got there you could all be speaking French,'

'I guess we could be, do you know any French?'

'Arrr, bon jour, mademoiselle.'

'What does that mean?'

'You're a pretty girl,' he lied.

Mike was already working on the gen-set which charged the batteries to power the Soanes Point navigation light, that, in conjunction with the Durham light, guided vessels into Petri Bay. By late afternoon they realized the job was taking longer than they thought so they set up camp in the shepherd's hut at Te Raki. The cod was easy to catch off the rocks and Mike volunteered to do be the chef so Dan and Molly, with the perfectly volcano shaped Monument Hill behind them walked, hand in hand, down to the beach. The rising ground behind them had created an amphitheater. With the low tide and emerging rocks in the lee of the SE wind created a stage-like setting. Once again, nature was the star of the show. At the high tide mark the paua shells glistened in the softening late afternoon sun; as their lengthening shadows became one, Dan, the master of understatement, simply said.

'Perfection.'

'Bella McLurg used to come to this remote place and loved it so much that she wrote a poem about the waves running up the beach and washing over the glistening paua shells, we learnt it a school,'

'Tell me.' he said.

Molly gathered her thoughts and said, 'It goes something like this'.

'The paua shell bride of the shore.
Her beauty glistening in the sun,
her groom as a wave,
running up the beach to kiss his bride,
to gaze at the wonder of her beauty.
He would back off then again
run up the beach to kiss her.
As the tide recedes
He reaches out to her
The tide turns and
he becomes stronger and stronger until
again, he can run up the beach and
kiss his bride.'

Their kiss was passionate.

Late the next afternoon they arrived at the Waitangi West homestead to be welcomed by Mikes wife Maria; she had been a teacher at the Pitt Island school and met Mike who was cod fishing around Pitt at that time. With the sudden death of his father Mike reluctantly gave up fishing to run the family farm, with saltwater running through his veins he had difficulty in tolerating life as a farmer, his passion was the ocean which is a far cry from managing 5,000 sheep on a 8,000 acre property. There was no school near this isolated part of the Chathams, so Maria homeschooled the few children of the area.

After dinner and with Dan and Molly being unmarried Maria showed them their sleeping arrangements, Molly had the spare bedroom and Dan was to sleep in the shearer's quarters, Maria said to Dan,

'No tippy-toeing in the night, you won't get away with that because the floorboards squeak and I'm a very light sleeper.'

Both Dan and Molly were at the stage of their relationship when each of them, for their own reasons were happy to keep their lives uncomplicated. However, they both knew that this uncomplication was unstoppable. Will Molly escape her bitter youth of a lost childhood?, would Dan put to rest the ghost of Rose, or were they both just dreaming?

Those few days with Mike and Maria were, for Molly, the lifting of the huge load that she had carried around for most of her life. She found a freedom that she had never known because of the responsibility of keeping her and her siblings safe. Good things happen when Dan is around.

Dan had brought the mail out from the Post Office which included a large parcel with American postage stamps, that had taken a year to get to the Chathams. The whole island was abuzz in gossip of what was in the parcel from the U.S. of A. Uncle Ned, in reference to Katey, Ray's American wife reconned it was another mail order bride.

It was more interesting than that, two masks, two snorkels, two sets of flippers and two thin rubber body suits with zips.

'What the hell do you do with this stuff?'

'Ever heard of a frogman?'

'A frogman?'

'Yes, a frogman. I saw them advertised in the American publication 'Popular Mechanics', Mike demonstrated by putting the mask over his head and the snorkel in his mouth.

'What do you do then?'

'You jump in the bloody water,'

'Like a frog?'

'That's the theory, you can swim along the surface with perfect visibility and breathe through the snorkel, the fins enable you to dive deep like a seal while holding your breath,'

'What will they think of next?'

'I first got interested from an article I read about these American Navy divers who would be dropped off at night by a submarine close to the German ports in the Baltic. They would dive down and attach explosives with a timer on the hulls of the German ships'.

'The Baltic? sounds cold and dangerous to me.'

'That's what the rubber suits are for, they wear full body woolen underwear which warms up the water inside the suit,'

Dan, thinking of the freezing North Sea, 'Do you think a couple of hot water bottles would fit inside the suit as well?'

'These divers,' said Mike, 'have a life expectancy of 3 months, that's how dangerous it is, anyway, I think we should go for a swim tomorrow.'

Molly's eyes brightened, 'If there is such a thing as a frogman then there has to be a frogwoman.'

Flat arse calm the next morning, so they all took turns in having a practice swim with the gear in the shallow rock pools down from the house. Fear was the first obstacle that quickly disappeared as they all discovered a whole new world that in the past they had never knew existed.

Dan had been hesitant at first but once he saw all the underwater food that was available at his fingertips he was hooked. Molly was so excited she said that after she died, she would reincarnate as a seal.

Maria said that her wish would be to reincarnate as a shag who had the ability to walk on land, swim in the sea and fly in the sky.

Mike's wish was to reincarnate as a lady's bicycle in Amsterdam.

'What about you Dan?'

'Me, well, with my luck I would probably reincarnate as myself.'

That night they prepared, with excitement building for the next day in the more challenging and deeper waters of Tubung, Mike gave his opinion of life under the water.

'Four-fifths of this planet is covered in water which the people of the world never get to see, for us, it's like having another planet at our doorstep that we are going to be part of. Sleep well because tomorrow we will be exploring our planet.'

At low tide the next morning Mike got his ancient Fordson tractor fired up with Dan on the crank handle, they hitched the flatdeck trailer loaded with gear for their big day out in the briny along the beach to Tubung. This extensive schist point was home to an abundance of bird and marine mammal life that because of their isolation they had little fear of humans.

Mike and Maria were first in the water while Dan and Molly set up camp, lighting three fires, one for cooking and the other two for warming cold bodies. The rubber suits were nowhere as efficient as the neoprene wetsuits of today. After about an hour in the water filling up a kete with kai moana the shivering Mike and Maria changed into warm clothing between the fires and handed the cold wet suits over, as divers know all too well that there is that one thing that is equal to a hovering shark was donning a wet wetsuit.

Mike handed Molly a spear,

'What am I supposed to do with this?'

'Fill the pantry.'

'Let's just go for a swim.' she said to Dan as she stuck the spear into the sand.

The soon to be lovers swam out to a depth of about 15 to 20 feet and became a part of this amazing environment. The long seaweed that was clamped onto the rocky seabed reached up towards the sunlit surface swayed in unison with the bull kelp that was attached to the shallower basalt that spread its fronds over the surface. The gentle surging swells of the sea likened the bull kelp to that of the long hair of a maiden swaying in a soft breeze. The ledges protected the inquisitive lobsters, the ravenous blue cod nibbling at any bare human flesh they could find, paua and kina sharing the abundant food on the seabed, a stingray swam between them at midwater checking out these intruders.

Dan, while swimming down to the seabed saw a flash of black out the corner of his mask, his brain told him the dreaded word 'Shark'. By the time he got to the surface he was hyperventilating, he looked around for Molly who was floating on the surface, he grabbed her shoulder and franticly pointed back to where he had come from, there was nothing to be seen. Molly then took a deep breath and dived down towards the seabed while the terrified Dan watched, then from nowhere a young seal appeared alongside Molly, he realized then that the seal was mimicking their diving to the seabed and then back to the surface again.

'I thought it was a shark!' Dan told her after he took his snorkel from his mouth.

She coughed and spluttered while laughing, 'Never, will I ever let you forget that one.'

Mike was in charge of the medley of fish that was sizzling in home-made butter in his cast iron pan, spuds were wrapped in bull kelp pouches and buried in the sand under the embers.

'Now I've seen the world as a fish sees the world, tough life, eat or be eaten, starting from the smallest through to the biggest.'

'Bit like us humans, sometimes we don't see the forest because the trees are in the way,'

'What the hell has that got to do with the price of fish?'

'He thinks he is that Greek philosopher Archimedes,'

'Archimedes was a mathematician.' Said Maria the schoolteacher. 'I think you mean Socrates.'

'He'll do, actually he invented a fast way of counting sheep,'

'So you're telling me he invented the abacus?'

'No, he didn't need one of those, all he did was to count their feet and divide by four.'

'Michael, you can be a pain at times.'

'I've changed my mind about reincarnation, I would like to be a spaceman and look at the world from outer space.'

'I think our lives would be pretty insignificant from out there.'

'Actually, I've always wondered if there is anybody out there watching us?'

'Maybe Jesus is coming, in that case maybe we better look busy.'

'Here we go again,' said Maria, 'Just remember not to believe everything you think.'

R.I.P. Mike

31

THE MAN IN THE BLACK BOWLER HAT

was leaning on the gunnel of the Rangatira as she tied up to the wharf. Dan was lifting the heavy mooring line onto the mid-ship bollard looked up to see a man staring intently at him. He initially felt unnerved at the intentness of the piercing eyes of this man who looked completely out of place on a ship in this remote part of the world. Then a stab of fear and horror cut into him.

'Impossible.' spurted out from his mouth.

Jack was working alongside him, asked. 'What's impossible?'

'Nothing.'

'That's not like you Dan, you once told me that nothing was impossible.'

'You hit a bullseye with that one Jack.'

The gangplank was lowered onto the wharf and as usual, Boson was the first to board. On his way up the steps leading up to the bridge he welcomed the man in the black bowler hat to the Chathams. The man just nodded without speaking. Not far behind Boson was the resident Commissioner, Bill who greeted the man, then they both walked down the gangplank to Bill's Landrover. Bill opened the passenger door and as he was climbing in the man said something to Bill, they both looked over towards Dan. Bill closed the passenger door and as the man walked around the back of the Rover he again looked intently at Dan.

Smoko time, so Dan climbed the steps to the bridge and was greeted by Capt. Ward. After the usual conversation which happens between seafarers on any ship in the world which is centered on sea conditions, weather forecast and even in this remote part of the world, the possibility or even the probability of enemy ships lurking of a soft target. Dan, as casual as he could muster up, asked him about the Man in the Black Bowler Hat.

'His name on the passenger list was George Gently, any conversation with him was one-sided, his response was mostly just a yes or a no. He had a Pommy accent and always wore that black bowler hat of his, even in the mess, the crew reckoned he probably even slept in it. He was met at the wharf by the Commissioner so he must be an official of some sort, maybe connected with the army...' He stopped when he saw the ashen look on Dan's face.

'I'd take care if I was you.'

When the Rangatira clewed up and set sail for Lyttelton Dan walked back to his jail which was slowly turning into a comfortable home. he cleaned up before heading to the pub for a warm beer. With a bit of luck maybe Bill Miller, a fisherman come barber, would give him a haircut in exchange for a bottle of Wards. As he walked out his front door, he looked to his left towards the Post Office and saw Molly collecting mail. He called out, both faces lit up. He hurried towards her as she, trying to be casual as, slowly locked her P.O. box and turned to face him, he slowed, also trying to look as casual as she was. It was all just a façade; he extended his arms, and she dropped her mail as they embraced, tight.

'I've missed you,' her voice broke as she spoke.

'I wake in the morning, you are on my mind, I go to bed at night, you are on my mind.'

They kissed, gently at first then with passion.

'Wow!'she said coming up for air. 'I'm sure I've got bruised lips,'

He laughed, 'Me too, feels like I've just done 10 rounds with Joe Louis,'

'I was hoping to see you, I knew you were working the ship so...'

'So, here we are, you're looking great,'

'I'm feeling great, I've got some great news to tell,'

He was holding both her hands and could feel excitement running through her fingers,

'Well, come on, out with it, don't keep me in suspense.'

'You know that job at Te One School I was telling you about? Well, I went for an interview with Judy, but I didn't think I had any show of getting it, but I can hardly believe it myself, but I've got the job,'

'You got it, Yah-bloody-hoo,' He kissed her forehead, 'That's fantastic, so, so you're on your way to being a teacher?'

'Well, a long way from that, for now I am Teachers Aid and Office Manager, can you believe it, a teacher and an office manager, all in one day, and, she said that if it all goes well, she will help me get into Ardmore Teachers Training College, that's in Auckland.'

Her words just kept tumbling out in excitement.

'Auckland, that's a far cry from Marakarpia, when do you start working at Te One school?'

'Monday, Judy is letting me a room at the school house for during the week and I go home on the weekends.' She was still gushing with excitement.

'Does this mean we'll see more of each other?'

'Yes, yes, yes, Dan, good things happen when you're around.'

'I think we should celebrate, you keen?'

'As mustard, maybe we could have dinner at the pub.'

'In that case I had better have a shower, I was going to get a haircut if Bill Millar is in the bar,'

'I've heard about this shower if yours, how does it work?'

'Simple as, come in and see for yourself if you like, actually, after I've finished I can stoke up the fire and the water should be hot enough in a couple of hours, you can try it out...' He realized that his mouth was running away from his brain, he stopped, then added.

'That's if you want to, come back, that is, you can try it out some other time, that's if you want to,'

'I want to.'

He was confused, 'did she want to come back tonight? or was it some other time? Go with the flow Dan.' the said to himself.

Of course Bill Millar was in the bar, is the Pope a Catholic? While Dan was having his hair cut Molly went into the kitchen to see if Ollie wanted a hand, 'Always.' she said. After the guests were fed and dish's done Ollie, the eternal matchmaker, said.

'From what you just told me let's make this a very special night, you go and get your man and I'll make up a table for you, my treat by the way.'

The clipped and shorn Dan left Bill chewing on his bottle of Wards as Molly entered the bar and told him that they had been invited for dinner, free of charge. The Tube overheard that one, and said,

'Happy Jack shouting! He's that miserable he wouldn't shout if he fell off a cliff.'

Molly had never dined out in her life, either had Dan come to think of it, she radiated as she saw the table set for two, a starched white tablecloth, the candle in a silver holder, a single red rose, a bottle of wine, the man of her life. Enchantment soared.

There was a chill wind in their faces as they, hand in hand, walked slowly along the beach, they didn't speak or more likely couldn't speak. It was if that words would break the magic spell that had enveloped them into a cocoon where they, and only them, existed.

They stood at his front door, each nervously looking to the other, he opened the door and ushered her in. His room was warmed by the peat fire that he had stoked before dinner.

'The water should be hot enough, that is, if you still want to check out the shower.'

'Tonight, has been a night of firsts,' said Molly, 'Let's keep going with it.'

To get the shower to work Dan had to run a small electric pump to circulate the water from the wetback in the stove to a small cylinder that he had made from an old copper and installed it above the shower. There was a cold water tap above a sprinkler that he had adapted from a galvanised watering can which adjusted the water temperature.

Molly didn't want the shower to end, she was afraid, coupled with a sense of nervous excitement; she had no control over what was happening between her brain and body, was this reality? It was if she was hovering from above as a spectator watching the night evolve and that any attempt to change course would be futile. The door clicked ajar, and a white towel appeared held by a hand that hooked it onto a nail, the hand retreated, and the door clicked shut. The shower cooled so she stepped out and picked up the warmed towel that had been heated from of the fire, wrapped it around herself with tingling fingers, took a deep breath and floated into the room to stand close to the stove.

Dan was standing in the open front door looking out at the night sky, he turned. Her skin was a deep brown actuated by the white towel and the dull light of the room. He had left the fire door open on the stove and the flash of flames played with her hazel eyes, sometimes green, sometimes brown.

'You are beautiful, like a dream, a dream that will last forever.'

'Let's just hold onto our dream,' she reached out to him as her towel fell to the floor, 'for the first time in my life I feel beautiful, come, hold me, kiss me.'

This was not the time for words, a kiss, a hundred kisses, a thousand kisses, a thousand kisses deep. (A thousand thanks to Leonard Cohen for that one).

The next day was a Sunday, they walked the beach to Red Bluff completely oblivious to the blue of the sea. The white waves were running up the beach to meet them, then retreating, hesitating, to run up the beach to once again kiss their toes; oblivious to the skylarks calling for a mate; oblivious to the mollymorks gliding and skimming the waves; oblivious to the squawking of seagulls riding the breeze; oblivious to the wagging of tongues transporting this latest bit of juicy gossip that travelled several laps around the island. With each lap a bit more would be added to the story; the girls in the telephone exchange were having a field day.

'Molly's probably pregnant by now,'
'Guaranteed to be twins,'
'Doubt it, I heard that the Irishman is gay,'
'He is on the run from the law,'
'Or a woman,'
'The Irish hate the English so he could be a spy for the Germans,'
'The Germans will be pissed off because there is no Jews here,'
'I wouldn't bet on that one, the new County Clerk has a Jewish nose and he's that mean that he wouldn't tell you the time, even if you asked him.'
'I ate some sauerkraut once, disgusting stuff,'
'The Island needs some new blood...'
And the gossip goes on, and the gossip goes on...

On their way back they waded barefoot crossing the Nairn River, with shoes in hands their pace quickened the closer they got to their own hidden world.

'Only you and I know love' (WBY)

That evening Molly rode to Te One to prepare for her first day at school. Dan spent the next few days organizing his new venture in the peat brick business. The hardest job was to convince the people who had burnt wood for cooking and heating for many generations, that peat was a better option, Each new customer got their first load of peat bricks free of charge.

Later in the week Dan found an excuse to ride out to Te One after school had finished for the day. Over a cuppa with Molly and Judy the subject of music lessons came up. Judy said that the Education Dept. had sent the school a supply of that basic wind instrument, the recorder. She had been trying to teach the children music without much success, the kids just didn't seem to get the hang of blowing into the recorder.

'My opinion, for what it's worth,' said Dan, 'Is that the recorder in an English concept that didn't sit with the rhythm and beat of Polynesia, a ukulele or guitar may be better suited.'

'It could be worth a try,'

'I think it may work,' said Molly, 'for our people music comes from within that has a beat and rhythm like the beating of the heart.'

'Good point, come to think about it I've never seen a recorder at a party or a Tangi.' Judy hesitated, the added while looking at both Molly and Dan, 'or a wedding...'

That was met with silence.

Judy carried on, 'Dan, if you're willing to be our music teacher, I'll round up all the stringed instruments I can find.'

'I'm keen, no violins please.'

Before Dan headed back to town that night he asked Molly, 'Would you care to be a guest in my humble abode over the weekend?'

'Does the sun rise from the east?'

Over the weekend and the following weeks Dan talked of his life in Ireland, of his bitter youth in 'Derry, of his travels south down to Dublin, his times at sea and adventures in the Deep South of Louisiana, Alabama and Tennessee, the people he had met on the way and the influences they had on him. He still lived a lie, he avoided his time in jail in 'Derry, his obsession with Anna in New Orleans, most of all he avoided the word 'Liverpool' and all the delirium that went with those dark days.

He saw in Molly's eyes the bitterness of her youth and the hurt that he would dump on her if and when the time came to stop living a life of lies. To Dan, Molly was a precious gift that he could not bear to hurt, he knew, deep down, that he, once again, would cause pain.

Molly, intuitively knew there were gaps in his story and that over time and bit by bit the truth will be told. She lived two lives, during the week it was total emersion into a life of children and education. Weekends were filled with the man she loved, she was in love, in love with life, love opened a whole new world, she dreamed of faraway places. Her existence was guided by an unseen power that she had no wish or ability to control, she didn't care, she was in love, a love that was blind.

'Dan?' she asked, 'Who is the man in the black bowler hat?'

Dan couldn't answer that one.

They stood together, shoulders touching both looking with unseeing eyes to the sea, it was as if they stood at the door of an eternal tunnel of sadness.

'Hello young lovers, wherever you are,
I hope your troubles, they are few,
Cling very close to each other tonight,
Yes, I've had a love like yours.'
'Hello young lovers, wherever you are,
Be brave, faithful and true.
All my memories, they are happy tonight,
Yes, I've had a love like yours.' (sung by old Blue Eyes, Frank Sinatra.

32

I'LL CRY TOMORROW

Over the next few weeks Dan had several expeditions using the Council surfboat and a couple of workers sourced from the Pub bar to cross the bay to dig and cut peat bricks. There was a 15-foot bank of peat handy on the beach which had been sufficiently wind dried to be able to be burnt without the lengthy process of stacking and drying.

They would beach the boat at ebbing half tide, cut and load the bricks and float off at the high tide; then reverse this on the beach outside his whare in Waitangi. He had no trouble in disposing his product with the Hotel being his best customer, not only in quantity but because he got paid on a regular basis. Often, he would supply government departments to replace their shortfall of coal if the ship was delayed; the government, being the government, always took many months to pay but at least he got paid, eventually. His local sales payments depended a lot on the local cashflow economy so often he was paid in kind or maybe just a bottle of Wards or two.

Dan kept weekends free, Friday afternoons were at Te One school for music lessons. When the bell rang at 3.00, he and Molly would ride along the beach to town and spend the weekends as a couple. Those precious two days and nights were spent in oblivion to the world around them. Long walks, hand in hand, as lovers do, evenings on the porch couch wrapped in a blanket watching the fat old sun abandon them to a long summer twilight. The town watched as their love deepened, the tut tutting gave in to nods of approval as their names became linked together.

One day she told him that, her birth name was Arona but was called Molly in memory of an ancestor.

'Arona, Arona,' said Dan, 'I like it, it just rolls off the tongue, does it have a meaning?'

'Well, it does, but for most of my life you wouldn't think so but in actual fact it means colorful.'

'I love it, Arona, I am very happy to make your acquaintance, can I call you Arona?'

'Call me anytime and I'll be there,' she stopped, then added, 'for you.'

One evening they were walking hand in hand up the hill to Tiki Tiki which overlooks the bay. They met George Hough on horseback who had been shearing at Shep Daymond's and was on his way to the pub, he stopped for a quick yarn for as long as his thirst would allow, his parting words...

'You can give her diamonds, you can give her pearls,
but there is no finer gift you can give a woman,
than to walk the street with her arm in yours,
so she can show her friends, that you are her man.' (Val)

After that one said George cantered off to the pub.

'He must have read my mind,' said Molly, 'there is no hiding human nature, is there?'

'So true, he's right in saying that I can't give you diamonds and pearls, just myself, and I lay myself at your feet.' (W B Yeats)

The Ghost of Rose watched from above.

After coming back down from Tiki Tiki they caught a glimpse of the man in the Black Bowler Hat standing in the gloom of the police station porch, watching.

The town rumor mill finally conceded that they were a fine couple that brought together the best of both races. Emerald and Greenstone.

One of Molly's friends asked her if Dan had proposed to her yet.

'Proposed what?' she was taken back, this was something she had never thought of, 'Marriage, Marriage?' She thought about this for a day or so, her life was perfect so why should he change it, or was it perfect? What was Dan hiding from her? and, did she want to know anyway? Was it that their differences attracted the other? Would, these differences, in time, repel?'

Molly wrestled with this for many weeks before deciding that she had one of two choices.

1 -- Look for a crystal ball and spend the rest of her life gazing into it.

2 – Ask him straight up and take the consequences, whatever they may be.

Life for Dan now was pretty good, but in the distant horizon he could sense dark clouds, there was no avoiding the fact that someday he would have to be honest with Molly about his murky past. The risk was huge but a risk he must take, whatever the consequences.

Over the weeks Dan unveiled his life and some of the events leading to his arrival on the Chathams. Now was the time to dig deeper to expose the real Dan, of being arrested for the murder of the policeman in 'Derry, of crime in Nashville, his mental breakdown after being torpedoed, the fight outside the Cave, it was there he stopped.

Molly struggled to get the words out and ask the question, but ask the question she must.

'Is there another woman in your life?'

She knew before he answered. He couldn't look her in the face, instead, he hung his head and told her, everything.

By the time he had run out of words her face had become an impenetrable mask, she stood and backed away, eyes soft with sorrow.

'Dan, I can't do this anymore, and, and I have to let you go.'

Dan was utterly drained, he struggled to lift his head to watch her back away, 'I love you, I've loved you from the very first time I saw you at Blind Jim's, I didn't know it then but it just happened, I didn't want it to, it just happened.'

'When my mum died, I was alone and survived, you came along and taught me to love, and now I am alone again, I've got to go.'

She wrapped her cloak around her shoulders, turned to walk out the door and said,'You are a Rhett Butler' and walked out without closing the door behind her.

'I'll cry tomorrow'. Arona said out loud to herself.

33

ALWAYS LOOK ON THE BRIGHTSIDE

Dan was in the pub when the Admiral walked in, he looked around, nodded to a few drinkers, leaned with both forearms on the bar, propped one foot on the long-galvanised cigarette butt tray and threw a few coins on the bar.

Happy Jack plonked a bottle of Wards and a glass in front of him.

'Why the long face?'[

The Admiral's eyes lit, he said, 'That's what the barman asked the horse when he asked for a beer.'

'What the hell are you talking about?'

'Why the long face.'

Jack, expressionless, wiped some imagery liquid off the bar.

'It's old Benji, things are not looking too good, I don't think he'll be with us much longer.' said the Admiral.

Dan overheard and walked over to the Admiral and shook his hand.

'Sorry to hear that, he is a good man, is there anything I can do?'

'Well, Bones, if you want to say your goodbye's you'd better head out our way pretty soon.'

'I might just do that, is there anything I should bring out with me?'

'Arrr, you can bring a bucket if you like.'

'A bucket, what do I do with a bucket?'

'Just put it at his feet for when he's ready to give it a good kick.'

Even Happy Jack couldn't resist a smile, he went out to the bottle store and came back with a bottle of Johnny Walker Black Label and handed it to the Admiral.

'Jack, Black Label? Wow, did you strike lotto? Happy Jack remained expressionless, 'anyway,' said the Admiral, 'that's very generous of you, much appreciated,'

'It's not for you, it's for the guys on the shovels.'

The Admiral studied the label and said, 'he's not dead yet.'

'Dan didn't quite cotton on to what was happening, but then 'that's the Admiral for you,' he thought.

When Dan arrived at Manakau he went straight up to the house and was shown to Benji's bedroom where his family surrounded him on matresses on the floor, some were sleeping, some were telling tales of times past. Benji was awake with eyes closed, occasionally a weak smile would crease his face.

His daughter said to him, 'it's Dan, Dan the Irish has come to see you.'

With eyes still closed he said, 'Dan, they tell me that you are pretty good with music, sing me an Irish song.'

'Find me a guitar?'

'Oh, Danny boy, the pipes, the pipes are calling,
from glen to glen, and down the mountainside
the summers gone, and all the roses falling,
It's you, it's you must go, and I must bide…

Ole Benji had nodded off.

Dan slept under canvas, close to the embers of the cooking fire when he was woken by a commotion from the front of the house. By the time he had walked up to the house the early dawn had thrust a few orange streaks across the sky, although the land and sea were still as one in the darkness. The family had brought Ole Benjie out from the house on a litter of woven supplejack padded with a feather mattress, he was propped up in a half sitting pose by a finely woven flax pillow stuffed with albatross down. Draped over his shoulders was a blanket spun with the wool of the Spanish Merino sheep that the family farmed on Manakau station. His litter was carried by his sons. The women accompanied him with karakia and soft wailing while he sat back serenely with eyes half closed. He was going home to his ancestors.

The entourage made their way up the hill where they nestled the litter on a prepared bed of the fronds of the punga. Ole Benji stirred, as he sat up his granddaughter propped pillows around to hold him comfortable, he straightened his shoulders and looked around beaming with pride. To his front was the lagoon entrance of Te Awapatiki, 'the path of the flounder'. He turned to his right to the island of Rangatira and the outcrops of the Star Keys, the Mangere islands, the Castle, Sail Rock and in in the distance guarding them all was Sentry reef. Beyond was the perfectly formed cone of the Pyramid. He was unable to see but imagined the hundreds of Mollymawks dipping and weaving around their home. His whole life was passing before his eyes as he prepared to travel to reunite with his ancestors.

Benji signaled to his family that he wanted to speak, the people hushed, all eyes and ears were intent not to miss a word, or a gesture, his voice strengthened so all could hear. This was the voice of a man of humble beginnings whose wisdom led him to become the reluctant leader of his people. Early in his youth he made an accusation to an innocent man, this man suffered immensely from this mistaken judgement. Benji learned from his terrible mistake that there were always two sides to all disputes and that each side must be heard without bias. He learned the importance of understanding the background of those involved and the motivations that led them to dispute. He did not judge, he looked for common ground and then searched for a solution in which there were no losers, and each party retained their respect and self-esteem. Over the years he became the man of the people who consulted his wisdom. He was regarded as their leader, a title he refused to acknowledge.

He spoke in the mixed-race language so all could understand.

'I look before me and see the path of the flounder, where our fore-fathers made the decision of peace, we suffered from that decision, it was and still is the right decision. Our covenant of peace resulted in terrible consequences, not only to ourselves but to all people, we cannot judge history from where we sit today. The Māori had been displaced from the land of their forefathers and came here as refugees. The white man came, and we suffered.

He stopped and looked at each person in the eye, as if he was talking to that person and that person alone.

'The time has come...'

There was a disturbance in the sea outside Manakau Reef as a pod of Blackfish thrashed the surface moving towards the shore, as they beached it was if the water was boiling. Before long they lay still in the ebbing tide. All eyes turned from Benji to the beach, the wailing of women was haunting. Benji regained his strength and spoke.

'The time has come, to wipe away our tears, to stand and be proud of our differences, we, as Moriori, Māori and Pakeha must at first learn to forgive ourselves, only then we can forgive the other...'

He faulted, his sons reached over to touch him to give him strength, he took in some deep breaths.

As he regained his strength he looked down to the beach, seabirds by the hundreds had appeared, soaring and dipping over the choppy sea, sometimes motionless, held by the wind. Some, like the Cape Pigeon fluttering excitedly, the Royal Albatross and the Mollymawks, majestic, looked piercingly to the entourage on the hill as they all circled the stranded whales. It didn't take long for the sharks to arrive on the scene.

Benji lifted his head with immense joy of the commotion from the seas, he looked to the northern sky to where his soul would return to a distant and forgotten land. The birds hushed and all motion and time froze, Benji was going home, the soft lament was at first felt rather than heard, then increased to enter the souls of all.

'Takahuihui wharehou e teretere

ana e runga o Rekohu e...'

Come the morning of the Tangi the men gathered at the Urapa to dig the grave where Ole Benji's remains were to be laid to rest. This Urapa was renowned for the difficulty of digging because of the intermittent layers of basalt. The shovel team came across a large slab of rock that was impossible to move or break, a brief discussion insisted that this was the only site for Benji to be close to his ancestors. After an hour of trying to dig around and under the slab without success somebody came up with a cunning plan of blowing the hole with dynamite. A message was sent to Pat, the County foreman to get the key to access the dangerous goods storage pit which was underground in an isolated spot near the Nairn River in Waitangi. He was to bring four sticks of dynamite out to Owenga.

'Four sticks queried Pat?'

'We need to make sure on this one,' stated Hydraulic Jack.

'No problem.'

The dynamite duly arrived at the gravesite and Hydralic Jack took charge.

'Can you handle this?' asked Pat.

'Do you all know why I am in charge around here?'

'Because you're an idiot.'

'Smartarse, I'm in charge because I know what I'm doing.'

'I can see that this is going to be very interesting.'

Jack did a quick mental calculation, instructed George Hough to dig a channel under the slab of basalt, fix the fuse wire onto the sticks of dynamite and run the wire to the detonator.

'Move back everybody, take shelter and get ready for the big bang.'

Jack stood over the detonator, spat on both hands, rubbed them together, anchored his boots to the ground, flexed his fingers and wrapped them around the handles of the detonator as if he was preparing to lift an enormous weight at the Olympic games. He looked around to make sure everybody was watching him, he then ceremoniously plunged the plunger.

There was a gi-normous explosion.

Jack was flattened by the percussion, there had been about a dozen horses grazing nearby and were last seen bolting for the hills. Flying debris punctured the radiator of a nearby tractor, the windscreen of Uncle Ned's Bedford was shattered into smithereens, the Police Landrover had holes punched all along one side. The grave diggers and spectators with ears ringing were splattered with dirt as they lay on the ground

In the house the women ducked for cover as four windows on the side of the house shattered with shards of glass spread all over the room. George Black, who happened to be at the house, panicked because he thought that the Germans were mounting an invasion. The Padre started praying while others were convinced that it was some sort of omen from the heavens, all the dogs were howling like their ancestorial wolves.

The gravediggers slowly made their way to their feet shaking the dirt off their clothing, some were too stunned to speak, others had ringing in their ears. They made their way over to a perfectly round hole in the ground. Jack, being the closest to the big bang staggered to his feet and then fell over again, something must have affected his balance. When he finally staggered over to his hole in the ground, he peered in and looked around at the others who were also peering down They were talking and he could see their mouths working but there was no sound.

'Hey Jack, the hole's the wrong shape.'

'What?'

Realising that Jack couldn't hear thing the voice said...

'You wouldn't even know how blow out a candle, you dumb bugger.'

Jack, recovering said, 'I heard that.'

'I said that the hole is the wrong shape.'

'Ole Benji is a pretty big man,'

'Yes, he is, but he's not as round as the hole that you just created,' said George Hough.

'We can fix that up, no problem,'

'I think we do have a problem.' They all looked over at George who had stated the obvious,

'What do we fill the hole up with?'

'Good question,' said Boof, 'Hey Jack, you told us you knew what you were doing, enlighten us?'

'No problem, first we'd better delay the service for a few hours while we go and find some dirt.'

'How do we do that

'Some mothers do have them,' said Jack, shaking his head. 'Dig another hole of course.'

'Not with dynamite, that's for sure,' said Bill the Policeman who had just discovered the gaping holes along the side of his Land rover.

Tommy Tomorrow piped up, 'We're going to need a lot of dirt to fill that hole, Jack my boy, I think you stuffed that one up,'

'I think I might have made a slight miscalculation on the margin of error.'

'Slight.' said Bo Jangles, 'This is the biggest fuckup since we gave women the vote.'

'Yeah, that was a miscalculation as well, anyway we got some work to do, lets crank up the tractor,'

'Tractors buggered,'

'Oh well, we will just have to use the use the truck,'

'The Bedford's buggered.'

'No problem, round up the picks, shovels and wheelbarrows.'

The women at the house were watching this circus of men walking in line from the Urapa down towards the woolshed pushing wheelbarrows and carrying shovels on their shoulders.

'What the hell are they up to now?'

'They need to have the shovels to lean on, otherwise they would have to lean on themselves,'

'The shovels are for shoveling up the bullshit they talk, and the wheelbarrows are to cart it away.'

'A few loads on my garden would be a help.'

'You can't live with them; you can't live without them.'

'You're not allowed to shoot em,'

'Men, I wouldn't put them in charge of a cat fight let alone something intelligent like digging a hole.'

'They're only good for one thing,'

'Half the time they mess that up as well.'

A few hours later there was a neat pile of soil alongside the now oblong hole. Happy Jack had closed the bar and the population had arrived several hours beforehand. The Clergy had talked about pastures green and the many mansions of the kingdom of heaven to his captured audience. As the men were about to lower the paua shell inlaid coffin into Benji's resting place George Hough called a halt to the proceedings.

'Today, we are not burying just a good man, we are burying a great man,' There was a rumble of approval from the people. 'A wise man, a humble man, to honor this man we must follow his wisdom, to set aside our differences, for good.' A soft mournful lament in the background. 'We all live on this island, Rekohu, Wharekauri, Chathams, this is our home, we are the people who will live in peace as one people, as Benji has guided us, united we stand.'

Benji was lowered into the ground and the men set to work with their shovels, Dan asked the Admiral if it would be appropriate if he too could hop on the end of a shovel.

'On one condition,' said the Admiral.

Dan looked at him, feeling that being an outsider, maybe he had broken protocol.

'On the condition that you don't hop in the hole with him.'

Dan's lips widened into a grin, then, realizing this was a Tangi, he was able to keep a straight face.

The Admiral, with the hint of a smile while looking at Dan struggling not to smile, he added.

'Always look on the bright side of life.'

Dan relieved Boof of his shovel and rhythmically helped fill the hole while thinking about the Admiral's words.

'Mmmm,' he thought, "Always look on the bright side of life," someday, these words may be turned into a good song.' (Eric Idle did so)

34

THE ROAD TO GLORY

was a road that Dan never thought he would travel, once again the fickle fingers of fate intervened. He was listlessly sitting at his table with pen in hand trying, but failing miserably to compose a letter to Molly. There was a knock on the door, thinking it might be Molly, he jumped up and did a 10 second tidy up before opening the front door. It took just one second for Dan to change from anticipation to disappointment.

'Why the long face?' asked the Admiral.

'It's a long story, I'll tell you about it sometime, come in and have a cuppa,'

'Looks to me like women problems.'

They were on their second cuppa when the Admiral got around to get to the point of his visit.

'Well Bones, I'm heading down to Pitt for a few days codding and I need a deckhand, looks like to me that you need a bit of fresh air, you keen?'

'Keen as mustard?'

Just as they had finished loading the Laurenel before dropping the mooring lines at the Owenga wharf the Police Landrover arrived, coming to a screeching halt. Bill, the cop, jerked the handbrake on as he held out his hand out the window, indicating to the Admiral to stop.

The Admiral walked out of his wheelhouse onto the deck, looked up at the cop, and put his hands up in mock surrender and said, 'Wasn't me!'

'It's not you, I've got the Doctor with me who needs to get to Pitt urgently, we have a sick child.'

Dr. Moss stood on the wharf looking down onto the Laurenel trying to figure out how to climb down to get on board the Admiral said, 'Throw down your bag and Dan with a bit of luck Dan catch it, then just wait until the swell lifts the boat and then jump,'

'You're joking, what if I break a leg?'

'You should know, you're the Doctor.'

Once on deck, Dr. Moss took a deep breath, relieved to land on the deck in one piece. He wished he hadn't, the smell of ancient fish bait, diesel, exhaust fumes mixed in with a pot of cod heads bubbling on the stove in the wheelhouse just about knocked him ever.

'I'm Gary,' said the Admiral, 'and this is Dan the man from the Emerald Isles.'

There was a heavy S.W. swell running as the Laurenel rounded Manakau Reef turning into Pitt Strait and into a headpunch for the hour-long journey to Flowerpot. Dr. Moss's face paled with seasickness. He stood at the door of the wheelhouse grimly hanging on while the Laurenel pitched and heaved on the steep waves caused by the wind against a running tide. There was no escaping the fumes of diesel, the cod heads and the heat of the wheelhouse mixed in with the ancient fish bait that was old enough to vote. The Admiral, at the wheel, turned and looked at Dr. Moss with quizzical eyebrows raised.

'I'm feeling pretty wowsey.' said the Doc,

'I've got the cure, that's if you're keen to give it a go.'

'I'll do whatever it takes.'

'The cure,' said the Admiral, 'well the cure is that you put one finger down your throat and another finger up you bum,'

The Doc looked at the Admiral, 'Oh yeah,' then he retched.

'And if that doesn't work reverse fingers.'

When that one sunk in Dr. Moss's face went white, he took a hurried step to the side of the boat and while grimly hanging onto the gunnel, he violently vomited. It took him a minute or so to stop retching, he straightened up, wiped his eyes and walked back into the wheelhouse, the Admiral asked.

'How you feeling?'

'Actually, I'm a lot better, you bastard,'

'It's called the "cure", and it never fails and I recon the 'cure' should be adopted by the medical profession.'

Once the Laurenel got into the lee of Pitt the seas calmed the Doctor regained his health and composure. He was met at the wharf by Tom with his Landrover that was amazingly still in one piece. He saluted the Admiral and took Dr. Moss's bag and threw it into the back of his vehicle. Once on the wharf Dr. Moss turned back down to the Admiral and said...

'Thanks for the ride, sorry, I'm not a very good sailor'.

'I fully understand,' replied the Admiral, 'simply because I'm not a very good Doctor.'

Leaving that bit of wisdom behind the Admiral steamed out of Flowerpot around to Northead to anchor for the night. The plan was to start codding at daybreak, head back to Flowerpot, pick up the Doctor, plus any other Pitt Islanders and back to Owenga to land the cod at the processing plant. Well, that was the plan anyway, as we all know Murphy's Law applies, especially at sea, 'what can go wrong, will.'

The next morning was still dark when Dan woke to the smell of cooking on the diesel stove where Chef Gary, as the Admiral called himself, was cooking up a storm.

'Rise and shine, wakey, wakey, wakey, hands off cocks and on with socks, I've got a heap of lamb chops, fried spuds and half a dozen eggs on toast ready to start our day.'

'What?' Dan groaned, 'At this time of the day I'm good for one chop, one spud, one egg, one toast washed down with one cup of tea.'

The Admiral's eyes lit up, 'In that case I suppose I'll have to eat the lot myself.'

He was a big man.

A day's codding was backbreaking work with the problem being the quantity of fish, in most parts of the world the problem is in the difficulty of finding fish, on the Chathams the problem was the abundance of fish. Each fisherman would work 2 lines, each line would have 4 hooks. Bait up and throw the weighted line overboard while hand hauling the second line. The hooks were modified so that once the fish were pulled up over the gunnel all that was needed to remove the fish off the hooks was to give the line a flick.

They had a reasonable load by midafternoon and with the fish stored in a ice slurry they returned to Flowerpot to pick up Dr. Moss. When they tied up to the wharf there was no sign of the Doc. After about half an hour Tom arrived in a flurry of dust to tell the Admiral that most of the Island population were queued up waiting to see the Doctor who said that he wouldn't be finished until later that night, could they wait until first thing in the morning.

'No.' said the Admiral, looking at Tom with a twinkle in his eye and then added, 'Sweat.'

They dropped anchor in Flowerpot Bay and rowed ashore and got a lift with from Tom to the farmhouse of the Patriarch and Matriarch of the Island, Ken and Eva Lanauze. The Admiral reckoned that they were always good for a big feed and a tipple or two. Although it was only about 6 miles to Northead it took the rest of the day to traverse the 8 gates with 2 cigarette rolling stops, a cup of tea at Auntie Bo's before heading for the Northead house.

After the left Auntie Bo's they met Dorsal at the Caravan Bush gate which meant time for a smoke and a yarn that went something like this...

Dorsal pulled out his packet of tobacco and began rolling a smoke,

'How ya doin' mate?'

'NOT bad,' Tom held out his hand for the tobacco pouch and began rolling his smoke,

'How you?'

'NOT too bad,' they shared the match, and both blew a stream of smoke.

'Hear the Misses is NOT well,'
'She's NOT too good,'
'Are the kids NOT going to school?'
'NOT if they can help it,'
'Has the Doctor NOT been yet?'
'NOT seen hide nor hair of him,'
'Weather's NOT good,'
'NOT too good at all,'
'Fish NOT running?'
'NOT yet.'
'I hear the ships NOT coming till next month,'
'NO way mate,'
'I kid you NOT.'
And so on...

Dan and the Admiral were both following the conversation as if they were watching a tennis match, when they finished their smokes...

'Better NOT hold you up,'
'We'd better NOT be late, see you,'
'NOT if I see you first'.'

It was dark by the time they got to Northead.

Unbeknown to the Admiral a heavy N.E. swell developed through the night and the Laurenel dragged her anchor and founded at the entrance of the cave in Flowerpot, she turned on her side, filled with water where she still lays to this day in her shallow grave.

The loss didn't seem to worry the Admiral too much who reckoned he was sick of fishing and should have stuck to farming anyway. He walked up to the Moffat homestead known as the 'Bluff' and asked old Jim for a job.

'You're hired', said Jim, 'We've got a cattle muster coming up so you're just in time, the only problem is that we have run out of cash and can't pay you until we get some wool out on the next ship, whenever that happens.'

'Sounds good to me, as long as you have a cattle beast hanging from that old Macrocarpa tree and some of that cowboy juice you make in that whisky still of yours to wash it down. Anyway there is not much point in having money because there ain't no shops around here.'

'You'll get paid, eventually, anyway if you need some stuff from the Waitangi Store, I can add it to the order I've got coming.'

'Some tobacco would be good, Oh, you may as well include a pair of boots while you are at it'.

The tight-fisted Moff said, 'What's wrong with the ones you got on?'

'Well, I've heard a bit about that cowboy juice that you brew in that still of yours, they say that it will rot your boots, so I'd better order another pair.'

'Hair on your chest, my boy, and lead in your pencil.'

Because of the heavy NE sea Doc. Moss had to wait a week or so to get a lift back to Owenga, no free lunches on Pitt, he became a dentist, a vet, a marriage guidance counselor, a shearing shed hand, he was even asked to preach at the Catholic Church on Sunday although it didn't matter that he was a Protestant.

After a couple of weeks Mugs arrived on his fishing boat, the 'Waitangi Three' to pick up the Doctor and a few passengers, Dan and the Admiral elected to stay on Pitt. Muggs never missed the opportunity to spend some time on Pitt where he had a romantic interest.

The was plenty of work for the Dan, every homestead had something that needed fixing, a genset, a leaking roof, tractor won't go and so on, his first job was the Northead tractor.

After dinner and over a cup of Irish coffee one night Dan asked Ken about the Lanauze history.

'We don't know a great deal other than my grandfather was a whaler who signed off after a summer season fishing down the ice and set up the whaling station at Owenga. That only lasted a couple of years before the whales were fished out. He went farming for a while and eventually became a registrar of the court and a Justice of the Peace.'

'Master of all trades,' said Dan

'Bit like you Dan, Jack of all trades,' said Eva

'Me, I may be a Jack of all trades but I'm Master of bugger all.'

Ken carried on, 'My Father once told me that their family name was La Nouze,' Ken spelled it out. 'Sounds French to me but also there is an Irish connection somewhere along the line, it has always been a bit of a mystery in the family.'

'Well Ken, you are not going to believe this, back in Ireland I worked for a farmer named Spud La Nouze who told me that he had an ancestor who went to America to escape the potato famine and ended up on a whaling ship out of Nantucket.'

'I wonder how the name La Nouze became landowners in Ireland?'

'According to Spud they were French Huguenots who had been persecuted by the Catholics who destroyed their Church's and stuff like that. They scattered to other countries in Europe and even as far as South Africa where there is still a Huguenot town. The La Nouze's arrived in Ireland as refugees and worked as farm laborers in a village called Clancy. They went on to become landowners and became respected around that part of Ireland, they are buried in the Catholic Cemetery in Clancy

'So, my ancestors could have Anglicized our name to Lanauze,'

'If I remember correctly Spud told me that they came from a small French village called, Alzon, I think, which is not far from the Huguenot town of La Vigon,'

'That's amazing,' said Auntie Eva, 'before the war we had a Priest come here claiming that his village of Alzon are the Antipodes of the Chathams.'

'What did he mean by that?'

'It means that if you were in Alzon and dug a hole through the center of the earth you would come out on the Chathams.'

'Looks to me like the Lanauze's tried to get as far away from their beginnings as they could, they then took a step even further by landing on Pitt.'

Dan looked up to the ceiling and said, 'That goes for me also.'

They both looked at Dan as Ken reached over and picked up the flagon of whisky, 'I think we need a nip of scotch.'

Early morning had Dan wandering the farm before breakfast which took him up the flat-topped Mt Hakepa, locally known as Walk-em-up which is one of the highest parts of the Chatham group. Its claim to fame is that it is the first inhabited place in the world to greet the new day. Dan got to the summit not long before sunrise, found a soft comfortable place to sit with his back on a smooth rock facing east. Warmed by the effort of the steep climb to the top he buttoned his jacket, put the jackets hood over his beanie and hands in pockets while he waited to be the first person in the world to witness the rising of the sun. On his left he could see in the distance the long flat line of the cliffs of the main island of Chathams. He imagined Molly looking to him from the top of Rangaikea, he could see beauty within the deep sadness on her face, he quietly wished her a good morning. He had never felt so alone. A light from the east broke the spell of imagination as the sun peeped its head over the horizon. Once again he was reminded of the ancient Greek poem that Pieter had read to him…

'Brave Phealus, wake up your steads.
Bring the warmth the countryside needs.'

The day he was due to depart Northead, Dan, for the last time walked up to his place on the hill, it was a grey day, and the sea mist melded the ocean and the sky so there was no chance of seeing the rising sun. He looked in the direction of the southern cliffs of the main island and wished Molly a good morning. As he turned to walk back down the south side of Walk-em-up he saw the smudge in the distance, it was the same image he had seen from the Horns, it was the same image he saw from the Liverrbird. Dan intently concentrated on the image of a ship as it faded into the distant haze, real or not, he felt a chill in the air, he shuddered and headed back down the steep hill to Northhead.

That afternoon the cattle musterers arrived at Northead from Bluff station in Flowerpot with old Jim Moff driving his horse drawn dray with a canvas covered load. Behind him about 10 good keen cattle musters and about 30 dogs of all shapes, sizes and breeds, also amongst them was the Admiral riding a Clydesdale gelding.

'Dan my boy, we're heading to Glory mustering wild cattle, are you keen?'

'It will be a first for me, but I'll give it a go.'

'You got no choice; I've even brought you a horse. He handed Dan the reigns, 'His name's St. Leonard, I guarantee he'll soon knock the Irish out of you.'

'So,' said Dan to Moff, 'Looks like I'm on my road to Glory.'

Moff looked up through his bushy eyebrows while rolling a cigarette that was shaped like a trumpet, rolled his eyes and spoke. 'Danny boy, after a couple of weeks of trying to tame these wild cattle, you will think you are on the road to hell.'

It didn't take long for Dan to find out that St. Leonard was no saint. Dan swung into the saddle trying to look nonchalant as the Saint reared backwards, pig jumped, snorted and did his best to be a ratbag, much to the entertainment of the mustering team. The Admiral reckoned that that if the horse farted he would get such a fright that he would bolt back to the Bluff.

Once they got underway the Saint settled down on the road to Glory where to wild cattle roamed the bush in this fenceless part of the island. There was a natural formation of limestone where a corral was built using Matipo pole fences to drive the cattle where they could be contained in the makeshift yards. The yearling bulls were marked and released until the next muster: the 2-year-old steers were contained until they quietened down, any unruly animals, including bulls that had missed the last years muster that were unsuitable for breeding were destroyed, hides removed, then salted and eventually shipped to a tannery in Canterbury. The 2-year-old steers were driven back to Flowerpot, then barged to Owenga and the meat processing plant at Sandstone.

The original farmer on the island, Fredrick Hunt, had introduced the Spanish Merino breed of sheep to the island. Several generations of farmers later the Romney breed was introduced and the Merino's were left to run wild. These descendants were rounded up, shorn for their fine wool and released back into the wild.

Around the campfire after a feed of Marino meat, spuds and watercress washed down by some of Moff's firewater Dan asked him how Glory got its name.

'She was a whaler that ended up on the rocks in the bay here, all the crew survived and got ashore; out of the wreck they built this hut that we are now sleeping in. The island was inhabited by a small settlement of Moriori who didn't have a suitable canoe to cross Pitt Strait. The crew's carpenters did a major rebuild of one of the longboats which included fitting a mast. They harvested mutton birds from Southeast Island, preserved them in their own fat, salted a heap of sow thistle to keep scurvy at bay and set sail for the 'Bay of islands.'

'Russell, Why Russell, why not Lyttelton or Port Nicholson?'

'They must have been concerned that if they landed anywhere else, they risked being attacked by Māori, they had originally provisioned at Russell so they knew that it was a safe port.'

'They made them tough in those days.'

'Those were the days when men were men and women were double breasted, and the birds flew backwards to keep the sleet out of their eyes. Anyway, their seamanship on that voyage was up there with Captain Bligh of the Bounty fame, these sailors were in an open boat, sailing against the prevailing winds of the roaring 40s with just a compass and sextant.'

'If I was them, I would have stayed right here.'

'There were no women at Glory back in those days,'

'There's none these days either.'

'Except sheep.'

Dan, survived two weeks on the back of St Leonard, living on a diet of meat, no broken bones, no bath except for a swim in the bay. Their bodies smelled of sweat, dirt, cattle blood, sheep shit and horse sweat, all that didn't matter too much as everybody smelt the same anyway. The sheep were shorn, cattle sorted, hides packed on Moff's horse drawn dray and the young steers had quietened down and became accustomed to human, horse and dog activity, All were ready for the drive back to Flowerpot the next day.

Well, everybody was ready except for the Admiral who had been keeping a close watch on Southeast Island and the sea conditions. There was a rowboat kept at Glory for the annual mutton-birding expeditions and with the weather looking good he reconned it was time for a feed. This meant rowing across to the island at the ebbing tide and spend a couple of nights birding.

It was April and the chicks, nearing adult, were fledging, they came out of their burrows in the evenings and began exercising their wings in preparation for their first flight. Once in the air the fledging's would join the adult birds to escape the Southern winter and migrate to Siberia, then next spring return to their birthplace for breeding. Once out of their burrows at night they were venerable to the hungry hunters who cooked and preserved them in their own fat, and fat they were.

Late afternoon on the second day Dan climbed to the steep summit of the island to watch the homecoming adult birds. There were 10's of thousands of birds blackening the sky coming back to their burrows to regurgitate their days fishing to feed their chicks. The Titi would crash-land on the canopy, fall ungainly to the ground and search for their individual burrows.

For Dan, compared to the concept of creation, nature was sublime with her infinite mysteries, these birds had been doing this for thousands of years before humanity emerged from the jungles of Africa. His existence on this earth was just dot in time and space of a force far greater than he could comprehend. He contemplated the twists and turns of his own life in relation with the sea, the mountains, the deserts. They were all here before we, as humans came, and will still be here long after we have gone. If he dies alone, so be it, his insignificance just doesn't really matter.

'Mmmm,' he thought, 'I'm overthinking, maybe I should stop walking up hills in contemplation.'

Or, better still, the writer should stop writing this rubbish and get on with the story.

Back in Flowerpot Dan had plenty of work to keep him accommodated and fed, he found himself constantly looking out to sea in the hope that a fishing boat working in the area would call into Flowerpot when he could hitch a ride to Owenga. He couldn't hide from his demons forever so was ready to go and front up to whatever fate had in store for him. He had to find out for sure if Molly would accept him, with all his baggage and allow him back into her life. He could do no more than to lay himself at her feet in the hope that she would tread softly. Another issue to deal with was the question of who was the man in the black bowler hat?

After several weeks the fishing vessel 'Waitangi' with Muggs at the helm tied up at the Flowerpot wharf and discharged a couple of Wildlife guys who were on their way to Mangere Island to do some work on the near extinct Black Robin.

Dan was at the wharf and arranged for a lift back to the Chathams,

'Sure Dan, but as you know there are no free lunch's around here, I need a deckhand for a few day's codding.'

By the next afternoon the fish bins were full of head and gutted cod Muggs set a course to steam around the horns and into the bay to Waitangi. As Pitt slowly receded from sight Dan looked back of his time on the island, he had been welcomed and warmed by the natural generosity that went with the humour of these isolated people. Behind all that there was a sense of the mysterious that lay beneath the surface, he shrugged it off, turned and walked up to the bow to face what fate had in store for him. 'Yesterday is history and tomorrow's a mystery.'

Night had fallen as the 'Waitangi' rounded Tiki Tiki with the lights of Waitangi slowly coming into view. After the dark nights of Pitt seeing the town lights of Waitangi, to Dan, it was like the lights of New York that he had once seen from the Liverbird. After the fish was unloaded and the 'Waitangi Three' on her mooring Dan and Muggs rowed ashore to land on the beach in front of Dan's abode. He threw down his backpack and made a beeline for the pub. For many weeks he had been imagining a cool bottle of Wards, with droplets of moisture on the bottle and the cold liquid wetting his throat. When Happy Jack saw him coming through the door, he had the bottle of Wards with a glass standing alongside, Dan didn't bother with the glass and swigged straight from the bottle.

'Just like mothers' milk.' Said the Tube.

After a loud belch Dan looked into the mirror behind the bar and saw a wild sight, he was shocked to see that he was looking at an unshaven, unwashed, uncombed stranger in dirty, tattered, work clothes smelling of sweat and fish.

'Look what the cat dragged in,' somebody said 'The wild man from Borneo.'

A few of the guys in the bar pretended not to know him and walked up and introduced themselves.

Dan had never thought about his appearance while on Pitt so coming into the Big Smoke of Waitangi took a bit of adjusting. The wake-up call was when Happy Jack told him it was about time he paid for his bottle of beer. Dan patted his pockets realizing that he hadn't thought of money so he had to ask Jack for credit. That was like having a conversation with a stone, Jacks expression darkened as he pulled out his black book and laboriously wrote Dan's name. It was not a good thing to have your name in Happy Jacks little black book.

When Dan opened his front door, he looked around and asked himself the question. 'What next?'

'If you don't know where you're going, any road will take you there', George Harrison once observed.

35

A FAINT HEART

never won a fair lady was the motivation that took Dan to go to the Post Office and ask Bob for some writing paper. Bob, of course guessed what Dan was up to so he went to a lot of trouble to hunt around his office to find several sheets of good quality embossed paper, a fountain pen and bottle of sky-blue Indian ink. Dan spent most of the afternoon composing the letter of his life, after many screwed up sheets of paper, he finally settled on…

'My dearest Molly, it would of the greatest pleasure to the writer if you could accompany him to the public reception in honor of the visiting Governor General Sir Bernard at 4 PM on the 21st inst.

'I am but an Albatross,
a bird of the foaming sea,
searching the Southern Ocean,
alone.
Soaring the highs and lows,
of nature, of life,
always.
With the vision of home.'

With affection, Dan.'

The Governor General arrived at the Chathams on the RNZN ship 'Philomel' which had been N.Zs first naval ship to serve in WW1. Sir Bernard's mission was to check out the Chathams as a possible POW camp and a strategic base for the Armed Forces. Along with the G.G. came all the pomp and ceremony of the King's representative to his Colonies.

The Philomel anchored in the bay and the old surfboat, which had been freshly painted, and was installed with comfortably cushioned seating for the dignitaries to be transferred ashore. After a heated debate in the Council Chambers the Commodore, Pete Saunders, was appointed to the helm of the surfboat which was now officially named as the 'Chatham'. The wives of the Councilors had designed and sewn their version of a Chatham Island flag which portrayed a rising sun over a calm sea. The flag was mounted on the stern of the 'Chatham'.

The Philomel hoisted her flags to signal that the G.G. was ready to be transferred ashore. Those ashore couldn't read the flags until one of the Philomelccrew could be seen gesturing with strange hand signals, they guessed it was time for the G.G. to be picked up. It took an hour to find the Commodore who had no sense of time and was having a siesta on his mates Mutu's couch. It took another hour for him to have a shave, dress and wander down to the wharf where the 'M.V. Chatham' was tied up with her single cylinder Lister chugging along patiently.

As the Commodore neared the Philomel the well-attended G.G. was lowered on a platform against the hull of the Philomel to just above the waterline making sure his feet were kept dry. The Commadore swung his boat around adjacent to the platform but misjudged his speed and crunched into the platform. This brought the G.G. to his knees as the platform tilted and seawater washed over at knee depth. He was saved from falling into the drink by his quick acting Adjacent. With the help of two of the ships officers who scrambled to stand him up and hovered around as they brushed imaginary dust from his ostentatiously adorned uniform. It took about half a minute to realize the G.G. was bareheaded, they all looked around for his hat that was laden with brass so was half submerged and floating away out to sea. An argument between the crew of the 'Chatham' was underway about who was going to jump into the drink and retrieve the hat. Nobody was keen so the Commadore gunned the Lister and tried to steer his boat in the direction of the hat. Eventually the hat was grappled aboard and while the Commadore's first mate, the Tube, was waving the hat around trying to dry it as they successfully tied up to the platform. With the Chatham secured the Commodore turned from the helm, stood to attention and faced the G.G., and saluted.

'Commodore Saunders at your service,' he paused, ' Sir.'

The bareheaded G.G. was escorted around the Island in the Police Landrover that still had holes along one side from the explosion at Ole Benji's gravesite. After inspecting the Courthouse, Hospital and Post Office the G.G. said he would like to meet some of these 'down to earth' Chatham Islanders.

'There is no better place for that than the pub.' suggested the cop.

As the entourage walked into the bar there was about a 10 second silence, then conversations all went back to normal. Bill Millar was cutting Bo Jangles hair, not that he had much hair anyway, the ladies kept on playing euchre, Mike Meo who was nicknamed Tonnage because he caught more crayfish in the bar than at sea, was yarning with Mutu who both were complaining that the pub was running out of beer.

The G.G. walked up to the bar, introduced himself as Bernard to Happy Jack and said to him.

'The gentleman over there said that the pub was running out of beer,'

Happy Jack glared at his clientele and said, 'Bernie, my boy, I don't give a stuff, and do you know why?'

The G.G. simply shook his head.

'It's because I don't drink that shit.'

George and Bob were at the bar and the G.G. walked over to them and said.

'I understand that the Chatham Islanders work very hard to sustain a living on the island.'

Both George and Bob disguised their embarrisment by taking a drink of Wards.

'My good man,' asked the G.G. looking at Bob. 'May I take the liberty to ask you what you do to provide sustenance for yourself and family?'

'Arrr, come to think of it, I don't do a great deal.'

He looked over at George. 'And you sir, what do you do?'

'Arr, I give him a hand.'

Kid Slow joined the group and shouted a round of Wards.

The bar had settled into normal, if there ever was such a thing, the G.G. downed a couple of glasses and his presence was accepted as any other visitor would be. He asked if rugby was played on the Island.

'Too bloody right,' said Kid Slow, 'We got some pretty good players here, some are good enough to play for the All Blacks,'

'All Blacks? that's impressive,'

'Competition is pretty keen, I play in the centers, you got to be pretty fast to play in that position,' replied Kid Slow.

'Any other sports played, like cricket?'

'Nah, takes all day,'

'We'd all be pissed by lunchtime.'

'Check out Uncle Ned over there,' he pointed to Ned at the other end of the bar, 'He often plays his favourite sport.'

They all looked at Ned who was investigating what was in his glass; he said nothing.

Somebody yelled out.

'His favourite sport is hide the sausage.'

Several days previous, Bob, the Postmaster, now nic-named Cupid, handed Dan a letter. In actual fact half the Island knew about the letter well before Dan received it. Bob stood at the door waiting for Dan to open the envelope,

'Thanks Bob, goodbye.'

'I thought you might like to reply,'

'Can I just read the letter first.'

'Oh, Arrr, good idea, see yuh.'

Dan's heart was in his mouth as he opened the envelope with his pocketknife, the page was folded and had one line written on it.

'Only on one condition.'

Dan's heart dropped like a lead balloon as he slowly opened the page. He saw the bottom half of the page first which depicted a small hand-painted watercolor of the wandering albatross, hovering in the wind over a beach with several volcanic peaks in the distance.

This time his heart skipped; the top part of the page had three wonderful words.

'My dearest Dan.'

His heart leapt as he read the following paragraph…

'Only on the condition that you accompany me, as my partner, to the birthday celebration of Judy Wright to be held at the Te One school at 7.00 PM on the 28th inst.'

RSVP at 4.00 PM on the 21st inst.'

It was unsigned, this time Dan's heart exploded. His front door was open and could see Bob on the beach pretending to search for shells, Bob looked up and asked. 'Have you got a reply?'

'Yaa-bloody-hoo.'

There was a 2-day holiday announced for the official dinner for the G.G. giving time for the hunter-gatherers-cooks to prep for the big day out. Even the band had a couple of practice sessions for the pre-dinner entertainment. Molly rode to town that morning and dressed for the function at Eddie and Lynn's where Dan was to pick her up.

Ollie made a lilac and maidenhair fern spray for Dan to give to Molly and pinned a pink carnation to the lapel of his jacket.

He knocked on Eddie and Lynn's door and nervously stood for what seemed like eternity, he knocked again. Molly kept him waiting, simply because that's what girls do, she opened the door and there she was, radiant, they both were unable to speak. Hesitantly he stepped forward and, without thinking he went to put his arms around her before realizing that he still had the lilac spray in his hand. He awkwardly handed it to her.

'It's lovely, thank you, did you walk up from your place holding this in your hand?'

'That I did, I felt as if the whole world was watching me, I tried putting it behind my back but that didn't work.'

'You're brave, come in while I pin it on.'

Eddie and Lynn were dressed to the nines ready to go, Eddie had his son crank up his new, well, new for Eddie anyway, 1928 Ford, and bring it round to the front door.

Billy, the chauffer for the occasion, pulled up in front of the hall and Dan reached for the inside door handle, Eddie told him to sit tight until Billy slowly got out and strolled around the shiny black Ford and opened the back door. The passengers made their grand entrance much to the amusement and catcalls from the smokers who were standing around outside the hall.

The entre' was served and all had to wait while Mayor David gave thanks to the Lord for this fine food. Naturally it is etiquette that the guest of honor to be the first to eat, so all had to wait while the G.G. plunged his fork into a kina roe. He lifted it up, studied it closely, sniffed, frowned, then with great effort and concentration managed to guide it past his nose to take a nibble, the milky juice ran down his chin, he involuntary sniffed as if he had a rotting fish under his nose, he smiled weakly and said. 'Delicious.'

There was a buzz in the hall as all the guests picked up their forks and gorged on the kina, some by-passed their forks and drank the kina straight from their bowls.

After the cream laden pudding was done the speech's started. Every male at the official table, in turn, stood, and said their bit, some went on, and on, and on till their wives gave them a nudge.

The Mayor brought the house down when he said that there are three major issues with the Chathams, he waited for effect... 'Gorse, pigs and rust.'

The man in the black bowler hat stood, with arms folded and intently observed all that was happening.

Dan and Molly held hands under the table, looked at one another, Dan nodded, Molly nodded, and they departed well before the show was over. Molly stayed with Dan that night, and the next, and the next as well. They sat on the porch on the ancient stuffed couch, sipping hot tea, wrapped in blankets. Dan asked her what she was currently reading.

'I am back to reading Somerset Maughan, a bit drawn out, he may take a whole chapter just to introduce a character, that person would have faults within their personality but doesn't mean that they are a bad person, it means that imperfections of character are just part of being human.'

'One thing I do know is that if you are looking for imperfection, I'm your man.'

'I guess we must accept that we are all different and that's something that we all just must learn to live with.'

'So are you saying that as time moves on, we don't change, over time our basic personalities are slowly revealed.'

'Opposites attract and then, over time, they repel.'

They were lost in their own thoughts with that one.

'It's like living on this Island, we all may have different beliefs and opinions, but we are all in the same boat, or in our case we are all Chatham Islanders,'

'I guess that's about it, we are all on the same journey to the same destination but each of us at our own pace.'

'So, where are we going on this journey that you are talking about?'

'Buggered if I know.' they both laughed.

'Anyway, Dan we should both live for this moment in time, if you ever get to buy me a present, don't give me a crystal ball.'

'As far as I'm concerned, don't you ever give me a rear vision mirror for a present.'

'The book I'm talking is called 'Of human Bondage.''

'Mmmm, sounds interesting, human bondage, how about we...?'

'Behave yourself Dan.'

The ghost of Rose looked upon them.

As the dawn lightened Dan walked Molly along the beach to start her new week at Te One school, they walked not only on the sandy shore but also on cloud nine.

As the months rolled by, they settled into Molly spending weekends with Dan, not only in Waitangi but, if the weather was good, they would trek for the weekend and camp overnight on the many beaches and coves around the lagoon. Although they could never seem to get enough of each other their conversations began to evolve into a future life together. Molly for the first time in her life had found freedom to be mistress of her own destiny, but what was the shape of her destiny? Even though she loved, or thought she loved Dan an uneasiness developed into the realization that there was more to life than this male, who may disappear as quickly as he appeared. She said to Dan one night…

'At birth a script was already written for me, being the eldest this script was that I am the caregiver, not only of my siblings but for my elders. I am bred not to have a life of my own. Now that I have been able to escape this script I feel as if I am now being drawn into a trap that I cannot change. I do not want to go back to a life of cooking, scrubbing and snotty nosed kids living in the shadow of a male like most, if not, all the women around here. I am not a doormat.

'Doormats are boring,' replied Dan

'Is that all you've got to say?'

'Do you know what I want from you?'

Annoyed, she asked, 'And what is that may I ask?'

'I want you to follow your dreams, sometimes in following your dreams you might getlost, but that's OK, in getting lost we often discover the good.'

'Are you lost Dan?'

'Yes, I got lost but I found you.'

'But that's not the be all, end all, is it?'

'No, it's not, so, what are your dreams?'

'I guess what I'm trying to tell you is that I have already made a start, with Judy's help I have applied for training at the Teachers Training

College in Auckland. Judy said that, if successful I will live on campus for the 2 years of training.' She stopped for a while to let that bombshell sink in.

'The collage has closed because of the war, but as the G.G. said in his speech that the war will be soon over, and life will get back to some sort of normality, then, he said, we will enter a brave new world. I want to be part of that world,'

This revelation knocked Dan for a six, however, what he did not know that his part in the war was far from over.

Over the next few weeks, Dan, the deliberator, thought about his own situation, would he return to Liverpool to face the possibility of spending the rest of his life in jail. Or does he stay on the Chathams or in NZ and follow his dreams, whatever they may be, basically, he didn't have a clue.

Another night of sitting on the couch warming their hands on a cup of scalding tea.

He broke a long silence, 'I've been thinking,'

'That's dangerous,' she said jokingly.

'You are right, I can't imagine us sitting on this couch the rest of our lives, I keep asking myself what do I want out of life, I think, besides yourself my passion in life is music. Maybe the time has come that I do something about it. 'What? that is the question.'

'Well, only you can answer that Dan she put her hand inside his thigh.'

'Molly, I'm trying to say something here and need to concentrate,'

'Ooops, sorry, my hand slipped.'

'To do what I want to do I cannot do on the Chathams, those words you used about a brave new world has sown a seed, that seed has actually sprouted into a song that's been in my head for some time, and I've been working on the music to go with it.'

'Does it have a name yet?'

'Not yet, but there is a line that goes something like...

"Yesterday is dead and gone,

and the future isn't what it used to be...'
'I guess that's why they call it the Blues'. (Elton John)

Several weeks later Molly received notice that she had been accepted into Ardmore Teachers Training College living on campus in Auckland, commencing in February 1946.

Dan's brain was a jumble, his eyes blurred and the first thing that came out of his mouth was, 'What are your thoughts about me coming with you?'

'I've given that a lot of thought, it'll be my first time in N.Z. and I want to give this everything I've got.'

'I think this is a fantastic opportunity, and, you are right, you'll need to be totally focused.'

'Actually, I'm terrified, you are the best thing that has happened to me and now, now I'm risking everything that I love and know for my own selfish self, and what if I fail?'

'Molly, we have but only one life, follow your gut feeling and if that takes you to Auckland, so be it.'

'You, what about you, what do you want?'

'You, I want you, but also sometime in the future I don't want to read on your headstone the words "What if" or "if only", or the word that you used to use often," but".

'Dan, I'll tell you something now so you'd better listen, I will never, ever, love anybody but you, no matter what.'

'Molly, we are not saying goodbye, I too, have a desire which has been wandering around in my brain ever since I left Lyttelton. It's vague, but now that you are going to do something with your life, it gives me the chance to get back into my music.'

'In Lyttelton?'

'Yes, Lyttelton, it reminds me of a version of New Orleans where there is all this artistic talent gets lost through the lack of opportunity,' He thought of a while then carried on. 'Like it or not, we all need to make money to survive and that's where artists and muso's often fail. My plan is to open a venue that has a permanent stage for music, stage shows or whatever. To finance this, I would need get a liquor license, and the icing on the cake would be to provide food with the emphasis being Chatham Island seafood.'

'Well done, Dan, actually you could get artists to display and sell their work from, from, what are you going to call your establishment?'

'I've been thinking about that, it has to have a Chatham connection,'

'What about the "Volcano,'

'Molly, you're a genius.'

'What a great idea, if anybody can make it work it would be you, what about money?'

'I've saved some, but I haven't figured that out yet.'

'So, the ship will be here in a few weeks, we could both go to Lyttelton and get you started and then I'll head to Auckland in the new year.'

Little did they both know that all this was just a pipe dream.

36

THE AQUARIUS

was originally a trader called the 'Brandeberg' before being commandeered by the Nazi sea-war machine. In 1935 the German Navy was taken over by Nazi Germany and renamed Kriegsmarine with the object of building a massive sea-war attacking force for the impending European war which eventually became WW11. The Kriegsmarine not only built their ships of war but also commandeered suitable trading ships to be refitted and repowered into fighting machines. The trader Brandenburg had her powertrain replaced by the engines of the passenger ship Luftwassar that was being dismantled in the German Baltic port of Lubbock. When her rebuild was completed she was launched and renamed the Aquarius by Hitler's naval commander Admiral Karl Donitz.

With her powerful engines, the Aquarius was one of the fastest vessels of her class of Auxiliary Cruisers, however, she was at the point of being overpowered and had continuing engine problems throughout her life. She was heavily armed with capabilities of firing torpedos and laying mines. Added to this she had storage for a small seaplane that could be lowered and raised over her side using the lifeboat derricks. With the help of plywood and false cranes, she could be made to look like the trader that she once was. Her cargo holds were fitted with large capacity fuel tanks which gave her a range of about 30,000 nautical miles. The Aquarius was a formidable weapon of war that was prized by Nazi Germany.

Her Master was the WW1 decorated Kaptain Kurt von Stryker, First Officer Theodore Eschenburg and the Chief Engineer was the overworked Otto Schultz.

The Aquarius, with her sister cruisers, were put to sea several months before Hitler invaded Poland which resulted in the British declaring war on Nazi Germany. These Cruisers, along with the feared U-Boats became a thorn in the side of the British Naval and Merchant ships throughout the North Atlantic in the early years of the war. When Japan allied with Germany and bombed Pearl Harbor bringing the U.S.A. into the war the battle for supremacy in the Atlantic brought the huge Battleships and Aircraft Carriers of both sides into the fray.

The first mission for the Aquarius was to patrol the North Sea to cripple the war effort supply chain from the East Coast of America to Liverpool. Her first kill was the sinking of a British Merchant ship North and West of Liverpool followed by the destruction and sinking of a troop carrier from the British colonies of Singapore, India and the Nepalese Ghurka's with all lives lost.

Kaptain Kurt of the Aquarius received a coded message directly from the Nazi headquarters in Berlin reading...

'Admiral Donitz has highly commended Kaptain von Stryker, his officers and crew for the sinking of the enemy ships, the Liverbird and the Princess Angela. Heil Hitler.'

The Aquarius had five more kills in the North Atlantic. With the Americans now helping to protect the Merchantmen the German High Command ordered the smaller Auxiliary Cruisers to relocate to the Pacific and Indian Oceans to concentrate on their hit and run tactics and the laying of mines.

The Aquarius, disguised as a trader had several more kills in heading well south of the Cape of Good Hope and into the Indian Ocean. Her speed and disguise made her a difficult target for Allied shipping although she had a couple of close shaves when laying mines on the sea routes when her engines gave trouble. This unreliable powertrain was a nightmare for Chief Otto and his hard-working crew down below.

With Singapore falling to the Japanese the Aquarius was able to dock in Keppel harbor to bunker, load provisions and add Japanese mines to their already substantial arsenal. The Raider then headed down into the Pacific to lay mines along the East Coast of Australia and then across the Tasman Sea to the North and East of N.Z. This part of the world was unsuspecting of the presence of a German raider who was able to sink many unarmed merchant vessels that were easy prey. If the ship surrendered, they would take off crew and passengers and drop them off at neutral ports in the Pacific. If the merchant ship tried to make a run for it she would end up in a watery grave.

The Aquarius was able to approach these merchant ships disguised as a trader before raising the Swastika flag which sent shudders of fear through the Pacific mariners who had thought they were relativity removed from the war in the Northern hemisphere. The sea plane would scout the oceans on the hunt, avoiding any ships that were obviously not involved in the war effort. Kaptain Kurt was after bigger game like the troop and supply ships that were operating from Australasia.

Although the German raider was a menace to the Pacific Traders, Captain Kurt became a somewhat cult hero because of his and his crews respect of civilian prisoners after taking them on board after the Aquarius had sunk their ship.

After laying mines off the edge of the Great Barrier Reef outside the coast of Queensland to assist the Japanese in the upcoming naval 'Battle of the Coral Sea', the Aquarius then made her way S.E. to the northern East Coast of N.Z. where she laid two lines of mines before disappearing south.

One of these mines was detected and destroyed by the steel hulled minesweeper, the RNZN Thomas Currell. The mine was detonated by a .303 rifle fired by a sharpshooter who was a fisherman from the Chathams, and, as we all know the fate of the Thomas Currell when she ended up on the rocks at Port Hutt.

The passenger ship Niagara, known as the Queen of the Pacific departed Auckland bound of Vancouver. She carried a cargo of troops, frozen meat and eight tonne of gold bullion that had come from the British Treasury to make payment to the USA for munitions before the Americans entered the war. The Niragra was just off the Whangarei Heads when she struck a mine and slowly sank to her grave without loss of human life. After the war the gold bullion was salvaged from the wreck and the Yanks eventually got their buck. The mines floated around the coast with several being found on the Northland beaches.

When the second ship, the Puriri struck a mine with loss of life Kaptain Kurt von Stryker lost his cult hero status.

The hunt for the Aquarius began in earnest as she went south to the Auckland Islands where she lay on anchor in Endeby Harbor. Her main engines were shut down for urgent maintaince, while fresh water was taken on and the crew did a bit of pig hunting and sealing for protein.

Through coded messengers Kaptain Kurt was ordered to return to the Northern Hemisphere to take part in the defense of the German ports in the Baltic. The Aquarius was running short on fuel and with the Americans now controlling the Pacific it was too dangerous to return to Singapore or Japan to bunker. To be able to head east to the of the Straits of Magellan and then to the north Atlantic they would have to refuel prior to entering the North Sea. Kaptain Kurt had no choice but to wait for a soft target to replenish fuel in the relative safety of the Southern Ocean. This was the ship that had sunk the Liverbird, this was the ship that Dan had seen from the top of the Horns and then again from Pitt.

The Rangatira had made the Waitangi Port call bound for Lyttelton loaded with wool destined to be made into military uniforms in Mosgiel. Also loaded on board was frozen fish, 150 lambs and 18 passengers including Dan and Molly. Local fishers had been chatting on SSB radio regarding weather conditions and the inconvenience of not being able to get alongside the Waitangi wharf because of the Rangatira loading cargo. This chatter was picked up by the radio operator of the Aquarius. There was a southerly gale forecast so Captain Ward sailed with the wind and took a northern semi-circle from Waitangi to Lyttelton. In turn Kaptain Kurt correctly estimated that this would be the case so he searched the area north of the Chathams. The further north both ships traveled the calmer became the sea. He launched his German built Fokker seaplane and at 12,000 feet sited a dot in the ocean, it was the mighty, reliable but unarmed Red Lady as Capt Ward called the Rangatira.

With the seaplane back on board his crew stripped her disguise and stood-by at battle stations, with guns readied she tracked her target throughout the night and pounced just before daylight. She fired shots over the bow of her prey and had ordered his signalman to raise the appropriate flags to instruct the Rangatira to shutdown propulsion. On siting the unidentifiable Aquarius, the Rangatira's radio operator franticly morse coded mayday calls which were being scrambled by the Germans, cunning buggars they were. The ships rafted together and the seaplane was once again launched to keep a lookout for any other shipping in the vicinity.

Cpt. Ward ordered all passengers to remain below deck, Dan was working his passage in the enginroom when Chief Harry was ordered to shut down the main engine, they both felt and heard the crunching of steel against steel as the two ships rafted. The engine-room crew were instructed to remain down below and set up the pumps and flexible hoses to transfer heavy diesel, oil and fresh water to the Aquarius. The sheep were winched aboard the Aquarius to be penned up on the deck, the contents of the galley and freezers were emptied and transferred. The passengers were ordered to gather belongings in one bag each and assemble on deck ready to board the Aquarius. The engine-room crew were instructed to assemble on deck Dan, on seeing Molly called out...

'You said that you were looking for adventure, well, your wish has been granted.'

As the passengers were being herded into the gangway to board the Aquarius, Molly stepped back to wait for Dan, she answered...

'This is not quite what I had in mind, but I think you did tell me once to be careful what we wish for.'

'Dan frowned, he had a bad feeling about all this, his instincts were telling him that the dark clouds of trouble had formed, he tried to make light of it by saying.

'And now for something completely different,'

'You can say that again,

'And now for...'

She put her hand over his mouth, 'We can do this together,'

By late afternoon the transfers were completed Kaptain Kurt sent his engineers aboard the Rangatira to open the seacocks. Captain Ward was invited onto the bridge where he was respectfully introduced to Kaptain von Stryker and his officers. The Kaptain spoke in accented English that he had learnt while attending the Maritime College in Greenwich before WW1.

'My good sir, I regretfully advise you that I have no choice but to sink your 'Rangatira', whom, without doubt, has served you well.'

Cpt. Ward did not trust himself to speak, he stood to attention and respectfully nodded while looking straight ahead at his Red Lady.

The Aquarius broadsided the Rangatira at a distance of a mile when her gunners, relishing the opportunity for target practice, opened fire. The mighty Rangatira was hit with a barrage of heavy artillery and lurched to on her side, in defiance she quickly righted, the power of the barrage forced her stern away and in defense her bow reared to face her attacker. All on board the Aquarius watched on as her stern lowered to slide gracefully into her watery grave. She died with the dignity she deserved.

Both Masters formally saluted, Captain Ward kept his composure and said to her as she disappeared below the surface. 'You are the lady, rest easy my sweetheart.'

'As we all know that in real life the destruction of the mighty Rangatira was far different from the honorable fate that has been portrayed in this fictional story.'

The somewhat excitedly nervous passengers and crew were squeezed into the mess sipping tea with pretzels when Kaptain Kurt, in full uniform, arrived in the mess with his first officer and introduced himself with the following announcement.

'Welcome aboard the Aquarius, Germany apologizes for this necessary inconvenience and we understand your apprehension, we are not at war with yourselves, we mean you no harm. Our intention is to land you safely on a tropical island where your government will be able to repatriate you all back to your island.'

At first there has a few grumblings of despair but all that changed when the word 'tropical' was mentioned.

'Honolulu,' 'Tahiti,' was conjured up, but all went quiet when Joe Goomes said, 'probably a place more like Alcatraz.'

The Kaptain patiently allowed all to quieten, then continued.

'If you have any questions to be asked, my first officer Oberleutnant Klaus Gunter, who is able to speak English will leaise with Captain Waitere.. Unless you are at working you must stay in your cabins. You will be allowed on deck three times a day for one hour. We soon will be in warmer climes so you will enjoy. We have a doctor on board who is very capable of mending. The Chef will need assistance so he will interview candidates. Men will be designated to slaughter the sheeps, and there is much maintenance to be done with paint brushes. He hesitated for effect,

'The men and the women will have separate cabins.'

A groan came from the men, the women, in defiance, cheered.

'Looks like we will be back to shagging the sheeps,' commented Geoff.

The Kaptain, in not understanding the word 'shagging' frowned and said, 'You will not have the time to be bored.'

When everybody quietened down, he continued. I thank you now for your attention and I introduce Oberleutnant Klaus to instruct the details.'

He stood to attention, clicking his heels and along with his officers raised their right arms, with palms outstretched.

'Heil Hitler.'

The Kaptain then returned to his bridge.

In silence, Oberleutnant Klaus looked at each and every person in the eye, then spoke with deliberation.

'If there is any disobedience, if you breach any designated areas, if you do not follow orders to perfection, you will be confined to the brig immediately where you will spend the rest of the voyage. If there is a siren sounding, you will immediately go to your cabins, you will stay there, I do not tolerate insubordinations.'

That lot was met with silence, his stern manner relaxed, just a little.

'I witnessed a member of your crew coming on board with a guitar on his back so we will have music and singing. Pretend that this is a tropical cruise for all of us to enjoy, tonight we will be having roasted lamb and you will be introduced to sauerkraut.'

He stopped and looked around for any response to his speech.

Somebody mumbled, 'Sauerkraut, I wonder who he is?'

'He must be the person who is in charge of the on-board entertainment,'

'Like a juggler, you mean?'

'Probably the man who pulls rabbits out of his hat,'

'He could be the magician who puts a girl into the box and saws her in half,'

'With a bit of luck, me Mrs. will volunteer for that job,'

With a blank face the Oberleutnant looked around. 'Are you making the joke?'

He straightened his shoulders and put on his most serious face.

'Your engineers will immediately report to the Bridge, after instructions you will be escorted to the engine-room where you will work under Chefingenieur Schlitz. You will be under constant guard and will obey him at all times. If you disobey, your penalty will be harsh

He, like his Kaptain clicked his heels and raised his arm.

'Heil Hitler.'

After he and his fellow officer left the mess Terry stood to attention, raised his right arm, with palm facing down. placed his left forefinger under his nose replicating a moustache. He then goose-stepped to the closed door that the German officers departed, swung his right leg which turned him around, then goose-stepped back again and said.

'Heil Hitler.'

The cruise was smooth sailing with the Aquarius disguised in her civilian clothing. The Chatham Islanders settled into a shipboard routine, several fishing vessels were sighted and ignored. Dan and Harry worked shifts and slept in hammocks adjacent to the engine-room. They had their meals with their fellow islanders and were permitted to be on deck in the evening music sessions and sing-along. It was just like Saturday night at the Pub in Waitangi except for the lack of beer.

The lovers, Dan and Molly had to carefully plan their time together. With Molly cooking in the galley and Dan in the engine-room eight hours on and four hours off had to be timed to suit the music sessions in the evenings. Although sleeping together was out of the question they were seen by the German night-watch scrambling into the life-raft that was on deck. The German crew jealously tolerated these nocturnal liaisons and turned a blind eye when the lovers were seen sneaking bedding into the life-raft.

Both the German crew and the Chatham Islanders made the most of the evening music sessions and were able to join in some of the common songs in both languages like for instance...

'She'll be coming round the mountain' and

'We're moving on', and

'Who will do me this time'.

The Germans were fascinated by the Haka so one was created for the occasion, this was followed by the women with poi's. The Polynesian rhythm and beat was something the Germans had never experienced, their musical background was of Wagner, Bach and Beethoven etc. To the German ears the Māori language seemed to flow smoothly off the tongue compared to their own tongue. One evening they requested a Māori orator to speak as they did in their village wearing traditional clothing. One of the women had her mother's cloak that she was taking to NZ, another weaved a headband to hold a feather. Joe Goomes, who could look the most fearsome was chosen to do the oration; the only problem was that Joe couldn't speak Māori. Dressed in the cloak, headband with feather and a borrowed walking stick that he used as a taia, he held forth. For reality he paced forwards and backwards with bulging eyes and protruding tongue. He began his oration…

'Timaru, Oamaru, Waipukarau,' he took a few steps forward into the face of the Germans.

'Owenga, Kaingapakaha, tutai, mimi,' he stepped back

Joe hissed, bulged his eyes and protruded his tongue, he stepped forward and challenged with his taia.

'Pukunui, kamatua, tuatua,Taranaki, Wharekauri, Wharekauri, Wharekauri.

The Germans gave him a standing ovation.

With confidence after Joe's performance, they rewrote a WW11 song and translated it into Māori which the group performed the next night.

Himete he te patunga to tahi raho'
Translates to…

'Hitler, has only got one ball,
Hitler, has only got one ball,
Hitler. has only got one ball,
And Herman Goering, has none at all'.

Everybody cheered and the Oberleutnant requested an encore. The second time around the Germans, who couldn't get their tongue around the Māori language hummed along with the tune.

The sea changed from green to blue, the day's lengthened, the sun warmed, they began to realize that their Pacific cruise could soon be over. Just like being back on the Chathams the gossip mill was in full swing, of course on board a ship it's called scuttlebutt…

'The Kaptain lied, we're heading for Germany,'

'We're going to be eating sauerkraut for the rest of our days,'

'They don't have luxuries like that in the concentration camps,'

'The men will be sent to the Russian front.'

'We'll probably be blown out of the water by a Yankee battleship.'

'Our women well be used as sex slaves.'

'Yahoo!' said somebody's wife, much to her husband's annoyance.

'I'm glad that I'm not Jewish.'

'We all know, you eat miles too much wild pork for that.'

'With a bit of luck this tropical island will have bare breasted hula girls.'

'You wouldn't know what to do with one even if she tripped you up and fell on the ground first,'

'Just ask your Mrs., she knows what I am capable of.'

'Smartarse.'

And so, on and on, into infinity the banter went.

One evening Kaptain Kurt stopped the music session with an announcement.

'Tonight, we will be at your destination, you will be taken ashore, you will wait until daylight and then you will walk to the village, this will take you one day.'

Everybody was silent, only sound that could be heard was the throb of the diesel engines, then a voice piped up,

'Where the fuck are we?

'Fucked if I know.' another voice responded,

'We'll probably be eaten by the 'where-the-fuck-are-we' tribe of cannibals.' quipped somebody else.

Kaptain Kurt, not understanding the funny side of that, carried on.

'You will assemble on deck at 22 hundred hours, you will not make noise, you will climb down the ladder, once you are in the lifeboats you will be under the command of your Captain Ward.' He paused,

'Auf Wiedersehen.'

After he left Captain Ward said just above a whisper to those close to him.

'Mmmm, did you notice that he didn't "Heil Hitler".'

'Sure did, I would say that Germany is losing the war.'

Dan and Molly quickly found one another in a quiet place on deck and held tight.

'Dan, I'm scared, but I guess this is just another one of life's twists and turns, I wonder what this island's got in store, for us?'

Dan's face hardened to a heavy frown, in the dark she couldn't see the fear on his face but had felt that his body was tense, he didn't answer.

'What's wrong?'

'Everything,' he was looking for the right words.

Molly suddenly had a premonition of what was coming.

'I've got a strong feeling that Otto needs Harry and me to stay on board,'

In horror she whispered, 'He, he can't do that to us?'

'I'm only guessing, but old Otto is just about at the end of his tether in trying to keep his engines going. He hinted that the ship could be heading into the Atlantic after they drop everybody off.'

Her face was an impassioned mask.

All he could come out with was…

'We don't know for sure yet, so, the best we can do is cross fingers and hope.'

By ten that night, the prisoners, although they felt more like passengers, were packed in the main mess waiting for instructions. Harry and Dan were told to be there as well, they had befriended Otto and he just told them to go and assemble with their fellow passengers. Dan saw that as a sign that they could be disembarking with everybody else; although he thought it a little strange that Otto didn't say farewell, he had just turned and went back to work.

A serious faced Captain Ward came down from the bridge and called everybody's attention. They all heard the main engines slow then become hardly audible as they settled into an idle, then stop, the only sound were the higher revving gen-sets. They waited for Captain Ward to speak, he cleared his throat.

'We have been ordered to proceed to the upper deck on our port side, the life-rafts will be lowered, and we will climb down the ladders and board. It will be overcrowded but the sea is calm and we have a full moon to guide us. Kaptain Kurt stated that this must be done in an orderly manner as quickly as possible. The galley has provided us with a little food and a jerry-can of water. It is my understanding is that we have a long walk ahead of us tomorrow. The Island is called Manus and is independent from the British and Germany. What he tells me is that it is a safe haven. Albeit, a long, long way from home,'

The captain was bombarded with questions.

He put both hands up for silence, 'You know just as much as I, except...' he had difficulty finding the words, he looked at his niece, Molly, 'except that Harry and Dan will not be coming with us.'

Absolute silence.

'Over my dead body.' said someone.

'Kaptain Kurt would not budge, he has ordered, on no uncertain terms that they must stay on board the ship, I asked him where they were heading, he ignored my question, but said that any insubordination will result in them being confined to the brig.'

Molly was hollow with fear, although, she felt it was something far deeper than fear, there was a stirring that was in her being which she couldn't understand or explain, even to herself. They had been holding hands as Captain Ward was speaking, she let go. Dan's eyes were brimming with tears as he turned to hold her body to his, even in her grief and anger her face was emotionless, Molly didn't have the strength of wrap her arms around him, to Dan, in her grief, she was never more beautiful.

A line had formed, and the people began climbing over the gunnel down to the two life boats, each with two German sailors to transition the passengers from the ladder onto the lifeboat. Dan and Molly kept going to the back of the line, when it was Molly's turn to climb over the gunnel she had one hand on the rope ladder as Dan held the other, she was shaking that much she missed her footing and swung on Dans hand. He steadied her and climbed onto the ladder to lower her into the raft, she found her footing and with Dan still holding her hand with his other hand holding onto the rope ladder.

There was a shout in German as two armed seamen leaned over the side pointing their rifles at Dans head. He stood in the raft and holding both her hands, he guided her onto the seat. They had no words, he kissed each hand while his eyes devoured her, then turned, and without looking back, climbed the ladder. Back on deck he called out.

'I will find you, wherever you are I will find you.'

As the raft pulled away, she put up one hand, he cupped his hands on his face and in her own tongue, shouted.

'Kia Kaha, aroha, Kia Kaha.'

Molly stood and remained standing, and as she faded into the dark, her last words, ever, to the man of her life,

'Murimuri, aroha.'

Little did they know that Molly was with child.

The man in the black bowler hat and his two uniformed cohorts had a long and fruitless wait on the Lyttelton wharf.

The war was nearing its end with Germany under siege from the West by the Allies and the East by the Russians. America was preparing for the final solution against the Japanese in the Pacific. The Auzzies and the Kiwi's had defeated Rommel's Desert Rats in Egypt and were chasing the Germans up through Italy. Mussolini had swung by his neck on the end of a rope. The Aquarius was ordered to return to the North Sea and defend the German ports in the Baltic. Dan and Harry had noticed the change in the mood of the crew, after they had discharged the Chatham Islanders there was a quiet excitement amongst the crew which slowly became somber and then to outright anger. Dan made the mistake in asking Otto how the war was going, in outright anger Otto immediately recoiled, he had a large spanner in his hand and Dan thought he was going to be hit on the head with it. On the side Harry's advice to Dan was...

'Don't mention the war.' (With thanks to John Cleese for that great one-liner).

After a couple of weeks, the crew settled down, they were heading home after being at sea for five long years: for better or for worse it didn't matter, they were going home. The Aquarius was the perfect modern-day pirate ship in the fact she could stay at sea and replenish fuel, oil, food, medical supplies and in the case of Harry and Dan a couple of engineers from the shipping she had captured. During these 5 years at sea she set 450 mines, some were anchored and held two or three fathoms below the surface so not to destroy the smaller fishing and passenger vessels. The magnetic mines were left to float around wherever the tides took them. These mines had sunk 13 ships that they knew of, there was probably many more. She fired 34 torpedoes sinking 14 allied cargo and troop ships and had captured and sunk, as with the Rangatira. In total she destroyed about 166,000 ton of enemy shipping.

The Aquarius and her crew were the unsung heroes of the Kriegs-marine.

By avoiding shipping lanes and by taking a wide birth around the Cape it took several weeks to zig-zag up the Atlantic and into the North Sea. When the icebergs became numerous, she turned SE to head into the dangerous waters of the Baltic. They sighted several small trawlers south of Greenland, hoping that their disguise and speed would keep them from the recognition of their true identity. Kaptain Kurt was fully aware of the possibility that these ships would report to the Allies the presence of an unknown vessel; and the hunt would be on. He had ad-vised the Kriegsmarine of his intentions but there was no protection as the Nazi war machine was being decimated on all fronts. The Aquarius had no choice but to run the gauntlet as they headed south, well off the Norwegian coast and towards the Baltic.

Late in the war the British had developed radar and installed this device on their larger ships and shore stations. The Germans were mystified of the British ability to see in the dark. The British spread a rumour via their intelligence agency that they had discovered that their ability to see in the dark and enhance their day vision was by eating carrots. The British destroyer, Amazon, had received a coded message that there was an unidentified vessel in the vicinity, also they were aware that there was radio activity between a German ship and the Kriegsmarine; the hunt swung into action. It was a black night when they picked up the zig-zagging Aquarius which was over the horizon as just a blip on their radar. To make sure of her identity they tracked her until first light and closed in, yes, this was the prize that had been a thorn in the side of the allies for five long years, there she was, a sitting duck.

In the gloom of first light First Officer Eschenberg saw a flash of light aft of starboard, as he sounded the alarm the explosions started in the sea close to his ship. As the Amazon gunners corrected their range, Kaptain Kurt ordered full speed ahead as his own gun crews returned fire with little effect because of being out of their range. The Aquarius shuddered from the impact of shells landing just yards from her stern, the enemy gunners had found their range.

The ship was zig-zagging and vibrating violently with her engines at full power, added to this was their continued change of direction which made it difficult for their own gunners now that the Amazon was within their range. It became a game of high-speed chess with all guns blazing. With the skill of Kaptain Kurt and his bridge officers and also the hard work on the engine-room crew they were slowly opening the gap between the two ships. Barrage after barrage of guns were crossing the space between both ships without a direct hit.

The noise in the engine-room was deafening, the fumes from the overworked engines were killing the oxygen in the air. Dans world became a vibrating hell as the ship's powertrain screamed in agony, another call from the bridge demanded more speed. Each time as the Aquarius changed course the engines screamed even louder. Otto's instruments shot up into the red danger zone as he pumped more fuel, more air and more oil into his tiring engines.

Both the engine-room and bridge crew knew that this was too much of an ask, but they had no choice but to keep going. After several long hours there was a terrible noise of metal grinding against metal as one of the pistons crumbled, Dan and Harry speedily isolated the cylinder. No sooner they did that another piston gave up the ghost, The Aquarius slowed, another piston gave up as the engineers realized that they could do no more.

On the bridge Kaptain Kurt realised it was all over, the first direct hit took out the aft guns which destroyed their defenses. As his ship slowed, she lost steerage and was not able to engage her forward guns. The terrifying noise of the siren to abandon ship sounded as the next hit destroyed the bridge and all personal.

Dan escaped the inferno of the engine-room and made it up to the deck and the utter devastation, the deafening sound of explosions, clouds of acidic smoke, the screaming of men dying. In the distance the enemy guns were still spewing out destruction and were becoming more and more accurate, the closer they got. The water alongside his ship was boiling from the red-hot metal.

Dan calmed in understanding and relief, he saw the ghost of Rose, hovering, and with immense joy he smiled and called her by her name.

The cruel North Sea finally claimed her man.

'Danny boy, oh, Danny boy
I love you so.'

R.I.P 1945

Val is married to Lois (Ngati Mutunga. Irish, Portuguese) living in suburbia Auckland with four children and a boring job.

In 1975, Lois, after returning from a visit to the Chathams with her mother Molly Remihana Taupae, the family, in a van and $100, moved to the Chathams.

Crayfishing and Paua diving for 15 years before they purchased the Hotel and, with family, developed group tourism in partnership with Air Chathams.

Now retired from the Hotel and with Lois, the passionate creative gardener and artist, they developed her 70-hectare property Marakarpia into a tourist destination.

A passion for adventure and walking up hills took Val to Nepal, Bhutan, India, Peru. On the many boring red-eye flights and a waning memory led to the writing of essays which became his published book 'Imagine'.

'The Call of the Chathams' is a book of fiction except for the bits that are true.

Coming Soon

CALL OF THE CHATHAMS
(MOLLYS STORY)

After being freed from the German Raider, Molly has been shipped from Manus Island in the northern Pacific and then to Auckland to face a city without pity by having a child out of wedlock, penniless and being Maori while she waits fruitlessly for her man. Dan has been held captive in the bowels of a German Raider, the Aquarius on her ill-fated return to Germany.

Mollys story starts with her ancestors who inhabited Uranui, an isolated enclave in north Taranaki, living in relative peace until the coming of a violent new world order in the early 1800s. Their peaceful existence is abruptly transformed by having to go into battle against the musket armed tribes rampaging from the north, then having to honour a covenant with the war monger Te Raparhau.

This part of the story is told through the eyes of Molly's grandmother Aronui and weaves its way to Parihaka, then imprisonment in Te Wai Pounamu. When the lands of Uranui are confiscated, Aronui, her brother Ngatuna and their people of Ngati Mutunga commandeer a ship from Port Nicolson to arrive on the Chathams as refugees.

Molly's daughter Pania reconnects with her Irish Liverpool ancestry which inspires her niece Rose to follow the footsteps of her grandfather Dan, who had absconded from the law in Liverpool to the obscurity of the Chathams. This is where Rose spreads her broken wings and learns to fly.

'Molly's Story' is the sequel to 'Call of the Chathams' and once again captures a glimpse of the melting pot of love, violence and humour that lay beneath the surface of these misty islands.

Acknowledgments

First and foremost, with respect I acknowledge the Chatham Islands and her people who have unwittingly created these fictional stories that are loosely based on actual events. Some characters portrayed may have some resemblance to actual people, some are named or nic-named. Other characters are compiled from the idiosyncrasies of several people into one person.

At all times I have aimed to respect all those who have participated in these events of the past, In portraying these events my aim is to respect the historic attitudes, beliefs and behaviours of those times which cannot be judged from a contemporary perspective.

To my family and especially my wife Lois, who is the basis from the original concept through to the publishing of this book. I found that the characters portrayed developed their own personalities with myself merely an observer who has descended into a world of fiction. In this detachment from reality, I often neglected the need of those around me and at times struggled to get back into the world of human connection. For allowing me this space I offer my heartfelt gratitude.

A chance meeting between David Johnson and Regina De Wolf in Gisborne led to the Chatham Island Tourism Coordinator, Jackie Gurden to organise a writers retreat on the Chathams. At that time, I was staggering in the dark, trying to transition a crude manuscript into a readable novel. To work with other writers from N.Z. and the

Chathams gave me the belief and confidence of what I had written was not such a load of tripe as I have, at times, believed. Over the four years of creating these stories which I believe are stories that must be told, albeit in a fictional form, has been an enlightening experience at this time of my life as I suffer battle with terminal ageism.

Regina, thank you for your creative, common-sense input that steered me through my poor understanding of modern technology, your expertise has realised my wildest dreams. Simone and Eve, well done with the book cover, Joselyn and Darian for their editing of my poor understanding of the English language. There are many who have read parts of the manuscript and offered their encouragement that has kept my enthusiasm alive. For this I offer my humble gratitude to Gill, Ross, Brian, Patria, Hamish, Buddy, Lois, Monique, Toni, Simone, Don and the many others who listened to my boring monolog about writing.

I find that the poets and songwriters of this world say it far better in less words than I. It is their wisdom and creativity that has enhanced theses stories.

Lois and I were wandering around Northern Ireland under the watchful eye of Ben Bulben and stumbled across a lonely churchyard to find William Butler Yates resting beneath his modest headstone. His wonderful words captured my imagination which is the basis of Part One of this story.

A thank you to Mary Hopkins for 'Those were the Days My Friend'.

Let's not forget the genius of Will Shakespeare, 'partings sweet sorrow.'

Good advice from Ray Charles to 'Hit the Road Jack'.

I tip my hat to the blues of Robert Johnson, who has, for around 100 years, been covered by the greats of today. 'Crossroads', Kind Hearted Woman', 'Me and the Devil Blues', to name just a few.

Isadora's 'House of the Rising Sun', was written by Ole Leadbelly while on the chain-gang is prison where he also found 'Rock Island Line', Cotton Fields, 'Midnight Special' , Irene Goodnight' etc.

'Where have all the Flowers Gone', by Pete Seager still applies to all those war mongering tyrants and despots of today.

'Marvin Gaye tells Cupid to 'Draw Back his Bow'.

Thank you Debbie Goomes for 'Ena rake teen ra'.

Selena Gomez advises us that 'The Heart Wants what it Wants'.

The late Leonard Cohen romances us with '1,000 Kisses Deep'.

Oscar Hammerstein ponders his own life with 'Hello Young Lovers, wherever you are, I hope your troubles they are few...

Eric Idle sings while hanging on a cross, 'Always Look on the Bright side of Life', good advice Eric.

Who can forget John Cleese's great one-liner 'Don't mention the war'.

Fredrick Weatherly laments with 'Danny Boy, oh Danny Boy, I love you so'.

Many thanks to 'Ingramspark' for taking this book into print through their on-line program, 'Bill Your Book'.

Val Croon 16/09/2024

www.ingramcontent.com/pod-product-compliance
Lightning Source LLC
Chambersburg PA
CBHW010713020826
48980CB00020B/814/J